# What Will Happen to You?

*A novel*

*by*

*Gary N. Lines*

Clink
Street

Published by Clink Street Publishing 2024

ISBNs
978-1-915229-96-0 – paperback
978-1-915229-97-7 – ebook

*To Maggi*

Beware that, when fighting monsters, you yourself do not become a monster...for when you gaze long into the abyss, the abyss gazes also into you.'

— Friedrich W. Nietzsche, German Philosopher.

'Wherever you go, there you are.'

— *Big Book of Jewish Humor* edited by Rep Moshe Waldoks and William Novak. This quote is generally acknowledged and accepted to be an apocryphal adage dating back to early Buddhist texts.

'He felt he was a character in someone's novel.'

— *One Hot Summer's Night*, a novel by Dunleavy de Boston and reproduced with his generous, if self-serving, permission.

# What Will Happen to You?
# (Brown Sauce)

*A novel*

*by*
#$%&^*@*

*The city rested during the sweltering nights. It ignored the stench from the rotting garbage on its streets. It ignored the strange birds in its parks. It watched the few citizens still in the city but it took no particular action against them. Not while it rested. Not in this heat. Your history, where you came from, how you existed before the city, these things were irrelevant. The only thing of relevance was 'what will happen to you?'*

# Austin Quinn

INT. AUSTIN'S APARTMENT—NIGHT

One hot summer's night, Austin Quinn, as he preferred to be called at night, sat alone in his apartment gazing at his computer screen in deep thought. It was late. He glanced up at the blue clock on the wall. It was 00.42. He turned his eyes back to the pulsing cursor. He watched it while he waited for inspiration, but all that came was perspiration. The light from the screen lit up his pallid face and made his Ken doll black hair darker. He wore a pair of cream tennis shorts. Sweat droplets ran down his chest and down the middle of his back. In his late twenties, single, and suffering from chronic loneliness, Austin Quinn hadn't written anything new for a long time. His life lacked form. He felt he was a character in someone's novel. The thought that it was not too late to escape hovered at the edges of his mind.

The city seemed to be melting in the heat, and Austin could detect the faint whiff of rotting garbage waiting to be collected on the sidewalks below. The city's inhabitants hated being in the city during the summer months. They disappeared to exotic beaches or cool mountain retreats for their holidays. They sat in auditoriums with sunburnt shoulders, listening to sweating comedians forcing laughs, or in chambers open to the night sky where they looked through fat telescopes at the constellations and sipped lemonade drinks with bobbing ice. During these times, the city was unusually quiet and less malevolent, not as voracious, not as capricious, as it was in cooler times.

In the heat, the city 'rested', as Austin had described it in the opening of his novel. He typed the paragraph more than once. He typed it at least once each night. He built its muscle with each repetition.

*The city rested during the sweltering nights. It ignored the stench from the rotting garbage on its streets. It ignored the strange birds in its parks. It watched the few citizens still in the city but it took no particular action against them. Not while it rested. Not in this heat. Your history, where you came from, how you existed before the city, these things were irrelevant. The only thing of relevance was, 'what will happen to you?'*

Austin Quinn didn't know what would happen to him.

He absorbed the city's heat as though it were a coded message. He kept his window open to catch the odd gentle waft of air. He stabbed his fork into a piece of rockmelon on a dish next to his computer. He rested the fruit on his lips before pushing it into his mouth. He crushed it with his teeth and swallowed.

He inhaled the stench from below. To Austin, that smell *was* the city. It was the smell of digestion, of the city's guts, of human detritus moving through its stomach bag, its duodenum, its jejunum, its ileum, its colon, and its working anus—city streets leading to the sewer. It was the smell of the city decomposing, of life rotting. It was the best of smells, it was the worst of smells.

The words *What will happen to you?* appeared on buildings, across billboards, on pavements, especially on the pavements, throughout the boroughs. People looked down when they hurried along the streets. *What will happen to you?* scrawled in white chalk. No one knew who the author was. Was it the work of an individual anarchist? Or was it the nocturnal city itself catching its population off guard and keeping them disconcerted, rattled, off kilter? No one knew the answer to the question. But the citizens found a strange ease in the words. Was the question from the past or was it for now? Or was it for the future? Or from its antecedent, *Eternity* in yellow chalk? It united everyone in an instinctive way. Everyone faced the same terrifying question, and the huddled citizens found some comfort and safety in the fact that no one had the answer, but everyone together had the question.

Tonight, like many nights, Austin couldn't write. Nothing new came. He sat still and waited. His bladder felt half full or fullish. It was difficult to be precise. He typed his opening paragraph again, his fingers flowing robotically across the keys. After a while, he crossed his forearms on his desk and rested his head on them. He wondered if a tarantula was eyeing him from some dark crevice in the room. He felt exhausted. On nights like this, he thought about Sophie Fanshawe and the privilege of kissing her. A long time ago, he took Sophie out a few times. He liked this memory. They went to dinner and had sushi. He drank cold *saké*, more *saké* than Austin knew to be optimal. He'd met her at The Writers Circle. The group met every Wednesday night at seven pm sharp. The moment he saw her, he recognised her. Sophie Fanshawe tended bar at the Stalwart pub in the city. Austin drank there Friday nights. He sat on the same stool at the bar and drank to excess and spoke to no one. He fell in love with Sophie from across the bar at the Stalwart, and again the first time he heard her dark voice in The Writers Circle, where he remained incognito. She pronounced every word. She elevated the verbs, as though they were alive and each deserved admiration. She spoke to the spellbound souls around the room. Sophie Fanshawe treated the members of The Writers Circle with reverence. They felt unique and singled out and appreciated, not pitied—as they pitied themselves, as the city pitied them.

The first time Austin attended the Circle, Sophie was invited to read snapshots of her work. Her beautiful prose left Austin stunned, with a dry mouth, fixed eyes, and a precise reduction of his usual sense of ambiguity. At times, Austin felt as though his existence was imaginary but Sophie, through her writing, made him feel real and not invented—unlike his fictional namesake 'Austin Quinn' in the lauded novel, *One Hot Summer's Night*, written by the American writer, Dunleavy de Boston. De Boston's fictional Austin Quinn's role cost him his identity within de Boston's novel—'identity' was one of de Boston's thematic obsessions.

It was no coincidence Austin's name happened to be the same as Dunleavy de Boston's character. Austin had chosen the name himself for The Writers Circle. It was a convenience for Austin that the convenor of The Writers Circle had set a writing exercise for everyone in the Circle, before Austin joined, which was to write a story that incorporated de Boston's reluctant anti-detective character, Austin Quinn. The task was to prompt the group into writing about an already fully formed literary character. Everyone laughed when Austin introduced himself on his first night. He made out he didn't understand why, and it was explained they were all writing stories about an 'Austin Quinn', Dunleavy de Boston's fictional 'Austin Quinn'.

And now they had their own real Austin Quinn in their circle. Austin didn't tell them he wasn't real and there was nothing accidental about his name. He'd known about their writing exercise before he joined and chose the name intentionally. It may have been the only time there was any laughter in the group, but not all had laughed. Some demurred, which required acting. Some wiped sweat from their foreheads with tentative fingers. Some adjusted clothing but to no purpose. Some felt diminished, grey, and looked down, and pinched their fleshy arms.

Austin fell in love with Sophie, as Austin Quinn, and this caused a complication for him and Sophie because his name was not Austin Quinn, and Sophie knew this.

But all that was long ago, and now Austin no longer attended The Writers Circle. He was beyond that. Austin missed Sophie. Sitting at his desk in his apartment, Austin thought of the absence Sophie had left in his life—a gigantic black abyss, an absence bigger than her presence. It made no sense. Right now though, Austin could taste her open lips. Her lips tasted of rockmelon. He thought of making love to her, caressing her, attending to her, then after, wrapping her in a white silk mantle. He thought of the female black widow spider eating the male after sex. After sex with Sophie, Austin knew he would have felt bereft, dislocated, lost, not himself, as though making love to her would have put quotation marks around his life and left him suspended and mute. Intimacy with Sophie would have shone a vivid beam on his life and exposed to him what it wasn't, rather than what it was. It was as though the intimacy acted as an inflection point to reinforce what he knew—that he barely existed, that what existence he tried to grasp was fictional, imaginary at best, and was only present in her company. Intimacy with Sophie would drain from him what little there was to drain. He didn't tell Sophie any of this, but he wished he had. She would have been gentle, and she would have smiled at the poetics of it, and she would have made him feel three-dimensional, and he could have told her who he was, although she already knew. She would have reassured him with her touch. One time, she told him he was her favourite character and, in so many ways, she told him she loved him. She used the word 'character' like people use the word 'person'. He lost her, but his enduring memory of Sophie resulted in a feeling of gratitude. After he admitted to himself, he loved her, Austin disappeared from her life. He had to. He would have accepted her devouring him after sex.

Austin walked past the Stalwart from time to time during the day, but not as Austin Quinn. He walked past as himself, and he may have imagined making love to Sophie. The melancholic sound of a double bass wafted through his open window as it did most nights. The low notes reminded him he was alone with his terrors, alone with too much information about himself. Alone.

\*\*\*

Austin's loneliness enclosed him like a fragile but stoic chrysalis. The cause of his loneliness was non-specific. His loneliness was his own, like everyone was lonely in his or her own Tolstoy way, but in this great eastern seaboard city, loneliness in all its incarnations was part of the fabric. It was omnipresent, like the heat. People expected it. They accepted it. Loneliness clung to your skin with a faint iridescent glow. You could feel it. You could sense it. It oozed from the buildings. If a laceration were gouged down the side of any of the city's silver skyscrapers, Austin thought, it would bleed loneliness. Loneliness was the city's blood. The people were its erythrocytes, leucocytes, and platelets (thrombocytes), and each had their job. Austin googled platelets—they were the blood cells that formed part of the clotting system—they prevented people bleeding to death by sacrificing themselves to form a clot, then a scab. Still, things could go wrong. Austin felt some sympathy for the noble platelet taking one for the team. Austin had manicured nails and cherry-black eyes and platelets ready to die for him. He had a constant trepidation that he was on the verge of disappearing, and he was fearful, but hopeful. His survival, such as it was, depended on vigilance—*everlasting vigilance*. He typed this on the white screen, then after a moment or two, deleted it. Then he typed *eternal vigilance.* Then he typed:

*What will happen to you, Austin?*

He left the cursor at the end of the sentence, pulsing, waiting, ridiculing. He deleted his name, it didn't look right, and it did no work. If he was to disappear, where would he go? Who would he be? Would he be someone else? Would he be better? Would he take his platelets with him? Would he find that 'wherever you go, there you are'?

He started typing the opening paragraph again.

*The city rested during the swelteri...*

# Robbie Carton

Robbie sat in his cubicle pretending to examine a column of figures until his eyes blurred. 'Pretending' was how Robbie spent a lot of his time—it was how he survived his day. He popped an antacid from the tin on his desk. He chomped down hard on the tablet. Snapping the tablet in two with his teeth produced an audible crunch. Robbie looked up and glanced to his left then to his right across the rows of cubicles, but no-one appeared to have noticed the sound, or if they did, they didn't show any signs of it bothering them, and it, the 'crunch', failed to disrupt the unrelenting accounting activity going on in the department. Robbie wasn't surprised that no one noticed—he preferred no one did, especially not Bentley.

Robbie Carton was a twenty-nine-year-old accountant with a slim build, a mop of black stylishly untidy hair and quiet dark eyes. He had clear pale unblemished skin and a boyish smile which wasn't often seen. He worked in a large mining company with offices and mines all over the world. Robbie didn't bother himself with the global reach of the company. He rarely thought about it and when he did think about it, he knew he was only pretending to think about it. What he did think about was how anxious being in his cubicle made him feel. He looked up to see if anyone else on the floor was showing signs of feeling anxious. He couldn't tell. He popped another antacid out of habit. He found the crunch satisfying on some primal level. 'Crunch'.

'You lose things, Carton.' This was Bentley Herbert, Robbie's supervisor. Bentley was three plus years older than Robbie, but Robbie thought, no wiser by any measurable measure—maybe Bentley was taller by a centimetre or two, with nostrils that flared at you at the end of his sentences. Bentley didn't wait for a response to his claim that Robbie lost things. The phone on Bentley's desk rang and he returned to his cubicle to answer it. Robbie felt some relief. Robbie had no response to Bentley's accusation—however vaguely plausible it sounded the moment Bentley said it. Robbie hoped no one else nearby on the floor had heard the annoying Bentley. Robbie had no idea what he'd lost, or if he did lose things, or how serious 'losing things' might be in life. He had no clue as to what Bentley was talking about. This worried Robbie. And this meant now he was worried as well as anxious. Robbie's degree of anxiousness was multi-layered, multi-dimensional, multi-faceted and probably ambidextrous, even multi-ambidextrous, he mused. The word *Panic*, typed in bold italics, but not with quotation marks, was pinned to his partition at eye level just above his laptop. Robbie Carton wanted more *for* himself and more *from* himself.

To be precise, Robbie Carton was a reluctant accountant—and so he delighted in anarchy, though as an accountant, anarchy made Robbie uneasy. But precision, he could handle. Existence also troubled him. He knew he was an accountant, 'but how do you know you exist?' He asked this question of anyone handy, but usually when he was drunk or well on his way to being drunk at the Stalwart pub most Friday nights.

He sent his question about existence out in an email to selected people in the office. He received no reply. He wasn't expecting any. Robbie, according to anyone who knew him, was squandering himself. Robbie agreed. The problem was that no one, himself included, knew what particular talents he might possess, if he possessed any at all. Indeed, being an accountant didn't amount to a talent of any note, he supposed. Other-self (his internal voice) was sure he was a talent-free zone. Robbie, on this matter, had to agree with other-self. Usually though, Robbie disagreed with other-self—it was dangerous to do otherwise. Other-self was a self-proclaimed actual anarchist, not a pretend anarchist like Robbie. Other-self was always trying to make trouble for Robbie.

So the question remained as to how these 'talents', if they did exist, might be used to the good of himself, or on a grander scale, to the good of the planet. Robbie's anxiety multiplied—not only did he have to worry about losing things, he also now had to worry about not using his 'talent', whatever it may be.

At the Stalwart pub on Friday nights, when Robbie had drunk too much, he would argue on the question of existence. 'Let's say you don't exist,' he would regale to no one in particular, 'then why would you "not exist" as an accountant, for crying out loud? Why not "not exist" as a matinee idol, or the inventor of the cure for cancer, or Mick Jagger and so forth? You get my drift? The fact that I'm an actual plodding accountant is insistent proof I must exist, or not, yes? I mean, it's an absurdity, is it not?'

He didn't expect an answer—he knew there was none. He was drunk and aware he was slurring his words. He also knew no one was listening. He knew Sophie Fanshawe couldn't hear his extemporaneous mumbling over the din in the pub while she tended the bar. He knew the two other regulars sitting along the bar from him would not indicate they had heard what Robbie had said—they feared engagement with a drunken accountant. They were drunk themselves and never spoke except to order their drinks, and even then, they would only scrape a finger on the beer mat or tap their empty glass once. Robbie both admired them for it and was frustrated by it.

The degree of love Robbie felt for Sophie Fanshawe increased in direct proportion to his inebriation. He could graph it if he put his accountant mind to it—love intensity versus degree of inebriation. He knew that thinking about graphing something as absurd as this confirmed his accountant credentials, and this depressed him, and caused him to order more drinks. Robbie hated being an accountant. Robbie hated being Robbie. Drinking at the Stalwart on Friday nights liberated Robbie from the tedium of both being Robbie and an accountant.

As was his habit, he pencilled the word 'Panic' above the column of figures on the sheet of paper in front of him and slid it into his outbox for Bentley to collect. Robbie glanced over at Bentley, who was still on the phone. Bentley was a surreal character, according to Robbie. If Bentley was surreal, that would mean everyone else in the department must be normal by comparison. Robbie thought that seemed improbable. Robbie argued Bentley would be hard to invent if he hadn't already existed—hard to invent, but not impossible. Bentley had heard Robbie's dissertation on 'existence' many times. Robbie had no idea where Bentley stood on the subject, but then neither did Bentley—for Bentley, according to Robbie, such notions were not the natural terrain of accountants. Bentley would have considered it a risky proposition to look too long and closely into such ideas, or into the abyss, as Robbie described it. Bentley was true to his profession and, as such, risk-averse—'risk' being an anathema to an accountant, but not to Robbie.

Robbie liked to think he was a risk-taker, even though that seemed not to be the case. Do risk-takers suffer from anxiety? Probably not, he had to admit.

On the rare occasion Robbie trusted himself, he thought that Bentley might be the sanest person he knew. That scared Robbie, who had legitimate concerns regarding his own sanity. According to other-self, Robbie's hold on sanity and reason was a joke. Robbie was inclined to agree. Robbie didn't smoke or wear singlets, but other-self did, and Robbie had no clue as to why.

Robbie was best described as forlorn. A man who lived alone in a one-bedroom rented flat in an inner-city suburb and worked during the day adding and subtracting numbers. At night, he could see the lights of his office building in the city from his apartment. During the day, Robbie could see his dark apartment from the east side of his office floor. Apart from Friday nights at the Stalwart, Robbie's life consisted of being in one of two places—his apartment, or his office. Wherever he was, he was looking at wherever he wasn't.

Robbie lived his life trying to minimise his discontent. In his apartment, Robbie kept little in his fridge apart from some bottled beer and the occasional half-empty container of leftover takeaway curry. He longed to find meaning in what seemed an absurd world, but so far, exhaustive examination had not revealed anything of substance, meaning-wise. 'Absurdity abounds, but meaning is in short supply,' he would often say. Nonetheless, he continued to hope that meaning did exist but so far he had failed to unearth any, especially in his department.

Bentley Herbert was still talking on his phone and, in his odd way, represented 'meaning', well, a kind of meaning, Robbie argued—the kind that tends to define something, in this case meaning itself, by not defining it. Robbie devised the notion that Bentley's meaning defined meaning more from what it wasn't than from what it was—its absence more than its presence. In the same way that a hole is defined by what's around it. This frustrated Robbie, as did many things, Bentley being prime among them. Robbie suspected there was a good chance meaning existed in his apartment, but whenever he opened the door, it disappeared. Meaning disappeared, not the door, or the apartment. Robbie added this for his own amusement—he loved a dangling modifier. Robbie was left with trying to find meaning in a fluid world, in particular, in a fictional world where you could reinvent yourself, if only temporarily. He worried though, that if you reinvent yourself, would you be someone else or still the same person? Could you be someone else? You would look the same. You would sound the same. Other-self was all for giving reinvention a try. Robbie typed, *'Absurdity abounds, but meaning is in short supply'*, and sent it as an internal email to Bentley. Bentley ignored it. Robbie followed up with, *'If your boomerang has come to the end of its usefulness, how do you throw it away?'* Bentley again made no indication he had read Robbie's email, but Robbie knew he had. Bentley read all of Robbie's emails. Robbie sent a third email with the statement, *'I've thrown my colander out, it leaked like a sieve, or like a colander.'* Again, no facial response from Bentley that Robbie could discern.

At this moment, Bentley Herbert was back and standing right behind Robbie. Bentley was dressed in body-hugging, iridescent green lycra. He was holding some files, a black bike helmet and his New England red lunchbox with the words 'Grafton Village Cheese Company' written on two of its sides. On one of the sides, the first letter of each word was missing. Such things exhausted and confounded Robbie. Robbie spent an inordinate amount of time being confounded by things that most other people wouldn't notice, or if they did, they wouldn't choose to be confounded by them. Robbie did, but it wasn't as though he had a choice.

'Did you hear me, Carton? I said you lose things.'

Robbie still had no immediate answer to Bentley's accusation and felt his stomach clench because he couldn't fathom if Bentley was joking, being sarcastic or deadly serious. It wasn't lunchtime, so why was Bentley carrying his lunch box? Robbie had no idea.

'I heard you the first time,' Robbie mumbled.

What had he lost? Did he lose things? Robbie worried about tone and inference. He had trouble reconciling these things. He didn't have any idea what Bentley was talking about, but it caused him to feel tense. He hated feeling tense, almost as much as he hated feeling forlorn, which was pretty much his default state, along with exhausted—tense, forlorn, exhausted, that was how Robbie felt most of the time. And now confounded.

'I was thinking about it, riding my bike, on my way in this morning. Yeah, you lose things.' Bentley Herbert said this with considerable smugness, as though he had found the key to Robbie. 'I don't know what will happen to you, Carton. I really don't.' Bentley, repeating the statement, reiterated each word with a strange emphasis on the word 'will' and with lengthy pauses between each word. 'What *Will* Happen to You?' Robbie assumed Bentley had capitalised the first letter of each word. Sweat formed on Robbie's brow. He felt light-headed.

Bentley spoke to himself and for his own amusement with a rhetorical flourish, though Robbie would argue that a rhetorical flourish was beyond Bentley's remit. Robbie felt there was an implied threat underpinning Bentley's words, but wasn't sure Bentley meant it that way or was even capable of such a thing. Nonetheless, Robbie felt threatened. And why had Bentley Herbert been thinking about him on his way to work? Tense, forlorn, exhausted, confounded and now worried and threatened, that was Robbie Carton in a nutshell. Robbie, for his own amusement, emphasised the word 'nut' in 'nutshell' but it provided no tangible relief.

'It's a worthy question and one you should ponder on, Carton. What will happen to you?' Bentley repeated to Robbie, who was at that moment in a land far, far away.

Robbie added to his stream of thought and typed the following words, *What Will Happen to You? A Novel by Robbie Carton.* The problem with this though, Robbie thought, as good a title as it was for a novel, was that it begged the question of how was he to write a novel with a title that asked a question he had no idea how to answer? That would indeed be a mystery novel, even to its author. Robbie considered the title for a second or two, and on the screen, removed the question mark. *What will happen to you.* Robbie typed the following question: *When a sentence is obviously a question as this one is, are not question marks redundant?*

Robbie typed this up and sent it as an email to Bentley even though Bentley was standing behind him. Robbie thought to strike-out the question mark after 'redundant?' but he couldn't.

Bentley, not a man to be distracted, nor one to concern himself with repetition, repeated, 'What will happen to you, Carton?'

Robbie knew Bentley would use a question mark because it was a grammatical rule. Bentley repeated the question on his way back to his cubicle, but with a grin in his demeanour, as though he had Robbie 'bang to rights', as they say on British police procedural shows. Robbie couldn't think of a reply, and this further unsettled him, and like anyone in an unsettled state, it was difficult to think of a good riposte, to use a word Bentley would favour. Robbie felt buzzy and nauseous. He hated feeling like that at work, or in his flat, or anywhere for that matter.

Later, for the sake of the exercise, Robbie mumbled Bentley's words to himself, 'What Will Happen to You?' And then he typed, *What Will Happen to You, Robbie?* Robbie deleted his name. It didn't look right, and it did no work, but some names do. Some names do a lot of work, but that was a topic for another time. If he disappeared and reinvented himself in another universe, he'd like to say to people, 'Call me Ishmael. You haven't seen a white whale anywhere, have you? A friend of mine is missing one.' This assumed that in the reinvention of himself, he retained his sense of the absurd—he would also hope not to lose things as Bentley had forewarned. But then it wouldn't matter because he would be in another universe, where Bentley wouldn't be. Robbie wondered if Bentley's absence would loom larger than his presence, or the other way round. Confounded again, Robbie popped an antacid and closed his eyes.

Robbie had a habit. He wrote random notes in a secret file on his computer, which was what he was doing when Bentley stopped behind him and accused him of losing things. The notes he kept in his secret file were about events and people and himself, but mostly his random thoughts. Sometimes they accumulated into micro stories—several micro stories. Robbie had no idea how this happened. He wondered if other-self had anything to do with it. Some of these thoughts Robbie might one day use in his novel, should he ever get around to writing one. A novel, any novel, he contended, was meant to be a stand-alone universe. His universe was far from 'stand-alone'. He felt it was savagely unstable. Robbie's universe lacked a central core. It was in a heightened state of near collapse, so he held little hope that he could write a novel given his limitations in his universe, such as it was. He also contended that writing a novel would take so much out of you, change you so much, that at its completion, you would be a different person—you would disappear as the author. He thought writing a novel might be one of the most dangerous things you could do. So, if not a novel, he thought, then he might consider writing a play, but he had no idea how to start such a thing. He typed *What Will Happen to You? A play by Robbie Carton* but it didn't make any more sense than it did as a novel, and seemed no less dangerous to its author. He thought, for the sake of this exercise, he might concentrate on writing micro stories, maybe a book of micro stories, but then he figured this would be harder than writing a novel, or a play, where you only needed one central idea. A book of micro stories would need many potent ideas, and he had none. He had a lot of micro stories, but none of them contained potent ideas, he didn't think. He could write something around Bentley or Sophie Fanshawe, or any number of characters he came across in his daily toil, but he was too exhausted, and he worried that it might change him into something, or someone, that might scare him, like a monster perhaps? Or perhaps it might reveal the monster he was.

For the amusement of all, himself in particular, Robbie truncated Bentley's last name to Bert. He did this because he knew it annoyed Supervisor Bentley Herbert and Bentley couldn't say it did because that would mean it did. To prove his childish petulance, as if he needed to, Robbie sometimes extended the truncated Bert to Bertram, or 'The Bertram' or 'The Bentley Bertram' or 'The Bentley Bert' or his *pièce de résistance*, 'The Bent Bert'. It all depended on his mood, or how unbusy he was at the time.

He typed *Unbusy* on a blank screen and watched the cursor pulse. He continued typing.

*'Unbusy'. Being 'unbusy' was the preferred state of the fluctuating forty or so accountants who worked in the department. 'Unbusy' wasn't just being idle, it was far more sophisticated than that—'unbusy' was when you were busy not achieving anything productive but looked as though you were. Accountants understood this concept and admired it in other accountants.*

Robbie stopped typing.

In and around bouts of 'unbusy' periods, Robbie's main job was to reconcile expense accounts across the mining company's distant divisions. That was pretty much all he did, outside of annoying Bentley, which he saw as his real job, if not his life's work. When he wasn't a bored accountant, he was a cinephile and a bookophile, or a hyperlexiphile, whatever the term was for someone who loved reading. If you loved reading, wouldn't you know what the term for excessive reading was? Robbie often imagined himself as the literary figures he read about. It was a way of getting through his day. On any given day or night, he spent hours being Patrick Bateman from *American Psycho* by Bret Easton Ellis and pictured himself taking an axe to some of the accountants, and thus purging the world of several number-cruncher types. Or Holden Caulfield, where Robbie would spend the day picking out all the phonies on the floor, starting with himself to be fair. Or Mark Twain, where Robbie imagined his desk was a raft floating through the aisles of accountants, or a white whale in a sea of accountants. Robbie did this often, but it left him feeling unsatisfied and still himself—still himself, wanting to be someone who wouldn't have any pending files in his in-tray. No in-tray at all, much better.

Robbie thought that absurdism was as prevalent as the air here, in the 'Department of Nonsense', a phrase Robbie favoured when talking about the office. Robbie's somewhat athletic build defied the fact that he did no exercise and spent most of his spare time reading and watching films, and drinking at the Stalwart pub, or standing in the dark in his apartment being watched by the twinkling lights of the city, feeling alone and forlorn, tense, and exhausted. This was on a good day. He didn't have good nights. All these activities, in their way, had a particular purpose. They abetted his desire to disappear and start again. He wished there was a 'disappear' button on his computer keyboard. He imagined being in the middle of working on a column of figures, or midway through a discussion with Bentley on something inane, like the previous conversation he had had with Bentley, with his finger poised over the 'disappear' button. Then when he couldn't take it anymore, he'd hit the button and 'puff', he'd be gone in a 'puff'. He imagined popping out of the miasma onto a beach in Key Largo or Madagascar wearing a colourful shirt and sporting a limp and needing a walking stick or finding himself on a tautologically frozen tundra in the black winter of a distant planet in another galaxy, somewhere where he wasn't known by any of the aliens and could start again. Of course, *he'd* be the alien, so no change there.

He typed, *Gone in a 'puff'* but decided not to send it to Bentley. *Gone in a puff.* Not that anyone in the department would notice he was missing. That was how it was on the floor—accountants kept to themselves and would consider the business of someone disappearing not something they should concern themselves with, unless they coveted the empty cubicle because their own was not as well sited in the hierarchy.

Robbie felt that the one person in the department who might notice he had disappeared would be Bentley, his arch-nemesis, or maybe Gloria, who worked two cubicles away from Robbie, next to Bentley's cubicle. Robbie looked over at Gloria. Her cubicle was smaller than Robbie's. He could see her shiny hair above the partition—it was captured by her usual ribbon, which today, or at the moment, was white. Robbie was guilty of sniffing Gloria whenever the opportunity presented itself, like when she leant near him to discuss a file or walked past him and left a trail of her perfume for him to inhale. Gloria smelt exotic in a way that made Robbie think of white sandy beaches, cocktail umbrellas, exotic white drinks, and a red and white striped beach towel. Gloria was all accountant but also all 'woman'. Robbie, together with all the other male accountants on the floor, and quite possibly one or two of the female accountants for all Robbie knew—wanted to ravish her, and Gloria knew that. In Robbie's view, the word 'accountant' and 'ravish' should not appear in the same sentence. It implied a competency not ordinarily associated with accountants—male or female—according to Robbie.

Whenever Gloria swished past, everyone—the men in this case—would bite down hard on a knuckle, or a pencil, or a bone, or a car part, or whatever was handy, to keep themselves controlled. Not that they would do anything to embarrass themselves, but they might develop a line of sweat across the top of their lip for those who didn't possess a pencil moustache or, worse, underarm damp patches might appear. The women in the department all eyed Gloria as she passed by, but no one knew what they were thinking—at least Robbie was sure he didn't. Gloria excelled at rendering an excellent 'swish'. As she swished down each aisle with her practised rhythm, it was like a Mexican wave of accountants—all, in turn, bending after her like flowers following the sun.

Gloria was smart, very smart, and universally understood to be destined for advancement in the department. She was already Bentley's deputy. Robbie found the juxtaposition of how smart she was with the way she looked, a conundrum—another conundrum in a life full of conundrums or conundra, as Bentley would mischievously point out, even though the dictionary cited 'conundrums' as the plural of conundrum because conundrum was not a Latin word, which Bentley would smugly reveal having suckered you into believing what he just said. '*Conundrums* is the plural, not conundra. It's not Latin, you *fatuus* [fool].' This was Bentley at full throttle. It was unspecified as to why or how Bentley knew any Latin, but he did, and he used it to make you look like an *idiota*—Latin for idiot, as he would disclose. Bentley could only be tolerated in *exiguis*—small amounts—Robbie thought. Robbie had looked up *exiguis*.

'Well, Carton, what *will* happen to you? Or have you left us for one of your fantasy worlds?' Bentley was back again, standing behind Robbie. Perhaps he'd never left. He repeated his question and laughed nervously to himself. Bentley, according to Robbie, had an infinite capacity to find himself amusing.

'This *is* a fantasy world,' Robbie muttered to himself.

Bentley remained behind Robbie. Bentley had primitive social skills, Robbie thought, and standing behind someone and waiting for a reply to what Robbie was sure was a rhetorical question, while others watched or tried to ignore the situation, wouldn't have occurred to Bentley as being bizarre, or embarrassing, or peculiar, or socially inept. Robbie wished Bentley would disappear along with the heat of embarrassment, which had risen to the top of Robbie's scalp and hovered like a heat-induced mirage over a dirt road in the middle distance on a hot outback day—Robbie enjoyed an overworked metaphor. Robbie searched his keyboard but failed to find a 'disappear' button labelled 'Bentley'.

'I heard you Bertie, loud and unclear.' Robbie tried to sound breezy and unperturbed by what Bentley had said, but he'd lost control of his voice, and it sounded too high. He didn't turn around to face Bentley, and he felt there was more agitation in his demeanour than he intended or wanted. This agitation escalated and graphed itself up to a more strident form of agitation, and the problem with that was Bentley might interpret it as proof he had gotten under Robbie's skin, which he had, but Robbie didn't want Bentley to know that. Robbie minimised the secret file he had up on his screen. At that point, Bentley turned away and walked back to his cubicle, with another inane thought wandering around his mind. Bentley, according to Robbie, had the concentration span of a gate off its latch.

Robbie exhaled and thought it wasn't the best start to his morning. Bentley had ambushed him, and Robbie preferred it the other way round. Robbie could smell warm cucumber sandwiches from somewhere in the department, but it didn't help.

# Gloria Penhale

Gloria understood the staff in the department. They were children. They were cowards. They were easily manipulated, and she knew she was smarter than all of them. She had one over-arching attitude to her fellow accounting colleagues—she had a warm affection for them. She considered they were redeemable in spite of themselves and their limitations. They limited themselves by their almost constant thoughts surrounding amusement, and accounting.

Gloria knew things about most of them, things they didn't know about themselves. Gloria made it her aim to help them be the best version of themselves, where she could. It would be a better outcome for them and for the department. She saw it as part of her job.

Apart from this, and as good as she was at inspiring people, Robbie Carton wasn't responding the way she had hoped—Robbie was a special case and she worried about him. Gloria was the second-in-charge in the department reporting to the department head, Bentley Herbert or the Bentster as he was affectionately known. When Gloria was a young girl, she put herself in charge of her younger sister and the other kids who lived nearby. She was a born benevolent manager of resources, and she considered the kids in the street she played with as her resources.

# Austin Quinn

INT. AUSTIN'S APARTMENT—NIGHT

The ubiquitous torn city poster hanging on Austin Quinn's wall showed how, on sunny days, the city had a sparkling harbour and commanding bridges. The breezy scene looked like the top of an enormous birthday cake. Yachts and ferries were racing across the dark blue icing and around the small island with its world-famous statue that might have been shaped out of foreign white chocolate. But this was how the city looked to the innocent—sublime, inviting, homogenised, and innocuous—grinning with decadent pleasure while shielding its malevolence. It was its own invitational poster. Austin had no idea how people prospered in the city. The city was about surviving, and if you didn't survive, you were consumed. You were swallowed by the indifference and the failure of hope. The shadows closed in on you, and you lost shape.

Austin had always lived alone, apart from the nameless white bird he kept in a cage hanging from a purpose-built stand at the end of his sofa. It was his habit to keep the lights off. His dark apartment overlooked a small park with peculiar trees. Sitting at his computer, he ignored the growing pile of white and brown envelopes on the floor by the door. When he entered or exited, he stepped over the letters. He knew none were for him. Even when he wasn't at home, the sound of the mail dropping through the letter flap and hitting the pile of letters on the floor was the only sound in Austin's apartment, apart from a soft murmur at night. He needed sounds in the same way a baby chick needed to hear its mother's heartbeat.

After dark, a pulsing neon invaded his apartment with red, blue, and green hues. On and off. On and off. On and off—permeating his life, his thinking, his moods, his thoughts, including, he thought, his biology and indeed his persona. He was Austin, then he was not, then he was Austin—like night and day. Austin couldn't see the neon sign from his apartment. He couldn't say what the deflected light advertised. He didn't know on any conscious level what its message was, but he knew it had one. Sometimes he imagined it said things like, 'God Created Suicide' or 'Are You *Prime?*' or 'Vigilance' or 'Live Long Insurance'.

The neon flashed across his naked back. Austin felt sure he could feel it, although he knew he couldn't. Perhaps the sign advertised camera equipment, or maybe a dark bar somewhere, where mouths distended, and lips jerked, and tongues clicked with sexual invitations. Austin didn't know but thinking about it was transporting. Time, to Austin, was elusive and uneven. He bit off chunks of time, like he might a big apple.

The neon washed through his darkened apartment and provided the only light in the sparsely furnished room, apart from the steady white glow from his computer. When needed, he sometimes flicked on the lamp next to the sofa. The lamplight was a warm yellow, more luminous than an actual light source. Its prominent effect enhanced his silhouette. It darkened his face and made him feel like he was Dick Tracy. 'Half hidden in dark contrasts under a yellow fedora,' he mumbled. The lamp didn't compete with the neon but added to the effect. For all Austin knew, the rest of the lights in his apartment might not work. In his apartment, questions remained unanswered, edges were blurred, cheeks were pale, lips were dangerously red, and nothing was as it seemed. It was its own world, and Austin preferred it that way. It was a world where he was one of the elements of the apartment, no more dominating than any other. Raindrops hit the glass and refracted the neon hues around the apartment. The rain outside ramped up the humidity and the white noise. Austin Quinn lived a film *noir* life.

When daylight infiltrated Austin's apartment, it was void of human life. Like other people in the city, Austin preferred the shadows. The city's citizens suspected that 'things' outside the shadows could kill you. The shadows were reprieve territory—demilitarised, non-political. Austin felt safe or safer in the shadows. Between the shadows, on the streets in the blinding light, real life—not the façade of city life—existed. Out there was where evil existed and danger threatened, where the way to survive was to look away, never meet the city head on. 'No direct eye contact' was the mantra of the bewildered citizens.

Safe in his apartment at night, or as safe as he could be, the neon flash and the muted city noises comforted Austin. The light and the sounds delivered the city's stories to him in a subliminal coded pulse. The pulse penetrated his brain. He heard the plaintive noises associated with murders, torture, and muggings—city crime—and the greatest of all, the sob and body heave of underutilised human endeavour. He heard the screams and moans and cries of anguish. He felt the human desolation, the sex gasp and the loneliness of loneliness. He felt the weight of surviving. Austin acknowledged and feared the off-stage declarative laughter. He absorbed the exasperation, the blind rage and, above all, the isolation. He felt the exhaustion of clinging hope. He felt the weight of this for himself and on behalf of everyone. For everyone in the city, hope was a lie, a con, an outright fraud. The city kept you in a state of sadness and punishing hope. You were expected to hope for relief, but none came, and this caused the sadness. The citizens knew hope would never solve anything, but no one spoke about it. If you gave up hope, you disappeared.

Austin felt the call to write the stories of the city, the baffling and, more often than not, desperate, disillusioned stories of its inhabitants. Writing the stories was the one uplifting thing in his life apart from the bird. The stories themselves were anything but uplifting.

He didn't trust the city. Nonetheless, he had an affinity with it. No one trusted the city. Everyone, on a subliminal level, knew that the city was retributive. Ironically, or perhaps not, this city, in so many ways, was perfect, and the citizens celebrated this fact with forced rictus. The citizenry was nameless and anonymous to Austin, as he was to them. He accepted his anonymity in silence with an existential fear. If your existence was not acknowledged, how would your absence be noticed? At night, when he looked out the window of his apartment, down at the dark-cloaked inhabitants moving in slow motion below, he understood that none of them knew him. They didn't know he watched them. They didn't know he listened to them. They dreamt of a redeeming life, but they couldn't admit this, not to themselves. And this was what Austin heard. He heard their muted dreams. He heard their futile hopes. On moonless nights, and when he allowed himself, Austin Quinn considered that 'Austin Quinn' was not his name and he was not Austin Quinn.

Austin kept the bird in its cage away from the windows. He fed the bird every second day and made sure it had water. '$H_2O$,' he repeated over and over in the hope the bird would say it back to him, '$H_2O$, $H_2O$, $H_2O$.' He did this in case the bird should ever need water. But after a while he said it for himself and couldn't stop repeating it for hours, until he went to sleep with a thirst and a dry mouth. Austin cleaned out the bottom of the cage every Saturday night at eleven pm. He didn't know what kind of bird it was. It was white. It wasn't a budgie or a canary. It was larger than those two species, and it didn't ask for water. It had a red-and-white coloured crest and a yellow beak. It didn't speak, sign or squawk. It made no noise at all during its waking day. Austin thought this might be because it had resigned itself to being alone. There was no other bird for it to attract with its song. It may not have understood there were other birds in the world—this was something Austin didn't know. One of the tenets of the city was that caged birds and humans alike knew 'we don't know what we don't know'.

Austin's bird wanted for nothing, except for its freedom perhaps, but that was questionable because it wouldn't have understood the concept of freedom since it had lived its life in a cage. Austin knew more than most that freedom could be terrifying. It might be the most terrifying concept in life. So maybe in resignation, or perhaps in protest, the bird remained silent except for a low murmuring sound it made when it slept at night. When it wasn't asleep, it sat on its perch and rocked and stared into, what Austin referred to as, the abyss of the middle distance. Austin thought one day he might release it into the park below, but he worried that as the bird had been kept in captivity all its life, it might not know how to survive. He thought this of himself. And this applied to the city's population. Austin came to realise that liberation can kill—freedom could be lethal. Only the true captive can know the terrors of freedom, and freedom can only be experienced by a true captive.

Austin unblurred his vision and focused on the cursor. He could taste the white screen hissing in his mouth. At that moment, in his dark apartment, at that precise time in his life, with his mouth open, Austin knew what would happen to him. He started typing.

# Robbie Carton

Outside it was a bright sunny day. The sunlight penetrated the office windows and quelled and consumed the interior fluoro lighting of the department. The battle was on. Robbie knew that everyone in the department understood that it was Bentley's mission in life to goad Robbie. A mission Robbie thought was, in Hamlet's words, 'more honoured in the breach than the observance'.

On one level, Robbie knew Bentley detested him, but on another level, he understood that Bentley wanted to be friends with him. Robbie had his suspicions about Bentley. He thought there might be more to Bentley than met the eye. On the other hand, there might be less. But Robbie knew he wasn't the best person to make such a determination. One thing Robbie did know about Bentley was that he could not be accused of not caring. Robbie admired this in Bentley and tried to emulate this in his own quiet, disguised way. As it turned out, Robbie was so proficient with his quiet disguised behaviour that for all anyone knew or considered, Robbie couldn't have cared less.

Robbie imagined a life for Bentley. Robbie imagined Bentley collected stamps and had a magnifying glass, and he polished brass late into his Saturday nights. And on the weekends Robbie imagined Bentley went bushwalking wearing a peaked beanie and carried sandwiches and a piece of fruit in a knapsack, perhaps a banana—definitely a banana. But Robbie couldn't say for sure. Maybe Bentley photographed birds or identified a particular brand of car. The truth of it was, Robbie knew little about Bentley despite their having worked in the same department for seven years. What little

Robbie did know about Bentley, Robbie had made up. Robbie opened a new screen and typed.

*It was strange that sometimes, more often than you might think, what you had made up, or imagined, was the truth, or soon became the truth—or at the least, indistinguishable from the truth.*

Robbie sometimes imagined Bentley as a fictional figure, not real like himself. Robbie wondered if he might have invented Bentley, written a backstory for him and developed him as his antagonist. But then that might be the biggest problem with Bentley, he was too real to be invented, even by Robbie.

Last Tuesday Robbie mischievously, and with exaggerated sincerity, said to Bentley, 'Why don't you try parting your hair on the other side of your head?' Robbie knew Bentley had no idea how to take statements like that. Later that morning however, Bentley had slipped into the men's room and parted his hair on the other side, and now it was standing on end, as Robbie predicted it would. This might be fashionable for a tortured sixteen-year-old dressed in black living in Melbourne near Palm Bay Florida, or in Llandudno, or in Tokyo under a bridge, but not so much for a thirty-three-year-old accountant supervisor for a multinational mining company, with the ability to flare his nostrils on demand. Still, Bentley was persistent with his hair because he wanted Robbie's approval—and Robbie knew that about Bentley, or thought he knew it.

There were times when Robbie felt sympathy for Bentley, perhaps something bordering on affection. For a start, Bentley was the kind of guy you could trust if you were ever in a pinch. He was the guy you'd want next to you in the trenches before you go over the top. Robbie hoped that people might think that sort of thing about him too—although Robbie couldn't see how you could easily get out of a trench. That aside, and because of thinking like that, he wasn't sure he would be able to deliver if he was needed. To be that kind of person, you needed to be a romantic. Robbie, according to Bentley, was a cynic and cynics don't generally believe in anything, especially romance. Robbie had to admit to himself that there was a lot to admire in the annoying Bentley, not the least of which was that Bentley was solid and a romantic, if not a fictional truth. And Bentley had great powers of concentration. Robbie was not confident about his ability to concentrate. Whenever Robbie tried to concentrate on a particular thought, or action, or matter, he found his mind wandering and questioning his ability to concentrate on any particular thought, or action, or matter.

'Hair looks good, Bertie,' Robbie said as he passed Bentley's cubicle later that day. Bentley was looking at himself in a hand mirror while trying to smooth his erect hair with his hand. Bentley put the mirror down next to a bike pedal and reached for an antacid. Robbie patted Bentley on his shoulder. 'Yeah, you look cool.' Robbie knew Bentley never knew how to take him.

Robbie looked at the antacids and asked, 'Can you spare one of those?' Bentley offered up the Vegemite jar full of antacids, Robbie took one and popped it in his mouth. 'Thanks, Mr B.' Robbie wandered off affecting a feigned jauntiness. He was proud of this. He considered that the business of pulling off 'jauntiness' in one's demeanour was hard enough, but to feign it was near impossible. He thought Bentley would be impressed and he hoped that Gloria might notice and admire his ability to render feignity, or feigness, and surely, she'd be impressed with his invention of these two new words. He sat down at his desk and felt the weight of the world crushing him.

Robbie's jet-black hair was permanently untidy, which currently made him 'on trend', whereas until recently his untidy hair made him 'untidy', as it did for Bentley. Only in Bentley's case, it was out of character. Now it seemed fashion had caught up with Robbie. Robbie felt unsettled by this. Not only by this. Many things unsettled him. Being unsettled, unsettled him. He felt a lightness in his tummy. Like everyone, Robbie dreamt of a different life for himself. He dreamt of a life he could understand. He dreamt of an exciting life, and he spent a lot of time thinking and designing what an exciting life might look like. At home in his flat at night, he liked to think he was someone else, and he was. But was he any better, or better off?

As annoying as Bentley was, Robbie envied Bentley's contented demeanour. Bentley loved being an accountant, and Robbie thought you had to admire someone who loved being an accountant, whether or not his hair looked ridiculous. At least Bentley was what he wanted to be. And more impressive still, Bentley knew what he wanted to be.

While Robbie and Bentley tended to rub against each other in mutual irritation, they nonetheless spoke often because being at odds with each other sort of came with the territory, and everyone in the department was okay with that.

*Robbie Carton and Bentley Herbert grind against each other like a ship against jetty pylons, back and forth with the slapping motion of the ink black sea.*

This appeared as an anonymous email on everyone's computer. Nobody disagreed with it. Nor did they own up to it or comment on it. Robbie thought it was overwritten and less than profound, although true enough.

Robbie looked over at Bentley, who was eating a sandwich and working one-handed on his keyboard. Next to Bentley's cubicle, Robbie could see the top of Gloria's head. She now had a purple ribbon in her hair, and her head was bobbing from side to side. He couldn't imagine why she was doing this, but it reminded him of caged birds.

Robbie worked in one of the many replicating cubicles in a large open-plan office—on the fifth floor of a four-storey building, as Robbie liked to say. He liked to say this to Bentley who, frankly, had no idea why Robbie would say something so nonsensical. Bentley was an accountant down to his bootstraps and demanded everything be accountable and pass the logic test. Bentley, according to Robbie during Robbie's lucid periods, was incapable of understanding irony, or sarcasm, or in particular, absurdism, and this made Bentley a ready target for Robbie. Targeting Bentley made Robbie uneasy— it was never as satisfying as Robbie thought it would be. Or should be. Why wasn't it?

'Can't you give Bentley a break, Carton?' Robbie looked up to see a gorilla walk away from him. The gorilla made Robbie feel bad about Bentley.

Later that morning, while he was away from his desk, a post-it note was stuck onto Robbie's screen. It read, 'What will happen to you?' Robbie worried that not having an answer to this might place him in some jeopardy. Robbie thought, with good reason, jeopardy was out to get him. If not jeopardy, then a gorilla. If not a gorilla, then everything Bentley stood for and was, was out to get him. Robbie argued with unnecessary mirth, when he was drunk at the Stalwart and suspected he was being watched, or listened to, that there was no point in wasting his highly developed sense of paranoia. No one around him responded, so he didn't know if they agreed with him or not, or what they thought of him.

Today felt like a Wednesday, but it was Thursday, late morning. Robbie popped his head up to look over his cubicle. He scanned the heads—lines of heads, up and down, back and forth—a grid of heads, all facing the same way. There were dozens of them—different hairstyles, different colours of hair, some with bows, others with their heads shaven. There were forty-two people in forty cubicles on the floor. Robbie had no idea what any of them did. Well, he knew what they *did*. They did accounting and administration jobs, but what any of them did in their life, Robbie had not a single clue. He could only guess at how they lived, what they thought, and how they existed. He pondered over things like, what was their best meal? their worst orgasm? what colour were their thoughts? Did they wish they were someone else? Did they smell their farts? What floor coverings did they have in their darkened bedrooms? Did any of them keep a pet? The answers to these questions and many others, Robbie could only guess at. He guessed at all this and much more in life, while getting drunk at the bar of the Stalwart, or sitting at his desk in the department. He couldn't fathom things as fundamental as the relationships between people. He had no comprehension about 'chemistry' between people and how it worked. He wasn't sure there was such a thing as 'chemistry'. He suspected 'chemistry' was the invention of the romantic.

As far as Robbie could discern, relationships, as such, didn't thrive in the department, or, if they did, they tended toward indifference at best. Indifference was the prime emotion in the department, and everyone tried hard to achieve it. Robbie thought indifference might be easier to achieve if you didn't try so hard to achieve it. Nonetheless, the more indifference you achieved, the better the accountant you were and the more you fitted in. In 'accountant world', the key to survival was 'oblivious indifference', and the key to success was 'amusement'. Accountants amused one another competitively. At least that was what they tried to do, or thought they were doing, or thought they were expected to do. In Robbie's view, way too much energy was expended on mindless accountant-style amusement.

Robbie thought the 'amusement' was puerile—not amusing at all and, at best, a nervous gesture to cover up fears of inadequacy. 'Amusement', or the execution of it, was necessary to be accepted by the accounting fraternity, but because accountants were incapable of causing amusement, it had to be faked. Some of the accountants in Robbie's department were so accomplished at faked amusement that it was, in some incidences, indistinguishable from actual amusement. He wrote this in an internal memo and sent it to Bentley for his comments. Bentley did not respond, not even with a 'no comment' or a 'non commento', which was neither Latin nor Italian, but a bastardisation of both and would have been how Bentley would have responded, had he responded, according to Robbie. After a while, Robbie sent a follow-up email to the Bentster asking, '*Non commento?*' But there was *non commento* from the El Bentmeisterio.

Everything Robbie sent to Bentley, he also copied to Gloria. She didn't respond either. This annoyed him because he was trying to impress Gloria. She'd taken a photograph of Robbie and hung it in the lunchroom, along with other portrait photographs she'd taken of people in the department. Robbie didn't recognise himself in her photo of him, but everyone else did. He thought the one she took of Bentley was spot on.

Robbie's theory about open-plan offices was that they were an unnatural habitat for the human condition to prosper—much like cages are an unnatural habitat for wild animals, and if you keep animals in cages long enough, and they are not in their cage alone, they go mad and eat one another. If they are in their cage alone, they just go mad.

Robbie looked around the department. He couldn't see anyone he fancied eating, with the possible exception of Gloria, whose cubicle was near enough to his that he could smell her wafting, exotic perfume. She had a red ribbon in her hair and deep purple lipstick, which meant it must have turned midday, because Gloria changed her ribbon at midday. She looked startling, and everyone in the department wanted her. Everyone except Bentley—solid Bentley, the romantic. But more on that later. Robbie considered Gloria eminently consumable, and she was the one attractive enigma in the open-plan landscape to drool over.

Robbie argued, to no one in particular, while sitting on his usual stool in the front bar of the Stalwart most Friday nights, that open-plan offices were like some sociological observer-effect experiment, where everyone felt they were watched and controlled, which in turn distorted their reactions to the degree they could be held in suspicion when there was nothing of which to be suspicious, and this could be confirmed if they didn't feel they were being watched. But then if you don't watch people, how can you confirm suspicion? Robbie loved to torture ideas, although he considered himself an amateur compared to his heroes, George Orwell, and Joseph Heller. On such occasions at the Stalwart, his strident opinions may have benefited, or not, from the alcoholic lubrication which flowed across the bar to him in the form of wine, beer, and spirits, or often all of the above, depending on his desperation and subsequent level of inebriation. The Stalwart was his favourite place to get drunk, and Sophie Fanshawe his favourite alcoholic server.

Robbie observed and made notes about the various behaviours of his colleagues—all the accountants, every one of them. Some had tics, some were prematurely grey, or bald, and not only the males. A few feigned dislocations, some majored in disinterest, others wore their stripes of absolutism on their sleeves. One of the females wore a wig but a different one each day, some-times a different wig during the day. Some mumbled to themselves—Robbie being one of them—some couldn't read without mouthing the words they were reading. Fingernails were chewed. Many stared into the middle dis-tance. Robbie wondered what was wrong with the near and far distance that nobody would stare into either. And where was the middle distance? Was it in the same place if you were long-sighted or short-sighted, and what was so fascinating about it that kept everyone staring into it?

*Beware the abyss*

Robbie typed this on his blank screen and emailed it to Bentley as an attach-ment. Bentley emailed back, *'Beware the monster'.*

Apart from the staring phenomenon, many of his colleagues couldn't sit still for an average of longer than six minutes and twenty-two seconds. Robbie had timed them, graphed them, and averaged it out, then pumped the results through an algorithm, which he wrote himself, to predict move-ment in the department. A few copycats polished a shoe. Another unpicked the hems of her skirts on odd days and hand-sewed them back again on even days. Her fingers were raw and bleeding, and Robbie felt she suffered the same anxiety as himself—but he couldn't help her. He tried to be especially kind to her.

One guy whose cubicle was way over the other side from Robbie wore a gorilla suit. At least Robbie thought it was a guy, but how would you know? The gorilla suit on the outside was male, you could tell by the muscular-ity and lack of breasts, but that didn't mean the person on the inside was also male. The gorilla suit might have been the only one available, or maybe all gorilla suits were male. Robbie didn't know the answers to any of these questions, and he wondered if the 'maleness' of the gorilla suit affected the person inside, or was it the other way around? All he could say with any con-viction was that no one knew who anyone was on the inside, or how much their exterior facade informed who they were and how they behaved, if at all, and vice versa, so forth and etcetera.

Robbie, looking around his immediate area, thought most of the staff on the floor were barely holding on to their sanity, but because they were all maladjusted and neurotic, no one noticed, and no one stood out unless they wore a gorilla suit and only then for the first few days. Robbie thought if they had any interest in themselves, or any self-respect, they would stand up from their cubicle and yell out, 'Enough already, brown sauce or not.' Then, having stood and yelled, they would walk out and do something worthwhile with their lives. Robbie thought he should, or would, do this himself— and he intended to, one day for sure. Robbie stood up. He did nothing, just stood still in front of his desk. He looked like he was going to say something or yell something, if it was possible to affect a look that suggested a yell was imminent.

'What are you doing, Carton?' Bentley asked, looking at Robbie.

'I have cramp.' Robbie sat down and started to type—not anything in particular, just anything to distract Bentley from thinking he was acting weird. Bentley looked back to his screen seemingly unconcerned and took a large bite from a fruit that looked like an apple but wasn't. Robbie could hear the crunch around the department. Robbie felt hungry but lunch was an hour away. Robbie typed:

*The fundamental problem was that everyone in the department knew they made no contribution to the betterment of humankind. They were boring, fastidious, pedantic accountants and in a lot of cases, excessive alcohol and antacids were how they survived every day—while affecting the notorious 'accountant's faked amusement'. That was crucial. They were all aficionados of self-loathing—it came with the portfolio.'*

In Robbie's view, it was the one thing they had in common—that, and the fact that only accountants would ever use the word 'betterment'.

Robbie stared into the middle distance. He had impeccable white shiny teeth. He amused himself by mouthing the word 'impeckable' in relation to his teeth. He repeated the word 'impeckable' several times for maybe an hour until his tongue tired, but even then, he kept repeating it. He repeated it until the word itself sounded ridiculous and hardly a word at all, but only a sound, and his tongue ached like hell. He hoped he wasn't as much of a coward as he feared, but he did know one thing, and that was that there was something he had to do. He didn't know what it was that he had to do, so far, but he knew there was something, and finding out would either be the making of him, or the end of him—he had no preference. 'Impeckable, impeckable, impeckable.'

Gloria looked up and over in Robbie's direction. Was Gloria looking at

Robbie or other-self? An email arrived on Robbie's computer. It contained the word 'impeckable', spelt accordingly. It was in the middle of an otherwise blank screen. It came from Gloria. It was lunchtime.

# Gloria Penhale

Gloria Penhale was a thirty-two-year-old (hurtling to thirty-three) accountant with a robust figure. Her 'robust figure' was other people's opinion, not hers, although she knew it to be the case and had long ago accepted it. She had three Degrees, including a Masters, and several industry-specific qualifications. In her spare time, she was a photographer. She took headshots of people, not to capture their presence, but to capture their essence. She was the youngest chairperson of the national body representing the accounting profession, and the chairperson of the company's social committee.

Among her duties in the department, and as second-in-charge, she ran the induction course for new accountants joining the department. Gloria had asked Robbie to script her welcome address.

This was her opening statement as written by Robbie Carton.

'Welcome. Today you will learn the company's protocols and policies and discuss the philosophy of life. By the end of the day, you are to speculate on the following questions.

How do we determine if fish work up a sweat after their morning swim and why do car workshops specialising in steering problems never prosper?

And we want to know what kind of accountant you are, so answer this: You run a company that makes new pallets, so if you have a stack of new pallets ready to ship to a customer, would you...

A. Consider the bottom pallet part of the stack, or

B. Consider the bottom pallet to be the pallet on which the stack sits and is used to transport the stack? And sell the bottom pallet with the stack at a discount, as it is now a used pallet? or

C. Brown sauce?

If you choose C, you will be drawing attention to yourself. There are no right or wrong answers.

In the meantime, let's start with office protocols before we tackle ethics. Oh, and during the break, I will take your photograph if you're game.'

Gloria left in the line, 'There are no right or wrong answers.' According to Robbie, these were the seven most terrifying words in the English language to any accountant. Gloria thought a little terror was not a bad thing. It tended to focus the mind.

# Austin Quinn

INT. AUSTIN'S APARTMENT—NIGHT

Austin didn't name the bird because a name was an intimate detail and could be prescriptive. He felt the bird's chances of freedom might be hampered if it had a name, even a false name like his own. He wondered how you could give a bird a false name. He also wondered why one's freedom might be contingent on a name. Austin chose his false name himself. He liked it, but it came with complexities. While there wasn't too much wrong with his chosen name at first glance, it did cause him some minor work. The name was solid with a certain style to it. It had no unfortunate construction that could be used or subverted into something derogatory, like people sometimes do—shortened or lengthened or obliterated in some accurate but cutting way. No, 'Austin Quinn' was a name that did not cause its owner too many difficulties. It was easy to spell so long as the double 'n' in Quinn was announced, not that spelling it to anyone ever happened. It's a little-known fact that Austin's initials were the same as Alonso Quixano (AQ), but that was rarely, if ever, noticed by anyone, and as such caused no particular inconvenience. Austin thought of this fact as his secret. Sophie Fanshawe may have noticed that Austin's initials were the same as Alsonso Quixano's the fantasist of Miguel de Cervantes' novel *Don Quixote*. In the novel, Alonso changes his name to the more regal name of Don Quixote de la Mancha. Austin found comfort in the fact that Alonso changed his name to become someone else, especially to Don Quixote a name which interpreted, meant someone who is determined to change and to right wrongs, but in the case of Don Quixote, he ends up making many silly mistakes. The parallels with Austin were eerie. Austin hoped Sophie might make herself available to him because of his initials—she would surely know that Alsono changed his name for noble reasons. Sophie wrote poetic prose. She was attuned to coincidence and serendipity. Austin tried to be Sophie's mysterious stranger. He wanted to be her knight. He felt he had failed her. He thought of Sophie often but especially when he sat in the dark, as he was doing now. Sophie Fanshawe was striking, and he couldn't help thinking of her creamy pale skin and her ample joyful breasts, and he was grateful for her generosity—she had helped him with his prose. He shuddered at using the word 'ample' to describe her breasts, but it rolled around in his mouth, and he licked it with his tongue. But his engagement with Sophie was a long time ago, and he couldn't remember what happened between them. He disappeared from her life, or she disappeared from his, he didn't know which. She was gone, but she left something. She left her absence.

The ongoing problem, if problem was the right word, with Austin's name was that he had deliberately borrowed it from Dunleavy de Boston's postmodern anti-detective fictional character in de Boston's celebrated book, *One Hot Summer's Night*. The fictional Austin Quinn was trapped in an *other*world by his god-author, Dunleavy de Boston. Austin felt he had a lot in common with his fictional namesake. He also had a god-author who had him trapped in a fictional world himself. The question which plagued Austin, was that when it came down to it, how do you know you aren't the invention of someone else's imagination—a character in their novel? A hero perhaps, or more likely an antihero, which was not to say you still can't be heroic. Even the writer of a novel might be a character in someone else's novel and not the writer at all, or, at best, a fictional writer—an implied writer for the implied reader. Does Dunleavy de Boston exist?

Austin asked this of The Writers Circle, but it was meant to be a provocative rhetorical question, not one to be answered. The character Dunleavy de Boston in Dunleavy de Boston's *One Hot Summer's Night* didn't exist. Nor did the character Gary N. Lines exist in Gary N. Lines' novel *Doing Life In Paradise*. Although it *was* true that Gary N. Lines the actual author of *Doing Life In Paradise* did live for a time on W57th Street in New York, not far from The Russian Tea Room, as did the fictional Gary N. Lines in his novel. Existence or otherwise was potentially as fictional as it was real. Austin felt exhausted. He felt he was everywhere. He felt he was read about, touched, understood, misunderstood, discussed, and expanded on, as was the case in The Writers Circle he attended for a time, every Wednesday night at seven pm sharp. Everyone in The Writers Circle wrote about him until he had reached his usefulness, then he was dropped out of everyone's narrative. Maybe Sophie had dropped him out. Perhaps that's what happened. If that *is* what happened, he wouldn't blame her.

Austin was an advocate of the 'free will' concept, so he invented himself. He believed in free will. He felt he had no choice but to believe in it. During thoughtful thoughts, he wasn't sure that it, free will, existed. Austin considered himself a person with a philosophical bent. He thought about things, but he didn't believe in anything. He didn't know he was a writer of philosophy, although he was a writer. And all writing was philosophical, categorically so, or so Austin believed. Sophie believed that too. Austin wanted a name that was his and his alone. He tried to recall anything he had thought deeply about, but he couldn't, and he thought deeply that this might be the reason he had lost Sophie from his life.

At one stage, Austin had thought to change his name again. He liked Tommy, or perhaps something less definite, like Robbie, but so far, he hadn't done much about it. He knew a 'Robbie', and this made it easier for Austin to consider the name. The 'Robbie' Austin knew drank at the Stalwart every Friday night. They'd never spoken. Such a conversation between them would have been impossible or insane. But Austin thought, most of the time, that Tommy would be a serviceable name for a writer. There was a man at The Writers Circle who Austin thought was called Tommy, or should be called Tommy. Austin called him Tommy. His actual name was Harry. Harry was Sophie's brother, who didn't mind being called Tommy.

'Tommy Fanshawe,' Austin Quinn murmured to Harry one night at The Writers Circle. Austin was trying out this potential new name for Harry. It had a touch of the Ernest Hemingways about it, he told Harry. Austin couldn't say why. He'd never been much of a Hemingway fan—the prose was too muscular and strained, too tight. It felt like propaganda to Austin. It felt like explaining. Hemingway, Austin had observed, excluded women from his stories and wrote to, and for, a 'male reader'.

'Robbie', Austin thought, as a name, was more avuncular and better represented Austin's writing style and interests. But Austin was probably wrong about that. Austin preferred his prose to writhe in pain on the page, like a decapitated snake in its death throes. And he abhorred overwriting too.

Only rarely in his work did Austin achieve anything like writhing prose, and it was often not on the page but inferred, implied, spectral. 'Robbie' was a good name for Austin's nom de plume, but he was yet to find the right surname to go with it. He wanted something literary, something that alluded to literary antecedents. 'Quinn' didn't work with 'Robbie'. Robbie Quinn. It seemed like Robbie and Quinn were in contention with each other, the same as Austin and Quinn. Austin felt sure Dunleavy de Boston chose the name 'Austin Quinn' for his protagonist with this contention in mind, and the fact that the initials were the same as Alonso Quixano's, which allowed de Boston to discuss Don Quixote in his novel. Clever, if obvious.

Austin kept working on the name. He felt the surname had to represent human endeavour, aspiration, and sacrifice. He would have gone for 'hope' except he hated the notion of hope. He didn't trust hope. For a second he considered the name Robbie Hope but thought it too cute, and it risked being shortened to Bob Hope, and that wouldn't do at all. Austin wrote a note to himself, 'all this name stuff, its complex, it's hard work, what work does it do?' He wondered why he had bothered.

Austin's routines were economical. He wrote at night when he could. He rose early every morning, showered, flossed, ironed his shirt, and dressed, then headed out to the café below for a croissant and latte. He imagined himself going to work. He imagined himself arriving at eight every morning at the florist shop he imagined he owned. He sold imaginary flowers to the workers in the building above his shop. Austin thought, Hemingway would have approved of Austin owning his own business. Hemingway's stories were about independence and freedoms, stories of men. But Hemingway wouldn't have made his protagonist a florist, Austin believed, or anything as boring as an accountant or a lawyer, and Hemingway's characters would never floss or iron a shirt. They would not drink lattes or eat croissants. They would drink beer or whiskey. Their shirts would be crumpled, not deliberately, but because it wouldn't matter.

Austin's imagined business survived because many women bought flowers for their respective offices every few days. Not only women, but also men bought flowers, perhaps more than expected. In the case of men, it was for their girlfriends, or wives or boyfriends and their mothers. Whereas women bought flowers for people who needed flowers, and for people who didn't especially need flowers. Austin thought about this a lot. He thought how it demonstrated that men were more targeted, less spontaneous and more purpose driven toward outcomes, with a survival instinct hard-wired into them—men strategised, women were less managed, less predictable. Women, he thought, were more generous and less confined, more community aware. Men were taut and often bewildered. Women were more relaxed, amenable and, if pressed, bewildered as to why men were so bewildered. Women understood compromise and bewilderment. Men were more fatalistic, more absolute, and thus doomed in a way that women weren't. Austin spent the day writing out imaginary cards to go with the bunches of imaginary flowers he was selling. Austin preferred the company of women, as did the self-imposed exiled Hemingway, who married four of them. Austin gave considerable thought to his customers, real or imagined—after all, putting a bunch of imaginary roses together in cellophane was hardly taxing and it left plenty of time to extract meaning from life around him and, in particular, from the human behaviour that walked the streets. None of it was real, though. In the early afternoons, the sun moved between two tall buildings to the south of Austin's shop and the flowers smiled and leant in the sun's direction. If he didn't know better, he would say his imaginary flowers were cheerful.

Austin invented himself as a florist. Being a florist wasn't what Austin wanted to be, which begged the question, if you are inventing yourself, why would you invent yourself as something you don't really want to be? Austin more or less fell into the florist idea, and he thought it rare that someone would feel they have a calling to arrange flowers. His parents, who both died in a mountain accident in the Netherlands—which seemed unlikely given the notorious lack of mountains in the Netherlands—left him with a modest legacy and, with this, he was able to invent the florist business and himself in it. In this concocted world, he taught himself how to arrange flowers. It wasn't that hard, but he had to admit, he wasn't a natural talent at it. Still, his arrangements were serviceable enough. It was roses that he imagined selling the most of. The city sought the spectre of love and rarely strayed from the comforts of *cliché*s. This truism, Austin felt sure, would apply to his imagined flower-selling business, and it did.

Austin's prose liberated loneliness by exposing it, but it didn't liberate Austin. His prose often converted itself into a character in its own right. He had wanted to write crime fiction because he loved to disappear into the mysteries of a constructed world. He used his downtime during the day thinking about character and plot. He loved the fallen, flawed private investigator characters who all seemed to Austin to be likeable and happy inventions of their author. His favourite was Jake J. Gittes from the film *Chinatown,* written by Robert Towne and starring Jack Nicholson as Jake Gittes. In some ways, Austin looked a little like Nicholson. He didn't have a moustache but then neither did Nicholson in the film. Austin did have a rakish smile, which he rarely used. Austin had adopted as a mantra the most famous and insightful quote from the film *Chinatown*—when a fellow police detective said to Gittes at the end of the movie, by way of an explanation of that which defies explanation, 'Forget it, Jake, it's Chinatown.' To Austin, this explained the inexplicable and often unfathomable randomness and absurdity that was life in the city. It contested how not everything was rational, not everything made sense in the world, and sometimes, perhaps often, the rules don't apply. Austin felt the weight of inexplicable events which combined to represent life, as though humans were not meant to be privy to the workings of life, and must accept their lot, however confusing and absurd it may seem. Free will was at risk, and writers like Ernest Hemingway and Dunleavy de Boston and Robert Towne knew that everything of importance was found in the section of the iceberg under the water, same as with people, and not everything appeared to make sense. Wearing a mask does not save you. It gives you freedom to be yourself but disguised—always disguised and disguised in all ways. Austin found comfort in a world that rarely made sense and exulted in its subtext. He thought that if the world didn't make sense, then he didn't need to either, and that this would mean he still had a chance to be himself. Making sense was hard work. And futile.

Austin had abandoned many stories. He tried to invent a private detective in the style of Gittes, but it wasn't as easy as he thought it would be. He imagined being the detective hired by someone anonymous, to search and track down himself, after he disappeared from his *noir* apartment one hot summer's night between torrential downpours in a seedy part of the city. This involved too much complication, and the idea fell apart. Austin came to the realisation that complexity was far better than complication. Complexity was complex, while complication was facile and too easily traceable. Complexity could be absurd and still work. Austin believed that that was how complexity *did* work.

Austin wrote his dark prose late at night. He favoured short sharp sentences. He sought to keep the meaning under the sentences. He ignored syntax rules. He wanted each sentence to stand alone as a dynamic universe—breaking rules when necessary. He allowed his sentences to be flawed. He wanted the flaws to be flawed. He didn't have any choice. His flawed sentences were reflections of the flawed people he always ended up writing about. He contended that it didn't seem possible to write perfect sentences about imperfect people, and all people were imperfect. Austin acknowledged his sentences deteriorated over time, much like the second law of thermodynamics predicted. They started with verve and punch and pure hope. They were imbued with a searing sense and stood like sentinels, but after a while they read as dark and chaotic. They were reduced to sense-lessness and sat on the screen alone, isolated, frayed, and abandoned, and above all, imperfect, lonely and pleading. Nonetheless, Austin dreamt of writing the perfect sentence. Often before he went to sleep, he imagined he would become world famous for his perfect sentence. He would win the Nobel Prize for literature with his one perfect sentence. All his sentences were perfect before they were written. Before they were written, they represented truth, innocence and hope in a three-act format committed to a journey and an arc. Only after his sentences had been written down did they reveal their failings, when entropy had set in—no adjective or adverb could inject sufficient energy to save them. Adverbs and adjectives had the effect of starving his sentences of their energy. His sentences lost their innocence, and hope disintegrated, and truth, such as it was, was ambiguous and compliant and almost never the truth. Eventually, his sentences withered with cynicism under the crushing weight of the truth, and this continued until the 'perfect' sentence became agonised and imperfect—a metaphor for life, he observed. Entropy was the real deity, if deity stood for 'management'. The universe exploded into existence. Perfect. No flaws. No crime. No sentiment. No human hope to be dashed. No betrayal. Then *the fall*.

Austin's perfect pre-written sentences followed this same pattern immediately he wrote them down. 'The fall' was perfect, or near to, but it was not a sentence, and it was not his. Austin resigned himself to the fact that while all sentences were perfect in the beginning, the elements they consisted of were all imperfect, and this was what prevailed as soon as they were read.

Austin had written a novel several years ago. It took him around five years to complete. It wasn't detective fiction. He didn't know what genre it was, and he had a lot of trouble explaining what it was about to anyone who asked. It was a mystery in the way that human behaviour was a mystery, not in the way that detective fiction was a mystery. The novel had been published and was languishing on websites all over the world. It had been translated into French. Austin came to acknowledge that the French appreciated novels that were off-balance, quirky, intriguing, and absurd, especially absurd. The French gave us Albert Camus and they have a wider variety of cheeses than any other country in the world. Austin felt this explained a lot about the French. The French understood, even embraced, excess. *Forget it, Jake, c'est Fromage, mon dieu.* Austin couldn't say if his novel was intriguing or not. He hoped it was, and he was happy the French might have thought so. He wrote, *Was this sentence a perfect sentence?* He wrote his Nobel literature award speech, which consisted only of one word, '*Thanks*'.

Occasionally, Austin received a random message through his website from some desolate reader somewhere in the world. He received an email from someone in Boardman, Oregon, who thought it imperative to point out she also had lived in Shadyside, Pittsburgh for a while, and worked as a colourist, or colorist as she had spelt it, in a salon called PureBeauty Salon and Spa, on Fifth Avenue in Pittsburgh, PA 15222. And before that, during her twenties, she lived in Corpus Christi, Texas. She lived on a street around the corner from Sandi's Diner, which her cousin, called Sandi, owned. She discussed her addresses but did not mention the novel except by name in the subject line of her email. Maybe she forgot, Austin thought. An email from another reader near Durban in South Africa was less precise regarding location specifics. But he was at pains to point out that he was tall and tended to walk on the balls of his feet due to some mild congenital birth defect for which no surgery or remedial efforts were effective in ameliorating. He stated he didn't mind too much having a defect, it had some disadvantages to be sure, but he claimed he was nonetheless poised and ready to run. Again, he offered no explanation as to why his readiness to run was an advantage, if indeed it was. He also, in a PS, stated that he had read the novel eleven times. He didn't make any other comment about the novel, or his experience of reading it eleven times, or why he had read it so often. Austin was asked odd things. Someone from Boise, Idaho, asked 'are potatoes grown commercially in your country?' He answered, yes. Another time he heard from a girl called Billie from Tahiti. She said his novel frightened her, but she didn't say why. He reread his novel. He agreed he could see why she might have been frightened, but then it was a story of a group of people who were themselves frightened. He wrote back to her and told her he never meant to write a novel that might frighten her. She wrote back and said, 'That's alright. I like to be frightened because it's the only time when I feel like I'm real and not a character in your novel.' She wrote this in French and Austin had to translate it using Google. He never heard from her again. One of the main characters in his novel was called Billie, and Billie lived her life fearfully. This may not have been a *coincidence*. Austin ran the French pronunciation of the word 'coincidence' through his mind for days, so much so that it felt like it had made a groove along his neural pathways. He thought of these neural pathways as dark empty roads with streetlights providing enough light to see an empty circle of illuminated bitumen.

Austin's novel was only marginally a detective story. It was not a whodunnit. It was a whowroteit. It had no private investigator and was not a mystery like *Chinatown*. The question the novel asked was, 'Who, out of the cast of characters, was the narrator?' But this was one of the many philosophical questions his novel asked and refused to answer.

The story of the novel was just what came out when Austin wrote it. He couldn't remember writing it and it seemed as though he might have been absent during the work, and, in some mysterious way, the novel wrote itself and the characters constructed their own life and dialogue. They didn't acknowledge he existed as the author. He consoled himself with the thought that his novel was a fictional world, in a place where normal everyday rules fail and things don't add up, and you can't make them add up, no matter how hard you try or yell into the silence. One day, Austin decided he would go to Sandi's Diner in Corpus Christi and have a burger and fries. He liked this idea because it felt like he was disappearing. No one would know who he was. He hoped the food was good.

Austin's novel had garnered some good reviews, but mostly from the academic end of the reviewing world and, as such, these reviews were not read by many of the book-buying public. Soon after the good reviews appeared in various newspapers and magazines, his sales slowed to a trickle and, eventually, to virtually nothing. He was still trying to write a PI story, but so far nothing like that had emerged from his imagination.

The city in which Austin Quinn lived was a place where things disappeared, and no one thought it odd. One night, Austin disappeared. His name was not Austin Quinn. Austin Quinn was his *nom de plume* or one of his *nom de plumes*. He thought for a while he'd like to call himself Winston Smith, after the protagonist in *1984*, who Austin considered a flawed hero, but he thought the name was too obvious, so he considered another name.

Austin considered himself flawed, but no hero.

These days, a young woman ran the imagined florist shop. She didn't know Austin but was good at flower arrangements. Her business was 'blooming', she liked to say. She had a small tattoo of a white bird on the back of her left knee. She took over the shop through a real-estate agency that had been appointed to find a tenant. The real-estate agency had never heard of Austin Quinn.

The neon light continued to search Austin's apartment at night. When the landlord entered the dark apartment to find out why the rent had stopped, all he found was a blue clock on the wall and, in the shadows, an empty bird-cage, a hand mirror up against the splashback on the kitchen bench and a pile of brown and white mail on the floor at the door. He found nothing else except a manuscript sitting in the dust on the floor, abandoned, as though someone had left their imagination on the floor to be covered in dust.

The blue and red neon light kept flashing through the apartment—its reversed message reflected on and off in the mirror. The landlord didn't notice. He bent down and grabbed the pile of letters at the door. He stuffed them into a garbage bag. He was about to drop the manuscript in the garbage bag but hesitated and left it on the kitchen bench. Taking the garbage bag, he closed the door behind him, generating a puff of random air. The title page of the manuscript broke free and floated down across the floor. The landlord was gone. The apartment was empty—no Austin, no bird, no trace. The neon light flashed across the title page on the floor. Intermittently, the words '*What Will Happen to You?*' appeared—on and off, on and off, on and off.

# Robbie Carton

Bentley's arm slid in next to Robbie, toward Robbie's outbox, to retrieve the files that were ready to leave. The word 'Panic', written in longhand, appeared at the top of each file. The 'arm slide', as Robbie called it, was one of the many annoying habits Bentley had. He didn't ask, he didn't say anything. Bentley's arm would slither from behind Robbie, and his hand would grab the files. Robbie thought of it as an extended tentacle, which could cantilever itself and reach unnatural human lengths for an arm. Robbie wanted to bite it, but he wasn't sure it was an actual arm, or what it would taste like, or if he had the teeth for such an operation. On the other hand—same hand, same arm—it might be no more than the normal business of Bentley collecting files from each outbox along the rows. Robbie could never be sure of what was, and what wasn't. And no one took any notice of Bentley collecting the files except Robbie, and Robbie didn't notice it all the time.

'What do you mean, I lose things?' Robbie asked Bentley again because it would take up a few minutes from what would otherwise be another mundane day, and because it had been eating away at him. Bentley didn't respond, so by way of a nervous diversion, Robbie said, 'It's an odd-shaped day, and time is running out.' Bentley stared at Robbie with what Robbie would describe as utter contempt. Robbie thought if Bentley's contempt were a colour, it would be blood red from an oversupply of red corpuscles, and if it had an odour, it would smell like sulphur or burning hair. Robbie imagined having a machete ready to chop off Bentley's arm before he could grab Robbie's files. He imagined the blood spurting out, covering the partition walls, and flooding the floor up to the casters on the chairs. Everyone would have sticky shoes and squelch as they walked around, creating an operatic symphony. Robbie's question, 'What do you mean, I lose things?' hung in the air for all to see.

'You know what I mean,' Bentley said with both amusement and authority. With that definitive explanation, Bentley collected the files from Robbie's out-tray, and ignoring Robbie's reference to time running out, headed back to his cubicle.

Robbie not only didn't know what the Bertleman meant, he wished Bentley hadn't said it in front of everyone in Robbie's immediate vicinity. 'I don't lose things. I am so organised and clear-headed most of the time that I know where everything is, and everything is where it should be, that is, except me. I shouldn't be here. I should be a private detective in a blurred wet nocturnal city somewhere, hiding in between neon flashes and eating dystopian food products.' Robbie thought he was whispering this to himself.

'So, what you're talking about is a mystery to me,' Robbie mumbled.

That was Robbie's take on what the Bertlepopstar said on one level. On another level, Robbie knew what Bentley meant. And Bentley was right. Robbie did lose things, not necessarily the things Bentley was talking about, but probably those too. This terrified Robbie when he thought about it. A lot of things terrified Robbie—losing things was one of them, especially if the thing he lost was himself. 'Himself' was all he had.

Robbie suffered from 'accountant's tummy'. Accountants, according to Robbie, tended to suffer from a state of near-permanent nausea and nervousness caused by a lack of control and meaningful purpose in their lives—in other words, 'accountant's tummy' occurred when, and because, they were not in charge of their world or because they were an accountant and their only contribution to the world was a boring balanced balance sheet. Robbie had decided that one day, as an act of absolute anarchy, he would produce an unbalanced balance sheet—although as an accountant, that was impossible. The top drawer of everyone's desk in the department contained a pack of antacids. Antacids were the accountant's drug of choice, apart from alcohol and fake amusement.

'Stop mumbling, Carton. The whole floor can hear you. And anyway, that was yesterday I said that, in case you hadn't noticed.' Bentley stood up to call this out to Robbie employing his full height for grammatical emphasis—as though he were a human exclamation point.

'One of the things you *lose* is track of time.' Bentley laughed as he drawled out the word 'lose' for effect. Then he flopped down in his hydraulic chair with a dramatic whoosh—no doubt representing some other melodramatic grammatical flourish.

Bentley looked pleased with himself. Bentley would have thought that any day you could get one over Robbie Carton was a good day, especially in front of everyone. This was what Robbie thought Bentley thought about Robbie, when, and if, Bentley thought about Robbie, which Robbie thought wouldn't have been often.

Robbie felt his tummy grip. He hadn't realised he'd been mumbling. He thought he'd been mouthing his words.

Typing the following, Robbie used his preferred third-person pronoun.

*He had untidy black hair, though fashionable, and was a twenty-nine-year-old accountant hurtling down a rabbit warren.*

Robbie highlighted 'rabbit warren', a paraphrased reference to Lewis Carroll's *Alice's Adventures in Wonderland* and inserted 'wormhole' instead. He continued.

*He probably had the most boring job in the two known universes, assuming there were two, or at least more than one. He lived alone in one of the universes—he didn't know which one. He had takeaway curry five out of every four nights. He drank too much and spent most of his time wishing he was somewhere else, maybe the other known universe. Looking around the department at his colleagues—misfits most of them—he couldn't be sure he wasn't already there, the other universe, that is. It was hard to tell, as absurdly, both universes were identical. They would be, wouldn't they? He wished he was doing anything but what he was doing, and that whatever it was he imagined he was doing, he always ended up getting 'the girl', like in a typical Hollywood film, like he was the hero and it was his job to save the world, and his reward was a woman who would love him forever and who he gave red roses to, in this Hollywood film he was in.*

Robbie was never happy ending a sentence with a preposition. He knew it was at least one grammatical rule he should break just to show he could. It was difficult though, and it unsettled him. He saved and closed the file. He opened a new page and wrote:

*I'm surrounded by bladders with various amounts of urine. How much urine is stored in bladders in this department at any given time? Why can't we hear it slosh about when people move? Probably a good thing because we wouldn't be able to hear much else.*

He saved and closed the file, then opened it again, then minimised it.

Robbie daydreamed about what it would be like to be loved by someone—someone who would love him forever. He realised he had never given a woman flowers, in particular, roses. He felt disappointed in himself, and regret landed by parachute in the darker corners of his stomach to sit next to the regret already there over the *preposition at the end of a sentence* event. White eyes blinked in the dark.

He wouldn't have thought Bentley would have had any disconcerting thoughts about Robbie, but with Bentley it was hard to tell what he was thinking. That was the thing about Bentley, he was a known unknown. Bentley could never end a sentence with a preposition. That much was known. Robbie looked over at Gloria. Robbie knew that Gloria was the only one in the department who wasn't stumped when it came to nailing the essential Bentley. Nailing people's essential selves was Gloria's speciality and an aspect of Gloria that Robbie admired.

Robbie reopened the bit about him being in a Hollywood film and deleted the last three words.

Robbie didn't daydream about giving roses to just any woman, or, say, a generic woman. He daydreamt about a specific woman—the incandescent Sophie Fanshawe, poet and bartender extraordinaire. She wore an alcohol-server nametag, that's how Robbie knew her name. She tended bar at the Stalwart pub. He saw her Friday nights when he went to the pub after work to meet up with the only two friends he had in the world, if indeed it was realistic to refer to either of them as 'friends'. They met Friday nights at the pub, but that wasn't a formal arrangement. It was more that they tended to sit in the same spots every Friday night, and those spots happened to be next to one another. Robbie had never spoken to either of them and he didn't know their names.

Anyway, he so far had never said anything to Sophie Fanshawe beyond ordering a beer, or a cocktail, when and if he felt buoyant, which wasn't often. Buoyancy required a lot of beer and a lot of beer erupted in melancholy, which had the effect of negating the buoyancy and thus the desire for something with personality, such as a cocktail. Not saying anything to Sophie was a deliberate strategy. He called it his 'slow burn' strategy, and he thought it was working. He couldn't be sure it was, as he hadn't yet developed an empirical test to determine its effectiveness. It was a strategy in progress, he conjectured. 'I won't know for sure if it is working, or not, until it doesn't, or does, work,' he told himself. He hoped he thought this, but, in retrospect, there's a chance he may have mumbled it. About all he could say was, at this juncture, it was either working or not working, or not not working. The whole thing had a touch of quantum mechanics about it. He thought of Schrödinger's cat. The only thing you can be sure of in this world, Robbie told himself, was that you can be simultaneously sure and unsure—sure of being unsure or unsure of being sure. And while this lacked originality, it was both the beauty of life and the pain in the arse bit of life. And both existed at least theoretically, like the cat in the box, at the same time, in the time/space continuum—whatever and wherever that was, he thought. He had mentioned this to Bentley two days ago when they were discussing end-of-months. No response from Bentley, but that wasn't unusual. Robbie wrote some of this in his special file, which he held open all day but kept minimised, unless he was working on it. He sent some of these thoughts to Gloria, but hadn't heard anything back from her either, but then Gloria did a lot of work in the department, and she was responsible for everyone's output.

Last Friday night, when Robbie was sitting in his usual place at the bar of the Stalwart, Sophie Fanshawe, with her bladder half full, or maybe ten per cent full, was serving on the other side of the bar. He thought of her as a kind of Helen of Troy—striking, dangerous, unattainable. She had started on his side of the bar, but then she was over the other side, pretending not to notice him. He wondered if that wasn't part of *her* strategy, to ignore him affectionately. He loved her all the more for it. He couldn't hear her urine sloshing about as she moved. Either she was low on urine at that moment, or the cacophony of the pub masked her slosh. He kept his eye on her. He settled on there being no slosh to speak of, as if it mattered, which it didn't. He felt buoyant and ordered a cocktail from one of the other bartenders, but then his previous alcohol intake started to take effect and caused him to lose his buoyancy, and he wished he hadn't ordered the cocktail. He downed it in three gulps to get rid of it. Sophie's presence alone gave him hope and made him feel uplifted, but the problem with him feeling uplifted was that mood-wise, he had further to fall. That's how Robbie felt sitting at the bar with a lot of urine on board and a skinful of alcohol. He wondered, 'Am I mumbling my thoughts?' He hoped he wasn't mumbling—Sophie would think he was mad. He thought better of asking her how much urine she had on board. She might not recognise it as small talk, or in his case, small mumble.

Small talk was a complete mystery to Robbie. He had never mastered it. He didn't know how to start it. He didn't know how to stop it. 'But without it, you're shot,' he mumbled. To meet women, Robbie agreed small talk was needed, but women of substance would see right through Robbie's small talk and reject him. Robbie couldn't blame them. His small talk, such as it was, was banal and that was putting the best spin on it. He concluded he would reject himself if he were a woman confronted by his small talk. Sophie was a woman of substance, and as such, Robbie knew small talk would not work on her, had he been capable of it, which he wasn't.

'Are you *still* mumbling, Carton?' Bentley yelled this out over several desks, emphasising the word 'still'. Everyone within earshot showed accountant 'amusement' on their faces and affected the accountant's equivalent of a fake wry smile. Robbie felt his face flush. He opened his secret file and started typing.

*Amusement. On this occasion though, the 'amusement' escalated spontaneously, and everyone on the floor shook their shoulders suggesting a giggle. A giggle in accountant-speak was bold and heroic. It was a wry smile on steroids, a supersonic gesture and, given its recklessness, shoulders quickly settled in unison so as not to chance drawing too much attention among the herd. It was thought to be dangerous for accountants to draw too much attention to themselves. No one knew precisely what would happen if they did draw too much attention to themselves because they were all accountants and, as such, didn't draw attention to themselves, but it was agreed that it would be dangerous if any of them did—as catastrophic as an ant breaking out of the column and taking up harness racing, wearing racing colours and a tiny, peaked cap. Everyone grabbed an antacid. The accountants, not the ants. The accountants performed these body rituals—shoulder shuddering, giggling, grasping for an antacid—without looking up from whatever it was they were doing, which was probably looking at porn or playing computer games. There are no right or wrong answers.*

Robbie stopped typing.

Robbie felt the heat of the flush again, rising and warming the roots of his hair follicles as it rose to the top of his head and continued upward as a perpetual thermal. Typing again, he wrote:

*Several soaring birds had gathered in the thermal above his head.*

He continued to type, referring to himself in the third person rather than using the first-person pronoun. This allowed him a fictional licence by establishing some fictional space between his actual self and his implied/fictional self. He thought of Sophie Fanshawe with not just a little angst and hope. He thought of her inner thighs. He was sure they were creamy and smooth and sensitive to a caress and a gentle bite—his caress and his gentle bite.

He thought someone at the pub had told him she was leaving and going to Paris, or something like that. He could have gotten it wrong given his state of inebriation at the time. Robbie admired Sophie Fanshawe. She was not beautiful in the classic sense, but she was striking, breathtakingly striking. Robbie remembered thinking this last Friday night, when he was at his usual place at the bar. He thought he might comment on how striking Sophie was to one of his friends sitting next to him, but he didn't. In Robbie's opinion, Sophie Fanshawe's lips looked like they had been designed for the specific purpose of being kissed—*lavishly* kissed. He typed '*lavishly*' on a blank page, then put it in italics. Robbie made an exception to his 'no adverbs' rule. When it came to Sophie Fanshawe, too many adverbs were never enough. Robbie wanted to believe he had been designed and destined to do the lavish kissing. If only he could hold her in his arms. He wanted to smell her skin, feel her soft feminine body and 'ample breasts' against his chest. He couldn't believe he used the word 'ample' to describe her ample breasts. He said these words to himself as he typed them.

*Sometimes unoriginal clichés worked. All clichés were unoriginal by definition—there was no such thing as an original cliché. If there were such a thing, it wouldn't be a cliché.*

He caught himself mumbling again and affected a throat-clearing distraction. *Ample.* He typed it next to *lavishly*.

Sophie Fanshawe was all-woman, no question about that. Referring to women as 'all-woman' or men as 'all-man' was a habit confined to accountants. It was obvious, puerile, childish, archaic, and politically incorrect, and these were the reasons the average single-celled male accountant found such things irresistible. Accountants said these things with alacrity but to an acceptable accountant's level of alacrity. The word 'alacrity', along with 'loquaciousness', was part of their armoury and both were accompanied by a fleeting all-knowing accountant's 'grin'. The all-knowing 'grin' was part of the accountant's coda—an addendum, or addenda if it was two or more accountants, or two or more grins—an accountant's excuse for a joke. A joke, which Robbie thought, Bentley would appreciate. He thought to send this joke in an email to Bentley but didn't. Instead, he sent the following to Bentley:

*Once upon a time, dinosaurs roamed the earth. Why so much roaming? Didn't they run sometimes? Go for a jog on a nice day? With all that roaming, didn't they enjoy a nice sit down occasionally? Watch the kids? Talk to friends? Maybe discuss the footy? Have an ice cream? Have a game of hypotheticals, like, 'What would you do if a meteor hits the planet, Dino?'*
*'Like that's going to happen.'*
*'That's why it's called a "hypothetical", roadkill breath. It's a "what if". Of course, it's never going to happen. Why is it so dark suddenly?'*

No response from Bentley, or Gloria.
Robbie posed the question,

*'How do you throw out a garbage bin?'*

He sent this to Bentley in another email.
Robbie's notoriety for being hopeless at small talk meant he confined himself to not doing it. He thought it was the least he could do for the women of his current universe. He never spoke to strange women he might be attracted to or accidentally bump into—not 'strange' women but women who might be a stranger to him, as in unknown to him. They may well be strange, but how would he know if he didn't talk to them? And what was 'strange'? One person's 'strange' was another person's endearing eccentricity. It was a minefield. He respected Sophie, and he didn't want her subjected to his inane attempts at small talk, so he resolved not to talk to her.

He wondered again, how *do* you throw out a garbage bin? The garbage truck comes along, empties the bin then leaves it there. You can't get rid of it. You can't make it disappear. Was this small talk, he wondered?

Robbie minimised his secret file and wrote on the top of a blank page on his computer the following:

*Micro story. Small talk. Change the names later.*

He decided to use his and Bentley's name in this micro story for convenience and because he wanted to get the story out while it was swirling about in his mind. Trying to think of two appropriate names would hold him up. He started typing.

*The characters. Robbie (not the Robbie) and Bentley (not the Bentley, but someone imagined and similar to Bentley proper).*

*Small Talk*
*The Meaning of Life Solved by Two Guys (as if)*

*Robbie and Bentley sat at an outside table of their local favourite café. It was a Saturday afternoon. The sun shone. It was not too hot. There was the gentlest of gentle breezes. Conditions were perfect for meeting women of the female inclination. To men, Robbie in particular, the business of meeting women was mysterious, disconcerting and required an innate ability for small talk. Men have been trying to master 'small talk' since Moses first realised, he was drowning in shit, and he couldn't say for sure how many chameleons were on board.*

*'How would you rate yourself at small talk?' Robbie asked Bentley.*

*'Superficial,' Bentley responded.*

*'That good?' Robbie was impressed.*

*Robbie and Bentley covertly eyed two beautiful women at a table nearby. This was not to suggest these women were particularly beautiful, they may well have been, but that wasn't the point. The point was that all women are beautiful on a Saturday afternoon when two guys are sitting in a café. Both men gestured to one another in the direction of the women. Their gestures ranged over the full gamut of male discussion without uttering a single word. The gestures were subtle—a nod, a wink, a pursing of one's lips, pushing air out through the pursed lips to make a whistling noise. These were universal gestures of the male language concerning women and were sufficient to carry the intended communication between two blokes. The women stood up and walked away, oblivious to the male gaze. That was what the men in this tale thought anyway—women are not oblivious creatures.*

*Robbie broke the silence and the ritual. 'You know, I'm no good at small talk. I try. I really try. I even try to approach the problem and deconstruct it logically, but nothing helps. I know others say they're also bad at small talk, but I don't know about them. I know I'm no good at it. No matter how hard I try and concentrate, I'm no good at it. Awkward is the best I seem to be able to achieve.'*

*'Women can live with awkward, mostly because they don't have a choice. Men are born with an "awkward" gene, and a "small talk" gene. Both are in contest with each other. We're compelled to try and chat women up utilising our "small talk" gene, then the "awkward" gene cuts in and makes the small talk look lame. Do you see? It's one of life's cruelties,' Bentley offered.*

*'Right.' Robbie looked at Bentley with cynicism, as though he had just invented a completely unworkable hypothesis, which strangely sounded plausible to Robbie, cognitive dissonance notwithstanding. Robbie continued, 'Yeah, whatever, but you want to do better for them than awkward. Besides, there's good awkward and bad awkward. I have mastered bad awkward.'*

*'One can only postulate on how you tell the difference between good awkward and bad awkward,' Bentley wondered out loud.*

*'Yeah, well, women know, trust me. But I suppose awkward is awkward, I guess. Good or bad, you're not getting anywhere with it.'*

*'Nobody is good at small talk,' Bentley observed. 'It's not a talent you want, is it? I mean, if your claim is that you're good at small talk, then by definition, you're superficial and lack substance. If your claim is you aren't any good at it, then you're indulging in small talk, and, as such, lay yourself open to the suggestion you are superficial, lack substance, are falsely modest and in your case, ugly,' Bentley concluded.*

*'For a start, I don't know what to say, what topics to raise, and how lightly I should deal with any particular topic given that it's small talk, not big talk,' Robbie said, ignoring Bentley's 'ugly' remark.*

*'Don't take offence when my eyes roll, will you, Moley?'*

*'When I meet someone on the street or in a more formal environment such as a cocktail party, not that I go to many of those...'*

*'Cocktail parties are rare these days,' Bentley observed philosophically.*

'...I fumble my way along. People, or more specifically women, who I might have met before and have shown some interest in me, however scant, say, "How's it going?" I say, "Yeah, good, you?" They say, "Fine, what have you been up to?" This is the question that gets me every time. I don't know what I've been up to. Since when, and what, if anything, I might've been up to, could be of any interest to anyone, even if I could think of something to report. And this also presupposes that the woman asking this question cares. It's more likely to be a question of small talk and not meant to signal their undying fascination and genuine interest in the episodes of my recent life, even if there were any—and if they, these women, might be sending out signals that I have no way of picking up and processing. I don't have a processing gene when it comes to women. So I answer, "Not much, you know. How about you? You been doing anything interesting?" They say, "Nah, you know how it is." I say, "Yeah." But I haven't a clue how it is, or even what "it" is.'

'You can overthink this subject, you know.' Bentley took a sip of his cappuccino, leaving white foam on his upper lip. Robbie didn't mention it.

'Then there's the other problem of how to get out of a small talk event. I don't know how to finish—how to relieve the situation and let the woman get away from me. Women, I've noticed, start saying things like, "Oh well, guess I should make a move." I say, "Sure yes, me too." They say, "What do you have on for the rest of the day?" I say, "Oh nothing much, you know, the usual." Talk about lame. It doesn't sound like I'm putting in an effort, but I am. I'm sweating bullets trying to sound genuine and interesting and interested, but it all comes out wrong and unconvincing in my view. What do you think?'

'I think I have identified "bad awkward".'

'Then the worst of it occurs when they say, "We should catch up soon." I say, "Yeah, we should, we could have dinner sometime, maybe I should call you." I say this knowing full well the last thing she wants is a call from me. She's being polite, as women do. But I remain resolute with the charade, undeterred, nothing will deter me. So this is when I make that stupid phone-hand, where you shape your hand into a handset and hold it up to your ear and mouth. You have your thumb to your ear and your pinkie to your mouth as if saying, "I should phone" isn't sufficient to get the concept through. I must stress the point with my phone-hand, which, I have to say, I have never mastered. To be brutally honest, I can't do it unless I use my other hand to press my middle fingers of my phone-hand into a fist and pull out my index finger and my pinkie finger and hope they stay in place long enough for me to get it all to the side of my face. I *invariably stick one of my rogue fingers up my nostril—the one that's meant to be part of the fist/handle, but point-blank refuses to stay closed. All this makes me look like a complete numbat. About the only part of this whole charade, I have mastered, is the bit where I, for reasons I don't have the slightest clue about, hold the elbow of my phone-hand out parallel to the horizon to act like an aerial, but which has the actual effect of making me look idiotic. And if it says anything at all, it says I'm overemphasising the whole "I should call you" bit because I have no real intention of calling because I know she doesn't want me to. And I know the woman I'm talking to knows I know she doesn't want me to call, and that's why I have to over-egg the pudding and exaggerate the whole gesture, when I just want to get my rogue finger out of my nose and myself out of the situation. But in reality, I'm sort of serious about calling. I want to call. And this is me making a complete hash of the encounter.'*

*'Right, and this is apropos of what, exactly?'*

*'The delicate art of "how to chat up the female of the species", I can't do it. When it comes to that specific "small talk" occasion, I fail catastrophically.'*

*'What about a plan, then?' Bentley asked, as though he might have stumbled on the secret of chatting up women. 'For men, a plan is all that is needed. It doesn't need to bog itself down with details or common sense. A lame plan is fine. More often than not, a lame plan is the most men can manage. Lame, though, is not a concept many men can identify. It is like they lack a lame-detecting gene. Some women claim this is one of the endearing features of the male of the species, which goes to show how generous women can be.'*

*'You think I haven't thought about a plan? But breaking it down into analysable and manageable bits to come up with a sound strategy has in itself been a disaster, and, if anything, has made things much worse. I did this. I broke it down to greeting, banter, farewell, and future arrangements. I wrote a script for myself, so I had actual words to say, planned words that convey sincerity, interest, and purpose, and don't involve any part of my anatomy shoved up my nose. And in their respective components, they sounded good...well, okay. But when strung together as is required in an actual small talk situation, they sounded stilted, lacking sincerity, interest, and purpose. I broke out into a sweat of torrential proportions, and the female concerned couldn't wait to get away before she drowned. Then I thought it might be better to have something interesting to say, something that women would not expect in a small talk exchange...you know, to stand out from the crowd, give myself an edge. This took me a while. First, you must choose a topic, but then you don't know what the other person*

*is interested in, so you keep the topic general, universal. I thought I came up with something both interesting and general enough to interest everyone. Here's what I came up with. Do you want to hear this?'*

*'Does free will exist?' Bentley's eyes followed a beautiful woman who swished by the café tables, leaving behind a trail of exquisite perfume that captivated Bentley and every man within the postcode. The 'eye follow' is something all men are used to and allow as an unwritten code. If a lovely lass is within sight, you are allowed to lose concentration and watch and enjoy the sight. The man talking will keep talking. He will slow down and try not to include vital information to allow for the break while the 'lovely lass' is in sight. Immediately after she has swished by and left the area, the ogler must re-engage his concentration with sincerity and earnestness.*

*'You have to admire a well-executed swish, don't you think?' Bentley asked.*

*'One of the joys of life,' Robbie said.*

*'You were saying?' Bentley enquired.*

Robbie tried to form his hand into a phone-hand. He had to press some fingers down and keep others erect. It wasn't easy. His middle fingers, the ones meant to be pressed down, insisted on popping out.

He worked on the piece for the rest of the day. He set aside his actual work. How would the world, his world, anyone's world, be better if he produced another set of figures? It wouldn't, so he didn't. He would get his actual work done after work. He preferred the office when everyone had left, when the light faded and only his cubicle light was on. He edited, cut and pasted, refined and rewrote the piece until he thought it was tight and hopeful. He knew he shouldn't try for 'hopeful'—he was no good at it, and he didn't believe in hope.

He thought he had to change the names of the two protagonists—it was too confusing, and neither were accurate depictions. He wasn't, and neither was Bentley, especially Bentley, and himself too. He thought for a while and changed his name to Jake, then to Don, and Bentley's to Austin. Later, in the early evening, he added more to the piece and gave it an ending. He introduced a woman who he called Sophie. He changed Sophie's name to Gloria, then thought, to hell with it and changed it back to Sophie. It was a good name, and the fact that he was fascinated with *a* Sophie, the actual Sophie, only he knew, and he didn't know that, so he left it. He changed his name back to his, and Bentley to his—it didn't seem that wrong, in fact it felt satisfying on some level he couldn't define. He closed the file as though that was an end to it, and it was. Earlier, about mid-afternoon, when everyone's sugar levels were fading, he looked over and saw Bentley talking to Gloria. They were discussing a file. Bentley never had to concern himself with small talk.

Later, in the dark, Robbie sat back in his chair and looked like he was thinking. He was thinking but not about anything to do with work. The office was dark and quiet. Robbie liked to think of himself as an unreliable narrator of his life, of life in general and of people in his life. And he was. He was so unreliable, he couldn't trust himself. He decided that when he next got some business cards printed, he would include the words 'and Unreliable Narrator', following 'Accountant'.

*Robbie Carton*
*Accountant and Unreliable Narrator*

There were days when Robbie wondered why Bentley put up with him. Robbie wrote a small piece for the company's monthly newsletter, called *Mine Yourself*. The newsletter was called *Mine Yourself*, not the small piece he wrote. Bentley had conceived the newsletter, come up with the name, and edited and produced it. Robbie had to concede that the Bentmeister did a good job in producing and editing the newsletter, although he would never admit this to Bentley. Some of the pieces Bentley wrote were not without a certain verve and style, Robbie thought. This both surprised him and didn't surprise him. The pieces Bentley wanted Robbie to write had to cover some aspect of the company, mainly employee focused. 'In the course of their work' sort of thing. 'Mine the human interest', as Bentley liked to say. 'Bring your quirky slant on life to bear.' When Bentley suggested potential titles in a conversation, he and Robbie had about a week ago, Bentley had held up two fingers from each hand in 'air quotes'. If that weren't bad enough, Supervisor Bentley formed those two fingers from each hand into two-fingered claws and bounced them up and down at the sides of his head for emphasis. This drove Robbie into hysterics, but there was something unauthentic about his hysterics. Not only did Robbie's shoulders shake, which in itself was concerning enough, but to further endanger himself among his brethren, he laughed out loud. This was more than alarming and nothing less than extreme accountant behaviour. Many on the floor within hearing distance sucked in their breath with accountant trepidation, and synchronised, as though in a chorus line, reaching for their antacids, popping the lid, and throwing down a tab or two. It could have been set to music.

Robbie knew Bentley had failed to see what was so funny and was too taken aback by Robbie's odd and bold behaviour of 'laughing out loud' that he demurred. Laughing out loud had caused Robbie to feel disorientated and queasy. Other-self remained silent. The room swirled about him as it did when he had drunk excessively at the Stalwart, and was replete with alcohol, as he liked to say. 'Replete' was one of his favourite words. To counter the room's swirl, he had to repair to his cubicle and hold on to his desk. 'Repair' was another of his favourite words. He felt guilty for embarrassing Bentley more than Bentley deserved. Robbie realised that Bentley had little by way of defence in the face of Robbie laughing out loud at him, and this made Robbie feel unsettled and a bully. There was a lot Robbie didn't like about himself. Again, no comment from other-self, which seemed disorientating in and of itself. That was all a week ago, or longer. Robbie was unreliable at determining time spans.

Robbie, seated at his desk in the darkening office, thought about Bentley and his newsletter. In recent days, writing for Bentley's newsletter was the one thing that kept Robbie from disappearing, though it failed to under-pin his sanity in any meaningful way. Robbie felt compelled to write. It was as though writing was something he had to do for his mental well-being. Robbie would like to write for a living. However, there was no money in writing even if he had any talent for it, which was dubious, and what with rent, takeaway curry, alcohol and women—not that he spent much money on women, but he liked to think he would if he could, if he met one that could survive his small talk and would agree to go out with him should he be bold enough to ask—he needed a job that paid a regular income. He became an accountant as a kind of protest against the fact that he couldn't expect to become a writer and earn a living. He couldn't do what he wanted, so in protest, he picked the most boring, least satisfying career he could think of to punish himself for not having the courage to do what he wanted. So accountancy it was. Accountancy was a self-imposed death sentence. Robbie liked metaphysical, over-blown metaphorical literary conceit, but it was eating away at him. There was a part of him, a large part that wished he could disappear. Disappear and start again but next time, he would do something exciting, which would result in him never feeling in jeopardy. He was sure that if he were to show his latest piece to Sophie Fanshawe, she might think kindly toward him. Sophie Fanshawe, Robbie had discovered, was a published writer—a published writer with ample breasts who wanted Robbie to kiss her lavishly. Why wouldn't she, Robbie supposed.

He resolved to write a micro story about Sophie Fanshawe. His first. Not his first micro story, and not a micro story about the celestial Miss Fanshawe, but a micro story inspired by her. He resolved never to show it to her, as such intimacy might alarm her, and he would never want to alarm her. Besides, he had little confidence in his writing talent, if 'talent' could be used in a sentence about himself. This notion caused other-self to laugh, but not maniacally this time. The laugh from other-self was more subdued than usual. Perhaps he was still recovering from Robbie's 'out-loud' laugh at Bentley. Even other-self was tremulous with Robbie's behaviour.

Bentley's incessant question popped into Robbie's head, and he wondered again what *will* happen to him. There were times when he wanted to hate Bentley. Right here, right now, in the office, could be one of those times. Perhaps his greatest fear in life was that the answer to the question of 'What will happen to you?' was *nothing*. *Nothing* will happen to him. So far in his life, *nothing* had happened to him, and *nothing* was killing him. If he could reinvent himself and start again, he would make sure *something* would happen to him, even if it were only the reinvention, after which nothing would happen to him again. Robbie sucked in a chunk of dark office air. He hadn't breathed for some time. He didn't hate Bentley. Bentley was annoying but not hateable. It wasn't Bentley he hated.

The darkness around Robbie thickened into a pearl-like cocoon, with a strict border between the darkness and the light glowing from the lamp on his desk. His head and shoulders were hunched over in the dark, the rest of him was in the light. Ideas floated through his mind. Robbie typed.

*(A micro story by Robbie Carton, as inspired by Sophie Fanshawe and other things. Lots of other things. None of the facts are true, unless they are. Names, places, and facts all transparently changed to protect the innocent/innocence, in that both innocents and innocence exist. You'll work it out.)*

*Distorted Perceptions*
*By*
*Robbie Carton*

*Question: 'How do you throw out a garbage bin?'*

*Rodney pondered the question after he said it out loud. No one answered. They stared at their beers, as though inspecting the amber fluid for any imperfections was their life's work. On tough days, Rodney thought of himself as a kind of garbage bin. Garbage bins start empty at the beginning of each week. They fill with rubbish, sometimes the odd treasure, then are emptied again, 'or renewed', as he liked to describe it on his positive days, to anyone who would listen. No one was listening. Spider webs and a fair bit of grime were characteristics of his garbage-bin-self these days and getting a bit worse for wear as the relentless juggernaut of life rolled along, emptying him, and leaving him behind. It didn't feel much like 'renewal' anymore. 'Juggernaut,' he said out loud. 'Juggernaut is a word that can hold its own. Let's face it, "juggernaut" is a word with muscle, don't you think?' Rodney said this to anyone in the bar and waited for some recognition but got none. 'You can't keep getting picked up, bashed, then thrown back down without taking a few hits, you know, losing a bit of yourself along the way. On the other hand, you also gain things too—dings, grime, busted hinges, spider webs, holes in the lid. Life, eh? Life, eh? Life but not as we know it,' Rodney said for the benefit of those nearby. 'Life was tough on the architecture.' He smiled conspiratorially at his fellow bar compatriots. None acknowledged him or one another for that matter. It was Tuesday night around ten o'clock in the local bar, as Rodney emptied his beer with several annoying musical swallows, his Adam's apple pumping its way up and down his throat like a useless piston. Rodney clung to his favourite barstool in his favourite bar with the same old comrades on their favourite barstools. Everyone was working hard to ignore one another and to be ignored. Rodney never let that deter him from enlightening them in the low-lit establishment.*

*'What are we doin' here?' Rodney asked anyone and no one. He didn't expect an answer. Frank, the bartender, kept on cleaning the glasses without looking over at Rodney. He tsked and rolled his eyes. Frank rarely looked at any of the regulars for fear of them taking that as a cue to start talking to him, so he made the half-hearted gesture of the 'tsk' and eye-roll with his head down and hoped for anonymity and peace. The truth of it was that the only risk of a conversation for Frank was from Rodney. Frank put the glass he was polishing back in the rack on the bar, flicked the tea towel over his shoulder, bent over, lifted the trapdoor, and scooted down the stairs into the cellar. Rodney thought he was probably checking the gauges on the kegs, or, more likely, trying to avoid the others at the bar. Rodney couldn't blame him for that—they were a draining*

lot. Rodney watched two of them drain their beers. Rodney peered over the bar and down into the dark cellar. 'The Abyss,' Rodney observed. 'Or an abyss.' He mumbled this, but that was okay.

Rodney looked around behind him at the waitress bending over a table, cleaning it with a cloth. Her name was Helen. Helen of Troy, he liked to say to himself. Helen of Troy, Rodney estimated, was in her thirties, or not. Maybe she was older, or younger, who knows these things? It was hard to tell. Rodney reckoned he had lost the ability to guess ages. Ever since he hit his more mature years there were several things he couldn't do anymore...well, couldn't do as well as he used to be able to, he should say. His balance, for a start. He couldn't put on his socks or shoes these days without leaning against something or knocking a building over. There was a time when he could have stood upright on one big toe while juggling, not that he could juggle, but you get the picture. Anyway, he reckoned that Helen of Troy was about the right age for him. She piled on the makeup a bit more than was necessary. He thought she did this to cover up blotchy skin and wrinkles around her eyes, that sort of thing. He admired her, though. She hadn't given up on life, or herself, he thought. She worked hard and put up with loudmouth drunks who slapped her bum as she served them. She smiled and told them to stop being naughty, but Rodney could tell she hated it. Rodney made sure he didn't touch her, not absently, or casually. He didn't rest his hand on her forearm or put his arm around her shoulders when he spoke to her. Not that he spoke to her that much, in fact, never, to be honest. He would love to caress her hair. But he never did that either. She didn't serve him, Frank did. She worked the tables, and Rodney never sat at a table. It was too isolating if you were by yourself, as Rodney invariably was—always was. Rodney kept a respectable distance between him and Helen of Troy, as much as he would have loved slipping his hand inside her blouse to tingle her nipples and feel the weight of her breasts. He imagined doing things to her, nice things, and he imagined her looking down, doing nothing to stop his hands. She would drop her arms as though they were dead, tied down and couldn't move. He masturbated a lot. Helen of Troy was his fantasy. She wore a gold ring on her wedding finger, but Rodney didn't know if it wasn't a ruse to stop men coming on to her all the time. He'd never asked her if she was married. For his own good, he tried not to get too personal with her. That sort of thing was how he had got himself into so much trouble in the past. He wanted to kiss Helen of Troy lavishly.

'Question: Why call them apartments when they are all jammed together? They are anything but apart.' No one responded.

*Rodney lived in a dark apartment. It was sparsely furnished with a blue clock on one of the walls. Rodney had served time twenty years ago. He had stolen a car for a joyride but ended up crashing into a tree and spending Christmas handcuffed to a hospital bed with his leg suspended by ropes and pulleys attached to a steel pin poking through his shin. After he got out of the hospital, he was transferred to Silverwater Prison and did nine months. It was stupid. The stupidest thing he had done in his life. He had a detectable limp, a criminal record and fear of driving, even though driving was how he earned his living.*

*The accident happened because he was feeling up a girl he'd met in a pub. He was driving with one hand, after way too many beers. She came, he liked to say, when telling his story, as he hit the tree. But it wasn't the tree, or the girl, or the beer that caused him to get into trouble throughout his adult life. It was his pre-dilection for falling in love. He spent six months of his nine months in prison, in love with the girl who came when he crashed the car. He didn't know her name. He called her Sophie when he thought of her at night in his cell.*

*Rodney earned an okay living driving a cab. He used to drive a cab, but now he drove for Uber. The money per ride wasn't as good but he got more business, and so he worked longer hours and took home more. The shifts and the passengers became a blur, and he would wake up in his flat having come off a twelve-hour shift through the night with no memory of the shift. He had no idea where he had been, who he had picked up, where he had taken them, or why once there was blood on the back seat.*

*Rodney spent a lot of time staring into the middle distance as he drove the city streets late at night.*

*'Question: Why the middle distance?'*

*Why not stare into the near or far distance? But that was how it was. When people were having vacant thoughts, it was the middle distance that held their attention. A lot of people in his cab would stare into the middle distance. He thought it was disrespectful but sometimes endearing and understandable. Sometimes he asked them, 'Where would you locate the middle distance, you know, if you had to?' But most times he drove in silence.*

*Frank re-emerged from the cellar and let the trapdoor fall into place, which made no noise as it fell shut. Rodney worried about that. It irritated him for some reason. Sometimes he got irritated and anxious and he never knew why. Just the impersonal vagaries of life, he supposed.*

*At the bar, mouths were distended, lips jerked, and tongues clicked with sexual invitations. The bar was replete with white noise—people talking, sharp outbursts of laughter, the constant bells and annoying rattling sounds of jackpot wins on the poker machines lining the eastern wall. Rodney thought of the white noise as a dense transparent liquid that dulled the senses and distorted perceptions. When he lifted his beer, it felt like he was working against a semi-solid atmosphere, and everything became muffled, thick, confusing.*

*'Replete' was one of Rodney's favourite words. He had many. 'That's me, replete,' he would say when he was finished drinking. He thought it sounded hoity-toity, although the expression 'hoity-toity' wasn't hoity-toity sounding. 'Repair' was another word he liked, as in, 'I think I'll repair to the little boy's room'. He thought Helen of Troy appreciated his superior word skills, though he had nothing concrete to substantiate such a notion. He thought she had to, given she spent her life surrounded by barflies who could barely string two words together most of the time. When their beers were empty, they didn't ask for another, they pointed or nodded when Frank looked in their direction, as though they were at an auction. As far as anyone could imagine, they might have been mute. Rodney had a collection of dictionaries in his flat, and he read them every day when he woke up. Today's word, 'imperceptible', or the adverb form with an 'ly' at the end. Rodney, as a general rule, despised adverbs— robustly so. Adverbs modified everything, and Rodney thought life was modified enough, dulled enough. He thought his life was, and it was a constant battle to give his life some meaning. He liked to say to his fellow barflies, 'Some days, I have an irresistible need to go on living.' He thought it was funny. No one laughed.*

*Rodney had decided to ask Helen of Troy out. He had practised in front of his bathroom mirror while shaving and inspecting himself. He had a plan. He would tell her he wouldn't be coming into the bar anymore and that he was going to stop drinking, for a while at least. He was pretty sure she was keen, though she never said so or did anything that Rodney, in his wildest fantasies, could interpret as interest in him. But still and all the same, how could she not be interested? Rodney determined her seeming lack of interest in him was her professionalism—she had to keep her distance from the bar's clientele. This made sense. He was sure she was ignoring him with purpose, that she had singled him out by ignoring him with deliberate intent more than she ignored anyone else in the bar. Clever, he thought.*

*Yes, he was confident she was keen. This was a problem Rodney had suffered most of his life. He assumed things about people, which rarely proved to be true.*

*He'd fallen in love with women he knew at various times in his life, but it often turned out that they weren't interested in him, or, if they were, it was fleeting and physical but nothing more. Time and time again, he'd get himself lathery over some girl he'd met and when he finally got around to popping the question and asking her out, she more often than not looked at him as though he was mad. Some women laughed in his face. He felt battered by it. Occasionally, he would get lucky. Occasionally, they might come home and have sex with him. But while he made love, they sought physical release, and when it was over, he was in love, and they were gone—and that empty feeling re-emerged like an opaque smog and smelt like a cold corpse and stayed. But that was in the past, Helen of Troy was different. He was enthusiastic about his prospects with the magnificent Helen of Troy. He was confident that she liked him, not just 'liked' but was flat-out interested. His vocabulary alone singled him out as a man of depth. The plan was due to be executed next week. He needed to shelve the drinking, get his hair cut and buy some new clobber. He intended to present himself in the best possible light.*

*He had worked out that if he made these manifest changes to his behaviour and appearance, she would see him as a replete man, changed and worthy, and she'd be anxious to go with him to his flat, or if she preferred, to her boudoir, where she would kiss him, and he would cover her in his kisses and tickle her with a clean, unused feather duster. He had the plan. He would ask her to dinner, after which he would suggest they repair to his or hers, whichever made her feel the most comfortable. He had bought a new six-pack of condoms—not that he thought he would need six, not for the one occasion, but he didn't want something so old from his top drawer that it might be faulty or look like he'd bought them when he was a teenager and hadn't had any call to use them before now. He didn't think that would send the best of messages and he didn't want to leave any of his little soldiers behind. He would slip two condoms into his wallet in case she chose her place to make love. No, wait, maybe not his wallet, his other back pocket. He didn't want the bloody things popping out when he went for his credit card to pay for dinner. However, if they did pop out of his wallet, she would at least know he was prepared and was being responsible, and there being two, would also tell her something about his ardour. He was in two minds about this—to pop or not to pop the condoms, that was the question. In the end, he thought better not to pop. He didn't want her thinking he was taking her for granted, or that he was entitled, or anything like that. He prided himself on being a gentleman at all times.*

*Rodney had spent months planning this. He'd fallen in love with Helen of Troy the first time he saw her smile, though he had never spoken to her or touched her, and she hadn't directed her smile in his specific direction. He knew nothing about her, except that she worked as a waitress at the bar at night. What she did during the day, he had no idea. But that meant he had so much to discover about her. It would be a 'magical mystery tour'. She had the best smile. That was what got him in the first place. She smiled easily, and he dreamt about her smile. And her perfume too. She smelt so feminine, so soft, so excruciating. Rodney took a picture of her on his phone—many pictures as it happens—while she worked her tables. He printed them out and blu-tacked them onto his bathroom mirror—in fact all around his flat, as he had a few. He thought she would be flattered if she chose to come back to his place after their first dinner.*

*Rodney had done this before—fallen in love, obsessed, stressed, masturbated. Many times. And every time, it had failed. But Rodney liked to think of himself as a 'glass half full' kind of person. No matter how many times he was let down, however bad that empty feeling was when he'd been rejected and however much it made him feel desperate, he bounced back, more or less. He would open himself up like a garbage bin and let life fill him up with its possibilities. He would cry when he was rejected by a woman that he was sure he was in love with. He would cry for days after—more so as he got older. When he was much younger, he copped the disappointment easier, but these days he took it a bit harder. He was more emotional. He blamed his meds. After these terrible times, he would swear off women. 'Never again', he would say to the others in the bar. He would feel the cobwebs clogging up his brain, clogging his thinking. He felt bruised and hurt. But eventually he'd come around again and get his mojo back.*

*He wasn't so sure how long he could keep going. He wanted companionship. He wanted to believe that if he kept trying, he would succeed. He'd always believed that. He was confident that Helen of Troy, with her flowing locks of red hair, would be the one. She was a down-to-earth woman, she had an easy way about her, and he was as sure as he could be that she was going to be receptive—even if she was a little resistant to start with. He was used to that. He would win her over and capture her. She'd like that. He imagined a replete life with her. They would live happily ever after.*

*He sat at the bar, ordered another beer, and started to plan his shopping excursion. He decided right then and there to go shopping tomorrow. This would be his last beer and tomorrow he would get a whole new wardrobe, clean his flat, change his sheets, do the washing, get some flowers, buy more condoms, get in some tinned pineapple. It was going to be perfect this time.*

*Rodney sat at the bar with a scary grin on his face as it came together in his mind. Frank looked at him, saw Rodney grinning and looked away. The others took a sideways glance at Rodney grinning and refocused on their beers and the wet beermat in front of them. One of them pushed his thumb into the beermat and made it squelch, over and over and over. Rodney thought if they knew what he was thinking, they would be cheering him on.*

*'You okay?' Helen of Troy stood next to him, as close to him as she had ever been. Her sleeve touched his shoulder. He could smell her perfume. It damn near knocked him out. He couldn't help but wonder how much urine she was carrying at the moment, while she stood so close to him. He saw her smile, and this time it was aimed at him, and it melted him. He widened his grin, chasing a smile. He wasn't confident about his grin. He coughed. He didn't know why—he had no tickle in his throat. He felt the heat rush to his face. He felt annoyed with himself for his hesitation.*

*'You dropped this?' She held up his wallet. He looked at it. He didn't know what to do or say. She put it on the bar in front of him and turned to walk away. He found his voice, as positive a voice as he could muster, trying for an upward lilt when he spoke to her. He wanted to sound friendly, familiar, earnest—in command.*

*He said, 'Why thanks, Helen.' She stopped and turned back. He had a whoosh. He had ringing in his ears, and it wasn't the pokies. He would ask her out right now. Yes. Strike while the iron was hot. 'He who dares wins,' he said under his breath.*

*'Helen, I was wondering if you...'*

*But before he could finish his question, she turned front-on to him and said, 'Sophie.'*

*Her smile waned, but not so anyone would notice, Rodney hoped. Rodney spoke again, but it came out a bit scratchy, not at as confident as he wanted. He hoped she wouldn't pick up the weakness in his voice.*

*'Sorry?' he said, not understanding what she was saying.*

*She pointed at the name tag on her blouse. 'Sophie...see?' she repeated.*

*He looked at the name tag. It said, 'Sophie'. She turned away, and in a flash of life's seconds, she was gone.*

*Frank walked past Rodney on his side of the bar and asked, 'How do you throw out a garbage bin then?' He laughed, amusing himself at Rodney's expense. Frank didn't wait for an answer from Rodney, he kept going to the end of the bar, leaving Rodney bashed and empty, much like a garbage bin, abandoned and full of nothing.*

Robbie had reinvented himself as Rodney, but in the end, Rodney was not in any material way any different from Robbie, or any better off. A little older, perhaps, with teeth that needed work. Robbie shuddered at the thought that he was Rodney and maybe Rodney was a picture of how Robbie was going to end up. Robbie sat motionless in his cubicle. He was bashed and empty. '*Nothing* was killing him.'

# Gloria Penhale

Gloria wanted a child. She didn't want a man. She wanted a child. Immediately, however, she wanted sperm. She would accept it in the conventional way if she found someone she could endure intimately. The conventional method was her preference. She had no definitive proof, but she had a feeling that sticking with the way nature intended would pay dividends in ways not readily apparent. Otherwise, she had googled 'turkey baster', and it all seemed good, if a little clinical. She bought a turkey baster, but she still needed a candidate. She had considered Robbie Carton, the resident office fish-out-of-water, but she suspected his stability, and she was perhaps too attracted to him. There was O'Brien, with his Arctic blue eyes. O'Brien had nothing much else going for him, which made him prime sperm-donating material. However, according to Robbie, O'Brien was not to be trusted, but Gloria feared Robbie's judgment was not to be trusted even more than O'Brien was not to be trusted.

Recently, Gloria had been bumped into by a man in the street. He had apologised in what seemed like a prepared statement, as though Gloria might not have been the first person he'd bumped into. Had it been possible, she would have absorbed his sperm right there and then. It wasn't possible, and the subject didn't come up. He apologised and then he was gone.

Gloria was determined to find the right candidate and have a child but continue with her career. She considered she would be a better mother that way. She hoped so. She had given it a lot of thought. She had started buying toys, nappies and clothes, and a beautiful baby rug. She didn't think this was obsessive or premature. She thought it felt right for her. She had no one with whom to discuss such matters.

# Sophie Fanshawe

Sophie, a published novelist with long red hair, stinging eyes, jet lag and a romantic nature had finally arrived in Paris to work on her second novel. Back home, she had lost her way with her writing. Her stomach tightened when she thought about how badly the work was going. She had never experienced this before. She loved writing. She loved being a writer. She felt so lucky to be doing something she loved. She hoped that time in Paris would solve her writing problems. She hoped for a breakthrough. She hoped to recover from her jet lag, foggy brain, and swollen feet.

Her second novel had unsolved plot problems and characters that treated her with indifference. One, her protagonist, had disappeared before he was supposed to. And now Sophie was in Paris to fix it but with no idea how. She felt lousy, light-headed, and her eyes were still stinging. She sneezed and hoped she wasn't getting a cold. The surprising idea she might be in love bubbled up in her thoughts. These were unexpected and complex thoughts, and she didn't understand why they were surfacing now. Was it because she was so far from home? Or maybe because she was having trouble with her work. Or was it because she was in romantic Paris? She didn't know.

Sophie was single and twenty-eight, and after only a few hours in Paris, she was ashamed to admit she was missing home. There were the swollen feet, and the Paris apartment she'd rented for three months was tiny, expensive, and mostly purple. It smelt of liquorice. It was a serious smell, sweet but not too sweet. Not sickly sweet, but almost. She thought it not unpleasant, but not pleasant either, just unexpected. The liquorice smell was alien in a way that emphasised how far from home Sophie was, but, on the other hand, she was in Paris where great writers had worked and where she had dreamt of writing all her life.

Standing at the windows of her tiny Parisian studio apartment, she contemplated her situation. She could only hope that this, coming to Paris, was not a big mistake. Unusually, she felt timid, apprehensive, out of sorts, as her mother Mel would say. Mel had warned her, Paris would be a disappointment. 'You'll feel flat', Mel had said matter-of-factly. Sophie's mother had her own agenda, and it didn't include having her daughter on the other side of the world for three months playing at being a writer, as Mel had described it to Sophie over the phone, before Sophie left for Paris. Mel's agenda would be more like, 'Move home with me and attend to my every need'. Sophie missed her mother at times. At other times, not as much.

Sophie thought of herself as an adventurous woman. She wasn't sure she qualified as adventurous, but she hoped so. She had clear frekled skin, and red hair that framed her magazine lips and iridescent eyes. She wasn't 'pretty' in the coy girlie sense—redheads rarely were, in her experience. There were the freckles, for a start, and she had her share. She knew she was striking in a way that suggested contemporary, if not modern. She was pleased about that. 'Striking' had been how Robbie Carton, one of the Friday night regulars in the Stalwart pub had described her. He had mumbled it to no one in particular. He was drunk at the time. He was drunk most of the time. He was also mad in ways that didn't scare her. He had never spoken to her in the pub, apart from ordering his drinks. She played along with his game—if it was a game. It seemed dangerous not to—dangerous for him, not her. She was happy with 'striking'. She thought of kissing him. Her body reacted with a tiny zing at the thought of her lips on his. He was a lost soul—a soul in trouble who might benefit from companionship. She hoped she could help him, if she got the chance—if he would be open to it. Right at this moment, standing alone, she craved his closeness and thought she could do with some companionship herself. Back home, Fridays were her favourite nights—when she wasn't writing, she was a part-time bartender at the Stalwart pub. She was careful with one and caring with the other.

Sophie smelt the coldness in the apartment. The stone-grey sunlight was weightless and transparent, and, in its insipid way, added to the chill. It cast indistinct and reluctant shadows around the room and struggled to penetrate the two tall grimy windows. Sophie thought the light was being timid, unsure whether to enter. She wondered if this was European light—weak and empty and shy. She thought of how the light back home was robust, weighty, and smiley—it felt like it could hold you up, like it wanted to hold you up, that holding you up was part of its job. A lone tear ran down her cheek. This caught her by surprise. She knew she shouldn't feel sorry for herself. It was her idea to come to Paris—her bold idea, her exciting adventurous idea. But at this moment, the idea made her feel small and insignificant, flat, to use Mel's word. Sophie put her overwrought emotions down to jet lag, cleared her throat as a gesture of her determined spirit and wiped her eyes with a tissue.

She needed a glass of wine. She needed something to eat. She needed to be warm, perhaps to be close to someone. She wanted her bunny rug, which sat waiting in her dark apartment at the end of her bed back home. She wanted it wrapped around her body while she watched rain spit at her French windows. She blew her nose and stiffened herself. 'This is not good,' she said with conviction. 'This is not good. Try harder, Sophie.' And with that, she felt a little better. She willed herself to feel better. She hadn't had intimacy with anyone in a while. She yearned to laugh with someone. Laughing with someone was in many ways as good as sex, and often led to the best kind of sex. The inside of her thighs tingled, but her eyes welled up again.

'How's the apartment?' Mel had asked across the oceans.

Sophie, using her mobile phone, and not the grimy phone on the wall, had called her mother in Melbourne to say she had arrived safely in Paris. She didn't mention she was exhausted, jet-lagged, cold, lonely, and trying to hold back her tears. She didn't mention she was also feeling a bit...well, sexual, or sexy. She didn't know which, and if there was a difference. Her mother would hear it in her voice soon enough—the loneliness, not the sexual business, she hoped. But then her mother could only hear such things if she listened instead of talking over the top of Sophie, jumping in to tell Sophie about herself, as was Mel's habit. It wasn't that Mel wanted to talk about herself, although that was part of it. It was more that she didn't want to hear what she didn't want to hear and talking over Sophie achieved that. Sophie knew Mel didn't want to hear about her daughter's state of horniness—Mel had enough problems with that herself.

Mel's habit of talking over everyone was known to her children. '*Back to me now*', Sophie and her brother Harry would mouth to each other, while Mel prattled on about shopping for a new television or how the neighbour's pants had fallen to his mid-thighs, or something about oestrogen, or grouting. Harry was less unforgiving toward Mel than Sophie. Harry was more generous and less judgemental. Sophie acknowledged that this said more about Harry than it did about Mel and said too much about herself and her impatience with her mother. Harry was more subdued these days, which was understandable given his recent history. Had Mel listened to Sophie, Sophie would have told Mel about the liquorice smell, but not the grimy windows or the purple, or anything about Harry, indeed not that especially. She also wouldn't tell Mel that so far, she felt so alone in Paris, and that she had a strong desire to be held, and to kiss someone. Sophie was a woman who liked to do the kissing. The urge of wanting to kiss someone, whenever the opportunity presented, was sudden and impulsive for Sophie and she had long ago decided not to deny it. So, she kissed when she could.

'The flat? I'm pretty sure it's a broom closet, with the broom removed to augment the available space, so I can't even have a sweep up.' Sophie relayed to her mother across the international delay. She knew her mother would not get her wry humour, such as it was. Wry? Wryish. Certainly, an exaggeration. And strained, perhaps more strained than anything else. There'd be a broom somewhere, Sophie thought. If not, she'd have to buy one. Her mother, by nature, was a cautious woman, and this made her literal.

'What do you mean you don't have a broom?' Mel's voice sounded frail and indignant. Sophie could hear her mother's legendary disinterest. The international delay on the phone didn't help their communication, but then nothing did. For Sophie's mother, not having a broom would be reason enough to leave Paris and come back home without unpacking. Sophie's mother wanted her daughter home, in Melbourne, living with her and being her friend—a friend with an infinite capacity to listen to Mel's grumbles and disappointments. Sophie, for her part, wanted to be exhilarated and adventurous. She wanted to reinvent herself. She wanted a fresh start. She came to Paris with more hope in her heart than she expected was good for her.

'You know you're just going to be lonely there,' Mel had repeated, experienced at being lonely. Mel had forgotten she had made this observation before Sophie left for Paris.

Mel's form of loneliness stemmed from two things—the absence of her children who both moved from Melbourne in their mid-twenties, and her need for purpose. Mel had lost her husband to a fake incident with a nail gun, and her son and daughter to their dreams, and Mel was left with nothing but cleaning and talk—her own.

'If being lonely occurs, it will give me the edge I need to work,' Sophie countered.

They fell into an international delayed silence before Sophie echoed, she had to go. She could hear the want from her mother's silence. They hung up both feeling emptier for the effort. Sophie thought, we're all lonely, and with that she didn't feel quite so alone.

This was what Sophie was thinking about, standing in the Paris apartment, so far from her home immediately after her phone call to her mother. She thought about the contradiction of feeling both trapped and liberated at the same time. They didn't cancel each other out but instead seemed to combine to make her feel light-headed and confused. She hadn't expected to feel this way. This was the way she had felt back home in her apartment—caught in the space between things. She had expected to feel exhilarated in Paris. Where was the exhilaration she had promised herself? She'd only been here for a few hours. She needed to orientate herself, get settled, start a routine. She needed to give it, Paris, and herself, a chance—it was nonsense to feel this way.

Her stomach groaned, reminding her she was hungry. It had been hours since she ate the inedible breakfast served over Turkmenistan, or one of the Stans, by a female flight attendant with soft eyes and powdery skin. Sophie needed food and wine and something to lean against.

She placed her hands palm down on the windowsill and transferred her weight through her arms to her hands. She felt the grit under her fingers and pressed harder.

A haunting, muffled sound of a phone ringing somewhere deep in the building seeped into her consciousness. She envisaged a shadowy, solemn apartment, perhaps lower in the building—a dark, musty room with ornate furnishings. For some reason, the ringing sound alarmed Sophie and struck at her heart. It was a different telephone ring to what she was used to back home. It rang and rang and went unanswered.

In that apartment somewhere deep in the building the ringing stopped. Sophie conjured a darkened room with vague speckled light—a *chiaroscuro* effect. She imagined a camera slowly pan across the plain room. Next to an empty, high-backed upholstered chair with a determined plumped cushion, was a small side table, she imagined. On the table was a shrivelled pink rose in a vase next to a yellowed, now silent, ivory phone. A few shrivelled petals had dropped. The table was covered by a white crocheted tablecloth with what looked like a faded cigarette burn to the left of the phone. A small curl of smoke might have once spiralled upwards. A still shadow hovered over the scene, casting no recognisable shape. Sophie felt a presence in the room. She wondered about the history of the room, its people, noises, and smells. The whole human story unrecorded. She pondered how this quiet apartment had existed when she was back in her apartment on the other side of the world. It was a space with its history sitting silently in wait. Her imagination conjured a decaying corpse with a funfair smile sitting next to the table.

Sophie's Paris apartment compressed her mood. Increasing the complexity, she could smell a faint linger of eucalyptus underneath the liquorice smell. Her sense of smell seemed heightened. She could smell smells hidden under other smells. The eucalyptus reminded her of home.

Back home in her high-rise building, her elevated apartment faced the city. Sophie often sat in the dark on the edge of her sofa, like a shadow, invisible to the world. The muscles on the sides of her mouth were dormant as she watched the city lights. She considered her place in the world. She felt safe but anxious. After one cold and wet day in the city, in her apartment that night, sitting in the dark, she puffed out her cheeks and asked herself, *'What will happen to you?'*—the question asked of her at her Writers Circle, which she attended every Wednesday night at seven pm sharp. She spoke out loud to give her words meat and a skeleton, and said, *'You must do things.'*

So she did. She came to Paris. She tried not to bring too much expectation with her, but that was difficult. Now in Paris, standing at the window, she missed her apartment. She missed the dark. She missed her job at the Stalwart. She missed the office men who drank too much and tried to ask her out while running their words together in an alcohol-induced drawl—attractive, she mused. She smiled. She knew they were drunk because they were lost. She saw her Friday night regulars sitting in their same places at the bar, like three birds on a clothesline. She saw them stunned by life. They never spoke to her apart from ordering their drinks, nor did they speak to one another. Robbie, the one that mumbled, was her favourite. The one she thought she could save. Robbie was the one she thought of kissing, whenever the thought of kissing anyone came to her. She knew his kiss would taste of beer, or wine, or whatever his choice on the night might have been. She didn't mind the taste. She wouldn't mind. It was the kiss for which she longed to revisit. She knew his kiss would tell her everything she needed to know about him.

Sophie looked out her Paris window straight into the building opposite, into other apartments spanning the width and height of the building. A middle-aged man stood at the window at eye level with his hand down the front of his pants. He was on the phone, looking out his window, down at the street below. While Sophie had waited at the front door for the letting agent, after the taxi dropped her off from *Charles de Gaulle* Airport, the street had appeared wider than it seemed now from up on the fourth floor. Down on the street, it was noisier, more impersonal, and there was safety in that. Up here, Sophie felt she could almost reach out and touch the building opposite or be touched herself. She felt faint fingers brush her cheek.

The windows opposite brought to mind a bank of muted television sets. They played out the silent drama of people's lives, like a soap opera. Much like her own life, to be honest. The truth of people's private lives fascinated Sophie, but not as much as the lies and self-delusion—the two natural states of the human psychological condition, she thought.

Harry, her brother, sometimes known as Tommy, hadn't responded to this insight, Sophie recalled. He had scars. He'd lost interest in discussions of this nature with her of late. Sophie thought that deluding himself suited him for this stage of his life. He considered it lucky if he could find a lie to disappear into. Sophie, by and large, allowed him this indulgence for the moment, but she was not ordinarily open to self-delusion—an example of self-delusion itself she reckoned.

Sophie heard things others didn't. She saw things others didn't. This was not to suggest anything extrasensory or magical. It was that she was open and astute to the small things, the 'tells' of human behaviour. She believed the key to understanding human nature was not to obsess with why people do things, but more with what they do. The key was to be found in their behaviour. She was charmed by the things people did, and where and when they did them. The character 'Austin Quinn', from The Writers Circle, fascinated her. She remained circumspect about the mystery surrounding him. She did not pry into his 'why'. She did not delve into his psyche. She wrote about him—well, his namesake—per the writing exercise given to the group, and she fell a little in love with him. Everyone in the Circle did. Harry, her brother, was unconvinced. It was Austin that thought Harry should be called Tommy.

Sophie was captivated by human spaces—*the spaces between things*—where thoughts, actions, relationships, feelings, especially feelings, loitered and hid themselves. She studied the space between intentions and their subsequent contrarian actions—sometimes the spaces were tiny, minute, other times vast, but they were traps and often silent, or if not, not audible if you weren't listening. These spaces, in Sophie's view, were where human purpose dwelt, the space between feeling trapped and liberated, where malevolent intent and good intentions stood apart from each other like contesting gladiators, where dreams, hopes, ambitions and fears resided. In Japanese culture, Sophie had once read, the space between things is called *Ma*, a concept that acknowledged that space was profound and essential to expression. In the case of Austin Quinn, Sophie saw the space between his behaviour and his truth as vast, and this made him fascinating. She knew who he was the moment he walked into the room and took his seat in the Circle. She was attracted to him. She was attracted to his sadness and his experimentation but most of all to his pause. She wanted to kiss him.

Sophie made a habit of noticing the absence of expected facts. Like when something should be there but wasn't or should be said but isn't. People tended to toil and worry and regret between these silent spaces. Sophie did. So did her mother. And so too did her brother, albeit in an annoyingly graceful manner, Sophie noted. Sophie was always trying to second-guess herself. Should I have done this, should I have said that? What do they think of me? Am I to lavishly kiss him? '*Will, I lavishly kiss him*?' she whispered. Pink or red toenail polish? She let her mind continue to wander—time slowed. Am I capable of love and hate? Something out of the freezer or should I cook something? Could I kill, yes or no? Sophie was convinced the motivations of everyday life were found in the curious spaces between life's binary opposites, and she listened out for them. Sophie heard her mother. Mel filled the spaces with her wishes, her dreams, and her disappointments, especially her disappointments. Sophie thought that pretty much anything Mel said could be substituted with the words, 'Do you love me?' Sophie and Harry often referred to their mother as 'the disappointed woman'. 'Mel, the disappointed woman,' they would say, and laugh together over a bottle of wine. This was back when Harry had reason in his life and laughing was easy. Nothing could make Mel happy, because she never wanted to be. To be happy would reduce her *reason*, and her willingness, to live. Disappointment was Mel's axle grease.

'Lavishly', bubbled up in Sophie's thoughts again. Where did that word come from? Sophie wondered. It felt like it had been placed in her brain to be used in conjunction with kissing. It wasn't a word she would have considered natural for her to use. Still, the idea to 'lavishly' kiss someone sounded wonderful. She thought again about Robbie from the Stalwart and Austin from The Writers Circle. It must be her jet lag. And loneliness. She had a flash that it might have been Robbie who had used the word 'lavishly'. She hoped he did. She paused her thoughts for a moment.

The man remained standing at the window opposite. He was so close that Sophie could pick out the grey stubble on his face and the mole on the left side of his cheek. On a woman, the mole would be called a beauty mark. Sophie regarded beauty marks with affection, in the same category as a lisp. They evoked mystery. She didn't have one herself, which from time to time was one of her regrets. One of the women who attended The Writers Circle had a beauty mark, and it mesmerised Sophie. Sophie had given a beauty mark to one of her characters in her novel. The character changed after the beauty mark had been added, subtly, but a definite change. With her newly acquired beauty mark, Sophie's character had more depth, and mystery, and an allure that was not previously there. She was surer of herself, more confident in some way. She had a greater appetite. She was more ample. Sophie found herself envious of her character, which posed the question: if Sophie could render such characteristics in one of her characters, why couldn't she manage these attributes for herself? Sophie wanted to be mysterious and alluring. Why not? If all it took was a beauty mark, then that was easily fixed. All you needed was a blunt mascara stick and a willing cheek. But a beauty mark was superficial, so how could it have such power? How could it manifest behavioural changes? Obviously, it couldn't. Nonetheless, she wished she had one.

'Ample'? Another word that seemed out of character for Sophie to use. 'Ample' had seeped into her consciousness from somewhere, or from someone.

The man opposite still had his hand down the front of his trousers, holding on with enthusiasm. She sighed with exhaustion at the fact that life was about sex, even when it wasn't. She gave some thought to slipping her hand down the front of her jeans in some sort of bizarre *simpatico* behaviour, but she was too exhausted.

Sophie recalled meeting a captivating woman from Savannah. This woman was elegant and regal and tall and had a faint but charming lisp. She was, in Sophie's opinion, a well-mannered woman living in a large eastern seaboard city. Sophie thought of her own city as iconic but indifferent to its inhabitants. Sophie's city didn't care about its population—a population of plump, languid flies buzzing with purpose about the buildings and entrances. Sitting in her dark apartment, with wet hair, her hand between her thighs as she took in the twinkling lights of the city, and wondering about her purpose, Sophie had felt alone—and now in Paris, where she thought things would be different, she still felt alone. Perhaps more so. The questions 'Does nothing change?' and 'How can you make things change?' wandered around her mind untethered like cattle in the outback.

# Mel Fanshawe

A long time ago, Mel had two fake children. They were seven and ten years old. Sophie, the younger, wanted to be a writer when she grew up. She also thought she would be beautiful when she grew up, as though being beautiful was a choice. She turned out to be striking, according to someone Sophie knew, which was far better than being beautiful because 'striking' had potential. 'Beautiful' was an end in itself and 'in the eye of the beholder' and treacherously temporary. These concepts should have been beyond Sophie at age seven. Her brother Harold, now known as Harry, or Tommy on occasion, wanted to be a writer also. This was due to the influence of his sister. Sophie ruled, even though she was younger than her brother. So, they both wrote stories in the red notebooks Mel had given them for Christmas. Before announcing they both wanted to be writers—in Sophie's case a famous writer, a famous beautiful writer, with a beauty mark or a lisp or perhaps a limp or a lazy eye—Sophie wanted to be a trauma nurse and Harold a black fireman. So, they wrote stories about trauma nurses and black fire fighters. Sophie's nurses had limps or lazy eyes and striking red hair. Sophie and Harold each received other presents for Christmas, but it was the red notebooks that held their attention the most. A red notebook, no batteries needed, only imagination, which Sophie had in abundance and shared with her brother. So they were fake children in the sense that they were wise beyond their years. They looked like children, they were the same size as children, they wore children's clothes, but Mel saw them both as being more sagacious than her, especially Sophie, and this unsettled Mel. She didn't think it was fair.

Mel could see the seeds of her children's personalities at their young ages and wondered how these things came about so early and what influenced their behaviours.

Sophie was independent and loved pretty dresses and demanded a bow in her hair before she would venture outside. She was unabashedly all-girl and, at seven, saw no conflict in this with her independence and bravery. Harold was stoic and a thinly disguised old man. He was responsible. The loss of his father to a nail gun accident had been hard on Harold. When the news came through that Mel's husband had died, Harold was old enough to understand, but not old enough to cope. He had worshipped his father and wanted to grow up to be like him, but after his father's death, Harold found he had no one to emulate, no role model to influence his morality and ethics. He was left to his own random experiences and his sister's influence. It was fair to say that Harold suffered the most over his father's death and for the longest time than anyone else in the family. Sophie was too young to grieve, and, if she had understood, she would have rationalised and compartmentalised it. In spite of Harold's suffering and prolonged grief, these things didn't help prepare him for the future. A future where he would accumulate personal items but lose the one thing he needed.

Harold changed after his father's death. He developed a habit of disappearing—not permanently, he was a young boy and needed to be fed and watered. Sophie knew this and so she never panicked when her brother disappeared, especially since she knew where he was. Harold would find a quiet, dark spot in the house, maybe a wardrobe or under something, and there he would stay for hours, or until Mel needed him for dinner or for him to have his bath. When the weather was fine and warm, he might hide in the recycle garbage bin when it was empty, or near empty. He would never do this on the first Wednesday of each month, which was recycle collection day.

Harold was good at hiding, disappearing that is, and Mel would look everywhere for him. She rarely found him. Sophie was the key. She always knew where her brother was hiding, or, in reality, sitting. It wasn't hiding, it was disappearing. But Sophie wouldn't tell Mel, until she deemed it time for Harold to come out. Then and only then would Sophie nod to Mel in the direction of where she might find her son. Mel, in the beginning, got cross with both her children, but she resigned herself to the peculiarities of their respective personalities. In some unsettling way, they seemed to know what they were doing. Mel accepted with some relief that her two children were nominally in charge. At times, she was sure they had banded together in a co-operative coalition to conspire against her. They both denied this while tucking into their favourite ice-cream desserts.

Mel, for her part, didn't miss her husband. She had felt relieved when she heard the news. She was elated. Her husband had been silent for many years. Occasionally, he might say 'pass the salt' or 'my shoes need cleaning', but otherwise he had resolved, for reasons Mel didn't understand, to stop talking to her. She asked him why, but as he wasn't talking, she never found out. She determined that he must have hated his life, or her.

He didn't die at the administration of a nail gun, that was the story Mel made up to disguise the real method of his death, which was that he died of a cerebral vascular accident, or a stroke as it was more commonly known, after a long drinking session by himself in the backyard shed. He must have lurched out of the shed and lost his balance, crashing into the Hills Hoist. Then one of the capillaries in Mel's husband's head popped. Mel thought this was an unseemly way to die. He had bumped into the pole of the clothesline, which caused it to shudder, which in turn, made the canopy rotate slowly. Several pegs were disturbed. Mel felt the nail gun story was less humiliating for her and more palatable for her children. She didn't want the whole street knowing her husband was a drunk. The nail gun story was shocking to most people and negated further discussion. People imagined it, and that was all they needed. Mel also felt that the truth might reflect poorly on her as a wife, as in she must have driven him to drink, and she didn't want that. It was Sophie who made the innocent observation about the sham nail gun story. 'But Dad doesn't have a nail gun. And he's a surveyor. Maybe his dumpy level fell on him, but that wouldn't kill him.' Mel ignored Sophie. She had no answer for her daughter's bothersome observations. Sophie was always picking out the flaws in things, it was one of her most irritating habits, in Mel's view. 'Are you sure it was a nail gun?' Sophie asked Mel again. Mel sighed with exhaustion. Mel knew her daughter never believed a word of it.

'As if anyone would make something like that up,' she said to Sophie.

In the conversation with Sophie about her father's death, Sophie asked Mel to define the word 'refreshing', as though the story about her father's death had been dealt with and it was time for a new topic. Sophie had never understood what 'refreshing' meant, she claimed. 'When you are "refreshed", how does that feel?' Sophie asked. This was another example of Sophie examining the territory between a word and its intent. Mel brushed her daughter's question aside. Sophie told her mother that the only way you can explain the meaning of a word is with other words, and in the case of 'refreshing' there didn't seem to be other words that adequately explained its meaning, at least, not as far as Sophie thought. Mel continued to boil some milk.

After Mel's husband died, Mel became dependent on Sophie and Harold. They were her life, everything she lived for and cherished. As they grew up, she serviced their life with food, shelter, clothes and all the extras that go with sustaining children. She derived immense pleasure in seeing them thrive. She watched them grow into teenagers, and while the usual rejection and teenage angst caused some static in her relationships with both of them from time to time, especially Sophie, it wasn't as bad as it might have been. That was what she told herself. She came to realise that her absolute love for them was so deep that she became her love. She was no longer an individual who might be described as 'Mel, the independent woman', a complete, free-standing person. No, she was 'Mel the receptacle', to house her all-consuming love for her children.

Both Sophie and Harold grew away from Mel as they got older, and thus were less troubled by her mothering. They grew closer together and so, by degrees, isolated her. At first, Mel didn't notice this. She was too busy attending to their every need, driving them to ballet or football—in Sophie's case, ballet, and football. Mel (not short for Melbourne) busied herself making costumes for their school plays and preparing party food for their birthdays. This kept Mel's focus on their needs, not on their demeanour toward her. It was when they were in their late teens that Mel started noticing how often she was left alone. She noticed that Sophie and Harold had developed their own lives, independently of each other to a degree. They remained close, but more specifically, independent of Mel. Mel found herself sitting in the darkened rooms of her house fretting and feeling disappointed. She felt that she was involuntarily disappearing. She grew her disappointment much like she grew her children, with love and nurture. Eventually it flourished into a full-grown competency. She resented her fake children. She grew to understand isolation but not the word 'refreshing'.

Eventually, Mel was no longer required to transport her children anywhere. They didn't have birthday parties at home anymore, and Mel wasn't consulted about the dilemmas in their lives, if indeed, they had any. Mel felt the sting of being abandoned. She thought to punish her children in some way for abandoning her, so she told them the real story of how their father died. But this truth had little or no effect on Sophie and Harold. They both preferred the nail gun story—the nail gun story had become their truth. Either way, the truth didn't force them to be closer to Mel. If anything, they treated her as a figure of some ridicule as though she had made up the so-called real story, or if she hadn't, so what? Who cares? Perhaps, they thought, Mel should have been a better wife. In their view, it was a fake story even if it was true. However, it being a fake story didn't concern Sophie in particular. Mel recognised her daughter was a writer, and as Sophie got older and more thoughtful, she claimed all stories were fake. Even when they contained truths, the stories were still fake, Sophie observed.

Sophie, as an adult and no longer living at home, had a friend, whom you might call an imaginary friend. Mel thought of him as imaginary, though she knew he existed. His name was Robbie—a fake name if ever there was one, according to Mel. There was a part of Mel that wanted a degree of quiet vengeance against her children, however much she loved them. Robbie, according to Mel, wasn't so much a friend, imaginary or otherwise, as he was a character in Sophie's life—her writing life. Someone who came into view but had little effect while he was there, compared to the effect he had when he wasn't there. Sophie modelled him on one of the regulars who sat at the bar on Friday nights at the Stalwart, whose name was also Robbie. This caused Mel to scoff.

Mel worried about Sophie's imagination—it bordered on the bizarre at times, perhaps slightly unhinged, in Mel's opinion. Mel worried a little about Sophie and her grasp on reality, or more specifically, her lack of grasp. Mel thought Sophie sometimes confused truth with fiction, but Sophie dismissed her concern by pointing out to Mel, 'There's no difference between truth and fiction, except that truth is harder to believe.'

Mel was aware there were two things Sophie didn't know about Robbie— the actual Robbie, the one who sat at the Stalwart's bar and mumbled to himself. The first was that he was in love with Sophie. Mel was sure that Robbie hadn't admitted this to himself. The second was that he was mad, and he wanted to disappear. Technically that was three things, but Mel didn't care about this kind of detail. She discerned these assumptions from the little Sophie had told her, and from the odd piece of writing she secretly read in Sophie's red notebook. When Mel met Robbie, she might have agreed he mumbled too much and that he was a lost soul barely holding onto reality, but this notwithstanding, he had potential. Mel was unsure if he was right for her daughter, though. And she couldn't be sure that one day Robbie might disappear and leave Sophie devastated. Mel knew what it was like to lose someone. She'd lost her husband to silence and a clothesline pole.

Mel felt jealous and sorry for her daughter. Mel thought being a novelist was a job you have while you're waiting to be discovered as a writer of note. In the meantime, Sophie survived pulling beers, mixing cocktails, and popping corks and, according to Mel, spent an excessive amount of time at her 'Writers Circle'. Mel felt that Sophie was obsessed with the members of the Circle, but then Mel was used to Sophie's obsessions. Mel had read in Sophie's red notebook that Sophie, the novelist, knew Robbie to be an accountant and she, Sophie, suspected he was deranged. Mel interpreted this to suggest that Sophie felt sympathy for Robbie. Sophie tried to write about Mel too, but to Mel, the writing seemed childish. Sophie made up a new life for Mel, a fake life and changed Mel's name to Syd, which wasn't short for anything as far as Mel knew. This new life bore little resemblance to Mel but was far more intriguing than the reality, Mel thought. But there was a part of Mel that resented this new incarnation of herself. It begged the question, wasn't her daughter satisfied with her mother? So unsatisfied was Sophie with her actual mother that she had to reinvent her. Mel was disappointed in her daughter. Sophie gave Mel/Syd one child, because in Sophie's view, Mel struggled to rear two children. So, she gave her a son, who she named Ignatius. She made Ignatius a private investigator, the profession Sophie would have chosen for herself had the ambition to be a famous writer not taken precedence. Mel recognised herself in many of the things Sophie wrote, but not all the things. Most definitely, not all the things.

Mel lamented that for all Sophie's talent and enterprise, she was only a bartender, working at the Stalwart pub. She worked the front bar, the busiest part of the pub. After hours, office workers from the buildings nearby disgorged from their foyers and poured across the streets and along footpaths to crowd into the Stalwart. Mel had dropped into the Stalwart one Friday night when she was in the city visiting her children. The pub was buzzy, and Mel saw how it was an excellent place for Sophie to disappear into the work and the throng. The more people, the more noise, the more alcohol, the wetter the beer mats, the easier it was to dissolve into the chaos. Sophie was too busy and hardworking to engage with anyone there. They were too enthralled with their after-work celebrations to engage with her. On the night Mel visited, there were birthdays, bucks and hens' gatherings, and send-offs for fellow workers who were leaving for greener pastures. Everyone disappeared into the rituals of these occasions. Mel couldn't help but notice this phenomenon, and she understood her daughter's preference for this life.

On the Friday night Mel had visited the Stalwart, she saw Robbie sitting at the bar watching Sophie's every move. Mel knew Sophie couldn't say if the facts she knew about Robbie were real, made up, or a combination of both. He might have been real, his name might well be Robbie, which it was, and he could also be an accountant. But Sophie might have made all this up in her fictional world. Mel didn't know the truth of the fiction, and such concepts annoyed her and stumped her. She preferred life ordered and linear, and black and white with no shades of grey.

Made up or not, constructed, or real, Robbie fascinated Sophie—Mel saw that. Robbie was lost, and Mel could see how Sophie thought it would be good to either join him in his lost world or save him from it—as one of Sophie's characters said in her first novel, 'In life there are many options, but only two alternatives. Yes or no. Go or stop. Do or don't. Live or die. Stay or disappear.' Mel saw all this on one night at the Stalwart while nursing a brandy and coke, and it depressed her. She kept her eye out for anyone who might replace her lost husband. The realisation and acceptance that Mel lost people was harsh. She sat at a table in the Stalwart, surrounded by people in love, in lust, or looking for either, and had to accept that she had lost her children to their adult lives, and she had lost her husband to alcohol. And before that to silence. Why did her husband stop talking to her? Was she so abominable? So disgusting? She didn't know the answer. She hoped it was more to do with him than her. For Mel, it hammered home her disappointment in herself. She downed her drink and ordered another from one of the male bartenders who she thought she might flirt with, then thought better of it. She was old enough to be his mother. For a moment she thought she'd like to fuck him, though. She found this a strange thought, inconsistent and incompatible with who she thought she was. She watched Robbie descend into an alcoholic haze.

Mel wanted Sophie to write about her, but in a loving daughter kind of way. Was that too much to ask? Mel wanted Sophie to declare her love and loyalty to her mother, but she knew this wasn't going to happen. Sophie wrote about a woman called Syd. Mel didn't want to recognise herself as Syd. Mel contended she had brought up Sophie, and Harry for that matter, in a happy, secure home, in spite of their father's silence and drinking, which Mel kept from her children as best she could. Sophie was encouraged to be an independent, confident girl. Mel took special care to ensure that Sophie would be strong enough to withstand all that life was likely to throw at a woman. Mel wanted Sophie never to find herself in a relationship like Mel had been with her husband. But Sophie seemed not to be able to find a man to suit her and her writing. Robbie Carton was not such a man for her daughter. Sophie's authorial voice, Mel thought, tended toward the distant. It was remote and pained, and evoked disappointment. This worried and hurt Mel. She wanted only the best, and as much happiness as the world could deliver, for both her children. But they seemed to be broken in some way. This was unfathomable and deeply upsetting. Her relationship with both her children was not as she imagined and hoped it would be. Mel, nursing a third cocktail at the Stalwart, wondered what had happened to her husband's dumpy level and if it could be used to survey humans.

Sophie and Harold both moved from Melbourne to pursue their respective careers. Sophie first, then Harold. Sophie to become a writer, which apparently couldn't be achieved in Melbourne, as Mel sarcastically pointed out the day Sophie came home, packed, and announced her plan to go north, or as far north as was needed. Harold, who was shocked to find his sister had left him alone with Mel, soon followed to become a creative writing teacher, which again was apparently not a job he could have found in Melbourne, as Mel found herself repeating to no avail.

Mel was aware that Sophie was writing her second novel, and Mel knew Sophie had no idea what it was about, and Sophie lived in a state of panic because of this. Not that Mel got any of this from her daughter. Mel knew—a mother knows things about her children. Harold's writing career shone after he won a short story contest. Mel was both happy for him and disappointed for him. She worried it would give him false hope that he might be a writer of some note one day. Mel, like all mothers, wanted her children to thrive, but she couldn't see how this would happen while each of them held on to this romantic notion of being writers. After the short story success, Harold wrote some advertising copy and was offered a job teaching creative writing at a suburban advanced education college, having completed a Master's in English literature. His thesis was on postmodernism, not that Mel had any idea what postmodernism might be when it was at home.

Mel understood that her son Harold knew that making a living from teaching saved him from confronting the knowledge that he wasn't talented enough to sustain a career as a writer and, more than that, he didn't have the temperament to be a writer. This last part was something about her son Mel knew but never discussed with him. He wrote his award-winning short story accidentally, he said. He told Mel he had felt a fake when he was told he had won, and when the short story judges asked him about his motivation, he obfuscated, and they seemed pleased with that.

Harold could be described as a comfortable old dusty leather couch—a bit worse for wear. The highlight of his life, and Mel's, was the time when he was to be married. Mel had tried to influence her children early in their lives, but to no avail. Mel felt responsible for why both her children moved north. They wanted to get away from her. This wasn't something she understood, or thought was fair. She thought it most unfair. She couldn't shake the feeling of guilt, as though her children leaving home to move to another city so far away was, in a way, her fault. She, from time to time, travelled north to visit them. It was a long journey through parched land and over rocking water. When she arrived, she was exhausted, as were the citizens of the city, according to her creative daughter.

When Mel wasn't visiting her children, she sat in her house—often the kitchen, but sometimes the lounge. She acquired a mobile phone but rarely used it. On the odd occasion when it rang, she hoped it was one of her children. One day while flicking through a lifestyle magazine, she saw an article on goats. The article explained how to milk a goat. She read it. She had nothing else to do. She thought you never know when knowing how to milk a goat might come in handy.

Mel waited in her Melbourne kitchen for the anticipated phone call from Paris. She had calculated the time zone difference. It was dark outside, but there were soft grey shadows as the sun advanced beyond the city's buildings. Mel sipped her hot tea and tore the page with the article on how to milk a goat out of the magazine. When the call came, Mel heard in Sophie's voice that Sophie needed comfort. Mel heard it over the phone in spite of the international delay. Mel hoped Sophie might come home before the three months were up, but Mel knew her daughter, and she knew in her heart that Sophie would complete her mission no matter what. Mel had always known Sophie to be stubborn and determined, much like her father had been, and unlike her brother Harold. Harold had lost his will to bother with life.

Mel didn't want to hear the loneliness in Sophie's voice, it unsettled her, so she talked about anything she could think of, but nothing relevant. It was better than hearing her daughter's pain. She couldn't stand when any of her children were in the slightest pain. It was too much for a mother to bear. She had just started getting over Harold's tragedy—she needed a rest.

'How's the apartment?' Mel asked. Sophie, using her mobile, had called her mother to say she had arrived safely in Paris. Mel heard the exhaustion, the jet lag and loneliness in her daughter's voice. Sophie tried to draw attention away from these things with superficial chat, something about there being no broom because of the smallness of the flat. Mel faked dismay, in sympathy with Sophie's joke, which Sophie used to mask her fragility. Mel knew her daughter and knew her resilience would soon cut in, that everything would be fine. Mel wished she could hug Sophie and make it all better. Mel knew there would be a broom somewhere and that her days of hugging her children to make it all better were over.

For some reason Mel couldn't fathom, she thought of liquorice after she had hung up the phone. She slipped the page on milking goats into a red folder.

# Harry Fanshawe

The clock struck two just before three o'clock in the afternoon. A knock at Harry's door jolted him awake. But then he wasn't sure if he heard a knock or if he'd dreamt it, or he had made the sound himself when his elbow fell off the arm of his chair, or if it mattered if he wore unmatching socks—he hadn't but would it matter? Harry wondered if he would find a purpose to his life soon. He wondered where you looked for purpose. Does it have a colour? A shape? A smell? Is it behind the door?

Harry was thirty-two and dishevelled in a distinct bachelor kind of way. His perpetual state of 'dishevel' didn't preclude cleanliness. As was the case with most single men, he was able to look after himself up to a point—the point at which personal hygiene was accomplished and dishevelment began. Harry had dark red short bristly hair and a pale complexion. He had a small but distinguishing chunk missing from the top of his left ear courtesy of an attack from a neighbour's angry dog when he was six. When Harry was six, not the dog. Harry didn't know how old the dog was, it didn't seem relevant at the time. The incident happened while he was fishing. Again, Harry, not the dog. The dog showed no particular interest in fishing, but significant interest in the top of Harry's left ear.

Harry hadn't always been called Harry. For most of his life, at least for thirty years of it, he had been called Harold. It was Beverly who changed his name. It was Beverly who destroyed his life.

Harry sat at his desk in his musk-filled, book-filled, dream-filled office. Not his dreams, but his musk and his books. He fought off mid-afternoon drowsiness but with little success. He had jolted awake several times while trying to concentrate on the assignments he was supposed to be marking. One jolt resulted in him biting his tongue, which was annoying, and painful. He glanced at his computer screen. The short story he'd been working on during the morning, and on and off for the past few months, sat in silence on the screen. He hadn't added anything to it for days, or perhaps months. He had dropped out of The Writers Circle he'd been attending with his sister Sophie, which was the reason he started the story in the first place. He couldn't be bothered with the Circle anymore. He couldn't be bothered with the exercise of writing about a character called Austin Quinn. He wasn't amazed by the fact that one of the members of the Circle was called Austin Quinn. Nothing much amazed Harry anymore. He had enough trouble writing this short story, much less a confected story about someone who existed in someone else's imagination. At The Writers Circle, he called himself Tommy. He offered no explanation as to why he used the name. How could he? He didn't know himself. But the charismatic member aka Austin Quinn had suggested this to him, in *sotto voce*. Harry detected a faint smell of rockmelon.

Harry's life seemed to be one long, endless timeline—something he couldn't understand. If you ran the months of the year together in one elongated, nonsensical word, you'd have Harry's life pretty much explained, or at least his relationship to the passage of time. He glanced with half-open eyes at the words on his computer screen and pressed the bit of his tongue he'd bitten onto the back of his bottom teeth. It hurt. He once told Sophie if words on a screen could gather dust, his would be covered. He said to her that this was especially the case in his office, where dust lived a full and robust life and 'purpose' was non-existent—not even necessary.

He re-read the words on the screen, without much optimism. He'd forgotten about the knock at his door.

*He had started wearing his bathers in the shower. Brenton's wife died two years ago. He had lived with her for forty-four years. She was the only woman he had ever loved. He was now sixty-six and lost. He worked this out by himself. He worked out the feeling of cavernous emptiness and total silence was loneliness, and it was, but then he came to realise that he was more than lonely, he was lost. He tried to spend as little time as possible naked these days. That's why he wore his bathers in the shower. It had occurred to him that if he were to drop dead in the shower, there would be no one to make sure he was clothed, or well presented. He didn't want to be found naked. He didn't want his worn sixty-six-year-old body being found naked by some young female ambulance officer. He wanted to die with some dignity at least.*

This was the opening paragraph of the story sitting on his computer. The story was about abandonment, something that Harry specialised in. It was the one thing all his stories had in common, and ironically, all of them had been abandoned.

At times, he thought he had enough abandoned short stories to fill a novel if he could find a way to link them together in a seamless, yet provocative way. They were all, in their way, about abandonment, so didn't that link them? But he thought better of this. For a start, he'd have to finish most of them, and that didn't seem as though it was going to happen, and it'd take someone with more talent than he had to pull it off. He didn't think he'd ever get away with it—a novel consisting of linked short stories. No chance of that working, he thought, so he abandoned the idea.

A shaft of dappled light landed on Harry's half-eaten sandwich. The sandwich sat on a pile of manuscripts on his desk. The sandwich featured two busy flies, both roughly the same size, with black rotating eyes. The smell of warm cucumber oozed through the room into Harry's nostrils. He was reminded of lunchtimes at primary school, when he was a small boy sitting alone in the hot sun in the school rectangle, eating his lunch. He missed his sister then, and now. Sophie was finishing her second novel in Paris. He envied Sophie, but more than that, he admired her. Sophie was the complete opposite to Harry. Sophie got things done. Harry didn't.

Another shaft of light landed on a book on his desk. It fell on the title, *Hope and Other Hopeless Pursuits*. Other shafts of light landed on the floor and on his arm, and on his shoulder. For a moment he felt as though these shafts were anchoring him and his life, such as it was, to his chair, much as the angry Lilliputians had done to Gulliver by tying him down. Harry's limbs felt heavy and unco-operative. Feeling oxygen-starved, he sucked in a slab of office air from one of the light shafts near his nose. It didn't help.

Harry heard the knock at his door again. This time it was softer, as though not to disturb the inhabitants of the room. The inhabitants were, in this case, Harry and the two flies—still fascinated with his sandwich. It was probably one of his students, Harry surmised. They would want to discuss some pedantic point about their attempt at flash fiction, which they would suggest Harry had failed to grasp. Had this been the case, if he had failed to grasp some poignant element of their work, it wouldn't have surprised Harry. His students were, without exception, smart, bright, eager and in some cases, talented. They exhausted him and absorbed what little concentration he had to offer. One of them always wore a shiny red raincoat. A knock at the door could be the beginning of an extraordinary adventure, one where Harry was the superhero, and finds the 'McGuffin' and saves the day. If only, he thought. If only his life had adventure, if only his name was Captain Ahab, and he had a white whale to pursue. At least the obsessed Captain Ahab had purpose.

Harry was aware that a name didn't automatically spell adventure. He picked up the sandwich and chucked it in the bin next to his desk. With the flat of his hand, he tried to capture the crumbs and push them over the edge of the desk into the bin. Some made it into the bin. Some didn't. 'Crumbs of life,' he said under his breath, 'are like people. Some make it, some don't.' The flies resettled on the top of his computer screen and watched Harry. There was no telling what they were thinking. Harry's tongue throbbed.

'Jus' a minuthe,' he croaked, his voice not up to its full working state, much like the rest of him, on top of which, he now spoke as though he was drunk or had a speech impediment due to the annoying bite to his tongue. 'Life's noth hard enough?' he mumbled and winced with pain.

He tried to compose himself to not look as though he'd been dozing. This was his office, third along the corridor wedged between Bridget, Head of English, and Alex, the medieval postmodern poetry terrorist—a contradiction in terms that Alex particularly enjoyed. Bridget and Alex, in their respective offices, would be fast asleep. Bridget would have crumbs of cake across her chin and chest, head back with her mouth open and snoring so loud she would be in breach of local noise restrictions. Alex would be slumped forward with his head on his desk and dribbling onto some student's too ardent attempt at exhausting poetry. Alex considered his dribble frequency equivalent to a comment written in iambic pentameter.

'Come in,' Harry said, and the door opened.

*** 

Earlier that ordinary day, Harry woke to the ordinary day. He didn't know this when he opened his eyes, but since every day was more or less ordinary there was no reason to suppose today would be any different. And it wasn't. Life was one ordinary day after another. The sun was up and prying its way through the gap in the curtains of his bedroom. It created a glare around the edges. Harry pulled himself up and sat on the edge of the bed, taking a minute or so to complete the process of waking up, starting with his eyes. They needed to get used to the light in the room. Then his body's stiffness, he had to get the blood rolling through his limbs. It didn't take long for this to happen. It was more a ritual of sorts than anything else—it mimicked a cold-blooded reptile stirring after a lengthy hibernation. He twisted his head and looked over at Beverly still sleeping. She was curled up in bed, sleeping in the foetal position for some deep psychological reason Harry didn't understand, but appreciated. He loved her. He loved her so much it caused him physical pain. She wasn't there. She hadn't been there for over a year at least. It could have been two years. Time was opportunistic and indifferent. Time kept going, with or without him, and didn't require Harry to keep track of it. Time preferred he didn't.

Harry knew the exact date. He knew where he was and what was happening around him when his life changed forever. He preferred to let it blur in his memory, as though not acknowledging it, or not thinking about it, would allow the exact date to disappear, along with the pain. He'd lost track of his life if he was to be honest. He still imagined her there every morning. While he waited for his pupils to adjust to the light in the room, he watched her, sleeping, only the faintest sound of her breathing evident and then only if he leant over and put his ear to her face. He smelt traces of her perfume. Then he woke up from his recurring dream.

Harry wondered how long this morning ritual would go on. He supposed his habit of dropping some of her perfume on her pillow every night wasn't helping. He didn't consider his sanity was slipping. People do far more bizarre things than the 'perfume on her pillow' habit. Harry could never think of bizarre things other people might do. But he was sure people did do bizarre things.

The phone rang and accelerated him out of his stupor. He leant over and picked it up.

'Yep?' Ordinarily he wouldn't answer the phone like this, but he knew who it was. Elbow called him around this time every morning. Harry knew why. It was okay, Harry thought. It did no harm.

'Did I wake you?' Elbow asked this every morning when he rang Harry.

'No, I had to wake up to answer the phone anyway.' Harry repeated this every morning to Elbow. Elbow's name wasn't Elbow. His surname was Joint. He had been known as Elbow since before time started, as far as Harry could remember.

'Good. I've been thinking.' Elbow said.

'What with?'

'I've been thinking about this ad you're writing, you know, to find a wife?'

'I haven't written it yet. I haven't even decided to write it. I think it's a silly idea, if you want to know what I think this time of the day, having woken up from a dream where I save the universe from evil using nothing more than my trick of raising my left eyebrow to indicate wry jocularity.'

'Yeah, I'm not sure you could even fake jocularity...'

After this morning ritual, when, and only when, Elbow was satisfied Harry was awake and had grasped the significance of life, Elbow would hang up.

Harry would lie back down and drift off to a time long long ago when there were damsels in distress aplenty, and every one of them could be saved with a cheeky raising of an eyebrow expressing a wry jocularity, fake or otherwise. Those were the days when a rakish smile said it all.

Elbow was a good friend, but he worried about Harry. Harry wasn't going to do anything 'silly'. He was going to live his life one way or another, in spite of Beverly's absence.

***

Many lives ago, Harry was due to be married to Beverly in one month. He pursed his lips and squinted his eyes whenever he thought of his impending wedding day. He got butterflies thinking about the life he was going to have with a woman so perfect that if he was able to invent her, he couldn't have gotten her more perfect. She was made for him. He explained this to his sister Sophie at one of her Sunday barbeques. He needn't have bothered, as Sophie already knew this about Beverly. Harry could hear Beverly's laughter from somewhere inside Sophie's apartment. She'd be making someone feel they were an extraordinary person, which was Beverly's gift to the world.

Harry and Sophie sat on the deck of Sophie's high-rise apartment with the winter sun low between the buildings. Harold loved his sister's barbeques. He loved the view of the bridges and the one visible tip of a sail of the white building you could see from the northern end of the balcony.

'Pretty happy with things at the moment, Soph.'

'Good to hear. Can I give you a hug, maybe some of it will rub off on me.' Sophie slid her arm across Harry's shoulders, as though rubbing a lucky charm.

'It's been so simple. It's more like it found me.'

'I've made the decision to go to Paris. I've got to finish this novel somehow.'

Harry didn't respond. He was lost in his thoughts. They both directed their attention to the distant glimpses of the harbour waters.

Harry thought Sophie was a brilliant writer, while his work was pedestrian at best. Teaching creative writing was more his style. He did this, ran creative writing classes, though he never believed you could teach people to write. No one had taught Sophie.

'You know, I guess I had sort of given up on getting married. Or I stopped thinking about it a few years ago.' Harry took a sip of his wine. 'So, Paris?'

'Yeah, time to take it by the jugular.'

'Sounds like you. I have no doubt you'll write a brilliant novel and win several prizes and become famous and get rich promoting cheese or socks. And people will come see you at Writers Festivals and ask you fascinating questions, like what you have for breakfast.'

Sophie laughed. 'Yeah, I look forward to that.'

Harry was in his early thirties when he met Beverly. It was on his flight to the Frankfurt Book Fair. He was to attend some lectures and get the feel of what it might be like to publish a novel and eat German food. This was what he told his colleagues at the college, who knew he had accumulated so much holiday time that he'd been told to use some of it, or else. No one knew what the 'or else' meant. In truth, he needed a holiday, but he wouldn't have taken one without being forced. Harry was not the type to holiday alone. He needed an excuse to travel, so the Frankfurt Book Fair was as good a destination as any.

Harry had settled in his aisle seat and waited for the meal service to begin. He'd selected a book for the journey from the airport bookshop-cum-newsagent, *One Hot Summer's Night*, by the American writer, Dunleavy de Boston. Harry figured since he was supposed to be writing about de Boston's character Austin Quinn, as per the exercise in the annoying Writers Circle, Sophie insisted he attend with her every Wednesday night at seven pm sharp, he had better refresh his memory. He'd read it before, but ages ago, and anyway, de Boston was such a good writer, you needed to read his work more than once to get the nuances. Harry liked that and tried to render nuances in his writing. Nuances, he thought, might be out of his reach.

Before boarding his flight, along with de Boston's novel, he also bought a newspaper. Once on board, he settled into his economy seat and opened the in-flight magazine to see what channel the comedy program was on and what films would be showing. Suddenly, a cold liquid splashed over him. It covered his tie and jacket and soaked through his white cotton shirt to his skin. He looked up in shock into the most angelic face he'd ever seen. Though he was disorientated by the halo of light around her blonde hair and the general surprise of the events, in that instant, he somehow knew his life would never be the same again. Flight Attendant Beverly Brown looked down at him with the biggest blue eyes you could imagine on this earth.

'My, who's a clumsy boy then?'

She said this in a soft American accent, as she scooped him up out of his seat, took off his wet jacket and started vigorously wiping him down. He let her take care of him. This made him feel guilty—he was savouring her attention and closeness. It dawned on him that he didn't have a glass of water and it must have come from another passenger, or perhaps Flight Attendant Brown. He realised she had meant her question as a joke.

She positioned him in the space opposite the galley, in front of the emergency door for a minute, and disappeared with his jacket. She returned with the purser, and they moved him to a spare business class seat for his trouble, and because his seat was still wet. A newspaper was folded and placed in the seat pocket in front of him.

'That's complimentary. For you.' Flight Attendant Brown said with a smile that could stop a war or start one. Harry wasn't sure, but he was sure his head was spinning. Flight Attendant Brown gently touched his shoulder before she disappeared down the aisle behind him. 'Back to economy,' she said. She didn't say it, she whispered it, as though there was some special meaning he should understand.

He looked back, but a curtain had been pulled across the aisle, separating him from the most enigmatic beauty he'd ever met. He felt a panic rise in his stomach. He had no idea what he should do, or if there was anything to do. He was flummoxed, and he was sure it was the first time he'd been flummoxed enough to use the word flummoxed. He had left his newspaper and de Boston's novel in the seat pocket of his economy seat and hoped Beverly might find the book and bring it to him, but she didn't.

He didn't see Beverly again because she remained in the economy class section and he was placed in the charge of Nicholas, who fussed over him like he was a member of the royal family. Harry enjoyed business class and the sumptuous meal. Nicholas anticipated his every need and kept the port and cheese coming until Harry felt so heavy and tired, he couldn't keep his eyes open. He drifted off to sleep dreaming about Beverly bending over and whispering to him, with her smile and disarming accent, like they had a secret. He knew he was in love and wanted to tell someone, but he didn't. He thought Nicholas would be the kind of guy who would understand and revel in the news, maybe do a little matchmaking. But he felt ridiculous, so he said nothing. What if he'd imagined the whole thing and Beverly was just being professional, same as Nicholas? He decided to see if he could get a moment with Beverly alone when they landed.

Unfortunately, not having flown business class before, he didn't realise he would be let off first. He was shuffled along and didn't have a chance of seeing her, much less catching her eye. Not that he had any idea what he would have said to her if he had gotten his chance. The words 'I love you' popped into his head. He couldn't say that to her. She'd think he was mad. The problem was he wasn't good with women, they made him nervous, and he found that if he got close enough to them, their perfume from their impossibly soft skin would overwhelm him so much he would be rendered speechless. So, he walked reluctantly off the plane into the frozen air of Frankfurt with its smells of hot pea soup and vinegar, convinced he would never see Beverly again. And that was that.

# Sophie Fanshawe

Sophie could hear the jet lag. It sounded like aircraft cabin roar, even though she'd landed in Paris five hours ago. But the roar was still there, in her head, far off and close by. She had to actively listen to hear it, but she could hear nothing else. It sounded like a forest fire or a medical condition affecting her hearing. Sophie scrunched her hands down into her pockets. She had a plan but now she was unsure if it would work.

Standing at the windows in her Paris apartment, Sophie was aware of several things. Her fingers tingled. Her eyes stung. Her feet were swollen. She looked at her swollen feet. She didn't know if she was hungry, or tired, or existentially dead. She knew one thing, though. She knew she had the 'can't-help-its', as her mother would say. But why? Was she scared? Was it jet lag? Was she homesick already? No, it was more than all that, she thought. But here she was, soon to be living the life. She felt so fraught but why? It was what she had wanted—coming to Paris to write.

On the other hand, was *this* what she wanted? she questioned. It was hard to say. What was 'want'? Was it hope disguised, poor man's hope, slum hope, hope-light, diet hope? Whatever it was, it was debilitating, relentless, existential hope. Hope promised all and delivered little, she thought. She once discussed this with her brother Harry. 'Hope is like a desalination plant,' she had told him. 'It's big, it takes a lot of energy to run, and then, for all that effort, it produces a disproportionately small amount of water. Not wine, not nectar, not even a lot of water.' She compared herself to a desalination plant, and she missed her conversations with her brother. She flicked her head and wondered if she was developing a tic, or a spasm, or an involuntary head flick.

At The Writers Circle, when Sophie had been asked to discuss her novel with the group, she discussed hope, and the human condition's dependence on it, and how it was one of the themes of her debut novel. 'The point the novel made,' she said to the group, 'or, ironically, hoped to make, was the absurdity that we regard hope as an essential human trait with value. Hope is a kind of depleted currency. But in reality, hope enslaves us, hope is high maintenance. You can't avoid it though. We are hard-wired to hope.' Sophie hoped she was wrong. The members of the Circle nodded, some didn't. Austin made notes at the time. She looked at him and felt he had understood her. She looked at him often.

Her publishers had made the point that the inherent discussion of 'hope', was one of the aspects of her debut novel they admired—they called it 'brave', one said 'heroic'. And some of her readers agreed and wrote to her to say as much. 'Your novel gives me hope,' one said. Another alluded to hope as a postmodern trope, which was all one can do with postmodernism, 'allude' to it, as they pointed out. The thing was, if you point something out, you've no longer alluded to it. Sophie did not take issue with this when it was said in The Writers Circle once. 'To dismiss hope is liberating,' another reader wrote. Then an Italian man wrote in Italian and provided the translation, *'a speranza è l'ultima a morire*—hope is the last to die.' He finished with, 'I didn't enjoy the vegetable metaphors. I didn't get it, *bella*.' Sophie scanned her novel. There was no mention of vegetables, and this worried her. She was not worried about the lack of vegetables in the narrative. She was worried about the lack of vegetable metaphors. Had she missed an opportunity for a postmodern literary allusion? Or as Austin mumbled in The Writers Circle, 'delusion?'.

For proof of the insidiousness of hope, Sophie had only to look at the damage 'hope' had done to Mel, Sophie's mother. Hope rendered her forever disappointed. Sophie recalled Albert Einstein's observation, 'The definition of insanity, is doing the same thing over and over again, but expecting different results.' You could say the same thing about Mel. She hoped. She hoped over and over again. And each time she hoped for better results, no matter how often 'hope' proved itself to be a disappointment, or at best, an anticlimax. At times, when Sophie might be solemn and sitting in her dark apartment with goosebumps and a dry swallow, she felt life might be just one damn anticlimax after another. Sophie hoped to work this into the text of her second novel. She was going for 'heroic' again.

With the grey light from the window landing on her, Sophie sighed. It wasn't the 'can't-help-its', it was jet lag, she assured herself. Sophie refused to give into negative thinking, even though she was thinking negatively.

Sophie thought she could call her brother but it was too early or too late. It was too late for him back home. He'd be asleep. And too early for her to reach out. She suddenly felt like a sandwich. Eating one that is, not being one. If her brother were present, he would argue that you can't know what it was like to be a sandwich if you haven't been one—substitute sandwich with anything you like, he would say. This was Harry misquoting Gloria Steinem, but he was close enough, and the sentiment was the same. This, though, was how life worked or didn't work, according to Harry, when he gave a damn—which wasn't often these days.

She imagined the phone call with Harry.

'It's here.' Sophie imagined saying to Harry over the phone, their two phones somehow connected between opposite ends of the planet by a long piece of string, like when they were kids.

'What is?' Harry would respond with both a delay and an echo.

'Me,' Sophie would say.

'That's disappointing.'

'Yeah, it is.'

'Wherever you go, there you are,' Harry would observe.

'Apparently,' Sophie would say with resignation, and then would hang up her end of the string.

For Sophie, the space between the romantic notion of thinking about doing something bold, like coming to Paris for three months, versus the actual reality of coming to Paris for three months was filled with her loneliness. Maybe she'd thought her loneliness would only be with her in the city where she lived, in her normal life. She hadn't considered it would come with her to Paris. But this was nonsense. Her loneliness followed her from Melbourne when she moved three years ago, so why wouldn't it come to Paris? It clearly liked to travel. She recalled a conversation she'd had with Harry recently. She was eating a carrot at the time. Harry wasn't.

'So what are you tellin' me?' Harry asked.

'I'm tellin' you it's not what I'm tellin' you that matters, it's what you think you hear that matters. It's the gap.'

'So what do I think I'm hearing then?' Harry asked with much the same level of disinterest he employed for the first question.

'I'm tellin' you the *Ma*, the space between things, in this case, what I tell you and what you think you hear or interpret, if you will, is where the emotional transaction exists. That's the sentence you need to write, which may not—almost never—appear to have anything to do with what I say and what you hear. But you need what I say, and what you hear, in the sentence, to get the emotional transaction out of it, if you're good enough, if you're intuitive enough.'

'Right. Pass the Vegemite, will ya'?' Harry said obtusely.

Life was full of juxtapositions. Sophie celebrated this fact. As a writer she needed there to be juxtapositions in life, and more than that, she needed paradoxes, absurdity, contradictions, and irony. These were the things she wrote about, and the things with which she was obsessed. Sophie believed that not to write about these things meant you were just writing a travel log—*I did this, then I did that*. Or a diary—*I felt this, then I felt that*. She didn't say these things to anyone because they sounded harsh and elitist, and that wasn't her at all, but that was what she had to believe. She accepted there was a place for that kind of writing, but it wasn't the way she wrote. Words were the retail frontage. It was what was behind the words that Sophie pursued.

Sophie's rented Paris apartment was on *Rue Jacob*, on the Left Bank, close to the Seine. The Louvre, on the other side of the river was a stone's throw away, if you could throw a stone a kilometre or so and you thought it safe or wise to do so. This was the sort of sentence construction Austin of The Writers Circle favoured in his work—she loved his way with words. A smile crept across her face at the thought of his syntax.

In the cab on the way to her Paris apartment from the airport, she had passed a loud street market with a stall overflowing with thick white asparagus. She hoped her apartment wasn't far away. She knew the apartment was near the Luxembourg Gardens, as she had seen the gardens in relation to her apartment on Google maps. It was April, springtime in Paris. Soon the spring buds would be starting to pop. Everything was a *cliché*, and that was reassuring. She was a stranger in a strange land, a *cliché* or two was comforting.

Before she would leave Paris, twelve weeks from now, the Luxembourg Gardens would be resplendent in leaves and flowers, a complete transformation during her proposed time in Paris. Maybe that would happen to her. Transformation. Everything was in a state of change and change was busy. Sophie came to Paris willing to change, wanting to change her life, but now she wasn't sure that would happen. She felt rushed and out of sorts. How do you change something you're not sure exists? Or, if it does, does it exist the way you think it does? Back home, in her city, she had felt an emptiness, but she had been busy, so it lurked in the background. Sophie believed everyone felt a similar emptiness. So, was it *her* emptiness or emptiness in general? Or was it a collective human emptiness? In her life back home, she had her routine. The routine wasn't elaborate. It didn't include eating offal or donning a mask for a party, or having sex outside in soft grass, or even having much sex at all. Perhaps that's what happens when you travel, she thought, particular parts of your personality come into focus, parts that were always there, but subdued, latent, only appearing when called upon. She wondered for a moment if she would have sex in Paris. She thought to jot some of these thoughts down, but she didn't.

Standing in her rented Parisian apartment, in her cold Parisian apartment, her loneliness had come to the fore and was sitting on her shoulder looking at the man opposite with his hand down the front of his pants. Why did her 'loneliness' seem like an entity in its own right? It was more assured, more confident, less threatened than Sophie herself felt here in Paris. Did her 'loneliness' have a beauty mark, or a lisp? Any physical flaw to give it an edge? She looked down at her swollen feet again. She couldn't tell if they were getting bigger. Would they keep expanding to the point she couldn't lift them to move? One of her toes seemed a bit purpleish. She needed a pedicure. She hoped her enlarged feet were a temporary condition to do with flying so far and sitting for so long.

French raindrops covered the window. She shivered, and goosebumps rose across her skin like a Mexican wave. She winced at not being able to think of anything other than a Mexican wave to describe her goosebumps. She hoped the apartment had heating. She'd forgotten to ask the agent, and it wasn't mentioned. She continued to watch the man opposite. She didn't seem to be able to move, or she didn't want to. It was like her body was locked, not from any fascination with his behaviour, but because doing nothing was the easy option. The man showed no sign of seeing her. Perhaps he couldn't make her out between both his and her grimy windows. Perhaps he didn't care. He was still on the phone occupied in conversation. Sophie imagined he was talking to his mother who, Sophie decided, was in her bedroom in a small French village, south of Paris. A grey-haired mum with pierced ears and a wonky eye, on the phone to her son who lived far away in Paris, on *Rue Jacob*, opposite Sophie.

Sophie imagined a pearl-backed hairbrush, bristles up, sitting on the old lady's bedside table and groceries propped on the counter in her beige kitchen. The old woman had forgotten about the ice cream, which was melting. Dark chocolate ice cream oozed out from under the shopping bag, like blood from a cracked head. A small raw liver soaked in water in a yellow bowl on the sink next to half a cup of white salt. The man opposite continued with the rigorous pursuit of his hard-to-get-hard penis, while his mother worked her finger deep into her ear.

Sophie wondered about this woman, where she might have spent her last birthday. Did she spend it with her son? Did she serve the food? What secrets did she live with, secrets she couldn't tell her family? When would she die? Of course, the man might not be talking to his mother. He might be talking to his girlfriend. Maybe it was phone sex? If it was phone sex then, so far, it didn't seem to be working for him, Sophie thought.

Sophie wondered about her own mother. Where was she? It was a rhetorical question. Sophie knew her mother was in Melbourne. Mel would be in bed asleep. She slept alone, propped up with two pillows. She slept in a Laura Ashley nightdress and kept the night-light on and her pearl-backed hairbrush on her bedside table. Bristles up. Weaponised.

'Mothers were a necessary evil in the lives of most adult children.' Sophie had raised this point with Harry on a few occasions when they were together. 'Not all the time.' Harry had scoffed. He wasn't much interested in conversations that had his mother as the subject. Sophie worried it wasn't only conversations about his mother he'd lost interest in. Harry had always liked obtuse questions, for example, 'did nomadic existence cease with the introduction of agriculture and did this create the need for permanent housing and, therefore, the invention of cement and the lunch box? If you were nomadic, you could gather your lunch as you went. If you went to the same place to work each day, you'd have to take your lunch with you and thus, you would find the need to invent a lunch box, and so agriculture caused the invention of the humble lunchbox.' However, Harry had lost interest in those kinds of questions of late. For a long time now.

Sophie's mother had advised Sophie not to go to Paris. 'Don't go to Paris,' she said many times. 'It's not safe for women to be alone.' But Sophie *was* alone. How was being alone in Paris any different? She'd asked her mother this question. Her mother, who had been alone for years, shrugged. 'That's not the point,' she said. 'Why do you want to go to Paris?' *And leave me.*

'What do you hope to achieve that you can't achieve here?' Sophie heard the words in the space between the said and the unsaid, loud and clear.

Sophie's vision had blurred, but when her consciousness returned, the man opposite was still on his mobile, and still had his hand down the front of his pants. He was scratching or searching for something down there, but nothing less innocent seemed to be happening. His body resembled a giant watermelon, with arms stuck on the sides and a rockmelon for a head. Sophie imagined his penis as a banana that was the aerial for his phone. He was adjusting it to achieve signal. The sight depressed Sophie. She would have this man, his phone, his rockmelon head, his watermelon body, and his banana penis in her life for the next three months. She had hoped for a more exotic, adventurous experience in Paris, not this raw fruit-based humanity.

In the next apartment along from the man and his penis obsession, a woman was standing in her bedroom, brushing her black hair with long, slow strokes. She was looking at herself in a mirror, side-on to Sophie. The man and the woman were separated by a single wall, oblivious to one another, like two television sets playing in separate universes on different channels with no sound.

Sophie guessed the woman's age to be around forty-five. Sophie could only see her from the waist up. She was beautiful. She wore a black bra. Sophie watched her roll deep red lipstick around her lips. The woman checked herself in the mirror, unaware of Sophie's gaze. She reminded Sophie of herself—alone, independent, but in Sophie's case, fearful. Sophie wouldn't mind being in as good a shape as this woman when she arrived in her mid-forties. The woman adjusted each breast in her bra. She slipped a black dress over her head, in a movement that precluded disturbing her hair. The dress fell down her body. She looked so elegant and French in that classic, sophisticated Frenchwoman kind of way that Sophie felt unsophisti-cated and crumpled in contrast. Sophie understood how this woman would fascinate men, and women. Sophie couldn't see the woman's eyes, but she imagined defiant tears in them. Sophie felt a desire to be hugged by this woman, to let the woman's tears release and be absorbed into Sophie's dress and run down between her breasts like sweat. Sophie felt the woman's life shudder—both life-shudder and life shudder. She watched the woman use a tissue to remove smeared lipstick from her teeth. She cupped her breasts again, as though her breasts were a crucial element to her appearance and she wanted them level, or full, or equal, or noticed. Sophie understood this and became aware of her own breasts.

Sophie missed her mother, even though her mother drove her mad. Mothers always drove their daughters mad. It was the way things were. Sophie resisted the tears in her own eyes. She squeezed her eyes shut to block out the woman and the man across from her and imagined herself at home at her window looking out at the city's buildings. She could pick out the tiny figures of people around the harbour. Here, in Paris, she was reflected like a ghost in the grimy window in front of her. She could hear seagulls squawking.

Sophie refocused her eyes and saw that both her neighbours had disappeared, and she was looking into two empty rooms.

She stepped back from her window and surveyed her tiny apartment. It was furnished sparsely but adequately. There was a small round wooden breakfast/dining table and four wooden chairs—one was mismatched. There was a print of an elegantly dressed Asian woman with a green face hanging on one of the walls. The kitchen was open plan and small, a galley kitchen, but it was as expected for an apartment of this size. Sophie assured herself she could deal with it.

Several harlequin masks were hanging on another wall. She felt like putting one of them on. She felt like putting on a mask and sitting on the beanbag in the corner of the room and never speaking or moving again. She imagined other guests coming into the apartment and noticing the sculpture in the corner sitting on what looked like a life-like beanbag. She would follow them around the room with her eyes. They would notice the sculpture's eyes following them, like eyes in paintings sometimes did. She would watch them live their life. She would make no assumptions. She would make no judgements. She would watch people come and go. She did this at the Stalwart. She wore her bartender mask. She was accustomed to wearing a mask. She observed the comings and goings at her bar. She watched lives. She made no judgements. She made no assumptions. She felt invisible, as though, behind her mask, she, Sophie Fanshawe, could not be Sophie Fanshawe. She felt dizzy.

Sophie's friends would describe Sophie as having a 'sunny disposition', but that was when she was at a Sunday afternoon barbeque overlooking the city's sparkling harbour, sipping on a glass of chilled *rosé,* and feeling the breezes waft through her hair and the sun on the top of her head. She was a character in a novel riding a stallion across a dark landscape with her red hair flowing back in the wind, in charge of her realm. On such an occasion, she felt confident, hopeful, and she found herself smiling. She knew this because the muscles around the side of her mouth felt extended, as though they were being pressed into unusual use. Her kiss muscles, she called them. It had been a while since they had been pressed into anything like a kiss. Sophie noticed an inexplicable metallic taste in her mouth.

Sophie couldn't remember the sequence of events, or the thinking she went through when she decided to come to Paris. As an adult, Sophie had trouble pinning her life down. What she did on any particular day, what and to whom she spoke to during the course of her life in the city, was often a mystery to her. She had trouble cataloguing things—dates and events, that sort of thing. It was a function of living in a big city, she thought. Or there was something wrong with her, something not right, not working correctly. She felt submerged in a blur of white noise and aircraft cabin roar. She felt homesick. And here on day one in Paris, she was feeling fainter, and fading, being absorbed by the over-real fairy tale city. She had looked forward to the anonymity and isolation, but now she was here, all she felt was anxious and not special. She felt the cold creeping into her body. Two seagulls landed on the railing outside the window. They looked at her. Birds did look at you, she had noticed this. Sophie wondered, when they looked at you, were they thinking about the meaning of life, or a chip with some Dijon mustard on the side?

Sophie had come to Paris with the plan to write, to finish her novel, to live the *cliché* of a writer's life in Paris, to escape, to disappear, to find herself, to mature, to find happiness, to succumb to the taste of white asparagus, to find love, to have sex, to find adventure, to learn how to shout 'foie gras' in a Peter Sellers' French accent—to find something she thought was missing in her real-life back home. She was open to it, she assured herself, not believing it as much as she needed to. She felt a surge of tenderness for Robbie Carton. She could see him sitting at the bar in the Stalwart getting drunk. Was Robbie a wasted opportunity? She didn't know, but she felt responsible in some way. But all in all, and all things being equal and considered, and when it came down to it, at the end of the day, she felt the same. And she couldn't accurately describe that—she'd run out of *cliché*s.

She had chosen her *Rue Jacob* apartment in Paris because it was five minutes from the two famous cafés, *Les Deux Magots* and *Café de Flore*, both in the *Saint-Germain-des-Prés* neighbourhood, on *Boulevard Saint-Germain*. James Joyce, Ernest Hemingway, and the absurdist Albert Camus had discussed their work and the issues of the day as they sat smoking Gauloise cigarettes in these Parisian cafés. And later, in the twenty-first century, an Australian writer, Gary N. Lines, moved temporarily from his W57th Street apartment, not far from The Russian Tea Room in New York, to Paris, to polish and edit his debut novel in these same cafés. Sophie suspected, without confirmation, that he wasn't a smoker. Sophie had read his novel many times. She was affected by his style, as strained as it was. He wrote about a young woman called Ruby. Sophie felt close to Ruby. She read in an interview with the author that he wished he had come up with a different name for Ruby. He thought Ruby was too fragile, too exposed, and he wanted her to have a more stoic name. He lamented he wasn't able to save Ruby. If that was going to happen, and he had his doubts, she would have to pull that off herself. He didn't think the name Ruby was hopeful enough. One of Ruby's problems was she struggled with the overwhelming elements of life. She didn't have the strength to fight life off, to mould it to her own will. Ruby, according to the author, in the same interview, lived her life frightened.

Sophie took great care when choosing names for her characters, but she was rarely happy with her choices. Names were an enigma, Sophie believed. Her brother Harry was never sure about his name. Lately, he preferred Tommy. And she knew Austin Quinn was not Austin Quinn. And Robbie? Well, that was a whole other story.

Outside her plan, Sophie had intentions. She intended to go to both famous cafés. She intended to sit with a coffee, make notes and watch Parisian life pass by. She intended to become a *cliché*—as in, a writer in Paris drinking coffee in the two famous cafés. She didn't mind this. She thought being a *cliché* was a workable outcome for someone without anyone in her life to love and nourish.

Ronny, a friend back in the city where she lived, who she did love and nourish platonically, had warned her the coffee at these two famous cafés was the most expensive in the world and she should think of it as renting real estate—they throw in the coffee for nothing. He then laughed his gay laugh. His laugh was not a laugh, *per se*, but a cynical comment on her life. She heard it punctuating her thoughts.

Sophie had two other ambitions while in Paris. One was to visit as many galleries and art museums as she could, starting with the Louvre. Ronny had said she would see a hundred metres of Jesus paintings at the Louvre. Ronny heralded, as only Ronny could, 'This is Jesus having dinner with his friends', 'This is Jesus with a torch held behind his head to give a halo effect', 'This is Jesus with unusable gifts from three weird gay guys', 'This is Jesus high up on a cross trying to watch the gay *Mardi Gras* for free'. 'This is Jesus coming out,' Ronny claimed. 'Everyone's gay, it's only a matter of time.' He also assured her that Parisians understood English. She wasn't so sure, but Ronny was no fool. She wanted to visit the Musée d'Orsay, which was walking distance from her apartment, as it turned out. She had read it was once a railway station. There were so many things she didn't know about, so many things. She wanted to see the museum's clock, which was originally the railway station's clock. She wanted to crawl in a warm hole and cease to exist. She believed looking at great artwork would forge her soul. The works would show artists have always suffered. She would see the suffering in their work and from this, she could reinvent herself and cope with her meagre suffering and, no doubt, meagre talent.

Her second ambition was to find love, or more specifically, find out if she was *in* love. She winced at the thought, the *cliché* of it all. She thought she was better than that. She thought she could rise above such mundane female dreams. But her mother was right, she couldn't. She wanted to be held by someone she loved and be lavishly kissed. She thought of Robbie Carton again. But Robbie was a lost drunk accountant and not in Paris. The whole thing about Robbie was complex, and she was at a loss to explain it. The men at the Stalwart were similar when they were drunk. They were drunk for a start. This made them similar in that regard. They revealed themselves to be boys rather than men. They were frightened and thus felt obsolete. When Robbie was drunk it was in a different way, though. Robbie started frightened and philosophically confused and ended up with his thinking clarified the more he drank. His sincere, hopeful nature came out. It was as if the excess alcohol released him from his sober self, which ordinarily drowned in the absurdity of life. His mumbles stuck in her mind. She had made love to him in another life, an imagined life. He was mad though, and she knew that and accepted it. The one big question was, how mad was he? How much madness could she accept? Was she not a little mad herself? That was three questions, but Robbie would have enjoyed the obfuscation, drunk or sober.

In Paris, she planned to establish a routine as quickly as possible, otherwise she feared she might flame out over the next twelve weeks, see nothing, achieve nothing, and return home less than she was before she came. Or more than she was. 'You'll be a disappointment,' her mother had remarked harshly. Sophie thought her mother's prediction was more or less accurate, except Sophie thought of herself as already a disappointment, so this meant she might return home more of a disappointment than she already considered herself to be. Her mother disguised her envy of her daughter's life with her infamous scoff. Sophie could hear the 'infamous scoff' across the equator. Without that 'infamous scoff' to motivate Sophie, she might not have bothered getting out of bed on any given day, and perhaps she might not have taken herself to Paris.

Sophie had thought through her plan. She would join the Parisian ritual and walk the Luxembourg Gardens every morning. She had brought a new sports bra and trainers for the purpose. She would then go to one of the cafés and have a *café Americano*, her body still buzzing from the walk. These two famous cafés reminded her of Cervantes' windmills. She would sit alone in the cafes and tilt her head. She would make notes in her current red notebook. She would make a conscious effort to make eye contact with people, or specifically, men, because she had read in a magazine that when in Paris it is acceptable to make eye contact with men, or to receive their attention without it resulting in actual engagement. Sophie thought this sounded exhilarating and mysterious and freeing, and it would help her writing. After spending time in the café, she would return to the apartment. She would be inspired, and she would write. She would write for three hours every day.

However, this part of her plan, the part where she wrote and completed her novel, was in trouble. Sophie had started her novel several times. She had significant plot problems to solve. There was a believability issue, and worst of all, her main character, Austin Quinn—she planned to change his name as soon as she could think of one that had some profound resonance—had disappeared.

In truth, Sophie had no idea what her novel was about. She had abandoned the first two chapters, the ones she had submitted to her publisher. Her stomach sank at the thought of writing. Maybe she should start a new project, something about Paris perhaps. A love story in Paris in the spring? That'd be original, she thought. But Sophie had spent so much time on this novel already, she needed to get something out of the effort. To be thinking of forsaking it felt like an act of betrayal. The novel worried her. Her characters had banded together. Back home, she was sure she could hear a muffled giggling sound in the darkness before dawn. Her eyes would open, and the giggling would stop. She would switch on the bedside light and look around, but the room was still. She would leave the light on. She was sure her characters were keeping something from her. Sophie believed this was her novel's last chance, maybe her last chance as a writer.

Sophie had picked up the signs her publisher was losing patience. She thought they were on the verge of asking for the return of her advance, and they might give her until the end of Paris to produce the completed manuscript, but no longer. There would be no advance left after three months in Paris. Surely, they must have realised that, she worried. She recalled the last meeting she'd had with them, to tell them she was going to Paris. The meeting was supposed to have been an update on her progress. But there was no update to give. When she told them she was going to Paris to finish it, they had looked at her like birds sitting on a ledge thinking philosophical thoughts. No one in the room said anything. Then one of them, her editor, said, 'Send us a postcard, you know, on how you're doing. We love Austin, you might want to rethink his last name.' Sophie had smiled, a smile intended to cover how depressed she was at their lack of enthusiasm. They had been patient, and full of enthusiasm when she had submitted her first two chapters. She didn't have the heart to tell them she had ditched those chapters and that her main character—the one they had enthused over, saying how much they'd like to have sex with him—was gone. In the lift after the meeting, Sophie had perspired all the way to the ground floor. Her butterflies had tried to escape from her stomach. They found the environment in her stomach too nerve-racking.

In the afternoons in Paris, after she'd written for most of the morning, she intended to return to one of the cafés for lunch. She might meet other writers. She might have a strange encounter with another person—it seemed probable. She might write about the encounter and how it would change everything. She would luxuriate in the feeling of satisfaction from having produced work.

She unpacked. She was here to stay, swollen feet and aircraft cabin roar included. There was no room in the tiny apartment to put anything, but she managed to empty the contents of her suitcase into an old orange chest of drawers in the bedroom. She stuffed her suitcase under the bed. She spread out her makeup on the top of the chest. She set up her laptop on the dining table. She plugged it in using the French plug she bought at the airport. She turned the computer on. The first page of a short story lit up the screen. She had been staring at that first page back home for several months. The short story was, as yet, untitled and was a distraction from the fact that she wasn't getting anywhere with her novel.

*My name is Valliant (Vally for short). I'm not so sure I have lived up to my name. I'm not so sure about anything much these days. I wish I were any age before my twenty-second birthday, to be honest. I wish someone would marry me and love me forever, as embarrassing as that is to admit.*

Sophie's finger hovered over the delete button, as it had several times in the past few months. The trouble with this story was she didn't know where it was going. Or, if it was going anywhere.

She flicked to the file that contained the remnants of her second novel. There were nine pages. Sitting in the chilly Paris apartment, on the other side of the world, far from her apartment, she thought she might find inspiration. If not in Paris, then where? She needed to find the truth in her novel. Maybe she could start with the story about Vally. There were remnants of truth in that story, and nothing works better for fiction than truth—well-modified truth, enhanced abridged truth. It wasn't a true story. In truth, truth was dangerous, especially when fictionalised. Sophie once said this to the members of The Writers Circle. It had just popped out of her at the time. Sophie had a style. She liked to throw in the unexpected. It kept the reader on notice and herself interested. She typed, *I've never had a threesome or eaten snails.* She was looking for intrigue and depth. She deleted the sentence. Vally was loosely based on herself, and a woman called Pamela, who Sophie met at her Writers Circle. She had interviewed Pamela, like she tended to do to everyone. Sophie had no idea what was going to happen to Vally, or Pamela, or herself.

Sophie was the kind of writer who wrote a sentence then stared at it for a month. She might change the comma or break it into two sentences. But then she was as likely to change it back again, or more likely, delete it altogether. She was brutal with her work. She knew her sentences cowered when she sat at her computer, as though they feared for their lives. As well they should. Sophie feared for herself and being a single woman only exaggerated her fear, so she took it out on her sentences.

Sophie looked around the kitchen and inspected the appliances. There was a half-size fridge making a noise better suited to a lawnmower. In the corner was a stove/oven combination that needed cleaning, a brushed aluminium toaster with burnt rust on its top surface and a plastic electric kettle with dark smears on its side. The cutlery drawer was full of mismatched cutlery, but nonetheless, it was workable. There was a corkscrew and a tape measure. In one cupboard there were four plates, two cups, two wineglasses and one drinking glass. Nothing special but adequate. There was also a brown plastic thing, which defied definition or usage. She figured it must be some French utensil that no one in the world used other than the French. The fridge stopped humming. It had become aware of how much noise it was producing and embarrassed itself.

This apartment was all she could find available for the full three months and all she could afford. She hadn't inspected the bathroom, but she knew the whole apartment would have to be cleaned before she could settle in, especially the bathroom. She hadn't felt like looking at it in her jet-lagged, cold state. She knew she might start crying. She knew she could not look at a depressing bathroom while feeling alone, lonely, tragically so, her writing life on the line, and without a bottle of wine in which to drown her self-pity.

Sophie had inherited a cleaning gene from her mother, who never stopped cleaning, even when she was in Sophie's super-clean apartment. Sophie checked under the sink for cleaning products. There was some dishwashing liquid, an old, twisted Brillo pad and a bottle of what looked like Brasso, but she couldn't be sure because she didn't know what the French word for Brasso might be, probably *Brasso*. And if that was the case then this bottle wasn't Brasso or *Brasso*.

Sophie grabbed her jacket, and purse from her handbag, and headed down the short hallway to the apartment's door. She considered calling her mother again but thought better of it. Her mother would hear the loneliness in her voice and would jump all over it. Along with cleaning products and flowers, she needed to get food and wine, especially wine. By the door, she found a gauge on the wall next to the bathroom. She hoped it was the heating. She hit the 'on' button, and it lit up. She dialled up numbers, which she assumed set the temperature. She set it at twenty-four and hoped by the time she got back, the chill would be gone, and the liquorice and eucalyptus smells would have settled. She hoped things wouldn't seem so desolate and bleak if she was warm. She thought, whatever existence hope relied upon, could only be maintained in a warm environment.

Out on the street, Sophie felt she was in the 'cone of silence'. She couldn't pick up conversations as she walked along. Everything she heard was muffled in a foreign language, not surprisingly. She felt anonymous. Her head felt thick, as though, when she moved her head, her brain lagged a second or two before it caught up and aligned itself with her eyes. No one knew her. In this entire city, as far as she was aware, no one knew her. She felt free, invisible, and liberated, even a little exhilarated. The air was damp, and the sky threatened more rain. It was cold. She inhaled the cold air. She dodged the dog shit on the footpaths and the small cars parked everywhere. She found herself squeezing past people and having to go around cars and scooters blocking the footpath. She searched for a food market and a wine shop, but all she saw were boutiques and art galleries. There were cafés on every corner. Heavily dressed people sat alone at the rows of cramped tables drinking coffee. Sophie heard scared loud American voices. She felt sorry for Americans abroad—they meant well, she thought, but they knew no one liked them. They didn't know why.

Sophie started to feel better as she strolled the streets. Here she was, an Aussie sheila in Paris—a writer in Paris. She decided to celebrate. A glass of bubbly perhaps, never mind the expense. She came upon a blue café and took a seat at one of the outside tables. She had failed French in high school. She hoped Ronny was right with his claim that the French spoke English but preferred not to. Who could blame them? She had intended to learn as much French as she could while she was in Paris, but she knew this was unlikely. She had enough to deal with just surviving.

A waiter floated by. '*Madam*?' That was all he said. Sophie answered in English, 'Err, a glass of champagne, *s'il vous plaît*?' She could at least use what little French she had as a gesture of goodwill. The waiter didn't answer but glided away to another table and took their order. She didn't know if he was going to attend to her, or if he was ignoring her because she was an ignorant tourist. She couldn't read anything on his face. Was that his 'waiter's' face or his 'can't be bothered engaging with the customers' face? Sophie noticed he smiled at the other customers. He reminded her of someone. She figured it out while she watched him move around the cramped tables. He reminded her of the main character in her novel. She was sure he was Austin Quinn, who had left her novel and ended up here in Paris, as an undercover detective posing as a rude French waiter. She had held out higher hopes for her main character. She wanted a relationship with him for a start, or to resume her relationship with him, but not as Austin Quinn. The waiter had a strong jaw and muscular body under his black shirt, like her fictional Austin. One of her girlfriends had asked, 'Isn't your protagonist a bit *cliché*? Good looking, muscular and mysterious.' Sophie's response came out sharper than she had meant. 'He's my protagonist. If he doesn't work for you, you can always write your own.' 'Okay,' came the response, 'but why has he disappeared? Can a protagonist disappear after a few pages?'

After what seemed a long time, the waiter returned carrying a tray with a glass of champagne. He put it in front of her and left. She had accomplished her first order of business. She had found a seat in a café, ordered her first glass of champagne in Paris, and been treated as though she didn't exist by a Parisian waiter who wouldn't exist if Sophie hadn't created him. She toasted herself and took a sip. She noticed a woman dressed in black sitting nearby. The woman looked at Sophie. It was more of a stare. She held Sophie's eyes. Sophie didn't know if she should look away. She didn't know what the intimate social café protocols were in Paris. Sophie examined the possibilities. Does she think she knows me? Should I smile? Sophie realised with surprise that she was the woman she had watched getting dressed. The waiter moved between them and stopped to speak to the woman. Sophie looked at the waiter's bum. She thought her girlfriend, the one who had complained about Sophie's protagonist's muscular physique, should see this *derrière*. He moved away. The woman was not looking at Sophie anymore. She was staring out into the street. A monkey wearing a red cap sat on a bench seat, but the woman wasn't looking at the monkey.

Sophie didn't know where she was, apart from the fact she was in Paris. Beyond that, she didn't know where she was in her writing life. She didn't know what she'd been thinking to commit to three months in Paris when her novel was in such dire straits. She wondered if she would last the distance. She didn't know what she would do next, right now and hereafter. She finished her champagne and, without thinking about the cost, ordered another. She thought of her empty dark flat back home and missed it. She wondered if she would achieve anything here or maybe she'd never be heard of again. This thought was comforting on some level. Wouldn't it be so easy to disappear? She took another mouthful of champagne in the hope the alcohol would help. It did. She felt disappearing was only half of it. She wanted to pop out of her life, to a warm tropical island, with a whole new life where she smiled a lot and was in love and felt sand between her toes and the warm sun on the top of her head instead of being in Paris, committed to finishing a novel that didn't exist.

A ball of freezing air hit her. It attacked her hair and would have blown over her glass of champagne had she not been holding it. She looked at the woman opposite. Her hair was unruffled by the wind, and she still looked elegant. There was something about her hair, something that hadn't occurred to Sophie before now. The woman was pale, as though she barely existed and might blow away in the next gust of wind. Sophie hadn't understood until this second that this woman was important. Sophie absorbed her stillness. She was enthralled by the woman's silence. Sophie wondered whether she was wearing a black wig. She was. Sophie suddenly realised that she knew this woman's name. It was Tilly. Sophie knew right at that moment that she had to complete her three months. She had to write her novel, and she had to get back home and do something about her love life before it was too late. The man she thought she loved might disappear at any moment. He already had once.

Sophie walked back to her apartment. She entered the warmth and opened a new page on her computer and started writing. She didn't notice the eucalyptus and liquorice smells had cancelled each other out or had been absorbed by the warm air. She recalled her childhood in Portsea, where she had played on the beach every day. She hadn't realised until she arrived in wet, cold Paris, how profound her innocent days in the sun, sand and coastal breezes had been. The best time was after the tourists had gone and before winter set in, when it seemed like the whole bay belonged to her, except for a woman who Sophie saw every day walking the empty beach. The woman had been alone and distant to Sophie. Sophie had never spoken to her, but the woman's presence had affected Sophie in ways she couldn't understand at the time. Sophie had been aware the woman was a sad person. It was known her husband had died suddenly. Sophie was thirteen, old enough to cry for this woman. In Sophie's memory, Sophie had squinted into the sun to catch a glimpse of this woman's face under her broad sunhat and dark sunglasses, but her features had remained indistinct. Sophie wrote the following story about the woman she named Tilly, short for 'until'.

*There Are No Pain Receptors in the Brain*
*By*
*Sophie Fanshawe*

*Tilly preferred Panorama Bay most of all when it turned into a ghost town after the final weekend of summer. Shacks were closed down, shutters were shuttered, and gates latched and padlocked. Packed cars headed back to the city with summer memories and sunburnt faces. Tilly walked the length of the bay along the water's edge and back again every day in the blustery wind and leftover sunshine. Only a young teenage girl who kept her distance in the sand dunes remained in Tilly's peripheral view—they never spoke or waved. Tilly hid under her floppy hat behind her mirrored sunglasses.*

*The dominating wind whistled along the only street between the low shacks. A loose shutter or unlocked front gate flapped somewhere, and the squawking seagulls hovered stationary in the air. To Tilly these sounds seemed louder after everyone had gone. They became the sounds of the bay at rest, replacing the innocent squeals and laughter of children and their parents playing on the sand along the water's edge.*

*Panorama Bay, or Pan Bay as it was known, comprised a row of stoic fibro shacks along the one flat dune and another row of shacks immediately behind the first line, with the short sandy street separating them. Silver-grey saltbush resisted the wind and clung in clumps along the low edge of sand separating the shacks from the sea. There was nothing much else. Tilly had come to accept, when it came down to it, things were what they were and nothing much else. It was a human desire to add meaning and to heighten experience, to try to make the most out of things, but in the end, life was indifferent to these human aspirations. It was just what it was.*

*Tilly was thirty-three, financially independent, widowed, and empty. She yearned for company, but not the company of anyone she knew. It was four years since Jack died. They had been married for seven years before he fell victim to an aggressive brain tumour and left her behind. She was coping with her widowhood, she would say, whenever someone asked how she was doing. She would never say it out loud, it wasn't the right response and people couldn't understand what she was going through. She had trouble making any sense of it herself and when she tried, her eyes flooded with her endless tears. Everyone had their own life and every life, as they say, comes with some pain. The truth of it, though, was she knew she hadn't coped with her widowhood. During the first few years, she lived in an agonising blur of relentless pain. She existed. That was the best she could say. She slept. She ate. She worked after a fashion. She was a zombie. Her plan of being married to the best man in the world for the rest of her life had vanished in what seemed like an instant. In truth, he took nine months to die.*

*She had kept their shack at Pan Bay. She needed to keep something to pre-serve Jack's memory. She could still smell him in the shack. She didn't want that to change. His fishing gear was still propped up against the wall in the shed. His dinghy still suspended from the rafters. His clothes still stuffed in the shelves in their bedroom. His pots of paint, left from the time he decided to paint the outside cladding, lined the back wall of the shed. He never got around to painting. The tumour had reared up and annihilated Jack's life. And without thought, without consideration, or notice, Tilly's life too.*

*She had spent a long time being angry with him. There was a part of her that couldn't forgive him for acquiescing to the tumour. She held him culpable for not trying harder. He could have tried harder. She would have for him.*

*In spite of his presence in the shack, she felt him slipping away from her as time passed, as she knew he would. In the weeks and months, then years, of Tilly's life after Jack, things changed but without her conscious involvement. Things occurred somehow. She didn't know how. She sold their house in the sub-urbs. It was too big for her, and it was haunted by memories of Jack she didn't want. The last few days and minutes he spent in the house were horrifying. They didn't want him and his tumour in the hospital. He was taking up a bed. They had given up on him. She remembered his eyes—his dead dark empty eyes. His life had moved on days before his body followed. She remembered her agony of those last few days, of seeing him lifeless, unable to recognise her. He had no physical pain. There are no pain receptors in the brain, the doctors assured her. They were talking about Jack as if he was dead.*

*She bought an apartment in the city. Two bedrooms and a small study, where she thought she might write. She wanted to write a book about Jack's life. Not that he had such a life it warranted a book, but more about his death. She didn't know why she felt she needed to write about it, maybe it would help her in some way, she thought, and she had some vague notion it might help others too.*

*The cancer had started as a baby but grew quickly to become a fully-fledged member of her family. Tilly had to stop herself from talking to the tumour rather than to her frail husband. It felt like the tumour had taken over, that it was so powerful it demanded she dealt directly with it and not the shell of a man it was occupying. It was not only killing Jack, it was also killing itself. Eating its host was guaranteeing its own death. It seemed to Tilly that the tumour knew what it was doing and didn't care. That was the nature of its short existence. Its purpose was to kill its host and having achieved that, it had no further purpose and died with its victim. This made no sense to Tilly. She tried to negotiate with it. Point out the stupidity of what it was doing. Stop killing my husband, and you can live on yourself. Have the spare room if you like, we can feed you mice or whatever it is you eat, buy you a car if you want.*

*But there was no negotiating with this entity. It was determined to kill Jack, and the more she tried to stop it, the harder it would go. So, it was this aspect of Jack's life she thought to write about. So far, she had written one chapter about the moments after Jack's diagnosis had been confirmed. After that, she had run out of steam. She came to realise his life, and hers, had changed when the doctor explained about the tumour and what it would do and how efficiently it would do it. She had sat in the doctor's office with a buzz in her ears and heard nothing else from then on. Her life had started and stopped in that one conversation with the doctor, and she had nothing more to say, in a book, or to herself or anyone.*

*Tilly ambled along the water's edge and let the wind blow her long red hair across her pale skin and whip her dress up around her body. She didn't bother to hold her dress down—there was no one to see her. It felt good to let it go, tentative and scary but good. She felt free but still somehow terrified, a feeling she didn't care to explain or understand.*

*All the shacks were sealed up and the curtains were drawn. There was the painted rock propped against each screen door to hold them closed in case the latch couldn't resist the wind. Tilly had nowhere to be or go, and no one to engage with. Pan Bay was hers and, eventually, even the young girl disappeared—probably back to the city to start school. Tilly missed her. Tilly was alone now except for the omnipresence of something. She felt it. She didn't wonder what it was. She knew what it was. She thought of it as the absence of life, as though the absence of life was so profound as to have an existence. That space between things, where she preferred to dwell. The space between Jack's absence and her presence. This is where she lived daily.*

*Except for the seagulls soaring above the shoreline and screeching to one another, there was nothing else, no other movement, no human sounds, no human demands. The human silence made its presence felt on Tilly. She could feel it over her skin and under her dress. She felt it brush between her legs. Her peripheral vision picked up a dark flash between the shacks, but there was nothing there. It was the echo of life, and she preferred not to look at it. An ice-cream wrapper had escaped one of the over-stuffed bins waiting for collection and skidded across the windswept street. It caught on the saltbush along the dune, then the breeze changed direction and pushed the wrapper back along the peeling palings of a picket fence. She repeated the alliteration. Peeling palings of a picket fence.*

*It was hot on the shoreline. The weather hadn't changed over the course of a day or so, just because the people had left, and the summer holidays were over. But still, the weather felt different to Tilly. The sun seemed lower in the azure sky than it had been last week, and the glare was more intense. Tilly had to squint. She couldn't recall the need to squint so much last week when the children were building their sandcastles. The wind howled louder and blew stronger than a few days ago. It whistled with independence and freedom. Apart from Tilly, the wind had the bay to itself. It blew into every nook and cranny. It blew out every last remnant of human presence. Summer had ended, and the wind was taking over, filling the empty spaces.*

*On days like this, Tilly found silence in the wind's roar. She could succumb to it. She let it seduce her. She let it blot out other sounds in her life. She stood still and felt the sea suck the sand from under her bare feet as each wave receded.*

*Tilly heard a loud crash. She scanned the front line of shacks against the glare of the sun. Nothing seemed out of place. There was no movement. She waited, but nothing revealed itself. She thought she saw a curtain move. The sound of the wind reached a crescendo and the relentless banging of a shutter or gate she couldn't see reassured her.*

*She turned back to the beach and continued walking. Bits of dried seaweed lifted in small twisters and stuck to her arms and legs. She listened to the sea through the deafening howling in her ears. She fantasised someone was watching her. She stood still. She conjured him with a smooth face, hidden in one of the darkened shacks. He held himself intimately while watching her from behind drawn curtains. She had to suck in a lungful of air, as though she had forgotten to breathe. She expelled the breath like an ejaculation. In that moment, Tilly wanted sex—raw penetrating, nihilistic, angry sex. She wanted unprotected sex. No names, no personalities, no engagement, no obligation, no future. She wanted male vigour.*

*Tilly sat in the shack after the summer season had long faded and listened to the birds, and on calmer winter days, she absorbed the lapping of the waves along the shoreline. She looked for the teenage girl in the dunes, but she wasn't there. She would pick some of the white roses Jack had planted along the front fence and arrange them in a vase on the kitchen table, as Jack had done for her, the full robust blooms profiting from Jack's ashes. She would lie on the sofa with her head propped up on a scatter cushion so she could see out the window and across the bay at the jumpy white caps. She remained quiet and still. She felt him caress her. She held one of Jack's sweaters to her face and took in his familiar disarming smell and closed her eyes. She would feel him enter her, and she arched her back in response. She wanted the feeling to last until she died.*

*She felt time was wearing her down. She knew she had no choice but to yield to the inevitability of change. So, one calm winter's day, when the low weak sun threw its light into the shack as best it could, she folded Jack's sweater and put it in a trunk along with the rest of his clothes and his favourite floppy hat. In the early days of her grief, she had contemplated all manner of things, but time passed, and she had survived. Not deliberately, not consciously, but on automatic pilot where there was no obvious button to press to eject herself. There was no point in time after his death when she had enough energy to slip away and join him.*

*Tilly felt like a ghost town herself, like Panorama Bay after the people had left. Like the shacks, she was alone and empty. She had nothing but the whistling wind and screeching seagulls to fill her ears, and the white caps to fill her vacant eyes.*

# Robbie Carton

Robbie sat in his cubicle. It was lunchtime on a Friday. Rain poured down on the city. Robbie, with a sore finger from slamming it in the hydraulic system of his chair, surrounded by grey accountants, with a hum but no buzz informing the white noise, a gorilla in his peripheral vision and absurdity at every turn, recalled he'd had two serious girlfriends in his life so far. This didn't include Sophie because, as things stood, he couldn't call Sophie a girlfriend, much as he would have liked to. Of these two girls, he had lost both of them. It was like he misplaced them, or worse, forgot about them. He felt he had let them down. But whatever, he had lost them. He sat back in his chair and pretended to be thinking about numbers, in that one can affect such a pretence. The thought of losing these two girls disturbed him. It disturbed him because losing things was annoying, and these two girls especially, he realised, both deserved better from him. It disturbed him also because it meant Bentley Herbert, his supervisor and daytime enemy, was right. One of the fluoro lights to his left flickered.

On the matter of Bentley, Bentley knew something about Robbie that was a truth that Robbie didn't know or did know now that Bentley had pointed it out. *Thanks, Bentley,* Robbie mumbled to himself. Robbie was sure Bentley would use it against him in some insidious Bentley Herberty way. Robbie glanced at Bentley sitting at his desk to see what he was up to. He wasn't up to anything. He was polishing something. Perhaps, though, Robbie did know deep in his psyche, wherever that was, that he did lose things but preferred to deny it. The thing about Bentley, Robbie thought, was that Bentley couldn't be underestimated. Robbie found this fact both troublesome and comforting. Robbie thought of himself as having a fractured psyche, in that he knew what a fractured psyche was, but whatever it was, he described it as his 'Robbie abyss'. He could have said this to Sophie one night at the Stalwart, but he didn't. It's possible he might have mumbled, 'Beware the Robbie abyss.' He would have been drunk at the time. He imagined there was no light in the 'Robbie abyss', just the echo of water dripping and his white eyes staring in the black. And somewhere in that black, Bentley lurked, as truth lurks.

Robbie felt tenuous. He felt tenuous all the time. The only thing he didn't feel tenuous about, was the column of figures he had in front of him. He was never tenuous about numbers, except when they didn't add up. These did. He wrote on the top of the page 'Panic', as was his habit and put the work in his outbox ready for Bentley to consume—Bentley was old school and insisted all work had to be in hard copy as well as digital. Robbie was tenuous because his outbox was full, and his in-tray was empty, and he had nothing much to do—nothing much he wanted to do. Life shouldn't be like this, he thought. He blamed Bentley. Robbie wondered what else Bentley knew about Robbie that Robbie didn't know.

'You can have your desires, but you can't want them, because they are you.' Bentley said to Robbie one day. It was apropos of nothing, but germane to everything. Apparently, it was a topic that had been discussed at The Writers Circle Bentley attended. 'To *want* something infers a choice, free will, get it?' Bentley added, 'No such thing, maybe?' Bentley was on a roll and smiling. Robbie got the impression Bentley was trying to be helpful, or he was corralling Robbie to a point where Bentley would hit Robbie with whatever zinger he had in store. Something with a Latin word in it, probably.

Robbie pondered Bentley's statement. He wasn't sure if Bentley meant it to refer to Robbie's life or to himself, or himself and Robbie. Or if Bentley was making a universal Arthur Schopenhauer kind of statement about the world and the paradox of free will. Did it exist or didn't it exist? Robbie found the question of whether or not free will existed one of the most profound, unanswerable concepts of life. If free will existed, would Robbie be listening to Bentley?

Robbie had distilled the free will question to the point where it had no answer. 'If you can't decide what you want, how can you decide what you want?' Robbie looked around his department at all the accountants and wondered if they all wanted to be accountants and where would the 'want' to be an accountant have come from in each of their cases? Or had they decided they wanted to be accountants? Robbie was sure he didn't want to be an accountant, and yet he was one. So this left him with the confirmation, 'you can't decide what you want', your 'want' *was* you. Or not.

Robbie felt like his proverbial garbage bin. He felt used, spent, worn out. He felt reminded of his status in the world—just existing—because he couldn't be thrown out, not because 'existing' was a choice. He was deteriorating, stuck in some kind of relentless Sisyphean cycle, the same thing over and over and never escaping his essential self, because how can you? You are you.

He thought about Sophie Fanshawe and imagined if he were someone else—someone mysterious, someone who might be able to raise an eyebrow, or own a florist shop, someone with prospects who might have a pet and was excellent at small talk—he would ask Sophie out. He would buy her flowers. That would be the first thing he would do. He would love her forever, which would be the second thing. But as Robbie Carton, accountant, single guy with half-empty curry takeaway containers in his fridge and a sore finger, he couldn't reach out to her. It was impossible. He had nothing to offer her as Robbie Carton. He had nothing to offer himself as Robbie Carton. And yet he was single and therefore free to be anyone he wanted. He was free to be anyone Sophie wanted, if she didn't want him as the Robster.

Gloria put a cup of coffee on Robbie's desk without saying a word. She headed back to her cubicle. Robbie took a sip and burnt his tongue. He was sure Gloria wanted a baby. He could offer his sperm if he thought his sperm could be trusted not to produce mini-versions of himself. He respected Gloria too much to do that to her. He raised his cup to her by way of a thank you. She nodded, then got back to work. Robbie didn't. He had a burnt tongue and a sore finger.

Back to the two girls he had lost. Whenever Robbie was walking around the city, he had two habits. The first was his search for these two past girlfriends he'd lost when he was a younger man, and the second was his habit of bumping into, or brushing up against people. He did this brushing/bumping thing both accidentally, in the ordinary course of moving about the city, and deliberately, but more often deliberately. Always deliberately. He would see someone, a woman, always a woman. She might be looking at flowers, at one of those flower stands on the sidewalk, or she might be standing outside an imaginary florist's looking at the window display of natives and grasses and clever flower arrangements, or the green sponge-like bricks that absorbed water. He would hover a bit before lurching forward, as though he had tripped on something, and bump gently into her. It was always gently. His intention was to have contact, not to hurt her or startle her in any way. The last thing he would want to do would be to startle or frighten anyone. He considered it a privilege to have contact with someone, however fleeting and innocent it was on his behalf. Actually, not innocent. Not innocent at all. Pathetic, certainly. He sought human warmth, contact with another person, to put it in its simplest terms. When he 'accidently' bumped into an unsuspecting woman, he was careful only to make contact with her arm or shoulders, never any area of her body that would be considered intimate contact. He accepted that this was wretched behaviour, transparent and puerile in the extreme, not to mention illegal probably, and intrusive, and abusive. Nonetheless, he still did it. He couldn't help himself. He could never confess this to anyone for obvious reasons—they'd think he was nuts or worse, a pervert. He didn't think of himself as a pervert. He felt he was at risk of admitting this ridiculous behaviour to Bentley and, for some inexplicable reason, he thought Bentley might understand, or maybe not judge him too harshly.

About the only thing Robbie could say in defence of his behaviour was that he was good at it. He was practised. He could pull it off without the women suspecting it was contrived. He prided himself he could do it without alarming them or frightening them. He made it look like the accident it wasn't, and it was this aspect he thought Bentley might admire. Setting Bentley's annoying personality aside, Bentley was the kind of person who admired technique. Bentley applauded endeavour. Bentley respected practice. Bentley understood things others wouldn't on levels unavailable to most people. Bentley would see actions for what they were, but more to the point, for what they weren't. Bentley was able to separate actions from the wider social interpretation, or the weight of social correctness. 'You bump into women to experience human contact with a female. Okay, I get that. And you have perfected the technique such that they are neither harmed, or alarmed, or any the wiser. All perfectly comprehensible.' Robbie predicted this conversation with Bentley, when and if it might ever take place. 'It's dangerous, though. You get that, don't you?' Robbie was again predicting Bentley's observation in this imaginary conversation. If such a conversation were to occur, which it wouldn't because Robbie couldn't tell Bentley about his 'bumping into women' habit, Robbie was one hundred per cent sure Bentley would get it, even though Bentley would still use it against him.

Using things against each other was the fundamental plank on which their relationship rested. It was an obligation, a social contract between them.

To the women Robbie bumped into, he would apologise profusely. He made a point of looking them in the eyes. He conflated a fake concerned look. He was sincere with his fake concern. He asked them if they were okay and when they said they were, he apologised again and walked on so as not to linger and cause them alarm or raise suspicion. This would convince them it was an innocent accident. Apologising was part of the ritual, a vital part. It was conversation. It was interaction. It was contact. He hoped they would be wearing perfume, and he could take it in for that instant he was near them. When he did this, bumping into women, he wondered about life and life's orbits. He wondered about the two girls he'd lost, who both were once his girlfriends and, in both cases, gave themselves to him. He wondered if either one of them might have been in the vicinity and might have recognised him, when he did the bumping thing.

He luxuriated in the electrical life force flowing through the strong feminine bodies of the women he bumped into. He felt the origins of their history, their dreams, their hopes, and disappointments. And he exulted in their success—just being a competent, coping member of the human species was in and of itself a success to celebrate, Robbie thought, and conceded it wasn't something he had managed himself. He rejoiced in their womanhood. He lamented their plight—always subject to male intervention, always having to calculate and strategise about where they were, what time it was, who was around, what anything meant. Men didn't have to do this. He hated the fact he was one of those males, intervening in their lives, and he felt let down by his behaviour. Why could he not rise above himself? He could not want what he wanted. He could not determine his wants, and so this made him part of the problem when he should have been part of the solution. Women deserved more from him. But this notwithstanding, he wondered what they might have had for breakfast that morning, when was the last time they cried alone or how they managed their finances and how they avoided loneliness.

He wondered if the bump caused an effect, an adrenaline surge that put them in 'fight or flight' standby mode. He wondered if he might have in some tiny way affected their destiny, caused the urine in their bladders to slosh about before settling. If he had affected them in some way, he hoped it was for the good. He wished them nothing but happiness and safety. How this would be achieved by deliberately bumping into them was unclear to Robbie. His good intentions were something to hope for while he stared into Friedrich Nietzsche's so-called black abyss and waited for it to stare back at him.

He favoured women whose personalities were evident in their demeanour. It might be the way they were dressed, or how they had their hair done, or their lipstick—maybe something as fleeting as a beauty mark on their cheek. Whatever it was, bumping was the highlight of his day. He knew this was wrong, so wrong on so many levels. He knew it would be viewed as misconceived, but it was his secret, so long as he didn't blurt it out to anyone.

He tried to stop, but he couldn't. Every time he did this, bumped into an unsuspecting woman on the street, he fell in love with her, just for a minute, just fleetingly. But he loved her, for sure. In much the same way as he loved the two girls he had lost. He knew if push came to shove, he would sacrifice himself for any woman who might need help. He acknowledged this as bordering on being patronising, but it was how he felt. He wondered if any of them could detect his love on some spiritual level. Maybe not consciously, but unconsciously. Perhaps they detected his love as a slight tiny electrical shock. If they did, perhaps they felt good, safe, appreciated—and loved him back just a little themselves. He trusted in human interaction, the frisson between the sexes, or more boldly, between human lives.

One time though, some time ago, or not that long ago, Robbie saw a blonde-haired girl buying flowers. It was a Friday. She had a beauty mark on her cheek. It was such a window into her personality. He loved her immediately. It was a bright, beautiful day in the city, one of the city's grand deceiving days. Robbie was about to feign a trip, but his foot caught the curb, and he did actually trip. The bump turned into an uncontrolled jolt. He fell into the girl with way too much force, and she collapsed under him. The flowers she was buying flew across the footpath. He grabbed her as best he could to try and stop her hitting the pavement and hurting herself. He worried he'd grabbed her too hard. He was careful to grab her around the waist and keep his hands off her body as best he could. It all happened quickly, in slow motion. He choreographed it in his mind as it was happening. He somehow managed to swing under her so she would land on him and not the concrete gutter. He panicked, as this was not intended. Sure, he was going to do his trip and bumping routine, but it was to be controlled and managed and gentle, always gentle. This actual trip was out of control and chaos ensued.

She was gorgeous and so gracious when he apologised while helping her to her feet. He came close to the beauty mark on her cheek and felt the heat coming off her body. He dreamt about her heat and beauty mark for many nights. She was unhurt, but he sprained his ankle on the kerb while trying to swing his body underneath her. A bruise, which appeared the next day on his hip, was so large he thought it might be visible from outer space, after the Great Wall of China and the Great Barrier Reef and now, the Great Bruise. The girl ended up helping him to a cab. She seemed genuinely sorry for him. He forgot to pay for her flowers. This annoyed him so much he resolved to stop this habit of bumping into women. He thought he would try and find her again and find out where she worked and deliver some flowers to her, to make amends. He would try to do this anonymously. He had already interfered in her life enough. He masturbated thinking about her, and he felt guilty about this too. He dreamt of her beauty mark while parts of his body, including his ankle, throbbed into the night.

It took some time to find her—several mornings in the end. Robbie positioned himself near the florist, thinking it might be a habit of hers to buy flowers there. He saw her one morning. She was buying flowers from the same florist—a young woman with a small tattoo of a white bird on the back of her knee, as Robbie observed while she was preparing the flowers. After the blonde girl left, Robbie approached the florist and asked if she happened to know the blonde girl's name. The one with the beauty mark, Robbie described. The florist looked at him for some time then smiled and said, 'Why do you want to know?' The florist's smile broadened but hovered on the side of distortion. It made Robbie feel uncomfortable asking a stranger this question. She had one yellow tooth that Robbie couldn't stop staring at. Robbie didn't want to admit to the whole 'bumping' thing for fear the florist might think him weird and wouldn't tell him if she knew the woman with the beauty mark's name. 'Not the beauty mark's name, the woman's name in possession of the beauty mark,' he mumbled. He hesitated, but before he could say anything further, the florist looked at his bandaged ankle.

'It's okay. I get it. It's the business I'm in. Do you want to take her some flowers?' Robbie nodded. The florist said, 'Pick red roses. They're the best for this sort of thing. She works in the building above us on the eighteenth floor. I think her name is Pamela.' Robbie managed a meek smile while the florist wrapped a bunch of long-stemmed roses, wrote out a card that said, 'For Pamela' and handed the roses with the card to Robbie. 'Is that okay? "For

126

Pamela"? You don't want to, you know, frighten her by being too forward. Do you want to include your name?' The florist looked conspiratorially at Robbie. Robbie shook his head no. He'd run out of words for this conversation. Robbie looked at her and said nothing. He took the roses. Pamela, if that was her name, wouldn't know who Robbie was, so there was no point in putting it on the card. Besides, no name on the card added to the mystery and was less intrusive for her, he thought.

'You know it seems to be happening a lot lately, people bumping into people. Is it a thing?' The florist smiled. Robbie felt his face flush and hoped she hadn't noticed. He tried to smile in concert, but that didn't work.

Robbie paid for the flowers but as he was now running late for work, decided to drop the roses off at lunchtime. He would leave them at the door anonymously so as not to alarm this innocent girl. He didn't want her to think he was stalking her, or that the whole, so-called bumping into her routine wasn't some puerile way to get close to her, even if it was, or would have been if things had gone to plan. She wouldn't know it was him who left the flowers, but at least, in some karmic, cosmos way, 'what goes around comes around way', the wrong would be righted, he thought. He thought she might get a kick out of the possibility of a secret admirer, rather than the disappointment of finding out it was the idiot who knocked her over in the street. He limped off in the direction of his office.

Robbie couldn't have known there were two women who worked in the same office who looked similar, especially on Fridays, when Bronnie, the girl he had bumped into, had taken to applying a beauty mark to her cheek on Fridays, identical to her workmate Pamela's. Robbie wanted to kiss Bronnie from the second his arms grabbed her waist, but he realised he couldn't do that. Social protocols prohibited kissing strangers in the street. One shouldn't be permitted to capitalise on accidental deliberate accidents. Robbie had an odd feeling, though. There was something familiar about the blonde he had crashed into. He often had that feeling about strangers. He imagined he knew them in some way or had known them, or there was something familiar about them. He once told Bentley this, but Bentley responded that Robbie might be reacting to humanity. That was deep for an accountant supervisor, Robbie thought, especially considering the number of bike parts Bentley had on his desk at any given time.

The whole incident of picking out a woman, in this case Bronnie, pretending to trip but then tripping for real, piling into her, seeing her flowers go in all directions, helping her to her feet and apologising, admiring her beauty mark, taking in her perfume and the heat of her body, her helping him to a cab as he hobbled next to her and him masturbating later while recalling the softness of her skin, made him ask why he couldn't remember how it was that he wasn't still with either of the two girls he had dated long ago. How had he lost them?

Robbie needed a pair of crutches for the next few days. His ankle had swollen up to the size of his thigh. Bentley saw the crutches and eyed Robbie but didn't say anything. He looked as though he suspected the story behind the sprained ankle was unlikely, or beyond belief, or the result of some event only an idiot like Robbie could cause. Bentley would be right on all counts. If Robbie didn't know better, he thought he detected a modicum of sympathy bordering on respect from Bentley, but that couldn't be right. It was as though Bentley thought, 'Whatever idiotic thing he did, at least he threw his whole self into it.' And that was true enough.

Robbie sent an email to Bentley, which asked the question, *What is the greatest invention of mankind?* Gloria responded with an email that said nothing more than *womankind?* Robbie looked over at Gloria. Robbie saw Gloria watching him. She winked at him and smiled. Robbie nodded to her.

Bentley, after a while, to placate Robbie, responded by return email with, *The wheel?*

Robbie smiled when he saw Bentley's response. He emailed back to Bentley, *Good guess but wrong. The second wheel.* He copied his response to Gloria.

Bentley replied with, *wouldn't you need to invent an axle?*

Robbie smiled again, relishing the exchange. *An axle? Isn't that just a stick? Do you want to go down in history as having invented the stick? Don't they just lie around on the ground?*

Robbie sent this off to Bentley. He watched the screen, waiting for Bentley's response. But none came—Bentley would have known better than to get into such an exchange with Robbie.

Robbie minimised his Mail screen, pushed his laptop forward on his desk, and slumped back in his chair with his hands together at the back of his head.

He looked over at Bentley concentrating on a screen full of figures, while eating an apple. Next to Bentley, Gloria was deep in conversation with Flanagan, about work, no doubt. Flanagan was wearing a Hawaiian shirt because it was 'End of month, Hawaiian shirt Friday' but no one else in the department was, as Robbie noted after a quick scan. Robbie conjectured, that either, as accountants, they don't have Hawaiian shirts, or they couldn't be bothered, or forgot, or the only Hawaiian shirt they have is still to be laundered after last month's 'End of month, Hawaiian shirt Friday'. Robbie didn't have any Hawaiian shirts, but had a particularly gaudy Hawaiian tie, which he wore loosely tied around his collar. Bentley was sporting an audacious colourful Hawaiian elastic head band. Gloria had a celebratory Hawaiian ribbon in her hair.

Robbie strained to hear Gloria and Flanagan's conversation but couldn't make out any words as they merged into the usual background noise of the department—the words were absorbed into the background noise, not Gloria and Flanagan. All Robbie could hear was the buzz and hum of people talking (mostly to themselves), or mumble-singing, dropping things, swearing, sharpening pencils, all against the punctuating snapping of Tupperware containers open, or the punctuating snapping of Tupperware containers shut, set to the orchestral clicking of many keyboards—music to an accountant's ears, Robbie considered.

The gorilla passed Robbie's cubicle and dropped a file into Robbie's empty inbox, gave Robbie a gorilla thumbs up, and continued through the department—not eating a banana, Robbie observed.

Robbie sat forward, pulled his laptop closer and lifted the new file from his otherwise empty inbox and set it down next to his computer and opened it. He rubbed his brow and got to work. His ankle throbbed, as did his head.

# Pamela Adams and her friend Bronnie

Pamela was twenty-eight, as was Bronnie. Pamela hoped one day to meet someone, as did Bronnie. Pamela wanted someone with whom she could enjoy life, someone with a mysterious name, like Austin Quinn, the literary figure who she was introduced to at The Writers Circle she attended every Wednesday night starting at seven pm sharp. By any measure, Pamela was a thinking person, as was Bronnie. Both women had firm muscles, soft skin and a mop of styled blonde hair. In Bronnie's case, her blonde hair was not her natural colour.

It was anachronistic to call Pamela and Bronnie pretty, but they were both attractive women, each in their own way. Pamela had two significant features—her natural blonde hair that framed her persuasive eyes, and a Marilyn Monroe beauty mark which guarded her left cheek. Both Pamela and Bronnie agreed that Bronnie's new blonde hair suited her better than her natural dark colour and contrasted dramatically with her black, architectural eyebrows. Bronnie pencilled in a beauty mark on her right cheek, but only on Fridays, which they called 'beauty mark Fridays'. On Fridays they could barely be told apart. Both women were good at their job and enjoyed each other's company. They occasionally spent time together after-hours, at a bar or a nightclub.

Their office sat high up in the city's canopy, as Bronnie liked to call it, where the air was rarefied, and the views bulbous, and the silence so profound you felt deaf. Their office window overlooked the harbour, and they could see the numerous bridges and glimpses of the white hero building and the famous statue in the harbour through the gaps between the city's skyscrapers.

Pamela's flat was three train stops from the office. Bronnie lived in the other direction, just over one of the muscular bridges. Neither had been to the other's flat. One day they timed themselves commuting to work, from front door to the building's entrance. They both arrived at the same time. This was how they expected it to be.

Pamela, and Bronnie for that matter, had no clue whatsoever as to how people met each other in the city. How men and women met and formed meaningful, lasting romantic relationships was a complete mystery. At times it seemed to Pamela that they lived like characters in a novel. Bronnie agreed but favoured 'windswept' characters. Bronnie liked the Bronte sisters/Jane Austen feel and advocated a deep theatrical sigh now and then. Bronnie enjoyed a dramatic flourish. Pamela enjoyed a 'dramatic flourish' as well, but in the absence of such an extravagance, they both claimed they would like a steady guy with an ordered life. They favoured good-looking guys with perfect haircuts and straight teeth, but none of these things were important. What was important was that the guy was true and had depth, and in Pamela's case, maybe a boat.

Pamela romanticised she would meet a man who lived on a boat moored in the city's reflective harbour. They would fall in love, and she would spend her days being gently rocked in his boat. The 'Austin Quinn' character invented by the American writer Dunleavy de Boston in his book *One Hot Summer's Night* was an anti-detective trapped in a postmodern tale. She had read this on the back of de Boston's novel. She wasn't sure she understood it, but she thought it sounded romantic. She would never have heard the name had it not been for The Writers Circle. Pamela held out hopes for her postmodern Austin Quinn, but Pamela was a pragmatist and knew her hopes were fantasy. However, she hoped she might meet someone someday—someone who might suggest a picnic. She considered a picnic a romantic trope. Sometime ago, Pamela saw a brochure highlighting a place called Hapgood Pond in Southern Vermont. It sounded romantic, far away, and looked ideal for a picnic. The brochure had been stuck to a beach ball. She peeled the brochure off the ball and put it in her purse and then later clipped it on her bathroom mirror. Pamela considered herself a devotee of romantic notions. Perhaps 'devotee' was too strong. She was a romantic enthusiast. Romanticism notwithstanding, Pamela would settle for someone who might not have such a mysterious name, someone with whom she could share her life and would love her forever—the picnic was optional.

The city in which Pamela and Bronnie lived and worked offered no obvious way to find a mate. 'White whales were hard to find.' Pamela remarked one day, soon after reading *Moby Dick*. Pamela and Bronnie discussed this often, the business of finding a mate. Pamela had a theory, or perhaps more a suspicion. She thought, or suspected, it might be the city itself. She speculated there were undercurrents in the city that worked against its inhabitants in some curious and dark way. 'Dark' was a word Bronnie appreciated. She liked 'sinister' too, but she thought it might be overused. According to Pamela's theory, the city sabotaged its citizens to keep them on edge. It got more out of its population if they were kept hopeful. The city, Pamela and Bronnie both agreed, was dangerous and anything but benign. As Bronnie observed, it was *dark* for a start and not only at night, during the bright days also. It watched you. This made them both shudder. Bronnie refused to use the word 'sinister', but it was implied.

Pamela and Bronnie had had boyfriends in the past, but not many, and not often, and nothing much came of any of them. They were each a disappointment one way or another. Some talked too much, some didn't talk enough, or had bad breath, or kept a caged bird.

'It's because men don't know how to deal with love,' Bronnie extrapolated.

'That sounds like nonsense costume drama theory to me.'

'Really?' Bronnie responded. 'Didn't Mr Darcy long for Miss Elizabeth? And wasn't it a fact that Darcy had no way of telling Miss Elizabeth about his feelings? Men are such blocks of concrete. But you gotta feel sorry for 'em.'

'Yes you do,' Pamela echoed the sentiment. They returned to their work.

Pamela lived alone in a white flat. Pamela's life, the one she lived, not the one she romanticised, never seemed to generate anyone, with or without a boat. She took the train to work and home again. She worked in an office, which was kept locked during the day, with her friend and colleague, Bronnie.

Pamela could not make her life feel real, and she bore a sense of doom. In her small flat, she kept her sheer curtains open. She kept no pets, and only enough cutlery for one person. Her kitchen drawers were full of plastic knives and forks, and small plastic fish-shaped soy sauce containers. At the end of the day, in her apartment, Pamela shed her work clothes and preferred to be semi-naked, wearing expensive black underwear. She felt free. She kept the heating off and allowed her nipples to swell. She would sit quietly on the end of her sofa in a semi-hypnotic state in the dark, contemplating the purpose of her life while she listened to the rain through the night. Pamela refused to have a television. She believed a television reflected you if it was off and represented you if it was on. She was averse to both. She didn't want to be confronted with that sharpness when she was alone in her apartment. When she wasn't contemplating the meaning of life and her role in it, she worked on a jigsaw puzzle, which she never seemed to finish. Sitting in the dark, she allowed the strobe effects of the city's advertising signs to blink at her body.

She never discussed her life in her apartment with anyone. She didn't discuss it with Bronnie, especially her swollen nipples. She was sure, though, that Bronnie would not have been shocked and probably knew a thing or two about nipples, swollen or otherwise. Bronnie was an extrovert and sometimes spoke loudly when she was making a point. Pamela was quieter by nature, which worked to make both women compatible. Pamela was superstitious and thought having enough cutlery for only two people might be bad luck, so she didn't. In her world, plastic cutlery didn't count.

Pamela was unable to visualise Bronnie's flat or Bronnie in her flat. Pamela suspected it was a dark chamber with some turquoise accents. Pamela assumed Bronnie's flat was much like her own, a place where you parked yourself overnight, where the question of whether the city continued to exist outside, remained uncertain. Pamela didn't know if Bronnie did, or didn't, have a television in her flat. It was never discussed. Nor was Bronnie's cutlery policy.

Pamela had been determined not to let life disappoint her, or overwhelm her, so for a time she took to joining things. At first, she joined a book club. The membership comprised of six other women and two gay guys. The club, unsurprisingly, required her to read books. She embraced this new obsession. She read *Moby Dick,* and *Killing Commendatore* by Haruki Murakami, and *The Information* by Martin Amis, and *The Pale King* by David Foster Wallace, until she found out Wallace killed himself. She thought this detracted from his authenticity as an observer of life, as an objective commentator. She couldn't say why she thought that, maybe she was just disappointed in him, or disappointed to have lost him. It was not just reading literature that was new to her, she also discovered deconstruction. She was good at finding the thematic undercurrents of the books she read. She'd never known this about herself. She discussed her interpretations with the group. She argued against the group selecting Foster Wallace. She wanted more Murakami.

She joined a local gym. She ran on the treadmills and rode the stationary bikes until the sweat stung her eyes, and her wet hair flopped over her face. Occasionally, a guy doing weights might look up and smile in her direction, but she couldn't be sure the smile wasn't a grimace from jerking his dumbbells. Then she quit the book club and joined The Writers Circle, not because she harboured any compelling desire to write or be a writer, but because she had read somewhere that writing can be therapeutic and she felt, at times, she might benefit from some soul searching. She hadn't expected to meet anyone, but one Wednesday night at the weekly meeting, soon after seven pm sharp, and after she had been a member of the group for around six months, a man called Austin Quinn joined the group. Everyone laughed when he introduced himself. The group had been given a writing exercise, to write a story in answer to the philosophical question 'What will happen to you?' and incorporate Dunleavy de Boston's character Austin Quinn, the same name as the man who had just joined the group. This astonished Pamela, but she didn't tell anyone that Austin Quinn, the name Austin Quinn, was the name of her fantasy man. This Austin Quinn in her opinion was not far away in looks from the fantasy Austin Quinn she had imagined after she had read de Boston's book some time ago. Life was confounding at times, and never strayed far from coincidence or the extraordinary. She felt a little in love with this new Austin Quinn. She felt she had a lot of history with him. This notwithstanding, she was still alone.

One night, after a meeting, she found herself in Austin's apartment. She drank tequila shots with him. She shouldn't have. Nothing happened. He didn't touch her. He didn't kiss her. She became woozy and lost her balance. He made up a bed on the sofa for her, took off her shoes and placed a throw rug over her with such gentleness it forced tears from her eyes. In the morning, he was gone, the coffee was on, and two slices of bread sat in the toaster ready to be pushed down. There was an array of jams, honey, and a jar of Vegemite in a huddle next to a white plate with a knife laying across the plate on an angle, and a paper napkin neatly folded under the knife. She poured some coffee and looked around the empty apartment. She felt like her hangover was a living entity in its own right—hell-bent on pushing her eyeballs out of their sockets. She noticed the unopened mail on the floor and wondered about this man whose apartment she was now in, alone. Why was his mail unopened? She finished her coffee and rinsed the cup and left it upside down to dry in the sink. She folded the throw rug, placed it on the arm of the sofa and plumped up the cushions.

There was a white bird in a cage at the end of the sofa. It watched her as she walked around the apartment. She felt it was making sure she didn't steal anything or do anything she shouldn't. She washed her face in the sink and used the paper towel under the knife to dry off. She thought the bird knew something. She said, 'Bye-bye, little one.' As she was leaving the apartment, the bird said, '$H_2O$, $H_2O$.' She stopped dead. She looked back at the bird still staring at her. She saw the bottom of its cage. There was a small empty plastic cup. The bird shuffled along its bar away from the door to the cage, as though allowing her access. She stared at the cup, then at the bird and back again. The bird did not break its stare. She put her bag down on the sofa and carefully opened the cage door, put her hand inside the cage and picked up the cup. The bird remained still. It watched her hand retrieve the cup. She closed the door of the cage and went to the sink and filled the cup with water. She placed it back at the bottom of the cage, removed her hand and closed the door again. The bird kept staring at her for a moment. It then made a murmuring sound and jumped down off its perch next to the cup and took a drink. After it had drunk its fill, it jumped back up on the perch and re-established eye contact with Pamela. Pamela picked up her bag and left.

She was glad nothing had happened between her and Austin. She thought Austin was disturbed and had some significant issues with life. Several weeks passed before she summoned the courage to return to The Writers Circle, but Austin wasn't there. He had disappeared from the Circle. Austin's disappearance turned up in everyone's story about their particular version of Austin Quinn. She never saw him again, but she felt close to him. She mourned him in a strange way. She wondered why the mail on the floor was not addressed to him.

Some weeks later, she noticed another member of the Circle. He hadn't said much, but he'd been in the Circle for some time. It was as though his presence had crept up on her. He called himself Tommy, and she came to realise he was Sophie Fanshawe's brother. Sophie, a published writer, had been a member of the Circle for as long as Pamela. Pamela loved to listen to Sophie read her work. It soothed her and made her think of escape in the sun and sea breezes on a deserted beach somewhere with a glaring sun low in the sky and seagulls squawking overhead. Sometimes she saw Tommy on this deserted beach, but he didn't see her. When she squinted her eyes in the glare, he wasn't there.

\*\*\*

'Do you want to go for a "Friday night drink' after work?' Bronnie asked Pamela while searching through one of her desk drawers for something. Bronnie and Pamela ritually referred to a drink after work as a *Friday night drink*, regardless of what night it was. 'I've got so much stuff in here. Do I use any of it?' she asked rhetorically.

Pamela watched Bronnie rummage through her drawer and wondered if the useless stuff in Bronnie's drawer was a metaphor for her and Bronnie's life in the city. They were superfluous stuff in the drawer of the city, and the city never shied away from reminding them of this fact.

Bronnie pulled out a hairbrush and small mirror and started brushing her hair. Her usual impeccable hair was ruffled.

'Did I tell you that last week I was bumped into by one of the city's citizens and almost fell? He grabbed my waist and saved me hitting the pavement, and order was restored, except a few strands of my hair had lost their place.'

'My my,' Pamela said without looking up.

'And I think he sprained his ankle.'

'No lasting harm was done?' Pamela asked.

'Not to me. But nothing will ever be the same again.' Bronnie repeated this after any incident, no matter how innocuous it might be. While regaling Pamela about this bumping incident, she recalled the guy's hair.

'His hair was chaotic. I couldn't be sure if it was the look he was going for or if he had forgotten to comb it before he left home. He had black-black eyes and he looked right through me, but he countered that with a nuclear smile.' This was how Bronnie described the incident and the guy. Pamela smiled at Bronnie, who was prone to a little amplification. To be fair, Bronnie did make him sound appealing.

'Where?' Pamela said, snapping out of her mesmeric state. 'For a drink?' she qualified.

'Oh, yeah, there's this new place called the Purple Parrot, or Orange, I can't remember what colour the parrot is,' Bronnie said, as she replaced her brush and mirror and closed her drawer.

'White?'

'What?'

'The parrot, it's white, isn't it?'

'What parrot? What are you talkin' about?'

Pamela mused. 'Never mind, I'm thinking of something else.'

'So, to drink or not to drink?'

'Out of a plastic cup?' Pamela said.

'Again, you've lost me,' Bronnie said.

'Don't worry,' Pamela answered.

'So, to drink or not to drink,' Bronnie repeated.

'What's the point?'

'That is the question,' Bronnie mumbled. She looked up at Pamela. 'We should take aim at our sea of troubles and accept there's no point. There never was, and there never will be. But if we go, nothing will ever be the same again, slings and arrows-wise.'

'Same as if we don't go,' Pamela said.

'True, 'tis nobler in the mind to suffer.' Bronnie continued to roll out her Shakespeare in whatever order suited her.

Bronnie always knew the latest clubs and bars and tried to get Pamela to come to them. Their building was two blocks from the notorious pick-up joint, the Stalwart pub, but they never went there. Bronnie contended that so-called 'pick-up joints' never resulted in anyone picking anyone up.

Pamela occasionally went with Bronnie for a drink to some new underground place, to break up the routine of her life. They would drink exotic translucent cocktails and do the puzzles in the daily paper. Pamela was good at the cryptic crosswords. She liked the obtuseness of how you might arrive at the word required. Hah, not the word 'required' but the required word.

The men they met required sex, and a souvenir. Pamela wanted sex, and she feared she was missing out, but she couldn't have sex with just anyone. That seemed too clinical and tedious and frightening. She wanted sex with someone who inspired her. She wanted to feel safe and dangerous at the same time. She wanted to be taken, but she wanted to be in control. She wanted to be examined by black-black eyes and to be disarmed by a nuclear smile. Perhaps someone with chaotic hair. This was hard to explain to men who only wanted to copulate, however hard they may try to attend to her pleasure before their own.

'The point is, this could be the night you meet Mister Right.' Bronnie smiled her enthusiastic, 'everything-will-be-fine' smile at Pamela. Bronnie had exhausted her Ophelia speech from *Hamlet*.

'You think?' But Pamela wasn't in the mood for a drink. She was preoccupied with the event that had occurred earlier that day.

There had been a knock at the locked office door. Bronnie and Pamela had exchanged looks. No one ever knocked at the door. They never got visitors. When Bronnie opened the door, the hallway was empty. The only movement was the flickering white fluoro. Bronnie looked down and saw a big bunch of red roses. She dragged them in before closing and relocking the door.

They both stared at the roses in silence as though, if they waited long enough, the roses would disappear, and they wouldn't have to think about them anymore. This was a city where things disappeared, and no one thought it odd. But the roses didn't disappear. Bronnie untangled a card from one of the stems and read it.

'"For Pamela".'

They both gasped. Neither of them gasped, it was only a bunch of roses.

'If there was ever an occasion that might be satisfied by a dramatic gasp, this is surely it,' Bronnie quipped.

Pamela agreed. 'A dramatic sigh would not be sufficient in these circumstances.'

Bronnie handed the card to Pamela. 'Read it for yourself.'

'Very curious?' Pamela whispered.

'It says "For Pamela". I kid you not.'

Pamela took the card and read the words. It didn't say from whom. Pamela turned the card over, nothing was written on the back.

'You have an admirer,' Bronnie said with discernible gusto, but no trace of a gasp or sigh.

'I don't think so,' Pamela said, hoping she did.

'A big bunch of red roses, with a card indicating they're for you, is irrefutable evidence of an admirer.'

'I suppose so.' Pamela felt light-headed. She had no idea who could have sent her roses or why. But whoever it was knew her name and where she worked, and this made her feel queer—a word sometimes found between words in cryptic crosswords signalling the hidden word starts with q.

Pamela didn't go for a drink that night with Bronnie after work. She didn't feel like it. She was preoccupied with the mystery of the roses. The thought of it made her feel heavy, immovable. She hauled herself home. She didn't want to deviate from her routine, in case her admirer was someone who she passed, or saw every day, and might reveal himself.

Pamela's thoughts whizzed and bucked. At one moment she felt positive about the whole thing—she thought, you must be inspired by someone who has a plan—but then she fell into a solemn state of melancholy, feeling more alone and isolated than usual. This was an example of what the city did to you. It set you up with hope and fear. It teased you, toyed with you and pestered you. Then it abandoned you. What if it was all a big mistake and the flowers were not meant for her but another Pamela? It would be a colossal coincidence, but nonetheless still possible. She conjectured to herself. Pamela was losing her faith in coincidence. Coincidence was all you had to fall back on in the city. The city used coincidence to keep you off kilter and unsure but encouraged you to be hopeful. It got you to hope for outrageous coincidences. It blinded you to the ridiculous odds of coincidences. It enticed you to want. She wished she had a television so she could sit in the dark and be washed by the flickering light of infomercials. She knew that if she had a television, she would never turn it on. Pamela had wants, she wished she didn't, but she did. This had been a lengthy discussion at The Writers Circle recently. In her own case, some of her wants, she didn't want.

\*\*\*

For days, maybe a month, Pamela hoped for someone to step forward and claim to be her admirer. But nothing happened. She thought, as someone had sent her flowers, it was therefore incumbent upon her to make herself approachable and findable. She wanted to be approached. She wanted to be found. No one approached her. No one found her. No one smiled at her. No one seemed to be her mysterious admirer. She struggled not to resent everyone in her path for not being her admirer. If he *did* admire her—how could she be sure of that?

Bronnie was also obsessed with the mystery and quizzed Pamela first thing every morning. 'Anything?' she would ask. Pamela would shrug, and they would both fall into silence for most of the morning. Disappointment grew. The admirer became the elephant in the room with dimensions, surface, ugliness. At lunchtime, they took it in turns to go to lunch, so the office wasn't left unmanned, or unwomanned, as Bronnie preferred. Then after Pamela returned from lunch. 'Well?' Bronnie would ask. As the days ticked over, her question became more wistful than urgent. Eventually, Bronnie's questions became tacit. The disappointment had grown to such a degree between them that, had it taken a solid form, they soon wouldn't be able to see each other across the office.

After two months had passed, Pamela recalled how liberating the arrival of the roses had been—the exciting prospect that someone might admire her enough to send flowers. Someone who might have had a plan to sweep her off her feet, where she would fall in love with this beautiful man and luxuriate in his generous kisses. But then she started thinking, if he were so beautiful, wouldn't she have noticed him in her daily routines? Maybe he wasn't so beautiful. But that wouldn't be critical to Pamela. His kisses didn't have to be generous—she'd work on that. She wouldn't ask much of him, if only he would reveal himself. She was growing tired with the disappointment. His shyness was charming in the beginning but now, two months on, was irritating and frustrating, and unnecessary. Why did he bother to send flowers, to make such a wonderful gesture if he wasn't going to take the next step? And what was the next step? All he had to do was say hello, introduce himself and see where things went from there. It wasn't so hard.

Pamela wanted sex. She craved it. But no sex was coming her way anytime soon. In the darkness of her apartment late at night, she saw to her own needs, but the act was empty. She didn't want to feel her own hand between her legs.

Bronnie had stopped asking the question altogether, both audibly and tacitly. The question had become redundant and annoying for Pamela and exhausting for Bronnie. The 'disappointment' in the room dissipated and their friendship regained its territory.

Pamela, feeling trapped, couldn't vary her routines in case she missed her admirer. She was stuck, doomed to do the same thing each day—'a Sisyphean dilemma' Bronnie called it. Bronnie was sometimes highly literate, and literary allusions popped out of her like involuntary spasms or bubbles, or 'literary farts', the description preferred by Bronnie.

Every day, Pamela left work dead on time, walked to the train along Park Avenue, on the left-hand side of the avenue, as she had always done. She caught the same train at the station on the corner of Park and 26th and got off at the same stop. She sat in the same seat, in the same carriage. People left her seat vacant as though they were trying to help. She walked home along her usual route. She stopped at the Chinese fruit and veg bodega along the way to pick up whatever she needed for dinner, and some rioja. She refused Bronnie's invitations to go out for a 'Friday night drink' or do anything on the weekends. She grew to resent her secret admirer. He was ruining her life by trapping her in it. It seemed so unfair.

But if she were honest, her behaviour was not any different from her life before the roses, and this realisation annoyed her because, in a way, this unknown 'admirer' had highlighted to her how mundane her life was, and how a mere bunch of roses could have such a disproportionate effect on her. But still, and all the same, why hadn't he made himself known? Why hadn't he at least sent a note if he knew her work address? Why didn't he step out in front of her, bump into her if necessary, announce he had been admiring her for so long, and tell her he loved her, and wanted her to be his bride? She had masturbated thinking about him. He owed her something.

'He could be dead,' Bronnie said one day, when the sun was lost behind grey clouds and rain pelted the city's buildings and streets in a way that suggested the city had been wicked and the rain was spanking it.

'What do you mean?' Pamela asked, alarmed.

'Think about it. This guy sends you flowers because he wants to impress you and get to know you. He harbours some romantic, or at the least, sexual fantasies about you. I mean, he wouldn't send an expensive bunch of red roses for nothing. I think we can assume that much.'

'I hadn't thought about his sexual motivation,' Pamela said somewhat distracted.

'I'm thinkin' out loud, you know. So why roses? Roses are a romantic gesture. So he was thinking romance, or sex, or both.'

'Maybe, I guess,' Pamela said, still thinking about sex.

'So there has to be some reason you never heard from him again.'

'He might have changed his mind,' Pamela mused. 'Or they weren't for me. A case of mistaken identity. It happens a lot in the city, people get mixed up, they get confused, it's the city, "Forget it, Jake. It's Chinatown.".' Pamela knew Bronnie would love the film *noir* allusion.

'Maybe. But I don't think so, it doesn't seem likely.'

'Thinking he might be dead also doesn't seem likely.'

'No, but it's possible. Mark Twain said, "The difference between reality and fiction is that fiction needs to be credible". At least I think it was Mark Twain...someone said it.' Bronnie went back to work, having said all she intended on the subject for now. The rain continued slapping the windows. Pamela looked at the drenched windows and thought the rain might be trying to get their attention and wanted help. Pamela thought about Bronnie's comments, but the whole thing, including Bronnie's attempt at analysing it, made her head hurt.

Pamela's thoughts ventured toward sex again. She thought of being caressed by a stranger whose face she couldn't see. She felt safe and compliant. She looked down at the paperwork on her desk and noticed the words and numbers were blurred, much like her life. She sighed. Bronnie sighed.

'Women who work together, sigh together,' Bronnie said without looking up.

Over the next few weeks, Pamela grieved for a man she'd never met and wasn't likely to meet, and she didn't know if he was dead or not. She spent the weekends tidying her flat. She painted her lampshade white again. One Saturday morning she spent polishing the bottoms of her shoes. She found one shoe still with a price tag on it. She cleaned her handbags inside and out and found a number of items she never knew she had. She threw out everything in her freezer, defrosted the fridge and wiped it inside with lemon juice, then took her clothes off and pleasured herself with a small vibrator she'd found in one of her handbags, after she replaced the dead battery with one she found in another handbag. She had always gotten a bit hot and bothered over the word 'pleasured'. It was one of Bronnie's favourite words, and she used it often as a battle cry for women. 'Pleasured.' Bronnie would often whisper the word under her breath, and on other occasions she would shout it out as if to warn all who needed warning. Sometimes Bronnie would hang up the phone after a long, difficult discussion with a client and say, 'Pleasured.' Then both of them would return to their work with an increased level of concentration.

\*\*\*

'I know, why don't we go crazy and go to the Stalwart for a drink?' Bronnie asked while scratching the side of one of her arms. 'It's Friday night and raining. The place will be heaving.'

Pamela looked at Bronnie considering the idea but then made a face and nodded no.

'Probably right,' Bronnie said.

\*\*\*

A few days before, Pamela was in the office at lunchtime covering for Bronnie's extended hairdressing appointment. Bronnie was going out to dinner that evening with her new boyfriend to celebrate their three-month anniversary, and her emerging black roots needed attention. Bronnie had found her new boyfriend when she was standing in front of the florist shop at the bottom of their building. It was lunchtime, and a guy bumped into her. This was the second time this had happened to her, but this bump was gentle, and she wasn't sent hurtling to the ground. And this time it was a different guy. He seemed surprised at the situation. Bronnie told Pamela about her suspicion that there was a bunch of men in the city who were bumping into women. She felt special she had been chosen as a bump target, twice. He apologised and asked her name. She told him her name.

According to Bronnie, this was how the story went, but it was worth remembering, Bronnie was prone to embellishment. Bronnie claimed that if you don't embellish the truth, you will lose your audience and thus your message will go unheralded. People will think it's fiction. Everything is, Pamela thought but didn't verbalise her thought. Nonetheless, Pamela remembered Bronnie's story word perfect with all the embellishments.

*'Bronnie.' He said my name and paused. His white smile intrigued. The pause continued. I had never experienced such a pause before. It made my nerve endings fizz and crackle. I must admit, I had a sudden vigour for pauses.*

*He looked at me in a curious way. He smiled and shook his head and repeated my name. 'Bronnie.' He said this in a way that suggested he was amazed or surprised. It was like he was tasting my name. 'Bronnieee,' he repeated. He lingered. I have never been lingered over before. It felt carnal. I experienced his tongue move over the contours of my name as he said it again—licking the peak of the capital B, then running it down over the protruding o and into the crevices of the ns, then hovering over the i before plunging his tongue into the spaces, then hovering again over the round top of the e. I felt my skin prickle, and I worried my face might have flushed. His eyes penetrated me, and I warmed in his electric smile. The guy said, 'Hello, Bronnie. I like the sound of your name, Bronnie. Do others comment on your name?'*

*'Not really,' I said and smiled.*

*He confessed he had seen me entering and leaving the building a few times before. 'You are a mysterious girl,' he said.*

*I said, 'Yes, sometimes.' I couldn't help but be impressed at being called mysterious by someone who seemed fascinated with my name, and who, it seemed, had a pressing need to get to know me. I didn't tell him I only had a beauty mark on Fridays. I felt the letters in my name harden. I asked him if he would like to have coffee. I wasn't letting the opportunity go this time. If men insisted on bumping into me, well, why not? I thought. I'd never thought much about serendipity before, but here it was standing in front of me and who was I to ignore it?*

Pamela, still alone in the office, heard a knock at the door. There hadn't been a knock since the roses. Pamela stared at the door. She had questions. Was it him? Was it another delivery of roses? Why had he taken so long to make contact with her, if indeed, that was who was knocking at the door? There was a second knock. It was softer, almost apologetic. She sat frozen. She couldn't move. She didn't want to move. She would have preferred the knock disappear into the city. She felt trapped again. She resented her so-called secret admirer. She didn't know whether she would love him or despise him. Either way, she felt sure she would be disappointed in him. She already was disappointed in him. She couldn't bring herself to get out of her chair. So she didn't. She sat frozen with heat arriving in her face. She felt her beauty mark throb. She worried the throb might make itself known on the other side of the door. She thought she had to do something to change her life.

Soon after, she heard the key turn in the door and Bronnie entered. Pamela peered into the corridor before Bronnie closed the door, but nothing and no one was there in the flickering white fluoro light. Bronnie checked her emails. Bronnie was in love. Pamela wasn't, and a small part of her resented Bronnie's luck, but a large part of her couldn't be happier for Bronnie. Pamela had hovered out on the street, in the hope some broken man would bump into her, but none did.

***

Pamela felt released to go out for a drink with Bronnie these days. And she cavalierly varied her way to and from work whenever the mood took her.

Sitting in her small flat, she opened her curtains to let in the grey light. She sat at the jigsaw table and wondered if Mr Dunleavy de Boston, the New York novelist, was married. She thought she could ask Siri on her phone, but she didn't.

***

Bronnie never spoke with Pamela about the red roses again. Bronnie didn't want to take the episode away from Pamela. It felt like theft and talking about it felt like it was lessening the romanticism. Bronnie wanted Pamela to have some romance in her life, even if it was unrequited. It was the city, the city did what it did, and it didn't bother with explanations or logic, or improbable coincidence. As for 'serendipity'—it handed out 'serendipity' with random disinterest and then, sparingly. The city rejoiced in absurdity. Its absurdity was not random—it was deliberate, antagonistic, and extravagant—as was discussed once in Pamela's Writers Circle, held every Wednesday night at seven pm sharp. In the city, as the discussion went, it wasn't what you did, it was about what *will* happen to you. That's all there was and that was nothing because whatever happens to you, the same question remained and was still unanswered, because there will always be something else that will happen to you, and no one knew what that was.

Bronnie stretched her arms. It was a gesture that things were back to normal. The next Friday, Bronnie put the beauty mark on the other side of her face, to shake things up a bit. Pamela noticed but didn't say anything. She felt better, though, without knowing why.

'Pleasured,' Bronnie whispered under her breath.

Pamela looked up before returning her attention to the *National Financial Review* newspaper spread out on her desk. She saw a small ad. It was directed at her. She clipped it out. The smallest things in the world could change everything, and nothing would ever be the same again.

# Harry Fanshawe

Harry had spent three days in Frankfurt and achieved nothing. Achieving nothing was not unusual for Harry. According to Harry, he was a world-class procrastinator. He could waste time for the country should there ever be a need for time wasting on a national level. The Frankfurt Book Fair was so huge, he was overwhelmed by it and decided to give the last day a miss. The combination of jet lag, too much stodgy food and too much schnapps at the various booths finally left him undone. He wandered back to his hotel and collapsed in his bed with flight attendant Beverly Brown's smile invading his thoughts. His return trip home was uneventful, no spilled water, no Beverly, not even a Nicholas, no upgrade to business class. He took up his aisle seat in economy and slept most of the way. He stirred when he imagined he heard a soft American accent seep through the hum in the dark cabin filling his dreams. He forgot to buy a newspaper, and when he disembarked in his home city, he had a stiff neck.

Harry had been back from Frankfurt for two weeks when he was to meet up with his mother, who was visiting from Melbourne. His sister wasn't available for some, no doubt, spurious reason. Sophie claimed there were times when she couldn't get along with Mel, which in Harry's mind was any time they were both in the same room.

Harry had arranged to meet his mother in the city for lunch. The purpose for this lunch was to catch up with her, so the obligatory unofficial interrogation about his life and why it wasn't working to Mel's satisfaction, could take place. He'd arrived early at the restaurant and took his seat and ordered a glass of wine when he received a text message. It was from Mel informing him she couldn't make lunch. That was peculiar. She had nothing to do other than to visit with her son and daughter. She offered no explanation why she was unable to make lunch. Harry thought it might have been the first text he'd ever received from Mel. He decided he would finish his wine and leave. He hated eating in restaurants alone. It made him feel more alone than he usually felt. He was aware of the new trend in the city, of singles taking themselves out to lunch, or dinner, and shouting themselves to the full service. He'd tried it once, but he felt so self-conscious, he decided it wasn't something he would take up. He was yet to master the business of holding a book open and using a knife and fork at the same time. Besides, he felt uncomfortable taking up a table for two and thus halving the restaurant's revenue from his table.

He was draining the last of his wine when he felt liquid spill into his lap. He jumped up and started to wipe his lap as the waiter standing next to him bent to help. He felt her presence. He smelt her. He smelt her perfume. She was next to him. The fabulous memory of Beverly came rushing back.

He heard a soft American accent whisper in his ear.

'Who's a clumsy boy, then?'

He looked around to find flight attendant Brown. She awarded him one of her brilliant smiles as she waited for him to remember who she was. She needn't have bothered. He knew before he saw her.

'Hello, I er...'

'So, you remember me?' Beverly asked.

'Yes, I do, yes, very much...' he blustered out as though he was a nervous schoolboy, which was how she made him feel. He felt the heat of a flush rush to his face.

'I'm not happy with you,' she castigated him good-naturedly. 'I get you upgraded to business, and you don't even come back and say thank you or offer to take me out to dinner in Frankfurt. I had a two-day layover.'

'I'm sorry. I wanted to, I really did, it's just...' Harry scrambled to his feet.

'I know, Nicholas wouldn't let you out of his sight. I can't say I blame him.'

Harry blushed red with embarrassment at the compliment. This was on top of the first flush of red. Combined, he thought he must be purple. At least he thought it was a compliment. If it was, it resulted in his schoolboy incoherent blustering. On top of which his shirt and tie were soaked. Beverly was direct, like a lot of Americans, or that had been Harry's experience with Americans. Even her smile was unambiguous. It told him everything he wanted to know. He found it at once refreshing, disarming, and alarming. If he didn't know better, not that he did, but if he did, he'd say she could use her smile to bring down an elephant, or shift a planet, if she aimed it accordingly.

Then something happened. Beverly, still smiling up at him, said, 'You *are* an angel, aren't you?' She stood on her toes and kissed him on the cheek. Harry's whole world ignited. He broke out into a sweat, his pulse sprinted, his temperature went into meltdown. He had the full Monty of emotions roaring around inside him, as though he was some tall dark stranger in a Mills & Boon novel. He felt like he was going to explode, faint, die, live, die again, and so on. He wanted to hug her and kiss her more than he had wanted these things with anyone else in his life.

'Harold Fanshawe 42c,' she said proprietarily. 'Harold,' she said again, as though she was trying it out in some way. 'Are you called Harold?'

'Yes,' he answered. He felt fortunate he'd got something out, even if it was only one word.

'Too stuffy. Harry is much better. Harry, are you going to ask me to join you, or are you waiting for someone? I know you're not waiting for your mother.' She held his left hand and looked directly into his eyes and smiled. Beverly let his hand go, pulled out a chair and sat down like she was moving into his life. She didn't wait for an answer to her question about whether or not Harry was waiting for anyone. Harry got the sense she'd decided he wasn't, or somehow already knew. The waiter brought her a glass of champagne without her asking for it. Harry sank back down onto his chair.

It turned out Beverly was from Los Angeles, 'The City of Angels' as she referred to it, a place where you arrive, walk out into the soft glow of the sun and disappear whenever you need to, she said. She looked at him and paused when she said this. He felt it meant something, but he didn't know what, and her smile and affection and attention toward him somehow didn't allow him to ask her. He tried to muster up coordination of lips, tongue, and brain to say something that might be remotely intelligent. He wondered if she had this paralysing effect on everyone she met.

'What about Tommy?' he asked.

'Who's Tommy?' she said.

'No, what about Tommy instead of Harry for my name?'

'Really? Hmm. Tommy, Tommy.' He watched Beverly think about it. 'Don't know. I'll have to think about it, okay?'

'Sure, it was a silly thought.'

'No, that's okay, silly thoughts are good. You know, I've thought about it. I discovered you as 'Harry', so that is what I'm sticking with.' She smiled at him and raised her champagne glass. 'Here's to us.' Harry hadn't known there was an 'us'. But he was glad there was. A glass of champagne had appeared on the table for him as well. He hadn't noticed that. He clinked his glass with hers and wondered how she knew his mother had cancelled, but then he realised he didn't care.

*** 

Harry noticed things. For a start, he noticed Beverly was happy, not now or this week, but she was the kind of person whose default disposition was 'happy'. Apart from this observation of his wife, the things he noticed didn't amount to too much, he thought. They were more angled than ground-breaking. He explained this to Beverly, or tried to one hot day a few years back, while they were spray-painting a table. Beverly had found the table on one of her rummaging 'recces' among the second-hand furniture shops on Emily Street. To be accurate, Beverly was doing the spraying. Harry was sitting nearby under the apricot tree in their backyard watching her and keeping the wineglasses topped up, mostly his wineglass. He described to her, in his warm inebriated state, his benign observational skill, if it could be called a skill. Beverly had more paint on herself than she had on the table. This observation alone confirmed for Harry everything he knew about his wife. She was passionate. She was full of life and fully into life. She had powers of concentration Harry could only marvel at. Harry admired his wife for all her qualities, which were too abundant to list. Nonetheless, he often found himself thinking about her various merits, things he loved about her, starting with her genuine interest in just about everything he said to her, however banal it might be. And after a few sherbets on a hot afternoon, he could be as banal as the best.

Beverly made him feel safe and gave him strength in his otherwise fragile existence. She saw things and understood things about him that Harry couldn't believe. He wanted to, but he couldn't grasp that he was anything like as fantastic as Beverly seemed to believe, but the fact that she believed such things about him made him feel complete in a way he had never felt before.

Saying he noticed 'things' was not strictly true. What Harry noticed wasn't things so much as extensions of things, consequences of things, the background to things or the gaps between things. This last one was Sophie's speciality. For example, yesterday when Harry switched on the television and flicked through the channels, he settled on a documentary. A reporter was doing a piece-to-camera on a local wine industry somewhere, it might have been France or the Southern Vales—all wine regions look similar. Harry had noticed a car way off in the distance, across the valley, behind the reporter. The car drove with purpose along the distant country road. It was silent. This fascinated Harry. He was interested in the driver of the car more than anything the reporter might be saying. The driver would have been unaware he or she was being filmed from afar. Harry watched the car travel across the screen, behind trees, around a bend, behind a farmhouse. It looked like a small mouse—everything seems out of proportion if you let your eyes glaze a bit. He wondered where that driver was right now, where he or she was going on that day. Harry mused about this person. He wondered about their hopes and dreams, their everyday stuff. The car passed behind another farmhouse. Harry wondered about the master bedroom inside the farmhouse, what bedside table facility had been settled upon? What was on their bedside table? Harry was fascinated in the quiet privacy of people's lives. Everyone has a bedside table with more or less the same objects on it, or in its top drawer, but while these objects are of the same category—a lamp, a coaster, a digital clock, book, a collected rock—each person has their own particular objects—perhaps they chose while on holiday in Rome, or while hiking through Acadia National Park in Maine. Harry had discussed this with his sister Sophie, and she incorporated it into one of her short stories she read out at The Writers Circle. Sophie understood. She was interested in these same things. The members of the Circle made notes. Austin made extensive notes.

People have lives, Harry observed to Beverly. Yet, peoples' lives, in all their infinite private detail, were rarely acknowledged, rarely thought about, rarely noticed. More recently, when Harry was trying on 'Tommy' for a name, he discussed it in The Writers Circle. Austin Quinn seemed to be obsessed with this observation. In this fast-paced world, who had the time to give to thinking about the nuances that are representative of individual lives, their everyday stuff? The quiet mysteries that make up people's daily lives are what Harry noticed, or maybe not so much the mysteries but their secrets.

*All families have secrets.* He had read this in the novel, *One Hot Summer's Night* by Dunleavy de Boston—de Boston meant it malevolently.

Beverly didn't indulge in such trifles. She lived in the moment, took people as she found them. Beverly was the practical to Harry's esoteric mutterings on the unobserved. Someone had to arrange for the plumber when 'Dean the Dishwasher', as Beverly liked to call it, started making those noises as if it was digesting the dishes, not just washing them. Beverly, when she met people for the first time, was generous. She expected the best from them while Harry was more cynical and expected the worst—the yin and yang, black and white, the binary couplings. Harry wondered what it was about his and his sister's childhood, growing up under Mel's supervision with a disconnected father, that led them to both want to be writers, with an interest in the intimacies of people's lives.

Beverly was never called Bev. Always Beverly. Harry thought she was a full to overflowing person. She needed her full name.

Harry and Beverly were two peas in a pod. Harry liked alliteration. It was his literary background. Beverly didn't so much, he thought, or at least she made no mention when Harry came up with one. Harry and Beverly had been married for some time. They were greater than the sum of their parts, and less than half, if apart. Harry knew that applied more to him than to Beverly. That was how Harry felt on this day, less than half of himself, just sitting and watching Beverly instead of reading his students' work or working on his manuscript. How could he write anything worthy when he was less than half of himself? He pondered the prospect of his writing being less than half it could be, and if he couldn't write as a whole, complete, well-adjusted person then he was doing a disservice to his readers, should he find himself with any readers, that is. Harry would be happy to get one sentence out that didn't fail on some level. His sentences formed conspiracies with his other sentences and accumulated into a threatening lifeless paragraph, which defied, or just couldn't manage, any attempt to act. He'd made the protagonist in his unfinished novella a writer/private detective who found himself in a mystery while writing a mystery, and the two invaded each other to the degree where it was no longer possible to tell which was real and which wasn't. Harry wasn't getting anywhere with it. He read what he had, to The Writers Circle—but only because he had to.

Harry got up from his chair, left the shade of the apricot tree and Beverly sanding something, went inside to his desk and opened a letter from the top of the pile. It was a bill. No one sent letters these days. Anything personal came in the form of an impersonal email, text, or WhatsApp. Only regular bills used snail mail.

Harry didn't consider himself to be an academic, despite his job as an academic at the college where he worked. The feeling of being a fraud when he won the short story competition was pretty much how he felt all the time. Winning the competition had highlighted this. Harry considered he hadn't won because he wrote a short story so fantastic it stood out head and shoulders above the thousands that were submitted. He considered he won because he survived the cut and won the toss. Harry taught the creative writing class at the college. He also taught postmodern theory to the rare, bespectacled misfits who had any interest in such an undefinable topic. He thought of his students as representative of postmodernism, for just turning up and showing an interest in a topic that had no particular interest in them, nor any interest in explaining the human condition, and point-blank refusing to be defined. Postmodernism, Harry contended, merely observed human nature, without passion, without interest, without favour or bias. It was only interested in commentary about itself. It overworked irony, self-reflexivity, and parody, and it did this with a smirk on its face, as though it thought itself relevant, or still relevant if it had reached the pinnacle of relevance. About the only thing going for postmodernism these days, Harry thought, was it did notice stuff, much like Harry.

Harry spent hours with his friend Elbow discussing his students—Harry's students, not Elbow's. With the exception of irony, the youth of today were mere human representatives, simulacra, or people palimpsests. They took endless selfies and sent these captured images to anyone on their contacts list, as though the world was interested in their mundane, self-obsessed lives. But everyone did it, so everyone did it. They surrendered having anything meaningful to say for the artifice of a selfie. If it wasn't the ubiquitous selfie, then they were 'twittering' their life away, Harry felt. They were, according to Harry, forever diluting themselves with selfies and tweets. Harry thought that few people 'thought' these days, they just were, they just did, they just happened, but they didn't think, strategise, or plan. Actual thinking was archaic. Thinking had been replaced with talking—incessant, meaningless but still urgent, talking. Talking, selfies and tweets, that was how they lived their life. By and large, Harry thought most of the youth were redacted and uneducated, including the students at his college. Harry noticed they never noticed anything other than themselves noticing themselves. He mused over the irony of the ultimate postmodern iconic image—looking in a mirror while taking a selfie of your mirror reflection of yourself, then Instagramming your image to all your 'followers', as though this proved your existence. It didn't. Harry argued people don't exist by just existing.

He glanced up at the photo in the gilded frame of Beverly, standing behind him, posing for the camera with her arms around his neck. A photo taken when photos were meaningful and not diluted by the proliferation of the narcissistic selfie. She looked happy and contented, and not like she would disappear. Harry wondered how he had anything to do with that, her happiness, if he did. He didn't understand happiness, not in relation to himself. It wasn't as though he could say he was unhappy, certainly not, he had his life with Beverly. Nonetheless, he was unable to define happiness. Beverly was happy in a way that suggested her 'happiness' was an entity in its own right. It lived and breathed, had an existence beyond both her and him. Her happiness defied definition and explanation. It was the kind of happiness that glowed, and if you stepped into its glow, you felt it. It was warm and safe and embracing. Harry had never felt anything like it, or how it made him feel in general, before, or since. He assured himself this feeling might be as good a definition of happiness as he was likely to get, a definition that existed in the radiance of someone else's happiness.

***

Harry was driving to college one winter morning about two years ago. He was thinking through the travel arrangements for his and Beverly's upcoming road trip through North America's National Parks. They planned to visit Yosemite, Death Valley, Zion, Monument Valley and the big daddy, the Grand Canyon. Their own road trip, Jack Kerouac style, minus the drugs, excessive typing, and mindlessness. It had been something Beverly had wanted to do all her life, so Harry decided he would take her. Harry was excited. Tingling could have been a bit too big a call, but he did get a buzz out of thinking about the trip. Being a postmodernist, he knew the dangers of this kind of thinking. Large raindrops started splashing across the windscreen. His phone rang. It was his new Head of Department, Professor Wendy Gogh, pronounced Goff, or Gog, or Go, he never was sure. He called her Wendy. He pulled the car over and listened. He had to strain to hear over the rain pelting down on the roof of his car. But he did hear the words 'Beverly is dead'. Maybe that wasn't what Wendy had said exactly, but that was what he heard. 'Beverly is dead. I'm so sorry, Harry.'

Huge sheets of water slashed across the bonnet of his car and up his windscreen with such force his view was obscured. Everything blurred. He sat in his car, the engine still running. The sound of the rain slapping the roof and the swoosh of cars passing, penetrated his consciousness. He looked through the veil of water at an alien world. He felt a sudden drop in temperature and smelt the new rain. Beverly loved the smell of new rain. It made her happy.

\*\*\*

Harry had a theory about how the roads of any country reflected the nature of that country's people. Harry had a lot of theories, and this was one of them. His road theory went like this. In America, it was multi-laned freeways and exits. Americans were obsessed with exits. They worried about missing the right exit. They gave directions according to exits. They highlighted their address by telling people the exit, as though they had some ownership over it. Their exit was theirs, or they were their exit. In Germany, the Germans had their autobahns where it was possible to travel at any speed you liked, or your vehicle was capable of. If you couldn't keep up, you had to stay on the inside lane. To do otherwise was to risk being run over by the numerous intercontinental trucks. The Germans were in a hurry, and no one had better get in their way. The same could be said for the Italians, except the Italians didn't seem to be so destination-oriented, they were going fast chaotically. The French wanted to see how fast they could get around the *Peripherique* or see how many near misses they could achieve while entering and exiting their grand roundabouts, of the *Arc de Triumph* and *Place de la Concorde*. In England, the streets were tiny and cramped—the cars frustrated by slow, small, inhibited narrow roads. Harry could go on, but to whom? Elbow? Elbow had heard it before. Sophie? She laughed at her brother and pointed out the inherent dangers of generalisations. To Harry, travelling along the silent, stoic roads of the Australian outback provided a luxury of quiet thinking time, where he was at liberty to indulge such generalisations. Beverly would have listened to him. Topics like these were the sort of observational conversations he would have with Beverly. She was so good at giving him the impression she was hanging off every word. Harry spent time after her death, driving through the Australian outback. He drove for days. He noted the average time between country towns was about an hour of driving time at one hundred kilometres per hour, the speed limit in most states. He figured that that was about as far as you could get in a day riding a horse, when horses were the mode of transport. He just drove. He wasn't going anywhere. He may have been trying to disappear. He can't remember what he was thinking. Maybe he was trying to drive away from the pain of his life.

Harry's thoughts went back to the day when he introduced Beverly to Mel. It was at a restaurant in the city. Beverly breezed into Mel's life and blew away Mel's inherent stuffiness with her smile, and expectation that all would be well. And it was. Harry was amazed at how good Beverly was with people, making them feel relaxed and special. It was who she was—an angel. Harry remembered that she had his mother giggling like a schoolgirl, not a sight Harry had seen before. He knew Beverly had won over his mother, when, as they were leaving the restaurant, Mel leant over in *sotto voce* and said, 'She's a keeper, son. Don't muck it up.' In truth, Harry was astonished he had attracted someone like Beverly. She seemed like a gift from the gods. Mel had been disappointed in Harry when Beverly died, as though she held him responsible. Not directly, but in a universal way. Like he was careless. Mel and her disappointment didn't have to be logical. Harry agreed though, it was the ultimate act of carelessness for him to have lost Beverly. Not just for him and his life, but he felt the responsibility of having lost Beverly for the world. He should have looked after her better, kept his eye on her more. He should have tried harder. His grief counsellor didn't seem to understand his grief, as paradoxical as that was. She might have understood better if she'd met Beverly. Then she would also be suffering from the grief of Beverly's death.

***

'*Words are liars.*' Harry sat staring at this sentence. The light faded in the late afternoon. The muskiness of his cramped office hung in the air like thick soup. Dust, it seemed, was spreading out over his stacks of books, across the floor over the worn fake Persian carpet, and over his qualifications hanging on the wall near the small window. Harry wondered if he wasn't turning to dust.

Harry had been staring at these words for what seemed like a lifetime, whereas it was more like six months, which was a lifetime. The phone on his desk rang. 'Words are liars,' he whispered.

'Harry Fanshawe,' he said, as if it was necessary.

'How's the adverb-free zone going?' Elbow asked knowing this was one of Harry's pet hates, as it was for most writers.

'Swimmingly,' Harry responded and reached for his cold coffee. He took a sip and curled his lip at the brew. 'I may have the opening line for my novel.'

'Good for you. What are you doing?' Elbow asked.

'The usual, reading creative pieces from my writing class, trying not to fall asleep.'

'Okay, anything interesting?'

'Words are liars and life is dull.'

'Maybe,' Elbow responded, if with some caution.

'I may have the opening line of my next novel.'

'You said that. What is it?'

'If you have to ask, then it probably isn't working.'

'Oh, that was it, was it?'

'Yeah.'

'Words are liars, and what did you say?'

'Life is dull.'

'Yeah well, you got that right, especially this conversation. I was calling about your birthday Friday. Do you want to do something?'

'Not really.'

'I knew you'd want to. We can double date. You know how you love that.' Elbow said this as though there were two ready-to-go women available and arranging this double date would be no more difficult than brushing your teeth.

Harry hadn't been in love as he understood love to be, until he met Beverly. She had swept him off his feet. He felt literally unbalanced, however Doris Dayish that may sound. The scent of Beverly's perfume, her smile, and the way her crystal eyes seemed to sparkle when she looked at him, combined to reduce him to tears. He knew he was a walking *cliché* of a man in love and everything he experienced with her was nothing new in the world, but it was new to him. He didn't for a second think about what would happen if he lost her. When it happened, he was unprepared and had no hope of recovering. In The Writers Circle, he was asked to examine the question, 'What will happen to you?' He had no idea, and he didn't care.

\*\*\*

Harry had looked away from the casket when it started to lower. He couldn't watch her disappear from his life. Instead, he watched the seagulls hang in mid-air over the harbour's inlets. He couldn't remember much of the day. It went past in a blur. He remembered the wake after the funeral as sombre, in spite of it being in Sophie's apartment where he felt safe. He remembered plates of food being handed around. He saw Mel serving people drinks. He didn't remember much else. He recalled a fragmented conversation he had with Sophie as the sun set over the backyards to the west.

'What will happen to you?' Sophie asked tentatively.

'What will happen to me?' Harry responded without much thought.

'Yeah.'

'Nothing.'

'Okay, that will work for a time, I guess.' They fell into silence and Harry couldn't recall much else of the day, or the days that followed.

Over the two or so years since Beverly's accident, not much had changed for Harry. Well, a lot had changed, but not much had changed. The changes that did occur were external. Harry was still walking around feeling like his life had been stolen from him, and he ached with the most intense pain possible at the loss of the one woman in his life he knew could not be replaced. He'd had some bad times, times when he questioned his own life, and whether it was worth the effort. But he knew Beverly would not countenance such thoughts. She would be disappointed in him if he didn't get on with it. So, in her memory, he continued with his life. It was excruciating at times and numb the rest of the time.

\*\*\*

Through his drowsy sleep, he heard the intercom crackle. He heard a soft American accent seep into his dreams. 'We are about to land at Los Angeles Airport, welcome to The City of Angels.' In his dream, Harry walked out of the airport and disappeared into the soft glow of the city's sun. Then he woke to the sound of a knock at his door. He glanced at his computer screen and saw the words he'd written many months ago. *What will happen to you?*

The question was meant to get him going, get him writing, but all it did for Harry was stop him dead. He had no idea what would happen to him or why anything should happen to him. Did someone knock at his door? He was sure he'd heard a knock. This time he was expecting someone. He jolted in his chair. He pulled out a drawer to his left and retrieved a small hand mirror. He checked his reflection and put the mirror back. He rubbed his face and eyes as if to wake himself up.

'Come in, please.'

He watched the door swing open. He saw someone who mattered to him. This fact startled him.

# Robbie Carton

They were both nice girls, the two girls from his past, but he'd lost both of them. He had also fucked both of them. He had caressed their breasts. He'd helped himself to their intimacy. He'd accepted their oral generosity. He'd taught them how to dangle a modifier and split an infinitive, should such a need ever arise in their lives, but he was just showing off. He described 'undeserved misfortune' to them. He didn't have to teach them 'suspension of disbelief'. They'd mastered that—they were dating him. He saw the sparkle in their youthful eyes and took advantage of them. This behaviour he had dismissed as the wayward behaviour of a wanton youth. But, as he hurtled toward his thirties, this behaviour horrified him. Losing these two girls caused him to feel bereft, confounded, and anxious. He felt abject embarrassment at his callousness. He owed them an apology. He owed them a lot more than an apology.

He'd felt honoured by their unguarded affection. He could say with confidence they were both in love with him. They had both told him of their love for him early in each relationship. He didn't know what it was he represented to them, but he could see what a hopeless phoney he was, so why couldn't they? This made him sad. Sad for himself because he didn't, indeed couldn't, say he loved them in return. He didn't feel it. He wanted to, but it wasn't there. He was also sad for them because he was never going to fulfil whatever dreams they had, that might have included him. He held them both in the highest esteem and affection, but he couldn't say in his heart he loved them. It wasn't a lot to ask from the world, to be loved. He was sure they were seeing him through their hope glasses. They would have thought he was the marrying kind, but he'd never been the marrying kind. He didn't know what 'the marrying kind' was or looked like. Why couldn't they see that? Now they would have forgotten about him, and their heartache was his heartache whenever he thought of them. And that's as it should be, he conceded.

He imagined them now in their late twenties, probably married with children. He visualised them as beautiful, sexy, wise, intelligent fully developed human beings contributing to the world. They would have opinions, hobbies, attitudes, and affection. Robbie didn't have these things in his life. He was empty.

Robbie went out with the first of these two girls for seven months and the second girl, sometime after the first, for four and a half months. In both cases, he'd got to the stage of meeting their parents, and again, in both cases, he knew their parents considered him as potential son-in-law material. That was because Robbie, with all his foibles and insecurities, was good with people. Well, older people—specifically, parents of girls he might be dating.

Robbie knew he wasn't much good with people at all. The thing was, he didn't understand anyone. When people told him things about themselves, it was as though they were speaking a foreign tongue without subtitles. He heard them, but he struggled to understand their motivations. He couldn't figure out why people did the things they did. So little made sense to him. This, he thought, was infuriating. It caused his breathing to labour. Had he been Bentley, he'd have flared his nostrils. The parents of these two girls saw him as intelligent and mostly well-adjusted, on some levels at least—on some superficial levels at best. But most importantly, they saw him as a respectful male of marrying age. Best of all, he was an accountant, a valued if dull career.

Not understanding people and having a blank spot when it came to interpreting people and their actions, was no disadvantage if all you wanted to be was an accountant but was problematic for someone who wanted to be a writer. How could he write about people if he couldn't understand human motivation? This was a significant reason Robbie had not seriously pursued a career as a writer. He wrote, he always wrote, but he had stopped sending work out, apart from 'Small Talk', which, on a whim, he'd sent to an international short story competition. He'd had no response yet and didn't expect one.

Robbie had a lot of micro stories, and he kept writing them. His stories were philosophical by nature. He didn't know the answer to almost any question of a philosophical nature. He once told Bentley that whatever the philosophical question was, the answer was brown sauce, or this was as good an answer as any. But this was nonsense and meant to confound Bentley, which it did. Bentley wondered why the sauce had to be brown. Bentley countered with, 'Any sauce was just as likely to be the answer as brown, or just as unlikely.' Robbie had to concede Bentley had a point.

Robbie thought, and argued rhetorically at the Stalwart, about philosophy. He said that philosophy sought answers to the meaning or meaningless components of life but, ironically, philosophy would fail to exist if it came up with any meaningful answers, and could be dismissed with the words, 'What's the point?' In spite of his cynical existentialism, he wrote down his philosophical thoughts and formed them into stories and kept them in his special secret file on his computer under the file name 'Absurd'. He thought he wanted to write a story about a guy who deliberately bumps into women so he can feel something in his heart. Or he could write about Bentley—a story about an insane sane accountant who couldn't be trusted, but who was completely reliable.

The parents of these two girlfriends had been easy marks for Robbie. They just wanted a bloke who would take their precious daughter off their hands and look after her. So all that was necessary was a glimmer of reassurance that this was what Robbie represented, and they were won over, dead easy. Robbie knew the parents didn't mind when, during dinner, he would nick out to their garage between main course and pudding, slide across the cool back seat of their Ford or Mitsubishi and plug their precious little daughter. They would sit at the dining room table with their pudding going cold, tapping their index finger on a book of matches they'd picked up from a New York Italian restaurant where Peter Carey eats, or from the front desk of the Ritz Carlton Hotel in New Orleans a long time ago, as they waited for Robbie and their daughter, with ruffled hair, to return to the table. So, Robbie charmed the parents of any girl he was dating. He would talk to them as though they were his only focus. He made them laugh. He appeared serious when it was needed. He discussed politics, philosophy, or sports, whatever was called for, but he was careful not to be controversial. He delivered this with just the right combination of confidence and humbleness, and a lot of silent guilt. He did the dishes. He could see them exchange looks with each other, signalling thoughts like, 'Is this guy for real?' or 'Where did she find this guy, and can we keep him?' or 'Maybe we should whisper to our daughter, her hair is ruffled.' But it was an act. Mostly it was an act. Some of it was an act. After all, the way you act is who you are, so was it acting? Robbie wondered. Robbie had no idea what the answer might be. Brown sauce?

Robbie remembered and typed the following:

*Both girls had let him slide his hand up their short skirts and between their legs under the dining table on the basis their respective parents approved of him so enthusiastically. He loved how both girls had held themselves still, to not give away what was happening under the table. He loved when they acquiesced and parted their legs enough to allow him access. He felt so privileged, so honoured they would do that, and so sorry for them that they thought it was necessary. He loved how a thin smear of sweat formed on their strained faces as he continued his conversation with their parents as though nothing was amiss, discussing the latest in string theory, or fascinating them with the question of which came first, fire or language, while at the same time having one of his fingers plunged into their daughter's most intimate space—the space where notionally, metaphorically and philosophically, all their hopes and dreams resided. He spoke with enthusiastic expression to their parents, diverting their attention to cover their daughter's breathlessness and inexplicable perspiration, even the odd suppressed groan. This parental enthusiasm for Robbie, which Robbie knew to be unmerited, allowed each daughter to satisfy him with a quick handjob or blowjob if there was enough space for her head not to hit the underside of the table with the tell-tale rhythm, to give away the activity. This occurred whenever either of their parents weren't watching, but were talking fast, or had retired to the lounge to watch "Sixty Minutes", to give the 'young people' some 'privacy'.*

Robbie couldn't remember what happened to bring each of these relationships to an end. It was as if they just got lost. Did he just forget about them? Robbie's affection for these two girls remained, and he thought of them often. He felt ashamed of the way he'd treated each of them. He felt the most shame at the faked behaviour he utilised to impress their parents. It was despicable. These were sweet, complex girls who had aspirations and probably not an unrealistic expectation of something permanent with Robbie, he thought. A future with this guy who they had allowed to finger their clitorises wouldn't have seemed an unreasonable expectation in life. Robbie wondered how often the plural of clitoris was needed in any discourse on life.

Robbie's life was a blur. He couldn't seem to remember things in detail. He worried about this. He worried maybe he had already disappeared, and no one realised it yet, himself included. Sometimes, perhaps often, he would sit on the sofa in his flat, in the dark, and mouth the words from Cilla Black's song 'Alfie', written by his favourite composers, Burt Bacharach and Hal David, from his favourite Michael Caine movie of the same name. He didn't know why he told people Bacharach and David were his favourite songwriters—he couldn't name another song they had written, but the lyrics from the song 'Alfie', were a perfect description of Robbie's life.

Robbie wanted to be kind, and he was desperate to make amends. He still loved both of those girls. They deserved his kindness. When he thought of them, tears formed in his eyes and he despised himself, and this made him feel better about himself. A little better. Not much better. He often thought of them when he was drunk at the Stalwart on Friday nights. What he wouldn't give to be able to stick his finger in their cunts again but this time sincerely and respectfully—he would never say this out loud to anyone. Perhaps Bentley. Bentley would get it.

It was hardly a mystery why Sophie wasn't interested in him and why Bentley thought he was a self-obsessed nihilist if that's what Bentley thought of Robbie. Bentley hadn't said such a thing, but Robbie figured that had to be how Bentley saw him.

Robbie had to concede that Supervisor Bentley was right—Robbie lost things. It was official. Not that it hadn't been official, but now it was declared so by Robbie himself. Robbie felt a grudging respect for Bentley for identifying this about him. Even the two friends he drank with on Friday nights at the pub were new. They replaced another two friends he'd had for a while, who'd sat at the same places at the bar, but he didn't know what happened to them either. He lost them both. He never knew their names. The reality was, for the sake of convenience, he referred to both of them as Austin, not so they could hear him, but just in his thoughts. But he'd lost them both.

\*\*\*

A while ago, sometime after he had accidentally on purpose bumped into Bronnie, whose name he thought was Pamela, Robbie found himself on her floor in her office building, standing in the white light. There were two office doors at either end of the corridor outside the lifts. One had the words 'Dr Solo, Dentist to the Stars (keep on smilin')' written on the wavy glass panel to the right. He looked at the missing 'g' from 'smilin', like it was a missing tooth. Was this dental humour? Was there dental humour? There was no writing on the other door. He stood in front of the door without any writing. It was the same door where he had once left roses. He knocked and waited. No one answered. He was sure he could sense the presence of a beauty mark on the other side of the door. Was it throbbing? It might have been, anything was possible. All it took was suspension of disbelief.

He knocked at the door again, softer this time. He thought he had to knock once more, but also, he didn't want to disturb anyone in the office. No answer again. He left. He felt the disappointment of loss, a general loss that he couldn't attribute to anything in particular. He felt the disappointment of not making amends. He had a lot to make amends for in his life, starting with his two lost girlfriends. He thought 'the not making amends' was in some profound way a summation of his life, endless and futile. He felt defeated. He felt he'd lost something important. He lost lots of things, but this time he thought it was something critical. If he kept losing things, eventually what he lost would be critical.

He travelled down the elevator, standing alone in the metal cube. He felt annoyed. He felt annoyed with Bentley, while also feeling a rush of affection for him. He slumped against one of the internal walls of the lift to brace himself. Right at that moment, in that elevator, by himself, he felt exhausted and drained and thought about his death. Robbie wanted to engage with people, but when he did, it never turned out the way he wanted. To Robbie, in that instant, going down in the elevator of this nondescript building, Bentley represented the truth. He was matter to Robbie's dark matter. Robbie would like to confide in Bentley, but he knew that wasn't going to happen. How much burden did he want to be to Bentley? To anyone? And what would he tell Bentley? Robbie had no idea. Robbie thought if he could do one decent thing in his life for someone, even a stranger, especially a stranger, it might make the difference. It might make him feel worthwhile. That's something he could tell Bentley.

***

164

'We're having a few drinks in the boardroom tonight for Flanagan's birthday, you comin'?' The Bertymeister was hanging over Robbie's cubicle divider, and Robbie could hear it creaking under Bentley's weight.

'I suppose. What time?' Robbie said while not taking his eyes from his screen. He wasn't looking at anything in particular—not focusing, that is. His screen saver was of a galaxy far, far away, with the word 'No' floating around and bouncing off the sides of his screen.

'After work. When do you think, moron? Have you finished with the spreadsheet on the northern mines' expenses? We didn't send you up there just to get red dust up your arse, you know.'

'Not yet.' Robbie said this absently, which was pretty much how he said most things to Bentley. 'Not yet, Bertyblaster.' He emphasised this under his breath.

'Send it through as soon as it's done. I need it finished today, ready for end of month.'

'Sent, Bertlebrox.' Calling Bentley Bertlebrox exhausted Robbie. He didn't know why he said it, to be honest. Robbie pressed the send button with some considerable pomp and far more circumstance than the effort warranted. He liked to make Bentley's life as difficult as he could. It was something to do to liven up his otherwise dull days. Lately, doing this, shortening Bentley's name, caused Robbie a headache, or a sudden need to rest. Everyone in the office called Bentley 'The Bentster' or one of the variations on a theme Robbie had introduced. No one did this to Bentley's face. At least Robbie had been the instigator of something in his life, however impoverished it might be and however depleted it made him feel. It was his particular contribution to the 'amusement' level on the floor, which at times reached the designation level of 'Critical' but mostly it sat at 'Unsatisfactory', or, the accountant's favourite, 'Pending'.

Robbie placed the word 'Panic' at the top of every file he sent Bentley, which Bentley hated. He hated it because he didn't get it. Bentley wasn't capable of getting references that weren't strictly out of the accounting textbook. For a start, he didn't see the point of such things. Accountancy, to Bentley, was sacrosanct. Robbie would wager Bentley would not have seen *Casablanca*, or read *1984*, or *Animal Farm*, or *Fahrenheit 451*, or *Lord of the Flies*, or *The Hitchhiker's Guide to the Galaxy*, or *One Hot Summer's Night* or *Catcher in the Rye*, or any other of a hundred seminal novels and films representing dystopia, which Robbie considered essential to anyone's education.

The chances were, Bentley would not know what 451 degrees represented. Bentley probably didn't even know who Ray Bradbury was. On the other hand, Robbie could see how he could be completely wrong about Bentley.

As much as Robbie liked to make Bentley's life difficult, whatever he did, resulted in Robbie feeling empty and without purpose. Robbie loved irony, but not always. It simultaneously gave him joy and depressed him. Playing with Bentley's name suddenly seemed lame.

'Oh, and can you say a few words tonight about Flanagan, and say something funny for once?' Bentley asked.

'Me? I don't know Flanagan,' Robbie said with some panic in his voice.

'Might I remind you, you were at his wedding. You were a groomsman. You have to know him some?' With this, Bentley gave Robbie one of his smart-ass smiles and walked back to his cubicle. 'Got him,' he said as he passed Gloria. Gloria looked up and over at Robbie, but only for a second, and with no discernible emotion on her face. Robbie saw her face and felt she thought less of him at that moment, or worse, she might have thought more of Bentley.

'It is a far, far better thing that you do, Carton, my man.' Bentley spat this mangled quote from *A Tale of Two Cities* over his shoulder as he headed back to his cubicle. Bentley said this loud enough for all to hear. It was like he'd been planning and waiting for the right time to say it to Robbie, and he wanted it to hit the mark. Bentley wanted to let Robbie know he knew Robbie's last name was the same as the Dickens' character, Sydney Carton, in *The Tale of Two Cities* and that the famous line, 'It is a far, far better thing that I do', was uttered by Sydney Carton as he elected to make the ultimate sacrifice and be publicly executed in the place of his look-alike friend, Charles Darnay. The sound of Bentley chuckling made Robbie's head heat up again and nausea rise in his throat, though that might have been at the thought of having to speak publicly at Flanagan's do. Frankly, Robbie would rather face the guillotine.

Robbie hated public speaking. He thought he should say something funny, but when he tried to, it came out awkward and not funny at all. Bentley knew this and Robbie bet it was the reason Bentley had asked Robbie to speak. Bentley was sacrificing Robbie for his own amusement. And anyway, Robbie thought, he was only a groomsman at Flanagan's wedding because Flanagan ran out of friends right after he had appointed his best man, which was Bentley, of all people. As Robbie sat in the next closest cubicle to Flanagan after Bentley, Flanagan asked Robbie to be a groomsman and Robbie hadn't had the heart to say no.

So Robbie had agreed to be Flanagan's groomsman. It had seemed like a good idea anyway, because mythical urban consensus suggested that often the groomsman and the best man got lucky with the bridesmaids. But this didn't happen on the day, not that Bentley would have scored under these circumstances, or any circumstances come to that. For a start, Bentley was married to a beautiful woman who was a fuel specialist or specialised in some obscure specialisation that required a PhD and a higher intellect than could be found collectively in the department. Not only that, she had a body that could initiate nuclear fission or supercharge the Hadron Collider just by standing next to it. Robbie met her at last year's company Christmas party, and she accelerated his particles at such a rate that when he spoke to her, he made no sense at all. All he would have done was confirm he was the idiot Bentley would have described him as. She was way too beautiful and brainy to be married to a pod like Bentley. She was also nice. When she spoke to Robbie, she touched his arm and seemed to want to hear everything he had to say, as though what he was saying was fascinating and not the rubbish he was spewing out. She seemed unspoilt by her beauty or her intellect. Her being married to Bentley made no sense. It begged the question, why would she be married to an accountant? Why would she be married to a Bentley? It was unfathomable. Did Bentley have hidden depths? Surely not. If she hadn't been so highly intellectual, she could have been a supermodel, or an actor, or something not requiring such an intellect. She was so gorgeous. And this wasn't only Robbie's opinion. It was the accepted opinion among the accountants on the floor who had stared at her at the same Christmas party—drooling, staring accountants with horn-rimmed glasses and several pens in their top pockets. Now there was a sight to behold. She must have been standing in the middle distance. The accountant's default position was to seethe with envy and jealousy and agree in unison, and so they did, when it came to their opinion of Bentley's wife, Sabrina. So Bentley wasn't going to strike it lucky with the maid of honour, not because he couldn't, proba- bly he could, although this seemed unlikely, but because he wouldn't. Why would he, when he had a wife like Sabrina?

Robbie thought he had a much better chance of success and looked for- ward to meeting his corresponding bridesmaid. Not *his* bridesmaid as such, but *the* bridesmaid. The one he had every intention of plugging in a toilet cubicle at the reception if she was willing. He'd made sure to have a condom or two just in case.

He came up with the idea that perhaps when Flanagan and his bride were cutting the cake, he and his bridesmaid could each slide down under the table and meet in the middle underneath the cake, hidden by the tablecloth, and make whoopee. This didn't happen, though.

Robbie's bridesmaid was a substantial girl and might not have fitted under the table. She had a line of sweat across her busy top lip. Busy because she also had a moustache that if shorn, would have made a reasonably decent cat. She was dressed in a pink taffeta balloon-like constriction. She looked like she was about to explode, and for reasons that defy explanation, she took an intense and immediate dislike to Robbie. Robbie knew he wasn't everyone's cup of tea, but she didn't even know him and anyway, who was she to be looking down on people? She was the bridesmaid, not the bride. She had a nice smile, but she didn't point it in Robbie's direction. Robbie observed there wasn't a big difference between a smile and a sneer when it came down to it. It was the same look, but with different intent. When she walked, her dress made a loud, scraping kind of noise. At least he thought it was coming from her dress. He hoped it was coming from her dress. It upset him she could dislike him so intensely before he'd even spoken to her. He smiled at her, but she looked away. It made him feel disjointed and sad, but in particular, anxious. Okay, she didn't have to fall in love with him, she didn't have to have sex with him, but she didn't have to detest him, not without getting to know him. After she'd been exposed to his corrosive personality, then she could detest him.

'She hates you, Carton,' Bentley had whispered to Robbie. 'What did you do to her?'

'I didn't do anything, honestly.'

'Must have been your dynamic personality then.' Bentley slapped Robbie on the shoulder. 'She's filthy on you, no bunga bunga for you tonight.' Bentley laughed his Bentley laugh.

Robbie cruised the Net for speeches for accountant types who were having a birthday. He figured he could change the names and insert Flanagan's. He found several sites that looked kind of promising but then he got bored, and Bentley started sneezing, and Gloria came over and leant over his divider, which made her breasts bulge out the top of her blouse.

He liked Gloria, she was smart and funny and had wonderful bulging breasts, and Robbie was partial to bulging breasts, especially Gloria's. As she stood overlooking him and giving him a stiff neck, he thought of asking her out. Still, he had decided long ago, he didn't think it was a good idea to get involved with fellow workers. Besides, she had a piece of lettuce stuck to her front tooth and it put him right off. Robbie thought he could tell her about the lettuce, but he didn't. It was a rare person that would, and no one on his floor would. He looked back at his computer screen to avoid the lettuce and also to relieve his stiff neck, but then he thought that was rude, so he looked at her bulging breasts instead.

'You going to Flanagan's send-off?' she asked.

'Yeah, probably, maybe,' Robbie said with not much enthusiasm. 'I thought it was his birthday?' The lettuce was scaring him, so he concentrated on her breasts. Robbie did this deliberately, and with intent, so she would either get offended and leave or keep doing it. She kept doing it. What the hell does that mean? Robbie wondered. Robbie had a vision of the lettuce growing into a gigantic green ball and exploding out of her mouth, and everyone and everything getting covered in soggy lettuce, then people just wiping it off their monitors to keep working, or doing whatever they were doing on their computers, which probably didn't have anything to do with work.

'What are you doin' after?' Gloria asked. She smiled when she spoke, which revealed the piece of lettuce was still there.

'No idea, will there be an after?' Robbie avoided looking at her lettucey tooth.

'Whaddya mean?'

'I mean, after Flanagan's bash, won't it go on, won't we be pissed, what else is there and how do you grow seedless grapes in ensuing years?'

'Yeah sure, whatever you say.' She ignored his 'seedless grapes' comment. Robbie often did his non sequitur thing, so he thought she probably recognised it was one of his quirks and ignored him. She wandered back to her cubicle. Robbie had a fantasy involving Gloria. He captures her, after a fashion, she goes along with it. She's not stressed about it. She's more inquisitive. He somehow gets her in a dark warehouse somewhere. Where the hell he found a dark warehouse was never defined in the fantasy. He invites her to lie on the bed naked and allow herself to be tied up, and she can't leave until she's had five genuine orgasms. 'Only five?' she asks. He doesn't know where he got the five from, but it seemed like enough. He tells her she will not be harmed but tantalised by his feather duster and an array of vibrators he happens to have on hand. So, in his fantasy, she giggles and shrugs and takes off her clothes, and willingly lies on the bed naked. She doesn't resist or protest. He remembered, he kind of did this to one of those girls he was dating, not precisely the same but near enough. He didn't think to tie her up. She suggested that. She liked it and wanted to do it again. But it wasn't in a warehouse, it was in his flat. And he didn't have an array of vibrators, but he did have the feather duster, which he used for the purpose, and with some distinction, he thought. He had no idea where that feather duster was today. He wondered if she hadn't taken it.

'It's just that maybe you want to go for a curry after?' Gloria was back, and the lettuce was gone. Robbie looked at her and thought of feather dusters. He thought of feather dusters cleaning up soggy bits of lettuce.

'Why didn't you tell me I had a piece of spinach stuck in my teeth?'

'I thought it was lettuce.'

'Right, that explains it then. Anyway, you want to come for a curry or not?'

'Maybe. Who else is coming?' He knew she meant her and him, but he liked to make her work for it. Her lying naked on a bed waiting for his feather duster flashed into his head.

'Judy said she and O'Brien would come, and Makepeace also said he would come?' This pissed Robbie off. He hated when he tried to be a smart-arse and it didn't work, and he hated O'Brien. O'Brien acted like he was some kind of actor waiting to be discovered, or something like that. Anyway, he was always acting. But then wasn't everyone? Still, Robbie hated it when O'Brien did it. Robbie suspected, like his namesake in *1984*, O'Brien was an informant.

'Will Makepeace come in his gorilla outfit?' Robbie asked.

'She's not Makepeace.'

'Okay,' Robbie said. 'I'm giving the farewell birthday speech, so it'll have to be after that.'

'Cool.' Gloria started to wander back to her cubicle. 'And what about seedless watermelons too?' She said this as an aside walking away, with evocative mischievousness, emphasising the words 'bulging watermelons'. Maybe she didn't say 'bulging', Robbie might have had the word 'bulging' in his head.

Robbie smiled in Gloria's direction as she turned away from him. He said to her, 'It's brown sauce, it's brown sauce all the way down.' Gloria, without turning back to him, gave him a thumbs-up as she sat down on her chair in her cubicle. Robbie wondered if she swallowed the spinach or retrieved it and threw it away. He wondered where it was right at that moment.

*** 

Robbie was at the Stalwart. It was Friday night. He'd just returned from Paris. Paris, France, not Paris the mine, which was the affectionate name of one of the company's mines in the outback. Robbie had been in Paris for five days attending the conference Bentley mysteriously couldn't attend. Robbie was jet-lagged, and his two friends hadn't shown up, and it was raining outside, which translated to dampness inside, and the atmosphere was hot, humid, and steamy. Torrential, unrelenting rains caused Robbie to think the end of the world was nigh. He liked how the rain distorted the city lights, where neon signs became blurred and unreadable. The Stalwart was pumping its own version of dystopia. Robbie was being jostled by people coming up to the bar to order their drinks. Some of them wore loosened ties and various little badges in their lapels. They smelt humid and alcoholic. Their upper lips and foreheads were beaded with sweat. He tried to spread his elbows to mark his territory, but it was no use. They were drunk, like he was, and they didn't get that he owned the beer mat territory from the bottle top over to the Foster's beer logo. He spilt some of his beer on the beer mat to either side of him in the hope they would get beer on their hands and money and leave his territory alone. But they were too drunk to notice, or if they did, they didn't care.

Someone bumped into his back as though they had tripped and fallen onto him 'accidentally'. He jolted with the bump and lost half his drink over the rest of the beer mat in front of him. That pissed him off. He turned, but he couldn't be sure who had bumped into him. There were tall, loud bodies around him, several of them women, and he wondered if his little habit of bumping into women had gained traction in the city, only on this occasion he was the target and women were making their own arrangements. He returned his attention to the beer mat logo in front of him. It was all he could do to focus on that, his head was spinning, and he felt nauseous. He thought it must be his jet lag, or the combination of jet lag and a skinful of alcohol. Paris seemed like a lifetime away, but it was roughly the same travelling time as Paris the mine. This fact confounded Robbie, more so because of his alcohol consumption.

Thinking about life, his life, he wondered what was the use of it. He downed what was left of his beer and resolved to get a curry and go home. He squeezed out backwards, pushing against bodies behind him. He had his hands on the bar and his arms outstretched. He thought how this might be the last time he came to this pub. That was the thing about life—you never knew when things were going to finish, or you were going to just disappear. The people's faces were distorted, laughing, sneering, hooting and dribbling. For all Robbie knew and understood, he might already be dead, or, more profoundly, he might not have ever existed. He thought he should ask someone. He turned to the person next to him and spoke to his back. 'Hi, can you confirm my existence?' 'Certainly Robbie, I will be right back to you on that important question,' he mouthed the person's response. He tried to catch sight of Sophie through the closing throng of grey suits. She was across the other side of the bar, impossible to see through the people. He wasn't sure if she was there.

'Hey, where you goin'?' Robbie didn't hear this at first, above all the din in the pub and the boozy haze in his head. Then it seeped into the point where he thought, 'Did someone say something to me?' He looked to his left and saw it wasn't other-self or HAL. It was Bentley. Through all the noise, he hadn't picked up Bentley's voice. Robbie found himself thinking Bentley was a sight for sore eyes. Robbie smiled at Bentley.

'I'm going to disappear, want to come?' Robbie said to Bentley.

'You're a fuckin' weirdo, Carton.' Bentley paused for a moment or two and looked off into the middle distance, such as it was in the Stalwart. 'No one understands you, Robbie,' he said with a typical senior-supervisor's exhausted-with-life-and-columns kind of exhalation, while still staring into the middle distance. 'You're just wastin' yourself. And I don't mean people don't understand what you say, although that's the case often, I mean they don't understand you, what you're doin' to yourself, you know?' There was an 'affection' in Bentley's voice, and his demeanour changed at that instant. It was as though he was being sympathetic, and he knew stuff about Robbie that Robbie didn't know, and that when Bentley wasn't pissed off with Robbie, he felt sorry for him. Robbie worried that Bentley's wife, Sabrina, might feel sorry for him too. If she did, it would make him feel bad. He didn't want his angst invading her life. She was too pure, and he wanted her to stay that way. It was enough she had to be married to Bentley, the accountant supervisor, she didn't need Robbie's corrupted disposition creeping into

172

her life. He hoped Bentley didn't tell her what an idiot he was whenever they were having dinner together with a nice glass of red.

'Not such a bad thing, not being understood,' Robbie answered weakly because he couldn't think of anything pithy to follow up with, which was always the case. He was usually a one-line pithy sentence guy. After the first line he had nothing. He often had nothing in the first instance if he were to be honest. Absolutely nothing. Nada. Zero. He wondered if his brain was lame, crippled or hampered in some pithy-saying way. Right at that moment, he imagined slitting Bentley's throat and seeing his blood spurt over the oblivious girls and boys drinking and shouting in the pub. He saw globules of Bentley's blood drop into glasses of beer. He saw blood running down the cleavages of the girls. He saw a lot of blood and a lot of cleavages. But this was a cheap metaphor not worthy of some schlock made-for-tv movie, much less himself standing in the front bar of the Stalwart, trying to be cool in front of Bentley who was trying to be nice to him. He thought schlock made-for-tv movies didn't trouble themselves with anything as existential as a metaphor of absurdity. And to be honest, if this was a metaphor for something, he had no idea what.

He tried a smile at Bentley in an effort to lighten the mood. His head started to swim. He felt bad imagining slitting Bentley's throat. Robbie wasn't violent to anyone, so where did such a thought come from? It had to be the alcohol and jet lag, he thought.

'What do you reckon's the difference between a nook and a cranny?' Robbie asked Bentley, slurring his words. 'You know, people never say things like, "I could use a nook or two right about now" or "where's a cranny when you need one?", but everyone refers to nooks and crannies, never nooks or crannies, so maybe no one knows the difference, do you think?' Bentley was still staring off into the middle distance and didn't respond to the question, but Robbie could tell Bentley was listening to him. Bentley snapped out of his mesmerised state as the volume in the pub went through the roof.

'Some of the office are here. You want to join us?' Bentley yelled into Robbie's ear. 'By the way, that piece you wrote about your last trip up to the mines, I'm running it in this month's newsletter. At first glance, it's got fuck all to do with the company, but then it's about the people out there, and anyway, I need material, and it's funny, yeah funny. Also, your end-of-month report and your Paris report today, thanks for getting both in on time and also, thanks for going to Paris at such short notice. So you comin' for a drink or not? Sabrina's here, she'd be pleased to see you. Come and say hello.'

Robbie shrugged. He didn't know what else to do. He couldn't see Sabrina and embarrass himself in his drunken stupor. Right at that moment, he realised something about himself and his life. He realised he was stuck in this pub with hundreds of office workers all drinking and shouting and licking one another, or trying to, and he had no one, and they were sending him deaf, and that, in life, people thought there was always some prick who was going to come along and fuck things up for you. But in reality, the prick was you. You were the prick, and you were fucking things up for yourself. And the question of whether you have a choice or not remains unanswered. Robbie's mind was closing down in the noise, lights, and heat. Bentley's edges started to blur, and his voice sounded distant and echoey.

Robbie heard a voice, or was it a thought? It was as sharp as a blade. It cut deep into his brain. He wondered if anyone else heard it. He wondered if Bentley heard it. This was unlikely in the din of the pub where no one was listening to anything but themselves. This voice, what it said, made the most amount of sense of anything Robbie had heard in his life. But the thing was, after he heard it, he couldn't recall what it said. Robbie felt dazed as he tried to recover the thought so he could tell Bentley. He knew Bentley would appreciate it, but nothing was coming.

'Well fuck off then, Carton. You can be a real prick, you know.' Bentley had got pissed off waiting for Robbie to behave like some kind of accountant's version of human. Robbie wasn't sure if that's what Bentley said, it was what Robbie heard, but that wasn't likely to be reliable. Bentley turned away, but then turned back and put his hand on Robbie's shoulder. 'Are you okay, Robbie? You know, if you need to talk, just you and...' Bentley either didn't finish his sentence or Robbie didn't hear what Bentley said. Robbie couldn't answer. His mouth seemed to have ceased working, or was it his brain? Bentley turned away and squeezed his way through the crowd, which carnally closed in behind him. Within seconds Robbie couldn't see him among the heads and naked, sweating skin and hair. Robbie felt bad, he wanted to go with Bentley, but it was too late.

***

Glowing from his computer screen, in the office after hours, in the dark, was a short story about meeting a girl and bladders and such. It might have been helpful for Robbie to read it now, when he needed something to anchor himself in his life, a life he had to admit was out of control, when he wasn't writing, but drinking at the Stalwart, as he was at this moment.

## COFFEE?
### By
### Robbie Carton

*Think of this scenario. Someone, a girl, accidentally bumps into you on the street and, after apologising, asks you for directions, or tells you your shoelace, which you leave undone deliberately, is undone. You imagine a nerdy girl, but reader, you can imagine whatever type of person you prefer. When this happens, you know you are standing close to a bladder containing urine, some urine, and equally, they, the person talking to you, the nerdy girl in this case, is also standing next to a bladder containing urine, yours, some urine, depending on when you last went to the toilet. Likely, in these scenarios, bladders, theirs and yours, anyone's, will be half-full or three-quarters full, or maybe contain only half a cup's worth. The urine will be sloshing about as they walk, or now that they are standing still next to you, it will be settling like liquid does after its container has come to rest. You wonder whose urine will come to rest first, hers or yours. You suppose it depends on who's got the most urine in their bladder at the time, and if you were just ambling or flat-out jogging. As you try to help her with the directions, you conjure up a dark rubbery bladdery thing, well just a bladder, and you are inside it, riding out the waves on a small open boat, getting sprayed with urine as the waves hit the chipped, red-painted gunwales. You also wonder if there's air inside the bladder, in this case, so you can breathe. You wouldn't think it could be a vacuum because the atmospheric pressure outside the bladder, whether inside or outside the body, would cause it, the bladder, to collapse. And if there was air inside the bladder, and assuming you were at sea level, the kidneys would have to produce urine at a pressure greater than one atmosphere or 101.325 kilopascals, in order to push the urine into the bladder and displace the air. And where would this displaced air go? That seems like a lot of work for two kidneys already tasked with a heavy load. There's no need to go into the four main jobs of the kidneys here but you, reader, can google it. If you do google the question about the bladder having air or not, you will find that usually the bladder doesn't have air, or gas, except when something is wrong. So no air. That's you dead in the boat from suffocation, if not urine inhalation.*

*You sometimes worry that if you're hit by a bicycle or a road train with canvassed sides—the canvassed sides are optional—and you die, and someone looks at your Google history and finds you have googled 'bladder gas' etc., what they would think of you. Maybe they would think you are some kind of weirdo, but you're not a weirdo, at least you don't think of yourself as a weirdo, you think of yourself as curious about things, is all. You think you should google some porn, so you don't look weird if someone goes into your history. The problem with porn, though, is it's got to be the same thing over and over, doesn't it? There are only so many scenarios in which women and men, or same-sex couples, can have sex. And the females aren't going off like nuclear bombs. They are acting, overacting in most cases, so porn isn't that sexy when you think about it. You like it when a woman goes off, but only if it's real. You like real things. Not that you have seen many women go off, so few as to be an embarrassment to admit to, but safe to say, you more or less know what happens. In the absence of hard experience, you use porn and speculation. As a scientist, you don't mind speculation, but you prefer confirmation. This is called unilateral dependence, where one element is dependent on another but not vice versa. Speculation doesn't need confirmation, but confirmation can't get off the ground without speculation—you speculate. You suppose it's not hard to guess why you have had so little experience with the opposite gender—long sentences can't help for a start.*

*Getting back to the bladder scenario, you suppose by extension that you could assume a bowel you happen to be standing next to in a train, or in a sky/ski gondola scenario, might have a 'compound' brewing. It will be moving, independently of the movement or otherwise of its host. It differs from urine in that urine doesn't move independently—urine needs to be jiggled about to get it moving. If you are still, your urine will be still, eventually, until you move or execute a long jump, for example. This is not the same for the bowel. You looked it up. It's called peristalsis. You knew it was called peristalsis, but you looked it up anyway. It's the wave-like action of the intestinal smooth muscle, which propels the contents forward. Bugger, that's another thing in your history someone is going to see when you happen to get stabbed, or your head explodes from a gunshot. You're not expecting to get stabbed or have your head explode from a gunshot, but it's a scenario, and alarming enough that someone might think to look up your Google history to create a profile of you while investigating who stabbed or shot you. And what will they find? A possible fetish for bladders and peristalsis. Yikes. (You will notice if you are observant an exclamation mark was not employed at the end of 'yikes' because the exclamation mark is implied by the word 'yikes' and thus the exclamation mark would be redundant. It would be like saying 'deja vu' twice.)*

*You're a nerd or nerdish. There's no getting around it. You're a nerd because you wear glasses, you have no fashion sense, you're supposed to be disconnected from the so-called 'real world', but you think this is unfair. For a start, you're rich. No one knows, except for your university professors, but you invented an app. What the app is you don't want to go into because you had to sign a confidentiality agreement with the corporation that bought the app. You're not allowed to talk to anyone about the app until after they launch it, and then you can't give details. It's the usual scenario with these things. You, dear reader, may have noticed the use of the word 'scenario' often in this piece. It has something to do with the app, but that's all that can be said about it, plus, let's face it, 'scenario' is a nerd's word, along with 'type', 'toilet', 'QED', 'bias', and 'pimple', to name only a few.*

*You'd like to meet a woman. You prefer the term 'girl' because you're a bit old-fashioned, behind the times, which is consistent with the nerd's credo. You aren't allowed to use the term 'girl(s)' anymore when describing girls. It's a pity because you feel the term 'girls' is a term of endearment and more casual than the more formal and somewhat impersonal 'woman', and to be sure, just as respectful. You think the feminists have stolen this description. You're not sure they meant to, it was an unnecessary over-reach, an unintended consequence if you like. Scientists love unintended consequences, most of the time. You kind of see yourself as a thirty-year-old boy, so a thirty-year-old, or thereabouts, girl is what you're looking for. You already used 'anyway' in this paragraph, but why can't you use the same word twice if you want to? The tyranny of rules, you call it. Anyway—third time, lol—ideally, you want a girl who is on the nerdy side herself. Not that you specifically need a nerdy girl for a particular scenario, like to help you develop an app that is female-specific or female sympathetic or female-centric. No, you're just being practical. You figure a nerdy girl will not reject you because you're a nerd, or might be less likely to reject you. She might recognise someone from the same herd. Maybe she will be less judgemental about dating a nerdish guy. You also figure a nerdy girl will not be so likely to fake her orgasm. You have no hard data to support this notion, but you think you can figure out some speculative reasons for it, and you would mention some of the reasons but for the fact that you have no empirical test to verify the reasons with an acceptable level of validity but still, speculatively, it seems like a nerdy girl would not fake her pleasure and she would be real. You guess attractive non-nerd girl-types are always having sex and they can't reach orgasm every time, you're guessing, but they don't want to make their partner feel bad, so they fake it occasionally. Again, you're guessing. Any scenario can feel right without needing empirical evidence. Don't misunderstand, reader, empirical evidence is handy, but limiting. It proves what it proves, or disproves what it disproves, and nothing else. You need to leave room for speculation. You need to trust in the value of speculation without necessarily trusting in the actual speculation itself, which would be unsound in a lot of cases.*

*In your daily routines, you don't see many nerdy girls, though, and that's because of the convention requiring girls/women to present themselves attractively and represent some kind of 'ideal', at least that's what it seems like. A whole industry of girl/woman-focused magazines exist for the prime purpose of establishing what girls/women need to look like to pass muster, as it were, and, in so doing, it underpins the point, don't you think? Whereas you're a male nerd, end of. Nerdy men are a category, documented and designated, and thus identified as such, and nothing beyond a demonstrated intelligence is expected of us. In this case the app you developed and commercialised and sold. Being a nerd gets you out of a lot of boring scenarios. Like no athletic prowess required, no mechanical aptitude, no dress sense, limited social skills and dirty glasses are almost expected. All these things and much more, are more or less accepted scenarios of a male nerd and are accepted by at least some girls/women and, let's face it, a lot of females like something to renovate, something to work on, to change for the better, to make the 'project' their own, so to speak, 'add their personal touch', and a male nerd is full of potential to be remade, although this is unlikely to succeed. So it's easy to identify a male nerd—look for army fatigues with an oversized Hawaiian shirt—but how do you identify a female nerd when most females try to conform to a much stricter and limiting code of appearance and behaviour?*

*You feel for nerdy girls/women. They must deny who they are or think they do, and the worst of this is they might think they have to hide their intelligence, but they don't need to do that for you. Intelligence is what you're looking for, intelligence and a quirky sense of humour. But still, it's a conundrum of how to identify a nerdy girl from under her makeup, with her uplifting bra, coiffed hair, and clean glasses—if she needs them and isn't using azure-coloured contacts. You need an empirical test, a test that will confirm your speculation when you meet a girl who you suspect might be a bit nerdy. You haven't come up with any test that would stand the scrutiny of scientific rigour or peer evaluation, but you do have a scenario that could work. It has potential at least. Next time you meet a girl, or talk to a girl casually, like in the street asking for directions or letting her know her shoelace is undone, if it is, and you hope she left it undone deliberately, and who you might suspect is a latent nerd. You have a question you can ask her which will reveal, by her reaction and response, if she might be a nerdy girl or not. Okay, it's never going to be one hundred per cent fool proof. Still, when combined with speculation, you calculate it's a working hypothesis with a better than even probability of success. In this world, sometimes you must go for it and damn the consequences and the statistical bias. So much science has been discovered this way. Sometimes you have to go with the serendipity. You're looking for a 'confirmation bias' scenario, a positive response. Ideally a smile of recognition, or at the least, not a horrified response. The question is this:*

*'I was wondering how much urine you calculate you have in your bladder at this time, and have you ever wondered why we can't hear it sloshing about?'*

Robbie took one last bleary-eyed look for Sophie before he lurched his way out of the pub. He saw her. She was dressed in her usual black T-shirt and black slacks, with her server's nametag pinned over her right breast. Her lustrous red hair electrified him. Robbie wanted to touch her, and he wanted to kiss her hair. He wanted to give her a rose. He wanted to caress her breasts and provide them with pleasure. He knew them intimately. She was on the other side of the bar, busy serving people. She looked up with a big smile, her eyes found him, and they seemed to make contact with him. He didn't know if her smile was for him, or if it was her bartending smile, or even if she happened to be smiling at someone else, or she thought he was someone else, or was she there at all? Maybe he imagined seeing her, and she was long gone from the pub. He lost his footing and fell away from the bar, and people closed the gap. 'Mind the gap,' he heard someone say in his head. He struggled to stay on his feet as he was pushed further away from the bar. He fell to the floor. He took a moment among the high heels and black leather shoes. He registered a small white tattoo of a bird on the back of a female knee. He saw elaborate socks. He started to *crawl* away, so Sophie, if indeed she was there (and he was confused as to whether or not she was), wouldn't see how pathetic he was.

He wondered how Sophie would respond if he asked her to marry him while he was on his hands and knees and thinking lowly of himself, drunk and dishevelled and trampled upon. He saw a stiletto puncture his hand. At least he saw it happen in his mind's eye. His bladder was sending 'full now' messages to his brain. He regained his feet and pushed back up between several bodies and staggered through the crowd, using them to keep him more or less upright as he lurched his way to the alley out the back. But he couldn't find the exit. He hated being so pathetic but having a full bladder and being in love with Sophie and being drunk and having an imagined stiletto wound in his hand, gave him no choice but to disappear before she saw him. Before anyone saw him. Why didn't anyone see him? Where was Sophie? Was she still in Paris? Robbie had no clue. Robbie was sick of being a prick to Bentley.

# Sophie Fanshawe

Sophie sat outside a café on the *Boulevard Raspail* in a mesmerised state. She shivered in the full morning Paris sunlight and felt the cold on her skin. Her eyes teared at the thought she'd failed. She felt alone, but more than that, she felt bereft of her talent, her life, her future. She fought back the desire to just sob. She believed that all that was left of her novel was the opening line— which wasn't even a complete sentence—and a few unconnected paragraphs. This was all she could remember. She didn't know what to do. She didn't know how to proceed, how to fix it, how the mess she was in was going to be resolved. She didn't understand how she got into this predicament. She felt weak, as though she hadn't eaten, and she felt demoralised. The state of her novel mirrored her own physical state, she thought. She needed a wax—her novel needed finishing. She needed body maintenance—hair, nails, face, the lot—her novel needed editing. Sophie couldn't fathom where the lost time had gone. The last two and a half months had vanished—museums, coffee, baguettes, cheap *steak frittes*, wine, white *asperges*—and the relentless pulsing cursor. She had written in new characters, but they were misbehaving, and none rang true. One was still absent. She found him working in a café near her Paris apartment. She'd given up on the question 'What will happen to you?' She'd given up on using Austin Quinn as a character to start her narrative. Nothing had worked, and most of it had gone under the delete button. The whole exercise terrified her.

Her time in Paris was almost up. She had two weeks left—but she wasn't sure. She'd lost track of time. She had looked at her itinerary more than once but couldn't hold the return date in her head. She'd used up most of her money, which included all her advance. It would have to be paid back. She stared at her reflection in the café's window and saw Blanche Dubois from Tennessee Williams' play *A Streetcar Named Desire*. Sophie wondered if, like Blanche, she was losing her grip on life. In recent days Sophie had become aware of her breathing, and she detected a ringing in her head. She thought she might get a tattoo, or a nose ring, or do anything to be someone else. She heard noises and saw movement but none of it was natural. She'd lost her sense of smell. She could no longer smell eucalyptus or liquorice. There had been slippage. She doubted herself. She questioned if she was a novelist. One novel does not make you a novelist, you must produce a second to be considered a 'novelist'. The second must be better than the first. She'd said this to Harry and now regretted saying it because it might be true.

She had visited many museums, one a day at least. She'd spent an excessive amount of time sitting at cafés thinking, sometimes not thinking—most times, not thinking. She wanted to go home but dreaded the thought. She felt her life was a blur and time had vanished. After nearly three months, no one in Paris knew her or cared about her. At the *Musée D'Orsay* she had visited Edouard Manet's *Olympia* and wept. She wept at the sheer talent one single person could have, a talent so profound it would last forever and talk to millions of people. She wept because her talent was so paltry by comparison. Not only paltry but did it exist? She wept because of her arrogance for thinking she could cause an effect in anyone's life with her work. She was not Virginia Woolf, or Sylvia Plath, or Anne Sexton. She was only Sophie Fanshawe. Those three famous writers had committed suicide. They had suffered from depression and shattering talent. Sophie had only mastered the depression—she excelled at feeling sorry for herself. When she stood in front of *Olympia* with tears in her eyes, a small woman patted her on her shoulder. She said something in French and wobbled away. Sophie hadn't understood what the old woman had said, but she dried her eyes. She felt embarrassed. She felt ashamed.

She had sat in *Les Deux Magots* and *Café de Flore*. She failed to write anything while hiding in both these famous cafés. She moved to other cafés that weren't famous and not anywhere near as expensive, but she still felt she hadn't written a word. She just drank cheaper coffee. Nothing creative came. She sat outside the less well-known and less expensive cafés with the breeze in her hair and a sense of hopelessness, but no sense of herself. She watched people sitting at nearby tables in the hope she might become inspired. They weren't tourists, nor were they other writers. They were local Parisians taking their daily coffees while contemplating their fate. She found the waiters less brusque, more helpful and patient with her terrible French. But still, she couldn't write. In her local *marché* she had relationships with the people who served her. They treated her well. They were strangers, and she had come to depend on their kindness. None of them asked her out, or home for dinner, or sex, but they served her with care and provided her with baguettes and fresh fruit and vegetables, and they filleted her fish. She craved company. She wanted to speak English to someone. But then, she thought, she had nothing to say. If she had anything to say, she would write it. She would write anything. If only something came. But she couldn't write—not as the Sophie Fanshawe who came to Paris with such hope. She was living such a mundane existence in Paris that her thoughts followed suit. Being in Paris had made it worse, not better. She had hoped for better. All the money and time, all wasted. These thoughts caused her stomach to grip and facial tics to launch.

She had had an expectation of producing publishable work in Paris, as so many other great writers had done, producing some of their best work in this city. Why was this not happening for her? She suffered from knowing that her friends, her mother in particular, would be expecting substantial output. Why shouldn't they? She came to Paris for that reason, but now Paris had defeated her. Her hair had produced grey strands. She had lost weight. Her legs had cuts where she had shaved and lost concentration. She had cried more in the past two and a half months than at any time in her adult life. She felt like turning into a cockroach if she hadn't already.

For reasons she couldn't explain, she often thought of Robbie Carton—in fact she had become obsessed with him. She thought he would understand without being too sympathetic. She needed him. She felt safe with his sense of humour. He was funny without trying. She thought about holding him. She thought about hugging him and kissing him. She wanted to disappear into the physical, no longer Sophie Fanshawe, but merely a body in the throes of ecstasy and, for a moment, no longer responsible for anything.

Sophie couldn't remember being blocked before. She had always had words waiting to come out. They would spill out onto her screen in the form of a short story that demanded to be written, or a character fully formed with her or his own story to tell. Back home, she wrote every day. She never knew what would emerge. She had no idea what story she would tell. It was as though it had little to do with her, that she was the mere typist, and the storyteller inside her did the work, and, after the work was finished, she didn't remember writing it. But this time she had nothing. This fact astounded her. She had heard other writers report the same thing. She felt so empty and exhausted. She missed home. She missed her mother. She rang her brother Harry a few times but didn't have the heart to tell him how bereft she was and how much she felt like a failure. He had his own problems, and they were far worse than hers. She hadn't felt in jeopardy until now. Her novel was killing her.

Sophie, sitting with a second coffee and nowhere to go or be, watched the people pulse along the street in front of her. She could sit like this for hours. But then, suddenly, she saw Robbie Carton, or a flash of Robbie Carton, through the clump of pedestrians across the intersection of *Rue de Babylone*, on the other side of the street. She recognised his hairstyle, if 'style' was the correct description, if style was the 'just got out of bed and didn't own a comb' look. He was an oasis, a beacon, a *cliché*. She loved him and wanted him. Her thoughts of having a life with him had taken hold somewhere in the back of her mind, behind her writing. She knew he was broken—she thought she might be a little broken herself.

Right at this moment, she was sure he was running along the street opposite. He carried a yellow case. Then she lost him in the crowd. She was sure it was Robbie Carton. Was it, though? Could it be? It seemed absurd the more she thought about it. Was it the same Robbie Carton who sat at the Stalwart bar on Friday nights, drinking excessively and not talking to anyone, often mumbling? If it was, what was he doing in Paris? It seemed so unlikely.

Her eyes strained to find him again among the crowds. She stood, knocking her chair over. The sight of him had exhilarated her. She felt a surge of intense affection for him. He was the perfect version of a lost little boy, and she felt like a lost little girl. In the bar on Friday nights, it was often all she could do to stop herself from putting her arms around him and hugging him to make him feel safe. But she didn't do that, she had hardly spoken to him, not in the pub. She took his drink order and delivered it to him and took his money and delivered his change, but nothing else. She felt it was up to him, because of the complication between the two of them, because she first knew him as Austin, not as Robbie. Sophie knew it had to come from him, for her to be sure he was ready for her. But it felt like a fairy tale. The longer they had no real engagement, any future engagement would be enhanced, but equally, as soon as they crossed the line and spoke, and became something more—friends, lovers, enemies—the sooner, she feared, it would collapse, and everything would be destroyed. He was, after all, unstable, and she could not be sure what he might do, or what might happen. She didn't know how she should address him. Should she call him Robbie, or Austin?

She continued to search through the moving pedestrians. He wasn't there. Then he was. She saw him again, waiting at the lights. People were milling between her and Robbie if that was who he was. She couldn't be sure—he was a shapeshifter. Not so much a shapeshifter but a personality-shifter, if such a thing existed. He was a long way from his favoured seat at the bar in the Stalwart, and she was a long way from The Writers Circle. Right at that moment, she wanted intimacy with him and felt a surge of electricity at the thought. She also thought it had been a long time since she'd had wild sex—any sex. She would have sex with Robbie, here or anywhere. He was volatile, though. There was something not right. It was as though he didn't fit into the world, and he had to work constantly to exist, and he did it by assuming another persona, but only at night. She knew this much about him, but it made him more attractive to her. There was a wretchedness that shrouded him like an army greatcoat. She thought she should run after him, but hesitated, and in her hesitation, she realised she didn't want to be with him. She didn't want the complexity. She didn't have the energy for him. Lethargy anchored her to her existence. It weighed her down like a thick, plastic sheet pinning her to the ground, preventing movement. She was unable to run across the street. She saw herself weave in and out of people, dodging women with prams and children skipping, and the monkey sitting on a bench near the pharmacy. She saw herself but she couldn't move. The weight of life bore down on her as she watched the back of Robbie's head bobbing in and out of view among the other Parisian heads bouncing along with their baguettes and dogs. She let him go. He disappeared.

James Joyce had discussed Jean-Paul Sartre's existentialism while drinking coffee in *Café de Flore* and *Café Les Deux Magots*. While Sophie wasn't sitting in either of these two cafés at this moment, she felt the same existentialism, a form of philosophical groundlessness, working its tragedy on her. She sat still. A slight Parisian breeze moved some loose hair across her forehead and caused the collar of her blouse to lift. She felt herself fading, disappearing from Robbie. She imagined, in a minute or two, her physical self would no longer be here on this seat, at this table, in this café, on the Left

Bank of the Seine, in Paris, France. Sitting so still, she felt herself to be an invisible portrait of the artist as a young woman. 'What will happen to you?' She mouthed the question but received no reply, only the traffic noise and people talking around her remained. *What will happen to you?* This relentless question from her, an innocent question that plagued and tormented her. 'Yeah, so what *will* happen to you?' That was the question hovering over every piece of writing, over the city, over every life. Answer this and you have a novel, a play, a poem, or a shopping list. You have something more precious, you have a life. She imagined that if she could still see Robbie, she would run after him through the wormhole into another universe. But Robbie was gone, and so was Sophie Fanshawe. She saw the yellow case disappear into the bodies of the pedestrians. Sophie closed her eyes and felt a slight chill from the breeze. She dropped into a sleep—everything went to black.

Back in her Parisian flat, the cursor on her screen pulsed in silence. It waited. It anticipated. The page number on the bottom of the screen read four hundred and twenty. The word count at the bottom bar read 135,325. The last two words on the page read 'The End'. Someone had been writing Sophie's novel. But it wasn't Sophie. It was Sophie implied.

She opened her eyes to find herself sitting at her kitchen table in front of her computer. She saw the words, 'The End'. She saw the page number and word count at the bottom of the screen. She scrolled backwards and found pages and pages of work. She realised her novel was finished. It had taken so much out of her, Sophie felt like a different person. She had disappeared as the author of this novel in front of her. She now realised writing this novel had been one of the most dangerous things she had ever done. She had no clue as to whether or not she would survive it.

She needed the safety of her brother and her mother. She needed the danger and risk of Robbie Carton. It was time to go home.

# Robbie Carton

Robbie—the Robster as Gloria was now calling him—told the accountants in his office that, to get to the company's outback mines you had to travel *North by Northwest*. This wasn't precisely accurate, although accurate for some of the time, but it satisfied the less than interested interest within the office, and Robbie got to reference the famous Hitchcock film for his own amusement.

It was a twenty-hour trip door-to-door that started in a plane and ended in a four-wheel drive. Robbie ate junk food and drank Diet Coke while he hurtled along the dirt roads. His vehicle flew over the corrugations as though surfing. He tossed the empty cans, paper bags and cardboard cartons over his shoulder into the back seat. He played The Beatles and The Beach Boys at near to full volume. He wound down the window and let the wind hit his face and he thought of Sophie.

Robbie savoured the sun's rays burning his right shoulder and arm. He smelt the freshness of the bush, and he felt confident. He inhaled the cool blast hitting his face. The bush knew what it stood for, and what it intended. You had to bend to it, it didn't bend to you. Singing the lyrics from The Beach Boys' song 'God Only Knows', God only knew, and Robbie knew too, the bush didn't make any allowances for you. Like living in the city, ever-lasting vigilance was needed to survive in the outback. It could sustain you, but it could also kill you in an instant, and it showed no leanings or prefer-ences one way or another. The outback didn't care—live or die, your choice. The city wanted you alive—psychologically chained, depleted, scared but alive—it needed numbers. Robbie preferred the outback's insouciance and absence of ambiguity. He loved the exhilaration of the jeopardy. It could kill you, and that was freedom to Robbie. Not being in his cubicle was another form of freedom. Robbie felt more like a person with purpose in the outback, than he did back in the city. In the city, Robbie felt blurred, indistinct, and unsure, like he had to hang on all the time, like he was a 'Nowhere Man', as the title of the Beatles' song described. Robbie flicked his phone to the Beatles' soundtrack and turned up the volume even more. He blasted 'Nowhere Man' through the car's speakers and out his open window. In the bush, he could just be—not himself, that wouldn't work, but not someone else either—that also wouldn't work out in the bush. Fakery, subterfuge, deception, disguise, none of these things would work in the outback. They were survival strategies for the city. The city celebrated these attributes. The city demanded them. The bush rejected them. They weren't needed in the bush. They weren't believed in the bush.

Robbie drove the dead-straight dirt road north toward the spirit level horizon. He sang along with 'Nowhere Man' at the top of his voice, pushing out the words against the constant blast of fresh wind in his face. He couldn't hear a thing.

He was three hours north of Oodnadatta, the last stop on the way to the company's mines. Through a clump of mallee trees off the track to Robbie's right, perhaps a hundred metres or so, in the middle of nowhere, near enough to the middle of the country, Robbie glimpsed a short fat man sitting on a log in the shade. Robbie slowed but didn't stop. The car shuddered as the slower speed resulted in him hitting each corrugation with force, instead of floating over the top.

Robbie watched the man watching Robbie bump by. The man's demeanour held no comment, it didn't change. Robbie understood. The man took a sip from a steel cup. He made eye contact with Robbie. Robbie observed his khaki shorts and the white dusty T-shirt stretched over his stomach. He had bulging eyes, surrounded by fat pale skin. He wore rough boots and a sweat-stained broad-brimmed hat with a red kerchief tied around his neck. There was no vehicle or horse anywhere that Robbie could see. Robbie didn't question it. It was the bush. The bush does not take questions. Robbie wondered what the Doppler-affected music of 'Nowhere Man' sounded like to the man sitting and drinking from a cup, while two kangaroos grazed nearby with time to kill. Robbie refocused his eyes to the road and absorbed the pounding corrugations. The man disappeared from view, as the bush closed in around him. Robbie pressed the accelerator to speed up and get away. He checked his rear-vision. All he could see in the mirror was the dust thrown up by the car. He strained to see that nothing was following him but if there was something there, would he know? He felt a presence. He felt he was in the opening scene of an Alfred Hitchcock movie.

'Call me The Robster,' he mouthed out loud. He wondered what Brian Wilson from the Beach Boys would have made of the outback, what lyrics he would have written to describe the enigmatic presence of the bush. He kept flicking a look in the rear-view mirror. There was nothing following him that he could see. He changed the music to 'Wouldn't It Be Nice' and sang along while imagining a life with Sophie.

He saw Sophie from the corner of his eye. She sat next to him in the car. She looked out her window at the mallee trees whizzing by. Then he saw her sitting with him on a cliff watching a sunset, sipping an exotic cocktail, and having inspiring conversations. She would be receptive to him. He imagined making love to her in soft grass. Sophie had a green flower in her red hair. She looked like perfection would look, if perfection were a beautiful woman in love with Robbie, with closed eyes, with the rays of the sunset bathing her body, with a green flower in her hair. It would be nice.

Robbie made this outback trip once a month to reconcile the expenses of both mines. He loved it. It was the one sane thing he had in his life. Everything was heightened—his sense of himself, his appetite, his appreciation of the outback, of his life, music, and junk food. Most of all, he appreciated, but not in a negative way, his total lack of importance in the world. If you weren't important, then nothing you did mattered. He couldn't disappoint anyone. All this was a relief, and 'relief' was new to him. It was freedom, or as close to freedom as was permitted by Robbie's personality. He loved the bush, but he was also terrified by it. He respected it as an alien environment. After too much alcohol, he was bound to exclaim this fact at the Stalwart to no one in particular. 'In the womb, you are an alien, a parasite, then after the womb, all environments are alien and you are an alien in them—humans are nothing more than a bacterial bloom,' he would mumble. He knew Sophie would get it. But she wasn't there.

In the city, Robbie lived his life with uncertainty, but in the outback, there was no uncertainty. He wasn't caged in the chook pen of an office. He didn't have to cope with Bentley and, to be fair, Bentley didn't have to cope with him. He missed Bentley though, but he doubted Bentley missed him.

Robbie thought Bentley would understand the bush or understand the effect the bush had on him. Perhaps that was why Bentley had chosen Robbie to make these trips. Out here, no gorillas spoke to him. He didn't have Gloria to look at and sniff. He supposed she had an agenda, he supposed it might be with O'Brien. In the outback, he didn't have Sophie, but he would never have Sophie. He didn't have her in the city.

A red kangaroo leapt across the track in front of him and disappeared into the bush. Several emus ran alongside the track before they deviated off into the scrub. A black kite rose from a gum tree in advance of his vehicle. It hovered over the track. It lived a black kite life. It had no understanding of the nature of air. Up ahead, celebrating crows danced around roadkill and bounced off the road to watch him pass. They waited for his approach and moved at the last second as he barrelled over the top of their roadkill. They bounced back after he passed. It was heading to mid-afternoon. The crows weren't expecting any more traffic at this time of day.

It was the red dust that had the greatest impact on him. The dust penetrated everything, including his psyche, especially his psyche. The dust and the heat, the flies and the cicadas made him feel liberated. When he returned to the city, when he was either in the office or at the Stalwart, he felt he understood something that others in the city didn't. He had a secret. Not an actual secret you could relate to someone, it was a sense of something, a sense of the bush, which was nonetheless a secret. The city knew this and rejected it—the city tried to talk him out of such a fanciful notion.

Robbie loved the psychological risk he felt so close to, when he was drinking in one of the mines' canteens after a day of reconciling the books. The dominating colour in the office back in the city was grey. In the mythical seductive bush, it was red—red enhanced by the blue of the clear, cloudless, horizon-to-horizon sky. His soul lifted and sank. He felt clear-eyed and lost. He felt smaller and bigger. Everything seemed noisier, but he couldn't hear anything. He wasn't sure if he would be heard of again. He liked how edgy he was and how happy it made him feel. In the city he was edgy, but it was internally generated. In the outback his edginess was external and not personal. It was him against the environment, not him against himself or Bentley. The intense red and the blue dominated his soul. The blazing sun shone in his eyes and crinkled his skin. A million or so flies landed on his face and crawled up his nose and nested in his eyes and ears. He appreciated the defining harmonic buzz of the trillion or so cicadas in the midday heat.

Combined, it made him feel brave. Everything came in vast uncountable numbers—flies, cicadas, stars and trees. Accountants couldn't cope with such vast numbers. Numbers that can't be reconciled or counted or managed, would destroy the fabric of any accountant—unaccountable numbers terrify accountants.

The red dust filled his nose, and for days after he got back to the city, he would blow his nose and globules of red dust would come out—the outback reminding him of where he had been. In the outback Robbie felt serious, tethered, and reliable. In the city he was flippant—adrift for most of his day, and at night, not himself.

He imagined an almighty contest. It went like this. The outback versus the city, and vice versa, for supremacy. Both had formidable but different lethal weapons. Both would fight to the death, inflicting massive damage to their opponent. He thought it ironic that fragile people could survive in either environment. Not easily, not well, not without danger, or being diminished, worn out, or just obliterated if you made a mistake, but nonetheless, people generally could survive so long as they employed everlasting vigilance.

To get to the first mine, Robbie had to leave the city. He found this difficult. It was as though the city was unhappy with his departure and he had to disgorge himself from it. He had to work against the city's pull—the city retarded his escape. It wasn't until he pulled into Oodnadatta's Pink Roadhouse that he felt the hold of the city lessen. And he could move more freely, and the seduction of the bush became palpable and overcame the paranoid demands of the city.

After Oodnadatta, he took the Dalhousie Springs track north, before turning east onto another dirt road, not sign-posted, and drove another two hours across more ruts. Just before his kidneys shattered from the corrugations, Robbie arrived at the gates of the first mine. Through the gates, it was another seventy-five minutes along a graded sandy track to the outpost of small buildings, consisting of dongas—single room demountable tin huts, affectionately known as suicide cells—with a toilet and shower block. This was where the employees slept, ate and washed after finishing their shifts in the mines, another ten kilometres away. At the end of the day, both men and women, were covered in dust and grease. They washed as much of the red dust off as was possible and after their showers, gathered in the canteen and ate sausages and steaks accompanied with great blobs of mashed potato, which they smothered with ketchup and brown sauce. They drank beer out of cans, a lot of beer. Robbie was included as one of the team. Robbie joined in the beer drinking with considerable enthusiasm. He loved the camaraderie, none of which existed back at the city office. He loved the sausages and mashed potato and the spurting ketchup. He loved the chunky slices of white bread thick with butter. He consumed lamingtons, a food from his childhood, and one that, as far as he knew, didn't exist in the city anymore. He ended up with bits of coconut stuck in his teeth from the lamingtons. The food tasted big. It matched his appetite. He loved the distance between him and his nondescript cubicle. He laughed at the staff's bawdy but clever humour. He heard himself laugh.

He thought of his DNA on his desk and on his computer in his cubicle. He existed there as a finger smear. But here, in the mining village, he existed large.

Drinking was mandatory in the canteen at the end of the day—never during the day. Robbie drank so much beer on these visits, that he could barely remember who he was, or if he was, or whether or not it mattered. This was a good thing, because back at the office he was confronted with who he was, or worse, who he wasn't, every second. And out here, no one cared. They took him at face value. They accepted him. They called him Abacus. Everyone had a nickname. Real names weren't used. He soon realised they were unofficially banned. Out here, you could be whoever you wanted to be—you could invent your history and that was fine, no one challenged you. He was happy with that. The staff kept snapping the tops off cans of beer for him. He spent the days poring over numbers with a headache he could hear. He loved the evenings when the flies subsided, and he celebrated the drinking. He seemed to be the only one with a constant hangover. The staff went about their jobs with verve and bush respect. Robbie admired them and envied their freedom and sense of cautious anarchy and capriciousness.

He gazed out the window of his makeshift office into the scrub and realised he could walk for five minutes in any direction and disappear. Could he ever live and work here permanently, though? This was one of those questions that sat silently in his head and waited for an answer. He was a city boy through and through, as far as he knew, but maybe he wasn't. How would he know? Robbie pondered this and other inexplicable philosophies while running numbers through his laptop. He wrote the words from Shakespeare's *Hamlet* on a clean page on his computer. There are more 'things in heaven and earth', Robbie Carton, 'than are dreamt of in your philosophy.'

The staff, both women and the men, slapped him hard on the back by way of affection, and to emphasise their point whenever they had something to say. He smiled at them in return and felt part of something. But his smile was forced. He knew he wasn't one of them and never could be, not for as long as he was an accountant in a cubicle.

One stocky woman, with a short back and sides haircut and a small scar across her left cheek, grabbed his upper arm hard by way of communication. She smiled a toothy grin at him and ran her hand through his hair. She made him feel solid, in a way that sitting at the Stalwart bar, drunk, did not. She smelt of soap.

'It's beer o'clock. Time to repair to the canteen. You commin'?' she said. 'Or you still got more number crunchin' to do?'

It was his last night before heading off for the other mine.

Robbie, still suffering from last night's hangover, answered, 'Just a sec', and noted her use of the phrasal verb 'repair to'. It shocked him in a small but happy way. She couldn't have known 'repair' was one of his favourite words. He wouldn't have expected her to use it the way she did. But then the call of the beer can was 'ritual', it was sacrosanct, and these were educated people, educated in life in a way people in the city weren't. He saved and minimised the file on his laptop and snapped the lid shut.

Robbie followed her and the rest of the staff out of the office, across the dusty bitumen pathway and into the air-conditioned, fly-free zone of the canteen to start drinking all over again. These drinking sessions destroyed his memory. The days merged into one long, bleary-eyed cacophony of loud voices, singing, backslapping, can popping distorted faces, a quacking duck, a soap smell, columns of numbers and fingers through his hair. He woke naked in the middle of the night. He was sure he saw a tarantula in his dark room. He saw two black orbs staring at him. The spider was huge, and it grinned at him. He felt ridiculed by the creature. He recalled dreaming it was on his penis about to sink its fangs into his erection. He recalled a soft caressing of his erection and how stimulated he had been while the ceiling fan turned so slowly above him, it seemed like it was dragging the room around with it. He fell back into a deep sleep.

He woke drenched in sweat. He heard distant thunder and his cot creaked when he moved under the rough blanket. He couldn't remember how he got to his cot. There was a distinct trace of semen on his sheet. His head felt thick and confused, and his mouth was as dry as a roll of sandpaper at Marble Bar in a heatwave. His memory was absent.

Next day, he packed up early and headed further north to the second mine, another five hours on a dirt track that barely existed. They knew he was coming and had his donga ready. The staff at the second mine drank as much as those at the first mine. More. They were determined to outdo one another. The competitiveness between the two mines amused Robbie. It was based on a spirit of good fun, not like the competitiveness back at the office, where it was snide, drenched in *schadenfreude* where everyone was happy to compete and succeed at their colleagues' expense. At the mines, Robbie joined in and declared his support and loyalty for whichever mine he was in at the time. He drank their corporate beer and ate their company steak sandwiches and stopped thinking. Robbie slept like he was in a coma.

He dreamt of tarantulas, of ejaculation, of female softness, of ample, of lavish. He missed Sophie during these times as Robbie Carton—intrepid bush accountant. He thought Sophie to be an adventurous woman and that she would love the outback. He resolved in his dream state to one day invite Sophie into the bush and lie next to her under the Southern Cross. He would give her a red rose every day of her life.

Sometimes, late at night in his apartment when Robbie was lying on his bed in the dark with the smell of half-eaten sandwiches on a plate next to him, and an erection he refused to touch, he would evoke his habit of imagining some of his favourite literary characters and how they might talk to one another. Not characters from the same novel, like Sherlock Holmes and Dr John Watson, but like Holden Caulfield talking to Winston Smith or maybe the Bret Easton Ellis character in *Luna Park*, who plays a version of the author, talking to the not-named character in *Bright Lights, Big City* about a girl called Amanda, or the values expressed by the business card choices you make. Or maybe Patrick Bateman in conversation with Dolores Haze. This was one of his favourites. Robbie would avoid the terrors of insomnia by making up whole conversations between these fictional characters. If Sophie had been in Robbie's room in the dark, maybe leaning against his football, or performing the plank in a bikini, or not noticing his erection, she would have heard his soliloquy. Robbie knew the characters in his favourite novels were made up, but their stories were true, and the only avenue of expression they had, he thought, for the expansion of their respective truths, was through Robbie's imagination late at night in his darkened bedroom *sans* or *avec* Sophie. He liberated them from their confined literary stories and released them to the universe. He wondered how the world might be different if literary characters were allowed to leave the constrictions of their literary lives and live among us. Austin Quinn came to mind. If released, would these literary characters still be altruistic, strong, capable, heroic, and compassionate or would they succumb to the chaos and corruption and debilitation of living in the real world with real people, like Robbie felt had happened to him?

Robbie didn't know the answers to these questions, but there was a part of him that hoped these heroes would fail too, as he was failing. On the other hand, maybe if they succeeded, they would take him along, and he might succeed in ways he seemed incapable of on his own.

On the way back from the mines, Robbie stopped at the Pink Roadhouse again for lunch, to complete the business of absorbing the alcohol in his system. He opened his computer while he waited for his buffalo burger and started writing a piece for Bentley's newsletter. He felt exhilarated. He felt alive. He felt he could be absurd. He thought it was the least he could do for the disjointed souls trapped in cubicle hell at Head Office. He knew the workers he'd just spent over a week with, enduring forty-degree heat infused with red dust, living with the constant satisfying hum of cicada rhythms, could never survive in Head Office. They couldn't, it would kill them in every sense. It was killing him. He felt in a small way privileged—he was something of a go-between for these two opposing universes. He felt he could exist, not flourish, but exist, in both these worlds. He could translate one for the other. He felt useful.

He wrote the piece knowing it was not strictly within the guidelines as prescribed by Bentley's air quotes. But it aspired to humour, the humour of the mines, and Robbie was sure Bentley would appreciate it on some level. The people of the mines were sardonic, irreverent, and clever. They affected a hard carapace to protect them from the glare of the sun, the heat, the dust, tarantulas, and the venomous snakes, but inside they were refined examples of the human condition.

They put on a smile, not so much on their face but from within their souls, as though they knew secrets to life the accountants in the city could neither know, nor grasp. Robbie acknowledged the humour of the bush, of laughing at yourself, then at your colleagues with affection, then in a general sense, at their lot, their plight. Not that they considered they were in any way disadvantaged by being in such a remote, unforgiving location—quite the opposite.

Because he knew Bentley probably wouldn't run it, he was able to write without the discipline of relevance and to demonstrate his respect for the people of the mines. In a strange way he couldn't explain, his time with the staff at the mines inspired him. He wrote about them because no one back in the sterile world of the office could understand how life was out at the mines, and he wanted to describe their philosophies and their fortunate universe. He would celebrate how they competed energetically with one another, their humour, and stoic dispositions, and in particular, their irreverence and how they took the piss out of themselves.

He sat in the Pink Roadhouse sipping his latte while writing a postcard, from himself, in the inexplicable outback, to his colleagues at head office. The English waitress hovered in his peripheral vision, but Robbie was unaware of her hover. When he did look at her while she delivered his food, he noticed she had a blushed tinge to her cheeks.

*Postcard from the Mines*

*To: Accounts Department: Reconciliations, Head Office.*

*From: Robbie Carton— Auditor on Location*

*Location: Just to the left of a gazillion mulga trees, and just to the right of the same amount, give or take.*

*To get to the mines, you will need a plane, a car, a love of kidney-crushing corrugations (thirteen hours of corrugations), plenty of water, and fear, a lot of fear—fear of the colossal, fear of cacophony, fear of vastness, and fear of yourself. The enigmatic Australian outback has a way of diminishing you, daring you to gaze into your soul. So be ready for your insignificance. Be prepared for the abyss.*

*Mine one, known as Bundanyabba, or Bundy for short, is a small village about six hours from Oodnadatta, or fifteen hours and five or six minutes from the nearest McDonalds, depending on traffic, wash-outs, kangaroos and corrugations. Paris, the other mine, is further out, four hours to the right. In the time it takes to get to the mines, you could be in Paris, France, almost.*

*Calling Bundy a 'village' according to Reg Taylor, chief engineer, and notional self-appointed Mayor of Bundy (aka 'Bluey' so known for his blazing red hair), might be to do an injustice to an actual village. It's a fifty-metre stretch of bitumen that runs between two rows of dongas (single room demountable tin huts affectionately known as suicide cells), five on each side. Four of them on the northern side are rammed together to make a canteen at the end of the street (or boulevard as the locals prefer), lovingly called the 'Chops Elysees'—chops being their favourite meat, and Elysees a direct send-up of their sister mine, Paris.*

*Back in Oodnadatta (pop. 204 at last count), which by comparison to the 'villages' of the mines is a thriving metropolis, a hundred or so demountable houses line its two hundred and seventy-two-metre bitumen main street. The residents, being very proud of every centimetre of bitumen, claim you'd have to go to Alice Springs to find the next bit of bitumen. But then you'd be in Alice Springs and not Oodnadatta. In Oodnadatta, known by the locals as the 'riviera of the outback', there's a way of telling locals (born and bred) from blow-ins (lived their life in the town but born elsewhere). The locals have a sofa on their front porch facing the main street in case anything happens (not that anything does, but they thrive on the anticipation), and the blow-ins have a sofa on the back porch facing the vast endless views of scrub stretching to the mountain range on the distant horizon. The locals have seen the view out the back. The view out the back never changes. They're interested in who comes to town, and who disappears.*

*You stop at the Pink Roadhouse in Oodnadatta before heading on to the mines, not just because it's your last known human contact, but you're coming to the company's mines to reconcile their accounts and are expected to pick up 'emergency stores' for both mines as you pass through. The pre-ordered stores, consisting of tinned food, meat, and beer (a lot of beer) are loaded into your rental car while you sip on a half decent latte. You can get a latte out here, out in the middle of nowhere, served by an English backpacker whose soft full-mouthed accent seems so out of place. But then everything is out of place. Only the red dust, mulga trees, deadly snakes, tarantulas, and flies belong. You are just tolerated—by the huge, by the din, by the vast, by the red. If you weren't so insignificant, the outback would crush you with indifference, and the scream of cicadas would mask your pathetic cries. Red dust penetrates every surface and infiltrates every orifice. The English backpacker smiles at you, or for you, you aren't sure which, but by the end of the trip, you suspect you will know. She acts as though she doesn't expect to see you again, even though you are back every month.*

*Competition between the two mines is intense, but by and large, good-natured. So far, the eight-burner barbecue has been stolen seventeen times. It*

197

*mysteriously emerged in Bundy, then just as mysteriously disappeared only to reappear, again mysteriously, back in Paris. No one expects it to stay in Paris long, especially the 'Parisians'. A barbecue is considered a civilising item at both mines. Why they wouldn't buy a second one and have one each, misses the point.*

*The second most contested resource at the mines is water. Mayor Reg, with tongue firmly planted in cheek, says everyone up there in Paris is particularly proud of their so-called 'spring', which is yet to flow. In response, the citizens of Paris reckon Bundy's 'spring' is a trickle of brackish water out next to the village dump—not even the 'roos drink it, and it only holds water once every eighty years or so after there's enough rain for the sewage to back up. Still, when it's all you have, you make the most of it. Reg says, 'at least we've got a spring, Paris has got seven-eighths of four-fifths of sweet f\*ck all, if you don't count the mine or the eight-burner barbecue—when they've got it.'*

*The two mines produce a monthly newsletter, turn and turnabout. The newsletters are 'widely circulated' between each mine. The sole and only point of the newsletters are to outdo and send each other up. Last month Mine one (Bundy) lead with a story about their racing carnival, a grand day by any measure. The Bundy Outback Newsletter highlighted one of the races, which fielded two camels. One of the camels, the favourite, was facing the wrong way, and no amount of coaxing could encourage it to turn around, so when the starter pistol fired, it ran in the direction it was facing, throwing its jockey, and has not been seen since—the camel, not the jockey. The jockey was eventually found covered in dust with a beer in hand. The other camel came second to the joy of the only on-course bookie. The Bundy Outback Newsletter described their carnival as the 'Biggest and Best'. They had an unexplained surplus of 'B's' in the printing department that month. They went right off with 'Beaut' and 'Bonza', and a laboured 'Bociferous', which no one is sure is even a word, but it qualifies because it starts with a B. The highlights of the 'Biggest and Best' annual race meeting pushed the huge item of the week to the second page— the story about Dinger, one of the miners from Paris. Dinger, according to The Bundy Outback Newsletter's intrepid reporter, had a large wart on his nose that glowed at night, thus enabling Dinger to save on torch batteries and electricity—had there been any electricity, and assuming there was anything that needed looking at in Paris at night. Dinger, with his glowing wart, was pretty handy down the Paris mine whenever the generator failed or ran out of diesel, which was often, according to The Bundy Outback Newsletter's esteemed editorial. This was Dinger's story as told by the feature writer—the facts of which* were entirely made up, consistent with all the made-up facts as reported in both newsletters. It was a fact that if things weren't made up, there would be nothing to write about.

Anyway, the story goes thus: Dinger, resident miner in Paris, claimed his dingo Dietrich, had mastered the first chorus of Advance Australia Fair, although much to Dinger's regret, Dietrich refused to howl a single note of the anthem in public. Nonetheless, it was impressive, given that most Australians struggle with remembering the words and must acquit themselves by moving their mouth in a vague mime, pretty much as Dinger's dog did with a lot of howling. Dietrich covered off on the word 'girt' with some distinction while not knowing what the hell it meant and unable to use it in a sentence. He was a dog and struggled to use any word in a sentence unless it started with a W. The word 'girt' left him 'stonkered' to use a colloquialism.

Not to be outdone, this month, the Paris mine produced its newsletter The Paris Review Weekly—so called by this posh name even though it came out monthly. But not every month. It depended if there was any news or not. Let's face it, it isn't every week you get an eye-popper of a story like Dinger's dog Dietrich the songmeister, as gleefully reported in Bundy's newsletter. This month The Paris Review Weekly could not pass up the opportunity of re-reporting the Bundy race carnival, calling it a salutary affair featuring camels racing one another in the feature race of the day, the Outback Cup. The track, as described by The Paris Review Weekly, was so dusty that no one could see the camels or riders. Among the confusion and dust, no one noticed the riders had somehow swapped camels before they crossed the finish line, which tended to negate the result. 'The result is negated!' exclaimed the bookie. The Paris Review Weekly editorial team claimed with verve that they were sticklers for accurate reporting, wherever possible, and in particular, where the facts aligned with their mission to denigrate Bundy and its residents at every opportunity. They were themselves intending to lead with words containing several B's, but there was an inexplicable absence of B' at the printing press, which had disappeared days before the Bundy newsletter came out last month. The residents of Paris, which comprised a population totaling a thousand lives—including 981 wild goats, but not the billion or so ever-present flies, did not know for sure what had happened to the B's, but the reprobates who populated The Bundy Outback's newsroom were held in much suspicion by all who loved and revered The Paris Review Weekly.

The suspicion that the Bundy mine population was responsible for rifling

*The Paris Review's stock of B's came about because two years before, Bundy's two erasers went missing, and all the crossings-out and spelling errors had to be left in, making The Bundy Newsletter double its normal size to four pages that month. When The Paris Review Weekly reported on the missing erasers, it wasn't without a certain degree of snideness and celebration, and its next issue contained no crossings-out or errors. Soon after, Paris' eight-burner barbecue went missing, again.*

*This month The Paris Review Weekly suffered from the absence of Muggers, their usual headline writer. Muggers was out chasing one of his goats on his day off from detonation and blowing-up work. Doug, the goat, had swallowed Muggers' cigarette lighter (goats eat anything), and so Muggers had to follow the business end of Doug around for days waiting for his cigarette lighter to pop out, as it were. It's a dirty business, smoking. Anyway, this meant Doris, one of the cooks in the canteen, who had a light heart and an enigmatic beauty mark on her left cheek (which everyone confused with a fly), had to write The Paris Review Weekly's headline. Doris was better at writing her daily, weekly, or whenever, Page 3 column called 'Tips for the Lighthearted' where she would discuss such enlightened things as how to live a full and robust life in the outback without a peg or a pasta maker. She had a talent for teasing out the nuances of outback life.*

*The other story to run this month, also pushed to the second page, was the announcement that the Paris village committee had decided to name the village's only corner after the last tourist to have visited the dusty, main, and only street of Paris village. The committee took two years to reach the decision, by which time no one could remember several things. Chief among the several things no one could remember was who was on the committee. Finally, a committee was gathered in the front bar of the canteen, or enough committee that could be considered representational of the town's population, so the matter at hand could be dealt with, except now no one could remember the tourist's name, or even if there had ever been a tourist. So they decided to call the corner Doug, after Mugger's goat. To be honest, it wasn't much of a corner anyway; it turned off the main street and stopped, but even so, it needed a name, as everyone was sick of calling it 'the turn, off the main street that stops'. You can see how tedious that would be. The problem was, how would anyone know if you were talking about Doug the goat or Doug the corner? No one had an immediate answer, and the matter was referred to a sub-committee, which consisted of Dennis, the donga cleaner. Dennis had a suggestion.*

*Dennis, who cleaned all the dongas in Paris and Bundy, had been to Adelaide to have an impacted wisdom tooth removed from his ankle. The wisdom tooth had belonged to the dog Dietrich from Paris that had wandered down the track to visit Bundy on a day when Dennis happened to be cleaning the Bundy dongas. In a moment of confusion, Dietrich the dog, mistook Dennis's ankle with the dingo bone he was gnawing on—Dietrich was gnawing on, not Dennis. Dennis, who was the only member of either mine to have visited Adelaide, saw many amazing things in Adelaide, such as a roundabout, and pegs. Upon his return, he offered that the corner should be called Doug 1.0, which he overheard while in the surgery having the wisdom tooth retrieved. It seems that city folk distinguish things by adding a 1.0 or 2.0, or 2.1, to things. No joke. Anyway, Doug 1.0 it was, or just Doug for short. Everyone seemed happy with that. No one thought Doug the goat would last too long anyway. He had that lighter fluid in his system producing a prodigious amount of methane farts, enough to fill a blimp, so sooner or later, the methane farts would come into contact with a lighted flame from the lighter working its way through Doug's system and boom, no more Doug—Doug the goat that is, not Doug the corner.*

*It should be noted that both The Bundy Outback Newsletter and The Paris Review Weekly have been internationally recognised for their journalistic excellence, wherein both cases, the breaking out of secrets has kept both of these august newsletters at the forefront of investigative journalism for as long as... well since Muggers first noticed Doug the goat's penchant for cigarette lighters.*

*Accounts reconciled. Meat eaten. Beer drunk. A lot of beer drunk. You thought you could hear screaming in the night, but it might have been you.*

*PS All accounts reconciled. Congratulations to the office crew at both the Bundy mine and the Paris Mine for keeping their accounts in such good order and dust free, more or less. It was a great pleasure to visit and attend the racing carnival as an honoured guest. I could have lived without the hangover, the flies and the lost days and nights. On the other hand, I'm a changed person for the experience. I changed everything, but still the red dust persists.*

***

Robbie had submitted the piece to Bentley a while ago. Robbie was pleased to hear Bentley liked it. Bentley didn't say why he liked it, and Robbie was too drunk at the Stalwart to ask. Robbie had dismissed the piece. It wasn't his best work, but then nothing ever was. However hard he tried and wished he could do something worthwhile—he never did. He never produced his best work. What was his best work? He couldn't say because he hadn't produced it yet. He wanted to thank Bentley. That seemed like the right thing to do, but before he could, Bentley had merged into the Stalwart's throng.

After finally locating the door out of the Stalwart, Robbie staggered into the dark alley dazed and in trouble. He recalled Bentley talking to him about the outback piece. He recalled Sophie's black T-shirt, or someone's black T-shirt. He could still feel the throb of the bass from the music in the Stalwart, or was that the throb in his head? Or the distant call of a billion cicadas, or the shadow of a stalking tarantula? Do tarantulas stalk? He had no memory of how he got into the alley. He didn't recognise where he was. He slumped against a wall and closed his eyes, and thought for a confusing second, he was in a dark donga out in the seductive bush.

He opened his eyes. He was still in the alley. It was dark and shadowy, and freezing. His head hurt, like a narrator's head would hurt in these circumstances. There was no one around. The weird thing was, there was no noise. He couldn't hear a thing— no traffic, no people, no cicadas, no throb. It was as though noise hadn't been invented. Robbie felt something cold and hard against the side of his head. He moved his head and tried to sit upright and realised his head had been wedged against a garbage bin. He looked at its grimy dark side and noticed its lid was at an unnatural angle for a garbage bin lid. It was attached by only one hinge. Unhinged, he thought. Question: how do you throw out a garbage bin? Garbage bins are as much a function of the second law of thermodynamics as anyone, or anything, and must at some point degrade and need disposing of. How do you throw out a garbage bin? How do you dispose of a person? These questions, lubricated by alcohol, were rolling around in his head and around the alley. He had no answers.

That night in the alley behind the Stalwart, something came to him through the fog. It crept up on him. It was too dark, and he couldn't make out what it was. Robbie saw it from across the lane. It moved slowly but headed straight toward him. It reached his leg and disappeared under him. His head spun with alcoholic nausea. He recalled the noise and heat of the pub. He'd been talking to some people from the office, so he must have kept drinking after Bentley had spoken to him. He drank a lot, a herculean amount. Gloria was making out with O'Brien, and he remembered this pissed him off. He felt she should have known what a fake O'Brien was, and the fact that she didn't, or didn't care, made him feel bad. She must have known O'Brien was an informant. Gloria was an option in his life. She was a friend and he had failed to act in her best interest when it came to O'Brien. He wanted to help. He wanted to be of some material help to someone sometime in his life. He wanted Sophie Fanshawe, but he didn't deserve her.

He remembered talking to someone at the bar who told him Sophie Fanshawe was living in Paris, he knew that, but he was sure he saw her during his drinking session. Perhaps not. He recalled hearing this before, or he just dreamt it. He had no idea where Sophie was or if she was still in Paris. He'd looked for her across the bar, but she wasn't there, so maybe she'd left. Robbie wanted to have a conversation with Sophie. Bentley kept standing next to him, not saying anything, just waiting. Had he asked Robbie a question? Robbie couldn't say for sure if Bentley had asked him something. Bentley was standing between Robbie and where Robbie thought Sophie would be if she were there, which she wasn't.

In the Stalwart, Robbie had lost his balance as the room started to rotate around him. Bentley had gone, but then he was back. Bentley grabbed Robbie and held him up. Robbie brushed Bentley away and lurched in the general direction of the exit. Outside in the dark alley, Robbie noticed a woman far in front of him. She sashayed, Robbie thought. No one sashays anymore. Robbie imagined it might have been Sophie Fanshawe sashaying down the street, oblivious to the dark figure following her. Robbie felt a compulsion to save her, but he was in no shape to save anyone, including himself. He felt his head wobble and crash against the garbage bin. He would have 'bumped' into Sophie if he had any feeling in his legs.

Robbie squinted and tried to focus on the alley. The walls were covered in graffiti, in the form of a gigantic eye. There was an intense reflection of bright light in the eye, but he couldn't make out what the source of the light was. In a final realisation, it occurred to him that from this moment on, he couldn't exist. If he closed his eyes, the cold felt warm and the silence sounded loud, and he understood he had lost everything, and he thought that was a good thing. And he thought that was a bad thing. He felt seedless and impotent, like a discarded garbage bin with a broken lid, that couldn't disappear, and sounded hollow when his head crashed into it. He felt light in spite of, or because of, the giddy feeling in his head. He looked at the gigantic mesmerising unblinking graffiti eye with its bright white light and felt as though he was disappearing. And he thought he might have crossed over to the other universe.

He hoped Sophie Fanshawe was there to meet him. He felt himself slip away as he hit the 'disappear' button in his head. In the glaring light and the eye on the opposite wall, he watched with his eyes closed and dreamt. At least he thought it was a dream. He hoped it was, but maybe it was one of his micro stories, sitting on his computer, silently in the dark.

*Robbie's eyes sprang open and focused on his genitals. Not moving a muscle, he gazed down his nose at the most alarming sight he could imagine. Covered in sweat, his naked, ripped body glistened. The sheets under him were saturated. The liquid heat hung in the air and dripped down the dirty off-white walls in his room and caused the Christmas tinsel to cling flaccidly to the wall. The overhead fan rotated limply, suffering from heat exhaustion. Staring at his privates, Robbie saw a large black mound of fur. None of it was his. Robbie watched paralysed with fear as a massive tarantula settled on his penis. It was easily twenty centimetres in spread. The tarantula, not the penis. It laid its long furry legs either side of Robbie's member. Robbie knew he couldn't move. He knew this tarantula, not this one specifically but the outback tarantula, the deadliest spider in the world, or at least in these parts, and at this moment it sat on his growing erection. The tarantula was known to be easily spooked, and Robbie knew that if his penis moved, the tarantula would rear up on its hindquarters, punch out its deadly fangs, impale itself into Robbie's lively member and death would be swift.*

*Robbie's breathing fell silent, every muscle held tight as a rock. Hairs on his body rose like reeds across a marsh, or bristles on a new hairbrush. One of the tarantula's furry legs was unwittingly stimulating the underside of Robbie's penis, the part of Robbie's penis that was the most sensitive. We say 'unwittingly' but do we know? The tarantula's demeanour was suspicious, in that a tarantula's demeanour is able to be determined as suspicious or otherwise. Robbie watched in horror as his penis responded. He tried to think of other things. Ice-cream! No! Rubbish bins! Twistor Theory—the next thinking after String Theory! Postmodernism? Oh, my God. Not even thinking about postmodernism worked. Nothing could halt Robbie's inevitable erection. Robbie was all-man, and his erection would not be denied. He moaned with pleasure. Robbie could feel the weight of the tarantula. But as heavy as it was, Robbie knew his erection could support the weight of his football boots, or a bowl of soup, if need be, so the tarantula's weight would represent no problem.*

*Robbie could see more of the menacing creature as the elevation of his erection* rose. *The tarantula slipped. Robbie felt it grip more firmly, locking its legs onto Robbie's shaft, but still rubbing with its leg. Did it know what it was doing? Robbie knew he couldn't stop what was happening. How could he halt his manliness? How could any man?*

*The tarantula slipped again, against the rising angle. Robbie could see the tarantula was agitated. Robbie feared what was going to happen. The higher his erection, the more precarious it would be for the tarantula. Robbie bit his tongue like he would a soup spoon handle, had one been handy. He needed to create pain to deflect from the stimulation. Otherwise, Robbie knew that when his penis reached maximum hardness and height, it would twitch. His penis reached maximum hardness and height. It twitched, like it always did. The tarantula arched back and took up its strike position. Robbie looked into the tarantula's black glistening eyes, round reflecting orbs, like an astronaut's facemask, or two astronauts standing close together. The tarantula stared back at Robbie. It pushed out the ends of its fangs with menacing intent. Poison glistened in small droplets on the tip of each fang. If those fangs penetrated the head of his penis and pumped in the deadly venom, Robbie would be dead within thirty seconds. But not before he suffered intense pain, so great, it would rival childbirth, as he understood it, or if not childbirth, a paper cut. Those can really hurt.*

*Robbie spotted his machete gleaming on the bedside table. So did the tarantula. Robbie looked back at the tarantula. The tarantula shifted its gaze from the machete back to Robbie, daring Robbie to make the move. Robbie hesitated, squeezed his eyes shut, and in one astonishing synchronised movement, as the tarantula's back rippled and its head pounced, sinking its fangs deep deep into Robbie's cock, Robbie grasped the machete and slashed it across the top of his body, millimetres above the top of his thighs. The tarantula saw the machete coming, but defiantly, did not relax its grip or withdraw its fangs. Robbie felt the searing pain as the blade, like a scythe slashing through washing machine foam, or a cereal crop, severed his penis at the base, sending his pride and joy together with his deadly bed mate flying across the room.*

*Robbie watched in blood-spouting agony as the tarantula retracted its fangs from the dismembered member. The tarantula looked up at Robbie with what could only be described as admiration. Then, with particular attention to grooming, it cleaned its fangs using its two hairy front legs. For clarity, the tarantula had the hairy legs, not Robbie. When it was done, the tarantula crawled off Robbie's detached penis. It crouched low, but before brushing its stiff hairs under the bottom of the door on its way out, it stopped and gave Robbie one last look of recognition, as though in salute to him, then disappeared under the door.*

After this dream or story, Robbie did not wake up in the alley.

# Harry Fanshawe

Flash fiction piece as submitted to Harry Fanshawe, Creative Writing Teacher.

*The universe: 'What's it like for you to be profoundly lonely?' It sounded like a research question, asked by the retired Professor Emeritus. Yes, an odd and ironic surname for an emeritus professor of postmodernism, but then again, perhaps not.*

*'Me? Profoundly lonely? I don't know. Much as it is for you, I guess.' Answered by no one in particular or no one special. 'Why would you consider me to be profoundly lonely? I'm married. I have children. I have a busy life and a career. I have hobbies. I have purpose.'*

*'Don't we all.'*

*'So how does that make me "profoundly" lonely?'*

*'In this universe, we're all profoundly lonely, in our own way. Don't you think?'*

*'Oh.'*

*'So, what's it like for you to be profoundly lonely?'*

Harry read this flash fiction piece and felt in sympathy with it. It did some work—lame work if he was to be honest. The piece borrowed too heavily from Leo Tolstoy, he thought. It was trying too hard. The piece was from one of his jilted—jilted in the sense that life jilts us all—mature-age students who wore a shiny red raincoat when it was sunny out. She had a smile that could be confused with nervousness or confidence. Harry wasn't sure which.

'He'd met her before at The Writers Circle. It seemed to Harry that she used her smile like a scalpel to dismember the world for its meaning. Judging by this piece she'd submitted for Harry's flash fiction assignment, she wasn't doing too much smiling or discovering much latent world meaning. But then neither was Harry and perhaps she had sensed that and had written a piece that would have resonance to the 'abandoned' Harry. Clever*ish*, if transparent, Harry considered. He didn't like the piece much. It was too contrived, and the insight was a little on the insipid side, and the sentiment probably better placed on the side of a breakfast cereal box or a desk calendar. It was too aware of itself. He appreciated the bookend and the effort. He would never say this to her, though, not at least in those words. He resolved always to be encouraging where possible to his students. He didn't have the energy to be blunt.

Harry allowed himself to wonder for a moment if she might be naked under the red raincoat. She had a dark freckle on her cheek, which fascinated him, and he liked her blonde hair, and something was going on behind those eyes. The way she looked at him and smiled, he thought, she knows what I'm thinking. He felt disappointed with himself and a little embarrassed, but also surprised. He hadn't had any thoughts like that about a female for a long time. Harry's mind wandered and he invented the following conversation.

*'You look like a Tommy to me, not a Harry,' she said rhetorically. 'If you don't mind me saying? I'd like to call you Tommy. Do you mind if I take my raincoat off? I have nothing on underneath. Do you know who I am?'*

She didn't say any of this, Harry imagined it all. Such thoughts signalled Harry might be on the road to recovery, up to a point. Nothing was certain. He did know who she was. She was a member of The Writers Circle—but he hadn't taken much notice of her there. He couldn't fathom if she had joined The Writers Circle before she joined his creative writing class, or the other way round.

In Harry's mind, all his creative writing students homogenised into the one type—female, early to mid-thirties, disillusioned, harried, looking to escape her life, and herself more precisely. Most were married with children and with worries. They all worried, including the ones without children. This described most women in the world, so not that insightful, he admitted to himself.

Most of his students were female, and the few males he had in his class were ambivalent and, as such, if included in the curve, distorted the profile. Plus, most of the males didn't write much, a bit like Harry in that regard. He saw his students individually on Fridays in his office, in half-hour slots. It took most of the day. They came to discuss their work. The rest of the week, he had no idea what he did.

***

It was Friday. The student sitting in front of him, his ten-thirty, was in her thirties, early thirties, perhaps late twenties and fitted his generic description of his students to the letter. He went with late twenties. Harry had lost the ability to guess ages. She was married or perhaps divorced or single, had two children who caused her to be tired beyond mere lack of sleep, or no children but was tired just the same. She wore precise makeup and had a job she hated or didn't care about, or loved. She wasn't the type to have nothing on underneath her red raincoat, at least that was Harry's take on her, not that he'd given it much thought. As it turns out, he'd given it *some* thought, and she *was* naked under her raincoat. He knew none of the names of his students. He considered this made him an unworthy teacher. Such forgetfulness conjured an aura of standoffishness, or intellect, or disassociation. He didn't mind which image he projected. He didn't care. Life. His life. Their lives. All life, in general, was a tiresome mystery to Harry. Perhaps she's twenty-eight, he thought. He looked at her face with intent for the first time and saw how beautiful she was. Not just superficially. Something pinged inside him. What was that? It was the first time he'd heard a ping for such a long time. He wondered if she heard it too or was it just in his head.

Harry had always liked a mystery. When he was a young boy, he and his sister would write stories for each other. His were always mysteries, whodunnits, whosaidits, whowroteits, whostoleits. Nowadays he found the mysteries of life overwhelming. He wanted answers. He was sick of life being allowed to get away with its goddamn mysteries. Someone needed to hold life to account, make it answer for itself. Explain the inexplicable, the inscrutable—especially the fucking inscrutable. Life had to stop toying with its people, stop posing questions and never providing answers. Harry wanted to write a novel that asked questions and provided answers, but none of his work came out that way, because he had no answers and life knew that.

His creative writing students were also looking for answers, or, as some of them pleaded with too much earnestness, truth. They weren't looking for universal truth, as much as they claimed they were. They were much less ambitious than that. They were looking for truth in their lives, their own truth or any truth that would help them get through their days. Their fiction was in service to this quest. Harry was tired of reading and marking up, what, in most cases, amounted to autobiographical, thinly disguised fictional accounts of themselves hoping for a better life, or a different life. As if achieving anything resembling a different life would be any better, or they would be any happier, or more satisfied. They'd still be themselves, writing transparent, self-deluded work. 'Wherever you go, there you are,' as Austin from The Writers Circle would say. Harry looked at the woman in front of him. She was adjusting her bra strap. So, not naked under her raincoat, he thought. It might not be a bra strap, and anyway, if it was, she was naked under that.

'I read your flash fiction piece. It's okay.' He emphasised the word 'okay' by way of encouragement.

'Oh, only okay?'

'Okay is good. It's not bad. Good writing is rewriting. Try it again from the perspective of the implied author. She's not developed. I can't hear her. She's between the spaces. Sometimes that's where you'll find your voice, where you'll find what it is you're trying to say, which may not be what you think you were trying to say. Writing is often more of a discovery for the writer than it is for the reader. If you get it right, you'll be in danger. Try reading your own subtext.' This was Harry channelling his sister Sophie.

Her perfume lingered when she left. It made a difference to his office. He felt that ping again. What the hell was that? Double ping.

Out of sheer exhaustion and indifference, he set his students the same writing exercise he had been exposed to at The Writers Circle. He left the Circle because his sister was the only one who wrote anything worth listening to, and he didn't need to go out on hot nights to hear his sister's work.

Harry repeated to his class of students what the convenor of The Writers Circle had said to the Circle. Harry paraphrased and added his own bits. 'The title of your story is "What will happen to you?" If you prefer, start with Dunleavy de Boston's character, Austin Quinn, or if you like, pick Miss Jean Brodie or Anna Karenina, or create your own protagonist, if you're scared enough. You can choose any other literary character if you prefer or write whatever you want. Delete the character or replace him/her once you have reached a plot point or whenever it feels right. You can choose a short story or flash fiction format. Deadline is one week. Good luck.' Harry felt he had it covered with this instruction.

This was pure laziness on Harry's behalf. He couldn't be bothered to think of anything else. When he'd tackled this exercise himself, he got nowhere. Sophie, on the other hand, got her first novel out of it, *sans* Austin Quinn. She had replaced him in her narrative as she was meant to. She replaced him with a female protagonist, and it worked fine. Harry knew there was not as much difference between literary men and literary women as people like to suppose. Sophie started her second novel the same way, but this time it wasn't working. This time she lost Austin Quinn before she'd reached anything like a plot point. She went to Paris to finish her second novel in fear that her publisher might dump her. Harry knew she was in trouble with it. He could hear it in her voice on the phone. The international delay provided the space between her words that told the whole story. Harry felt sorry for her, but he couldn't help. Going to Paris might well have been her own plot point.

Sitting in his office, Harry knew what he had to do. And he was resolved to do it. The idea had been growing for a long time, at a slow evolutionary pace, but he'd ignored it, and he thought he had the perfect excuse to ignore it. Beverly was his perfect excuse. Beverly's death was his death, and the perfect pretext for Harry to do nothing, and he had achieved wads of nothing. But he knew his life, such as it was or had become, had to start moving. And that's what he had to do, start, or think about starting at least.

Beverly had been gone for well over three years, a long time to hold onto his grief. His grief felt like he was shackled to a grand piano, he told Sophie. It played beautiful music, but it was tough to lug around. It wouldn't go upstairs or through doors, and when he was lying in his bed at night trying to encourage an erection, the piano sat heavily outside his door, waiting. His grief was getting him nowhere, he'd started to see it that way. He knew it would be difficult to give up his grief—his grief had become part of him. The whole business, to be honest, scared him. If he thought about it, yes, he felt physically sick with a weakness in his muscles. He felt light-headed with sadness, and he had detected a sore nose, but that turned out to be a pimple in the making and not related. He knew in his heart he could no longer go on the way he was. How was he? He was alone. Worse still, he was lonely. He ate alone. He slept alone. He travelled to work alone. Most people do, so that wasn't of such import. He didn't go on holidays, apart from the forced holiday to Frankfurt that one time, because he would have to do it alone, and no one wanted to share holidays with no one. He didn't need selfies with no one else in the shot. Even when he was with his sister, who he adored and respected, he was still nonetheless alone—as much as she loved her brother and included him in her life. But that was the problem. It was her life not his, and when being included in someone else's life, it confirms your loneliness rather than extinguishing it. It says, 'You don't have much of a life of your own, so I'm inviting you into my life, so at least you will have a proxy, or worse, a borrowed life, but at least a life, however vicarious—by the way, welcome to my loneliness.'

People are kind, Harry believed. They invite you out, otherwise you would be sitting at home with no thoughts but those of how alone you are, and you are. When Harry was at the Stalwart pub with Elbow, he basked in the light of his best friend's unequivocal friendship, but basking wasn't living. Harry had to find someone to love. He couldn't replace Beverly, but he had to find a reason to bother continuing. He knew Beverly wouldn't want him to vegetate his life away.

Harry knew that finding someone to love, while difficult, would be the easy part. The hard part would be finding someone to love him. Not that there was anything wrong with him. He wasn't ugly, nor obnoxious, and not poor, but to be clear, not rich, more just right. Or, if truth be known, not just right—to be 'just right' would imply some ideal or degree of perfection, if 'perfection' can be considered in degrees, and wasn't absolute, as he suspected it was.

In any description of himself, Harry had to accept the word 'not' preceded the element he was describing. Not perfect, pretty much summed him up. On his more enlightened occasions, however, not that there were many of those, he considered with some confidence, that while he wasn't perfect, he was also not unpalatable. Sophie thought this also, but she was biased, and Elbow thought this too, not that he ever said so—too touchy-feely for Elbow. Elbow called him Goldilocks, the 'just right' man, like he was some kind of comic superhero, and his superpower was that he never caused anyone offence. Trouble with this though, was that when the world is in trouble, no one yells out for someone who never causes offence to save things. The whole comic book hero element summed up Elbow's sense of humour and his bent for nursery rhymes and comic book superheroes.

Harry prided himself with having a good imagination, and he lived a sober life, except for the times he spent with Elbow at the pub, and the other times when a glass or two of Shiraz found itself in his hand. All in all, he assumed he was okay, but how could he know? He thought some might say he was better than okay, and on occasions, he had wit and not just a little brilliance. Beverly thought so. And that was a point not to be dismissed. Beverly loved him. She adored him. If Beverly loved him, then, by definition, he had to be loveable on some level, he thought. He had to be worthy. Beverly was perfection, and while he'd known he was boxing above his weight, according to Elbow, he nonetheless held Beverly's love and adoration. So he must be just alright then. He would call himself 'Just Alrightman'. He opened a blank page on his computer and typed the following for his amusement, and while he had it in his head.

*A crowd gathered, and in unison yelled out, 'Quick, help, we need Just Alrightman to save us from this situation that is not quite right. We need Just Alrightman, who will save the day, or night, in the event it happened to be night-time when the not-quite-right trouble visited. Just Alrightman, who will save us by not offending anyone too much.' The crowd all yelled together but started to get out of sync by the end, when their voices tapered off a bit as you would expect. But they nonetheless knew they needed Just Alrightman— that was a given. Harry would swoop in—not that he'd perfected his swoop, but a swoop can't be that hard to perfect—and save the day, or night, with his superpowers of being just alright, and his cunning ability to basically not offend anyone. Swoop.*

He thought he could send it to Elbow, who might get a kick out of it, he thought. But then maybe not.

Harry lived in a world where it seemed everyone was trying to find someone to love them. He felt the universal odds stacked against him. He thought, and often discussed this with Elbow at the pub or on their week-end run, that universal odds were stacked against everyone. It was a law of the universe and, as such, inviolable. Harry recalled a conversation he'd had with Elbow last Friday night at the Stalwart. They were both drunk at the time. It went like this, more or less.

'These are the same universal odds that work against everyone when doing ordinary stuff in life, like putting the fitted sheet on the bed. It will always be the wrong way around.' Harry was regaling Elbow, who was leaning on his elbow against the bar at the Stalwart. 'Like plugging a phone into a charger—the plug end thingo will always be the wrong way round, and so on. Or when you reach a T-section looking for a particular place. Whichever turn you take, it will be the wrong way. I've given this a lot of thought.'

'Imagine that,' Elbow said.

'Yeah, I call it the "wrong way" law.'

'Clever.' Elbow said sarcastically.

'This law survives all attempts to disprove it, and so if the universal odds can't let you off with mundane stuff, like why does any dropped coin always end up under the sofa, or the fridge, and not just under it, but at the back and in the middle under it? Even if there's no fridge or sofa in sight, can't it once land in the middle of the room, not under anything?'

'Another drink, Goldilocks?' Elbow asked, trying to curb Harry's speech.

'This law prevails, it triumphs, it condescends, it laughs. And, by definition, if it does this with the unimportant stuff, then what chance is there with the important stuff? Like finding a mate for life?'

Elbow signalled to the barman for two more beers.

'The difficult part,' Harry continued, 'the part that borders on impossible and falls into the category of miracle, is not only finding someone to love, and finding someone to love me, but finding these two things in the same person, and then finding that person.' Harry wasn't sure he believed in the notion that everyone has one perfect mate in the world somewhere. Harry's problem was if this were true, even partially true, then he was doomed to failure, as, by any measure, Harry had already had his perfect mate. He'd had Beverly. But she was gone. And in her absence grew his loneliness and, annoyingly, a pimple on his nose.

'So what to do then?' Elbow asked. 'Give up?'

'I've pretty much tried that over the past while, and all that achieved was nothing.'

'Beverly wouldn't sanction that if she could be consulted. She would want you to get on with your life,' Elbow said, slurping the froth off his beer, ending up with froth on his top lip.

Harry knew this was true. He was sure she would want him to find another mate. If she were around, she would help select the perfect partner for him. But then he wouldn't need her help for that, if she was still around.

\*\*\*

Earlier that day in his office, Harry was jolted out of his snooze by his ring-ing phone.

'What are you up to?' Elbow clearly with some downtime at his disposal.

'Reading flash fiction.'

'Sounds riveting,' Elbow said. 'I was wondering, shall we go to the Stalwart tonight for a sherbet?'

'I don't want to go there. It's too loud and desperate.'

'Yeah, and your point is?' Elbow asked.

'I've got another plan.'

'Okay, I'm up for a plan. You have some other hot-tottie stacked place in mind?'

'I'm not sure women are still referred to as "tottie", hot or otherwise. Anyway, that's not the plan.'

'I somehow didn't think it would be.'

'This plan is much bigger than relying on the haphazard business of going to any pub or bar, stalking innocent women with our beer-breath, and won-dering at the end of the night why we didn't get anywhere. No, I have an actual plan, one that has a much better chance of success. It has structure, wisdom, and if I might be so bold, it has just a bit of elegance to it.'

'Oh yeah? Elegance? I can't wait to hear this.'

'It's to do with the ad I've been threatening, you know, to find a woman.'

'Oh, that again. An ad to find a mate? No one's thought to do that,' Elbow said sarcastically.

'I realise it isn't new but running it in the *National Financial Review* is new.'

'Terrific, so you'll end up with an accountant. That sounds exciting.'

'That's a possibility, but it's not only accountants who read the *National Financial Review*. And anyway, there's no law stating accountants can't be interesting.'

'Sure. Who else?'

'Who else what?'

'Who else reads the *National Financial Review*?'

'I don't know. Doctors, nurses, architects, office workers. Regular people are interested in finance, you know, not just accountants.'

'The Stalwart's starting to look like a compelling option if you ask me.'

'Look, I'm not just advertising for a mate. I'm advertising for a travelling companion, or I may not mention the travel idea, see how it goes first.'

'Really?'

'Yes. You're always going on about how I should take a holiday. I'm taking your advice.'

'Yes, I meant with me to some place full of single hot tottie women of the gorgeous female persuasion.'

'I couldn't think of anything worse than some hedonistic pick-up resort.'

'When are you doing this then?'

'I've done it.'

'Really, any responses?'

'No.'

'Okay, the Stalwart it is?'

'I can't go to the Stalwart.'

'This ad hasn't managed to attract Miss Accountant Beauty Queen?'

'Not yet, but I live in hope. And she doesn't have to be a beauty queen.'

'No risk of that. Beauty queens are not known for their patronage of the financial papers, I wouldn't have thought.'

'I'm only looking for a companion. Let's keep the ambition modest.'

'Modest is the word.'

'Correct.'

'See you at the Stalwart later?'

'Okay.'

Harry sat alone in the dusty silence of his choked office and wondered if his life would have been better if his name had been Tommy. If his first name was to be Tommy, what would his last name be? He could choose whatever he wanted, but could he choose to be whomever he wanted? He somehow doubted it.

# Robbie Carton

At first it was a distant sound. Robbie listened. If it were possible to listen harder, he would have. He kept his eyes closed, it seemed safest, and he felt it aided his listening—the sound/noise was still distant and indistinct. The noise was muffled, alien, but somehow reassuring. That didn't make any sense. Robbie wasn't sure he was listening to it at first, but he could hear it. It was in his head maybe. He didn't know. It was a hum, he thought, or perhaps it was more a buzz. Buzz or hum? He loved language. If he was an academic, in particular an etymologist, he'd do a thesis on the difference and evolution of the words 'buzz' and 'hum'. He fell asleep.

\*\*\*

He was in bed, but it wasn't his bed. It was narrower. Still with his eyes closed, several questions lined up in a queue. Was he still in Paris? Was he in his donga at one of the mines? Was he home? Was he in another universe? The sheets were tight, deliberate and smelt white. Definitely not the out-back, no rough blanket. By way of a policy, he decided to keep his eyes shut. He had a suspicion he'd had his eyes closed for a long time. How long? He couldn't say for sure, but long. He was more or less sure of that.

He didn't want to open his eyes because then he might find there were more unanswered questions. He might discover where he was, and he might not want to be where he was. He was sure his eyes would hurt if he did open them. Bright light threatened through his veiny eyelids. He wondered if his penis was still attached. His timing with his life, and with everyone else in his life, was out of whack. It hurt his brain, trying to get it straight. He had an erection, so the penis question was answered. He tried to smell the white again, but white had no smell.

He felt light and hungry. Perhaps he'd lost weight. He realised his fists were clenched. He relaxed them. He mentally scanned his body. When he got to the side of his head, he realised he had something fixed to it, something tight, perhaps a bandage. It throbbed. His head, not the bandage. Apart from the throb, his body was pain free, so that was encouraging, but the buzz he could hear, was that significant? He didn't feel like moving, which was good because the tight sheets had hold of him and being held had a comforting element to it. He felt safe. There was a vague smell of antiseptic in the air. Can a smell be vague? he wondered. A part of his brain argued he should stay put. Don't move. Wait. 'Keep your eyes closed at all cost', his other-self said. Other-self was untrustworthy. Other-self was self-serving and tricky. Other-self was unreliable. Other-self was vocal and demanding. Other-self exploited Robbie's fragility. Other-self endorsed using a new name, a new persona. Robbie had to fight to resist other-self from winning. Robbie had to hold firm. It was difficult, and it took concentration, which he wasn't sure he had. Often when he was drunk, Robbie wondered if he might ever be happy, or happier, and if he was to reach the level of 'happier', might he achieve something. He thought it unlikely. 'Happy' seemed like a stupid word. He could sense other-self wandering around inside his brain, looking to make trouble for sure. Looking for a weak spot to dig into. Other-self was ordering in, probably pizza with pineapple—pineapple on pizza, typical. Other-self would make a mess, leaving pizza boxes lying around in Robbie's head.

Robbie thought, if he couldn't find a way to live a full and valuable life, even a happy life, and not happy all the time but some of the time, then who would want him as Robbie Carton? Would Sophie want him as Robbie Carton, or would she be disappointed in him? He felt all the people he knew were disappointed in him. It was true enough, Robbie Carton was squandering himself. The distant hum or buzz either subsided or he stopped hearing it. He drifted off. He drifted off, feeling distraught and hungry for a pizza. A single tear formed in both his closed eyes, but he was asleep. Other-self fell silent and slept surrounded by his accumulated rubbish including a few missed bits of pineapple and a few bent empty beer cans.

***

The hum or buzz was still there, but it seemed harmless. It was background noise. Robbie could hear actual voices, but he couldn't make out what was being said, he didn't recognise any of the voices, and it felt exhausting trying to decipher what anyone might be saying. He heard someone snoring. It was nearby, maybe in the room with him. He heard a word, no two words, *Merde, Merde*. Perhaps he didn't hear them. Perhaps it was other-self again, in his head. Then *Rue Bonaparte* flashed in his mind on a street sign. He was on the street, the sun was shining, but there was a chill in the wind. He was cold. He saw many people on the street. Beautiful women everywhere, *Belles femmes partout*. He saw a *vendeur des fleurs*. He thought to buy some roses, and this made him think of a woman. He saw her fall, and he wanted to reach out to grab her, but he couldn't move. He couldn't see her face. He saw a beauty mark, *marque de beauté*, on her cheek, but not a real one. Strange, he thought. He couldn't make her out. He felt disappointed, and still cold. He held his hand out to her. His last thought was Sophie Fanshawe. Was it her he was reaching out to? Where was he? He blacked out.

Some indeterminate time later, his eyes still closed. Okay, he felt peculiar, not himself, but not his other-self, just not himself, not Robbie Carton. Nothing made much sense. He might consider never opening his eyes again. His other senses were heightened. He felt okay in a physical sense, but light. His mouth tasted of stale something, sawdust perhaps. He wasn't sure sawdust went stale, or, to be more precise, what stale sawdust tasted like, or even what fresh sawdust tasted like, for that matter. Ah, his brain had started to act normal, normal for him. His thoughts were colliding and achieving little but further confusion. He was Robbie Carton. He knew that for sure now. He didn't need to look in a mirror to realise that, so he kept his eyes shut. Disappointment lingered.

The snoring continued. He'd located it. It was to his right, no left. It stopped. He heard someone walk to his bed. He heard the squeak of her shoes. He assumed it was a female from the perfume. She was a sweet-smelling female with purpose. He heard some liquid poured into a glass. Robbie felt a warm hand on his forehead. She was feeling for his temperature, he assumed. She un-smoothed his hair with her fingers then left. He heard the squeak of her shoes on the linoleum floor fade, Doppler-like, as she left the room. The Doppler effect. His mouth repeated the words 'Doppler effect', then in French, '*effet Doppler*'. He held tight in his left hand a yellow briefcase, *mallete jaune*. As far as he was aware, he didn't own a yellow briefcase, but it seemed familiar, and he had no idea why he was using French phrasing. Ordinarily, he couldn't speak a word of French.

*Am I dead? Is this death?*

He heard this asked, but not audibly, just in his head. He didn't think he was dead. There was no *Inferno*. He was aware he had a half-hearted erection, *une érection à demi sincere*, under the stiff sheets and he couldn't imagine you would have an erection if you were dead, *demi sincere* or not. He thought the French were mad—why would *une érection* take the feminine article? His *érection* led him to believe it was morning, and he had woken from his sleep. He often woke with half-hearted erections, but in his own bed, not someone else's. On the rare occasion when he might have woken up in someone else's bed, or in his bed with someone else, his erection was anything but half-hearted. The snoring started up again and put an end to his erection event, for which he was grateful. He didn't want to embarrass himself, or anyone else for that matter, and he didn't know who the owner of the snore was. It sounded male, and this made it all the more urgent to quell his morning erection. The snore was final proof he wasn't dead. Who goes to heaven or hell and expects to hear snoring? He didn't believe in heaven, or hell either. He found them to be useful constructs, though. Still, he was sure the chances you would hear snoring after you're dead were unlikely. The death event seemed way too large to have snoring associated with it. So not dead then. Let's go with that. He wondered where the woman was who un-smoothed his hair. He imagined her standing in her apartment looking out at the world in which she lived. He drifted off again. She was ironing at her window.

When his consciousness next returned, he felt an intermittent breeze waft over his face. It reminded him of summer and grapevines. He could hear children's voices outside. He thought he might be near a school. He had no idea how long he'd been asleep.

There was no snoring or squeaky shoes this time. There was perfume, but not the same as before. He thought he recognised it. He started to worry about what had happened to him. The last thing he remembered was the cold dark lane and being slumped against a damaged garbage bin. He remembered something about a tarantula, but that was confused with a turning ceiling fan, and being in a small room. It had been hot then. He wasn't hot now. Then nothing. Before that, he remembered Bentley. He heard Bentley speak to him. He thought he could remember Bentley had said, 'Are you okay, Robbie?' A good question, he thought. If only he knew the answer.

'Are you okay, Robbie?' Robbie recognised Bentley's voice. 'Robbie? Are you awake? Are you okay?'

Robbie felt compelled to ease his eyes open. Opening his eyes caused him to feel disappointed because he knew once he opened his eyes, he would exist, and everything would start again. He felt the pain of the light and the throb at the side of his head. He blinked and moved his hand to shade his eyes. He looked in the direction of Bentley's voice. He could barely make out Bentley's shape. He heard the squeaking shoes, but far off down a corridor, not near him. The hum was still there but harder to hear. He couldn't hear a buzz. The buzz had forsaken the hum, the buzz had migrated to a beehive. He felt a hand on his forehead. After a few seconds, his eyes adjusted to the light, and he could make out this beautiful woman to his left with her hand on his forehead, smoothing his hair. He smelt her perfume and fell in love with her and started thinking maybe he *was* in heaven. He felt an over-whelming sense of safety and comfort. He was glad Bentley was there. They couldn't both be dead, he thought, so not in heaven.

'Robbie, you remember Sabrina?'

'Hi Robbie, we met at the wedding, do you remember?' Robbie looked up and focused on her phaser, planet exploding, Hadron Super Collider-initiating smile. He was glad to see her. She stopped smoothing his hair. He thought he might cry but he forced himself not to. He felt the tears gather in his eyes. He was embarrassed on so many levels. He wished he was someplace else, maybe on a beach somewhere, next to crystal-clear water, or any place but here, wherever 'here' was. Bentley was right about Robbie when he once said, 'Carton, you haven't a clue.' Robbie didn't have a clue.

Bentley repeated his question, 'Robbie, you do remember my wife Sabrina, don't you? You met at Flanagan's wedding, remember?'

'Sure...yes.' Robbie's voice crackled. He had no idea how long it had been since he'd used it.

'Can I get you some water?' Sabrina asked him with a voice that made honey seem abrasive.

She picked up the glass of water next to him and held her hand at the back of his head to help him sip from the glass. Robbie took several sips. He felt exhausted. He hadn't realised how thirsty he was.

'How you feelin', Robbie?' Bentley asked. 'You had us a bit worried for a while.'

'What happened to me?' Robbie scratched out his question without a lot of conviction.

'We can't tell you,' Bentley said. 'The doctor wants you to remember yourself if you can. Besides, we don't know. The last time I saw you was in the Stalwart. You were pretty well gone. That was five days ago.'

'Don't worry, Robbie,' Sabrina said. 'You're fine, just a little bump on your head. We want to have you around for dinner as soon as you get out of the hospital and you're feeling better. Would you like that?' Sabrina asked.

'Yes...yes, thank you,' Robbie croaked out, sounding, and feeling like a little boy. At least he now knew where he was. 'I think I'm a bit tired.' He could feel the side of his head pull at the bandage, if that was what it was. It didn't cause him any pain though, apart from the throb. He had a nuclear headache.

'Of course, Robbie, you need to rest. We'll go and let you get some sleep.' Sabrina touched Robbie's shoulder and smiled an efficacious smile at him. 'Efficacious?' A smile that could cure leprosy, let's just say that. Bentley was one lucky fucker. Robbie's other self was working as per usual. Robbie smiled at Sabrina. She could get a smile out of a rock. Other-self went silent in the presence of Sabrina.

'Robbie, we're so sorry you've been through this.' Sabrina bent over and kissed Robbie on his forehead. It might be the first time in his adult life he had felt loved.

'Yeah, you get some rest,' Bentley said. 'We're expecting you back in the office as soon as you're ready. There's no one there who can make my life as difficult as you can. I'm losing my will to live.' Bentley smiled, as though his little joke might not be as obviously a joke as he wanted it to be. Robbie smiled back as a function of reassurance. 'And don't worry about your trip to the mines this month. I've sent O'Brien. He's been nagging about wanting to go. So he can do it this time. See how he goes, eh? He might not find he has the stomach for it.' Bentley chuckled.

Bentley spoke with no malice in his voice, but Robbie felt a niggle of discomfort. He didn't want O'Brien getting the mines. O'Brien wouldn't understand the people there, and they wouldn't trust him. O'Brien couldn't be trusted, and the people out there could see right into your heart in an instant. They'd pick O'Brien for a phoney. This got Robbie thinking. He wondered if they also knew how much of a phoney he was. He felt weak.

Sabrina said goodbye and signalled to Bentley she would meet him outside, or downstairs, or at the car. Robbie got the gist. She left. Robbie started to drift off but not without panicking about his semi-erection and whether

Sabrina had seen the bump under the sheets. Holy crap, he thought. Bentley remained and leaned over to Robbie.

'You said some weird stuff while you were out of it.'

Robbie looked at Bentley. Robbie understood what it was like to be a startled rabbit caught in headlights.

'Yeah, French words. I didn't know you could speak French,' Bentley said.

'I can't, as far as I know.'

'Well, you were speaking French.'

'What did I say?'

'No idea,' Bentley said with little inflection. 'No idea at all. But Sab speaks fluent French, and Mandarin, German, and Italian, and she can read and recite Latin too. She interpreted.'

'Oh, okay but...'

'Some weird stuff, about some street sign in Paris, we assume, Rue de something, and beautiful women. That sounded like you. Something about a yellow briefcase, and a flower seller, we think, something about a flower seller. Then you were talking about some character called Doppler, and something else about a beauty mark, like it was false or something. Very odd. A hangover from your Paris trip, I guess. Your trip to Paris the French capital, not Paris the mine out in the middle of nowhere, I presume.'

'Did I mention anything about a garbage bin?'

'No, not that I recall.'

'Okay...anything else?'

'Something about a limp erection? Bizarre.'

'Christ! Really? I hope I didn't embarrass Sabrina. I...'

'No, she's fine. I've told her about you. I show her your emails. She gets it.' Bentley said this not in a nasty way, as Robbie might have expected but in a reassuring way, and Bentley saying that made Robbie feel good, as though he and Bentley had a relationship different from the public one in the office, different from the one Robbie thought he had with Bentley. But still, Robbie felt humiliated to have said such things in Sabrina's presence, even if he had said them in his best French.

He felt exhausted again and closed his eyes. Robbie drifted off. He saw Sophie standing in a grove of mallee trees in the outback drinking from a cup. She had a red kerchief around her neck and nothing in her eyes. She started fading away. Robbie wanted to go to her, but his legs wouldn't move. A breeze carried the waft of warm sunshine across his face.

When he woke, he could smell perfume again. He hoped it would be Sabrina, but he knew it wasn't. It was different perfume, still nice, still reassuring, but not the same as Sabrina's. He recognised this perfume. It was Gloria's. He kept his eyes closed.

\*\*\*

Robbie had a flash memory of Paris. He strained to remember when, and as much of the trip as he could, but it all seemed so blurry. He decided it was important to try to remember.

*Robbie Goes to Paris*

That's how Robbie conjured his trip, like a chapter out of a book. Not a chapter, just a section of a chapter. *Robbie Goes to Paris*. When he thought of it, he thought of it in italics, like it was formatted in a children's book where the main character does things in each new chapter. *Robbie eats steak and mashed potatoes. Robbie hits his head on a garbage bin and knocks himself out. Robbie is lost somewhere. Robbie hasn't a fucking clue. Robbie tries out his small talk. Robbie has a full bladder. Robbie loses his penis. Robbie is in love. Robbie disappears.* That sort of thing. Not that Robbie thought his life and its various events warranted chapters in a book—subheadings at a stretch but not whole chapters. But thinking of it this way seemed to assist his memory.

Robbie recalled Bentley had sent him an email, just after he had returned from his last outback audit.

*Carton*

*You're going to Paris. You leave tomorrow on the five o'clock flight on Qantas. Economy seat. You'll attend an international conference (five days) in my place. Further details to follow. Start packing. I'll need a comprehensive report on your return, write it on the flight back. Don't get pissed and miss the conference. I'm counting on you. Find your passport. Did I mention not to get pissed?*

*Bon voyage*

*PS Apologies for the short notice but you're the only one I can count on. Gloria will be running the department.*

*B.*

Bentley wasn't at his desk when Robbie received the email, so Robbie couldn't ask any questions. Like, why wasn't Bentley going? What's the conference about, and where was he staying and where was his passport, and endless questions, none of which could be answered because Bentley was nowhere to be found. Prime among the questions was, why did Bentley choose Robbie? Why wouldn't he send someone else, anyone else? And since when did Bentley feel he could count on Robbie Carton, the office anarchist and resident idiot? Robbie liked the thought that Bentley thought he could count on him, but then he wasn't so confident it was such a good idea. Robbie felt he wouldn't want to let Bentley down, but then he thought he was bound to fuck up somehow and this made him feel distressed.

When Robbie had come to work the next day, after having spent most of the night searching for his passport and packing, there was a thin yellow case on his desk with the conference details inside. Bentley was still absent, and enquiries with Gloria revealed Bentley was taking personal time. But what for? No one knew. Gloria knew he was out of the office for an indefinite period, and she was in charge in his absence, being his second-in-charge. This was un-Bentley-like, and a buzz or a hum went around the floor. It was difficult to separate buzzes from hums, but universes were in jeopardy, Robbie knew that much. Robbie worried about Sabrina. He worried if she was okay. For Bentley to be absent would mean something alarming and potentially catastrophic must have occurred. Gloria agreed but had no insight and was herself concerned. Robbie hovered near Gloria's desk. Gloria kept working.

'Bentley would give up breathing before he'd miss a day in the office.'

Gloria nodded and refocused on her work, as though she had to work faster and harder to cover the chasm created by Bentley's absence. Was Bentley's absence larger than his presence? Robbie observed Gloria frowning more than usual. She wouldn't want to let Bentley down either. Robbie returned to his desk. He had a lot to finish if he was going to be away for a week, and he needed to be as efficient as he could to assist Gloria. He felt a little exhilarated by the tasks in front of him. He wanted to call Bentley to see if he and Sabrina were okay, but then he realised he didn't have Bentley's mobile.

Maybe Gloria should do that on behalf of the department. He wasn't sure. He opened an email to Bentley but didn't write anything, so there wasn't a lot of point in sending it—so he didn't. He got back to work. He had about six hours before his flight and at least ten or more hours of work to get done. Otherwise, Gloria would be left with it. He got the work done because he got on with it and didn't waste time sending emails to Bentley, or just generally wasting time writing stuff.

His time in Paris was pretty much uneventful, as far as Robbie could remember. He was jetlagged the whole time he was there. He picked up food poisoning on the flight over and was vomiting up unrecognisable chunks for the first twenty-four hours. Jetlagged and sick, he attended the conference about international regulations on tax declarations in various jurisdictions, a guaranteed cure for insomnia. He took notes for the report Bentley wanted. He attended all the sessions, including the ones in French. His food poisoning caused him to throw up several times the first day in the bathroom near the conference room, but he tried to time this for the breaks. While leaning into the toilet bowl waiting for the next wave of vomit to burst out of him, he thought about Sophie Fanshawe. She was in Paris somewhere. On the way to and from the conference centre, he looked for Sophie but never saw her. He had no way of contacting her. It registered with him that for some time he hadn't seen Sophie at the Stalwart, but he assumed he'd just missed her, or she'd changed shifts, or he was too drunk to notice anything, much less keep dates and days in some order. He couldn't do that when he was sober. And he was sure he knew she'd gone to Paris, or was going, and yet he somehow hadn't married this with her absence until now. There were times when Robbie annoyed himself and let himself down. Too many times. He vomited again and felt the resulting euphoria post-vomit, until the next wave arrived. He had an itchy foot, but he was too sick to take his shoe off to scratch the itch. There was always something, never nothing. During another lull in the vomiting waves, he thought this could be on his headstone—*Always something, never nothing.*

After he stopped vomiting, he loved the smell of Paris. It smelt of coffee, patisseries, and diesel. He felt he was in a French film, with French being spoken everywhere but none of it making any sense to him. He'd recovered from the food poisoning, but he hadn't recovered from the jet lag, which prevented him from getting any sleep during the five days he was there. He found himself walking the streets of Paris at three in the morning. He looked for Sophie during his nocturnal wanderings. As he passed apartment buildings along *Rue Jacob*, he wondered if she might be sleeping in one of them. He wondered what she might be dreaming and what her hair looked like while she slept. He imagined slipping into her bed and touching her between her thighs while she slept, waking her like she was his 'Sleeping Beauty' and he, her 'Prince Charming'. When he returned to his hotel, he found he'd trodden in a lot of dog shit. Always something, never nothing.

After the conference each day, Robbie drank an enormous amount of wine from a small boutique wine shop not far from his hotel on the Left Bank, just off *Rue Jacob*. *La Dernière Goutte* specialised in small to medium-sized producers from Burgundy. He met an efficient woman there. Her name was Robyn, which seemed an unlikely name for a French woman. She treated him with impatience but did speak English and sold him a lot of wine. Robbie took the wine back to his tiny hotel room and drank himself into his jet lag, or out of his food poisoning, or into letting Bentley down by getting pissed. Bentley had arranged for him to stay at *Hôtel des Deux Continents* on *Rue Jacob*, a twenty-minute walk to the conference. His room was the size of the bed, plus about ten centimetres on either side. Robbie could step from the corridor onto his bed without touching the floor. The door only half-opened and stopped when it hit the end of the bed. There was a bathroom barely big enough for his toothbrush. The elevator was the same size as an upright coffin, and he had to send his one piece of luggage up, then walk up the stairs to get it. The hotel served pastries and croissants at breakfast with raspberry confiture. He scraped large dollops out of the pots it came in and plopped it on his croissant. It glistened and tasted sweet and lumpy with fruit. The coffee was the best coffee he'd ever had, and he needed it every morning to offset his hangover/jet lag and confused state. Bentley had told him not to get pissed, but he was jet-lagged, so he thought the drinking might offset his jet lag. It didn't. He wished he'd tried to find out where Sophie was in Paris, but he hadn't had time before he left, or he forgot about it. He wouldn't have tried to find her anyway.

On the last evening of the conference, at the official dinner, he was seated next to a woman from Indiana, who was born in the Hillcrest Baptist Medical Centre, in Waco, Texas, as she was at pains to explain. She was married with two children. Her husband was an oil rig worker. She touched Robbie's leg when she spoke to him. She touched him and talked to him with relentless American enthusiasm. He didn't mind. He let the conversation with her broad American accent flow over him like a bubbling black liquid. It wasn't bubbling but he couldn't resist the alliteration. He drank as much of the wine on the table as he could get hold of and looked down the front of her blouse at her bouncing breasts. To Robbie it seemed her breasts could also be described as enthusiastic, along with her conversation and personality and leg touching. He wondered if she would allow him to touch her leg, like she was doing to him. He felt a puppy-like affection for her and wanted to nuzzle his face between her breasts. He drank more wine.

By the end of the night, he was close to unconscious. The woman had turned to the person on her other side and was regaling him with her life story. Robbie didn't know if she tired of him or was evangelistic with her need tell people about her life. He couldn't see down her blouse anymore. He looked at her back and had an overwhelming desire to touch her. He placed his hand on her skin and leant over and put his cheek on her shoulder. He couldn't remember much after that, but he remembered her shouting at him, then he was in a taxi. He must have got back to his hotel because he woke up the next morning, lying on the floor, squished between the bed and the wall. He had an angry headache and a concrete stiff neck, no feeling in his left arm, and a badge thingy in his lapel. His hangover was as bad as it had ever been. He pulled himself up and flopped on the bed. He remembered the yellow case and looked around the room, but it wasn't anywhere. He panicked when he realised, he'd left the yellow case at the conference. It contained all his notes and was vital if he was to produce a report of any value for Bentley.

'Shit shit shitty shitty shit shit,' he mumbled. He cleaned his teeth and left. He hoped he was in one of his micro stories so he could write an ending where he finds the yellow case and Sophie. He didn't have to dress, since he hadn't undressed before ending up on the floor. He skipped the coffee and raspberry jam downstairs. He had to get the case, or he could never face Bentley again.

He missed his cubicle. He missed Gloria. He missed the office in general. He missed the Stalwart. He missed Sophie both in the Stalwart and in Paris. In Paris, he literally missed her, as well as emotionally. His life skated through the forest of disappointment, not so much a skate as a crash, a plunge, a clatter. He couldn't make anything work the way he wanted it to, or the way he thought it should. He got close, but never there. Something always conspired to keep him from getting anything he really wanted or thought he wanted. He knew in his heart, he was the reason for this. He sabotaged himself. He was better when he wasn't himself. He had no idea what he wanted. And without the yellow case, he wouldn't be able to write his report for Bentley, and letting Bentley down was the last thing he wanted.

He ran back to the conference room in the hope of retrieving the case. It was there, under his seat. He picked it up and held it close to his chest, as though it was the one thing in the world that could save him. He ran back to his hotel to pack and get to the airport. With this running and weaving in and around people and dog shit, he forgot to look for Sophie. The running was good for him. It cleared his head. He had to stop for the lights at the corner of *Boulevard Raspail* and *Rue de Babylone*. He saw a monkey wearing a red cap in front of a pharmacy. He had a sudden rush of affection for Sophie. He had no idea where she was at that moment, but he felt her.

Then he was back in his cubicle and jet-lagged again, a feeling that was indistinguishable from a hangover.

'Your report, Robbie. I need it today. There's a board meeting tomorrow, and I have to circulate it before the meeting,' Bentley said as he passed Robbie's cubicle. Bentley said this matter-of-factly, not with any malice, perhaps with some respect. There was no explanation from Bentley as to why he'd been away from the office. And there wasn't any accountant speculation. So Robbie thought, whatever it was, it was taken care of or didn't amount to anything of alarm. Robbie sat mesmerised by the cursor on his blank screen.

It was a Friday, and after completing the Paris report and emailing it through to Bentley, he found himself at the front bar of the Stalwart. His two friends hadn't shown up, and it was raining picks and shovels outside, which translated to moisture inside. The atmosphere was hot, humid, and steamy. The place was pumping. Robbie was jostled by people coming up to the bar to order drinks. Some of them wore loosened ties. They smelt humid and alcoholic. He tried to spread out his elbows to mark his territory, but it was no use. They were all drunk. They didn't get that he owned the beer mat territory from the bottle top across to the Foster's beer logo.

Robbie proceeded to drink himself to death. Not at one sitting, but slowly. He recalled talking to Bentley, but he couldn't say what it was Bentley had said, except there was something about his piece for the company newsletter, and something about his Paris report being 'excellent'. But anything else Bentley had said was gone. Also, something about whether he was okay or not, and nooks and crannies. Robbie couldn't get things in order. He couldn't.

He recalled he'd found a handwritten note in the yellow case when he was back in his cubicle. It was from the American woman born in Waco, Texas who had been sitting next to him at the conference dinner. The note said, 'Ophelia, L'Hotel, Room #210 where Mick Jagger stays.' It seemed an odd name for a hotel—a hotel calling itself 'the hotel'.

The more he thought about it the blurrier it became until, in the end, the word 'hotel' sounded ridiculous. And he wondered about her name, Ophelia. He hadn't heard of an American woman with this name. He also wondered if she had placed the note in his yellow case before he touched her back or after. Must have been before. Before he got drunk, or very drunk, he was already drunk. Robbie did not wake up in the alley.

***

He opened his eyes and saw Gloria sitting next to his hospital bed, reading a book. He looked down the bed at his crotch area to make sure he wasn't embarrassing himself again. Fortunately, there was nothing untoward. He hadn't thought of hospitals in an arousing way. He looked at Gloria reading her book and felt a surge of affection for her, but he didn't say anything. Gloria was a beautiful, intelligent woman, much more competent and reliable than Robbie. He squinted and watched her read. He wished he could do something for her, something worthwhile, something that would be special. But he couldn't think of anything. She wanted sperm, but he couldn't do that to her.

Gloria hadn't seen him open his eyes, so he closed them again, and the alley flashed into his mind. He recalled how dark it had been and how scared he'd been. He remembered something coming after him, but he couldn't remember what it was or where it went. He knew he was terrified and had cried out before he could stop himself. He opened his eyes again. Gloria moved to adjust her position. He saw her breasts move. She was unaware he was watching her.

Robbie thought about Gloria's breasts and how Gloria was her breasts. She loved them. She admired them. She used them to advantage. She relied on them to do a lot of work on her behalf, and they did, but they did this to such a degree of prominence that Gloria didn't need to rely on her intelligence, or personality, as much as someone without such assets—as might be the case with a beauty queen, who tended to spend her development years being beautiful and adored, and not spending time developing character to prepare herself for life's shit. When the beauty fades there's nothing to fall back on. One day, Robbie thought, Gloria's breasts will not be so prominent and valuable, they will be surpassed by younger, more pert breasts. But in Gloria's case it wouldn't matter, because Gloria not only looked fabulous, she was smarter and more competent than anyone in the department. Oddly though, Robbie felt sympathy for her. He squinted at her and watched her sitting next to his hospital bed, reading her book, pure in deed, oblivious to his potential erection. For this he was grateful. He worried about her though, and thought the question, 'What will happen to you?' was as profound for Gloria as anyone. At least Gloria was good at her job. She had that to fall back on when her breasts stopped working for her. He felt sorry for himself too, but for different and similar reasons. His life was also slipping by for him, but unlike Gloria, he had little talent to fall back on. He moaned at the thought. Maybe it was a sigh. But whatever it was, it must have been audible, as it disturbed Gloria.

Gloria looked up and smiled at him. She turned the top corner of the page down as a bookmark. Robbie winced. He hated that kind of brutal mistreatment of books. Her turning the corner of the page down was enough for Robbie to realise that he and Gloria could never be right for each other. That, and the fact she had exchanged tongues with the phoney informant O'Brien at the Stalwart, as he now remembered. Robbie thought memory, his in particular, was unreliable. Other-self filled his head with all sorts of poison and red herrings.

'Hello, stranger. How are you? You've been missing in action for some time, you know.'

Robbie misheard this. He thought she said, 'You've been missing an erection for some time, you know.' She didn't say that, but she could have, he thought. He tried to slide up the bed a bit. Then he tried to sit up, but he couldn't seem to make any of his muscles work, and his head started spinning.

'Here, let me help.' Gloria stood up and put her arms around his chest to help drag him up the bed. Her breasts surrounded his face. He wondered if he might have been a bit hasty in thinking they could never get together. Gloria grabbed a pillow from a nearby chair and put it behind his shoulders.

She smelt intoxicating, and he checked the sheet where his erection tended to pop up, to make sure it wasn't doing any independent thinking and going rogue. Christ, he hoped not. He couldn't see any suspicious bumps in his sheet, so that was good.

'Now, what can I get you?' Gloria had her hand on his bare chest. Why was his chest bare? 'Anything you want?'

'I think I'm okay,' Robbie said, knowing he wasn't.

'I hope so. The office has been pretty boring without you there. None of your esoteric alarmist, obscure emails full of literary references that almost no one gets.' She laughed and touched his cheek. 'Even Bentley misses you, I suspect. He was here, you know. He came every lunchtime and after work, every day. Who knew Bentley cared? Well, we all know he cares. I think it's easy to underestimate Bentley. Have you seen his wife? Why is someone as lovely as Sabrina with an accountant like Bentley? It makes you think, don't you think? I bet you'd like to fuck her. I would.' Gloria laughed and sort of clucked. It was odd.

Robbie hadn't heard her cluck before. He hadn't heard anyone cluck before. He interpreted the cluck as a cover for embarrassment. It didn't surprise him, but then nothing surprised him when it came to Gloria. So she clucks when she's embarrassed. The cluck was a flaw, but rather than diminish her in some way, it gave her depth, unlike Robbie's personality flaws, which did diminish him in ways he couldn't help.

'Bentley's not such a nobster though, is he?' Gloria said. 'He's bloody good at his job,' she added while reaching in her handbag and retrieving her lipstick, 'and he'd do anything for you.'

Gloria smeared thick red lipstick on her lips and smacked them together as though she was preparing for war. The smacking sound ricocheted around the room so loud, Robbie thought, it could be measured in decibels that would have knocked any hums or buzzes for six, had there been any in the room at that moment. Robbie reflected the whole lipstick routine was odd too, but not really. It went with the cluck and was maybe a little weird. But it was Gloria. She did things like that, and it evoked a heightened affection in Robbie for her. Robbie thought that people's personalities were dynamic, they added up, they made sense, they were representative, and engendered respect for the person or not, depending on the idiosyncrasy. This more so in Gloria. Still, he thought it odd she would be applying lipstick at that moment.

Robbie had a lot of time for Gloria. She was Bentley's second-in-charge. Gloria had a confidence about her, while Robbie wasn't comfortable in his own skin. Gloria knew who she was, what she was, what she wanted and how to get it. There was much to envy and admire, Robbie thought, as he watched her finish checking herself in her compact mirror.

'Are you and O'Brien...?' Robbie couldn't believe he heard himself asking Gloria about her relationship with O'Brien.

'Are we fucking?' Gloria asked while she made an attempt at rearranging the flowers in the vase next to Robbie's bed. 'Nah...not anymore. He was a dud fuck, as it turned out. He...you know, couldn't...you know, well not more than once at least.'

'Oh.' Robbie couldn't think of anything else that could be said in response to this. He didn't know if the 'not more than once' referred to per session, or if O'Brien was impotent after the first time they fucked, which seemed unlikely to Robbie. You couldn't put the word 'impotence' and Gloria in the same sentence. Gloria could defeat 'impotence' with one small wobble of her breasts, or by smiling at you, or rolling lipstick across her lips and smacking them together. He didn't feel disposed to ask for clarification about O'Brien's performance, so he let it go. He couldn't figure why he'd asked Gloria about O'Brien. It wasn't as though he cared that much, and well, it wasn't any of his business. In his current state of confusion, things seemed to pop out, or up, as it were.

Robbie felt people were making allowances for him out of kindness. He didn't know how to handle it, but he liked it. People didn't tend to make allowances for him. But then he was a prick to most people most of the time, so why would they?

'O'Brien's up at the mines, doin' your job. No one's heard from him. Maybe the flies got him,' Gloria said.

'Or the bush,' Robbie said.

'Okay,' Gloria said but not with much conviction. She looked like she wanted to say something else.

'What?' Robbie asked. He thought of O'Brien in the vast outback. He couldn't see how O'Brien could survive. Robbie was aware that he barely survived it himself. The outback confirmed your irrelevance. It made you as small as a fly, then that was compounded by the fact that you were one of a trillion trillion flies. There was a part of Robbie that hoped O'Brien didn't survive.

Gloria sighed and then giggled. She put her hands on her hips.

'You want me to get into bed with you?' she asked. 'Just this once? You know, might make you feel better, take your mind off yourself. What do you reckon?'

She indicated with her eyes toward the territory his erection was occupying under the sheets. He looked down and was mortified. Where did that come from? he asked himself. Did other-self operate the thing independently of him these days? He felt sheepish and embarrassed, but Gloria smiled at him and started to undo the buttons on her blouse. She opened it for Robbie to see her breasts that, as it turned out, were unhindered by the presence of a bra. Robbie noted they were perky, rude, solid, and creamy, all in a seductive, come-hither way, *and* it seemed her nipples were eager for contact. Robbie's erection started to fade, the exact opposite of what he would have expected. He felt a sudden weakness through his limbs and couldn't process it, and worried one of the nurses might come in to measure his temperature or blood pressure, both of which should be in the high range, but then he thought, worse than that, they might not be. Gloria closed and locked the door and then, in her own world, pulled her skirt off and stepped out of it. She had no underwear on. She removed her blouse and slid naked into bed with Robbie. She mounted her leg over his, and he felt her lips press against him. He was overwhelmed by her heat. She moved her hand down to his penis and held it. He was embarrassed that it wasn't erect. Just when he needed the damn thing to be doing its job, it was doing nothing, as though it was doing this deliberately to embarrass him. He figured other-self must be behind this, trying to humiliate him. He closed his eyes, and he felt safe and comforted by her caress. She whispered in his ear, 'Don't do anything, there's no need. Just cuddle if that's all you feel like. I'm sorry, you know if I've let you down, as a friend.'

Robbie put his arms around her and felt himself drift off to the dusty track between the mines. He felt the sun on his head. He felt Gloria remove her hand from his recalcitrant penis and lay it across his chest—her hand, not his penis, needless to say. He was standing in the red dust, a massive blue dome of sky reached over the top of him. The track disappeared over the horizon in both directions. He smelt the purity and coolness of the air and felt the flies crawl over his body with tiny caresses. The cicadas' scream blanketed him in a locked-in, resounding silence.

***

Bentley apologised for sending him to Paris on such short notice. Gloria apologised, for what, Robbie wasn't sure, but her apology affected him. Sabrina apologised for Robbie's strange little episode, despite it not being her fault. It brought tears to his eyes. Robbie couldn't remember anyone apologising to him before, for anything. He wondered how anyone could go through life without occasionally being apologised to by someone for something. Robbie felt this reflected poorly on him. Did it mean Robbie was such a pain to everyone that he never deserved an apology? An apology, for whatever reason, was a human reaction and a natural thing to do, if something was done that needed an apology, however innocent the transgression. Robbie already felt close to Gloria and Sabrina, but Bentley's apology made Robbie feel close to Bentley. It was as if they had an intimate exchange that would only occur with someone you care about. Robbie knew he had a different relationship with Bentley than the one he thought he had. He felt he should apologise to Gloria, but he didn't know for what especially. He knew he should apologise to Sabrina, not for anything in particular, but because she was so nice to him, and he never deserved someone like her being nice to him. The more he thought about it, the more he realised he needed to apologise to everyone in his life—the realisation of which lifted his spirits somewhat. Apologising was something he could do, a genuine act of selflessness.

Robbie sank into a coma, although he couldn't know that at the time. It wasn't a coma in the technical sense, as a doctor would define a coma. He was unconscious, but asleep. He slept as though he was catching up on all the sleep he'd missed in his life. When he woke, it was morning, much the same as it had been when he drifted off. But there was no indication if it was the same morning.

Gloria wasn't in the bed with him. He had no idea how long he'd been asleep. Hours? Days? Months? Robbie hadn't slept properly throughout his entire life. What the hell had he achieved in his life? What could he achieve?

He saw his laptop sitting open on the bedside table. He vaguely remembered Bentley had brought it in for him. A full page of words was on display, but he had no recollection of writing anything or using his laptop. He worked himself up the bed and tried to sit up against the pillows. He saw a cord and button thingy on the bed. He picked it up and pushed the button, and the pillow end of the bed started to raise itself. When he was in a more or less sitting position, he stopped the bed and rested. It seemed the smallest exertion exhausted him, and he couldn't imagine raising the energy to have sex with Gloria. He wondered what she must think of him. He shuddered at the thought she might see him in the same light as the impotent O'Brien. But at least O'Brien had managed it once. That was better than Robbie had achieved.

When he was sufficiently recovered, he reached for his laptop and rested it on his lap. He wanted to talk to Sophie, but he knew he was beyond that, and he would never know what to say to her that would change anything in the world, or his world for that matter. Sophie deserved much better than Robbie.

He didn't remember writing, and so as he read, it was like he read it for the first time. He must have been in a happier mood. It made him laugh. It didn't make him happy.

*Life's parable*

*A deadly tarantula has just bitten me, and I have thirty seconds to live. I should have written it as 30 seconds, it took longer than 30 seconds to write it out in fu*

*Legend:*

*Tarantula represents life.*

*Getting bitten represents life's cruelty and indifference. Both are much the same thing.*

*Having used up the thirty seconds writing in longhand represents the absurdity of life.*

Then this following on the same page.

*A Letter to Sophie Fanshawe*

*(never sent)*

*Hi Sophie, I hope you will remember me, it's been some time now. If you do remember me, you will remember me as Robbie Carton, barfly and drunk from the Stalwart. Apart from ordering drinks from you, you will remember me as someone who never spoke to you. Can I tell you, I always wanted to be a literary figure? I assumed living as someone else would be better for me, and everyone I know, than if I continued living my life as Robbie Carton. So that is why I choose a literary figure. Their author has done the work, given them a life, an enviable life. It seemed easy, at times, it seemed like it might be the only way out for me. I want to say goodbye now.*

*Robbie*

Robbie deleted the file then retrieved it from the waste bin, then deleted it again, then retrieved it again and gave it a file name only he would recognise. He called it 'Brown Sauce'. He closed his laptop and fell asleep. He dreamt he was bleeding. He dreamt he'd cut his penis off with a machete. He could hear the lazy click of the rotating ceiling fan. He woke in a sweat then drifted off again.

## Pamela and Bronnie

'It'd be like starting again, you know, doing something different, more exciting perhaps.' Pamela confessed to Bronnie one night out, a few weeks ago at the Stalwart. Pamela told Bronnie she was considering becoming an actor. She had no idea how to become an actor, but she liked the idea. She thought that invading someone else's psyche, producing a character, might be fun, even though it was make-believe. Make-believe was good because it wasn't permanent. 'I guess, I'm just looking for a change, something different.' Pamela mused.

There were some things Pamela wouldn't want to change. She loved her flat. She wouldn't want to lose Bronnie as a friend. She liked her job, for the most part. Recently though, she had entertained thoughts of wanting something a little more exciting, like the idea of being an actor, or a marine biologist. Not a marine biologist, she wouldn't want to be wet all the time. Perhaps a fashion designer, or a book reviewer. She would still want to keep her distinguishing beauty mark, and she wouldn't want to lose her essential self, but she felt changes had to be made.

'Yeah, an actor sounds interesting,' Bronnie said, 'but you don't have to become an actual actor, you know. You could just do something different, act different.'

'Perhaps, I suppose?' Pamela responded.

'Sure, it happens. People do other things all the time, no big deal.' Bronnie said.

'I don't know, it's all just a fantasy. I guess it isn't unusual to wonder what life could be like if...'

'Another Aperol spritz?' Bronnie interrupted.

'Sure. No. I'll have something else, something different. A martini, with an olive, extra extra dry.'

'Bold. I might join you.' Bronnie smiled at her best friend, as though having a martini was the beginning of something new.

Pamela considered Bronnie's observation that she could just do something different. She felt she needed change in her life—new challenges, new horizons. She could live in another city, yet she couldn't imagine leaving the city she lived in. She thought about different clothes, but there was nothing wrong with her current wardrobe, and would different clothes work anyway? She could change her makeup and get a new job, but that was only a superficial change. She might look different and work in a different place, but she would be the same person. The change she was discussing was more philosophical, more fundamental than makeup and clothes, and it didn't have to be permanent. That was why she thought becoming an actor might be transforming. She could try it out first, and, if it didn't work, she could always return to her existing life, which, to be honest, wasn't as bad as all that. It wasn't bad at all. It was familiar.

Bronnie returned with the drinks. 'You know, I think everyone feels that way from time to time, it's only natural to be dissatisfied with your life now and then.' It was Friday night, and Bronnie was sporting her beauty mark on her left cheek. She was more definite with her opinions on Fridays. The beauty mark gave her power. She felt it did.

Bronnie and Pamela rarely went to the Stalwart, or so they'd say to themselves. They agreed it was a noisy pick-up joint where no one met anyone. The truth was, they were there more often than they realised. Sitting at one of the tables, they congratulated themselves that they didn't come to the Stalwart often.

'This place is classic,' Bronnie said.

'Yeah,' Pamela replied.

The two women sat watching the crowd and sipping their martinis. Bronnie squinted, for no obvious reason. Pamela saw Bronnie's squint.

'I sometimes think of doing that myself. Not being an actor...I hadn't thought of that' Bronnie said. 'But making some significant change to ramp up the excitement a bit. That was before I met my current boyfriend and fell in love. Or fell in love with falling in love. The boyfriend may be merely an artifice. Or not.' Bronnie squinted again, but again, for no discernible reason.

Pamela started to feel the warming effect of the martinis.

'You know, with my temporary beauty mark and blonde hair, I feel a little disguised from my actual self, and I've gotten to experience, if in a small way, what it'd be like to be you. That's acting, don't you think?' Bronnie asked.

'Yeah, I suppose it is,' Pamela agreed. 'I suppose, a bit, I guess,' she mused and continued. 'But I'm not sure cosmetic changes are enough. None of these things answer the question of "What will happen to you?" That question applies to both your old self and to any new invention of yourself. That's the question, the big one, "What will happen to you?" They kept asking that question at my Writers Circle.'

'Good question. But there's no answer. All the good questions have no answers,' Bronnie mused rhetorically. They both finished their martinis. 'Do you think people know the difference between a rhetorical question, and an extemporaneous comment?' Bronnie ad-libbed.

'I wouldn't be at all surprised,' Pamela responded.

*** 

Pamela hadn't joined The Writers Circle to write but she found she enjoyed writing flash fiction. It was short, so needed much less commitment. It was a form of poetry, and it required a poetic rhythm. Every word had to do a lot of work, and the piece had to get started and finish all pretty much in the same breath. It had to describe a complete and dynamic universe. She liked this. She liked the brevity, and she liked how you could leave it behind if you weren't sure it was what you wanted to say. You could abandon it and start again without enormous effort, dedication, and work. She could re-invent herself as an implied writer and make up a different person as the author. The made-up implied writer, she could imagine, might be a male, have different ethics to her, live in a warehouse or contain his laughter or assign different meanings to words than Pamela would. She could be whomever she wanted. But the thought of this left Pamela with a nagging feeling of discomfort. It still didn't seem to be what she was seeking.

After her engagement with The Writers Circle, Pamela had decided she wanted to do more writing, so she enrolled in a creative writing class run by one of the members of The Writers Circle. She had little to do with him in the Circle, but she found out about his classes and resolved to join. She wondered if he would recognise her, as he seemed so disengaged. He was a disheveled man. Not so much disheveled in his appearance, although that certainly, but in his demeanour. He was tired and lost and exasperated. She called him Tommy, but that wasn't his name. It was the name he used in The Writers Circle. This fact intrigued her, and she reckoned there wasn't enough intrigue in life, and so, when something did intrigue her, she paid attention and she tried to accept it without prejudice. Tommy intrigued her, more than she had realised at first. His presence crept up on her.

Pamela wouldn't describe herself as an overtly sexual woman. She often wore a shiny red raincoat and occasionally, very occasionally, when she did feel a bit naughty, she went out naked underneath. When she did this, somewhat out of character, she felt liberated and free from herself, and a little sexy too. She had a sense of what it would be like to be someone else, someone more daring and adventurous. She thought about what it would be like to be the kind of person who might, under the right circumstances, take off her coat. But then if she took off her coat, wouldn't she still be Pamela, only naked? And what would that achieve?

One evening, over several martinis—Pamela and Bronnie had started to drink martinis regularly, it made them feel sophisticated—they were discussing the fantasy of reinventing their lives and becoming someone else. The discussion was fun and harmless, and interrupted only by Bronnie heading to the bar to get another round of martinis. Pamela had lost count of how many martinis they had drunk, but her face was flushed and hot. She thought of slipping into the ladies and removing her underwear, but then Bronnie returned, and the idea vanished. The idea of becoming an actor had flourished. Perhaps not so much becoming an actor, as the idea of acting as someone else more exciting and more daring.

'So, here's an idea Pammie. Let's swap.' Bronnie put the drinks on the table. One for Pamela and one for herself. The olives bobbed about in the viscous liquid leaving a translucent trail.

'Let's swap what?' Pamela asked.

'Lives. Each other's. You become me, and I'll become you.'

'That's silly,' Pamela said, with some caution. *No caution* was the natural consequence of drinking martinis, and they were heading in that direction, if they hadn't already passed it.

'Maybe. But should it be dismissed because it's silly?'

'It's impossible,' Pamela said with superficial conviction.

'Sometimes "I've believed as many as six impossible things before breakfast",' Bronnie said, quoting Lewis Carroll.

'How would it work?' Pamela asked intrigued.

'Simple. We swap lives. You live mine as me, and I'll live yours as you.'

Pamela laughed. Bronnie didn't. She stared back at Pamela. Bronnie, having opened the topic, was committed to it.

Pamela took in a long breath—a sigh in reverse. She locked eyes with Bronnie, took a large sip of her martini and resolutely put the glass down.

'Okay, let's do it. When do we start?'

'Tonight. When we go home. You go to my flat, and I'll go to yours.' Bronnie slammed her keys on the table in front of Pamela.

'Then what?'

'We do it. It's simple.'

'What about clothes?' Pamela queried.

'You wear mine, and I wear yours. We're both the same size.'

'You'll need to attend my creative writing sessions with my lecturer, and you'll have to wear my shiny red raincoat with nothing on underneath.' Pamela smiled.

'You didn't tell me about that.'

'No, nothing has happened yet, but it's going to.'

'What an intriguing life you have...I have.' Bronnie grinned.

'You can call him Tommy, it's not his name.'

'Whatever you say.'

'Okay. But what about your boyfriend?' Pamela asked.

'He's yours to do what you want with.' Bronnie laughed.

'Are you sure?'

'I'm sure. There has to be some dramatic changes, or this won't be worthwhile.'

'Don't you love him?'

'Maybe. I don't know. Probably not. Maybe you'll find out for me.' Bronnie smiled and raised her glass. 'A toast.'

Pamela raised her glass to Bronnie's, and they clinked.

'Maybe you'll find out if I love Tommy,' said Pamela. 'Here's to reinvention.'

'To that then.'

Bronnie took a sip from her martini and became Pamela.

'Will I have to make love to your boyfriend?' Pamela asked.

'You will. Often. Don't forget to cover your beauty mark every day other than Friday and keep your eyes open during sex. And purr, you will have to purr.'

'Okay. You don't think he'll notice that I'm not you?'

'Not if you purr. I wouldn't worry about that. He isn't who he is,' Bronnie responded with a cheeky laugh.

After another two martinis, Pamela and Bronnie parted at the front steps of the Stalwart and wobbled off in opposite directions.

Sometimes when sitting in the dark in her flat watching the twinkling skyline at night, Pamela saw herself in a different light. She loved sitting in the darkness of her apartment watching the city lights. These were the times in her life when she felt hopeful, positive, and happy. These were the times when she felt she deserved love and she would be good at it. She wondered how happy she'd be in Bronnie's flat.

# Robbie Carton

Another week passed before the doctors allowed Robbie to leave the hospital. During that time, Robbie wrote. Stories appeared on his laptop as if they had written themselves.

As far as he could fathom, he had slept, had numerous erections, and tried to recall what had happened to him, but without much success. He had vague flashes of scenes he couldn't make head nor tail of. He had visitors. Bentley and Sabrina came in every day and brought him presents. The last time, they brought a cake, which Sabrina had baked for him, and it was as delicious as he would have predicted. Bentley brought him an old book, *A Tale of Two Cities* by Charles Dickens.

'I saw this listed in an auction last weekend and went along out of curiosity and ended up getting it. You've probably got the book, but I thought this was a collector's item as it's a first edition, and you might like to have it. I know it's one of your favourites.'

Robbie ran his fingers along the old binding. The book was in pretty good shape for its age, he felt. He didn't know what to say. No one had given him such a gift in his life. Robbie was overwhelmed and couldn't find any words to say to Bentley.

Bentley patted Robbie on his shoulder. 'Enough of that, when are you getting out?'

After Bentley and Sabrina left, Robbie opened the book and read the first paragraph. Dickens starts several sentences with the words, 'It was the...'. Robbie recognised and enjoyed Dickens' use of the grammatical affectation known as anaphora—repetition, used to slow the read for emphasis. You can never get enough anaphora. You can never get enough repetition. You can never get enough emphasis in your life, he thought.

'It was the best of times, it was the worst of times, it was the age of wisdom, it was the age of foolishness, it was the epoch of belief, it was the epoch of incredulity, it was the season of Light, it was the season of Darkness, it was the spring of hope, it was the winter of despair, we had everything before us, we had nothing before us, we were all going direct to Heaven, we were all going direct the other way—in short, the period was so far like the present period, that some of its noisiest authorities insisted on its being received, for good or for evil, in the superlative degree of comparison only.'

Robbie thought that this opening paragraph of *A Tale of Two Cities*, one of the best books ever written, seemed as though it had been written with his life in mind. Robbie realised while re-reading it that it even resembled Robbie's style as a writer, also as a human being. He saw and identified the ambivalence of life, life and all its binary and diametric opposites. *It was the best of times, it was the worst of times, it was the age of wisdom, it was the age of foolishness.* Robbie had read this opening sentence of the great novel many times, but until this second, he hadn't seen himself in the philosophy. He realised that life was simultaneously opposite and in conflict with itself. And life, unlike Robbie, thought nothing of this. It wasn't concerned. It didn't mind, nor did it feel the need to explain the contradictions that exist in every nook and cranny of life. Robbie was astounded by this revelation. He had lived his whole life trying to be one or other of himself, when all the time he lived in a universe where that was not required, where contradictions were the norm, and not your enemy. He finally realized that people couldn't exist, and not be a mass of contradictions, and that was perfectly okay.

Robbie had lived his life trying to figure out why life was so confounding and inexplicable. He was forever railing against the 'why', thinking that fighting for understanding was important. Robbie drifted off to sleep with the book open to the last line, where Sydney Carton says, 'It is a far, far better thing that I do, than I have ever done; it is a far, far better rest that I go to, than I have ever known.' Anaphora again. Robbie Carton smiled in his sleep at this tautology.

***

His sleep was fitful, same as always. When Robbie woke, he was still alive. He was still Robbie, he was still anxious but somehow wiser, less agitated, and this gave him some comfort. He looked at his computer screen and saw he had written another flash piece. He assumed he wrote it. It was there, on the screen, completed with a title. The piece read like something he would write. It was his style, in that he could say he had a style.

### PLANET42
#### By
#### Robbie Carton

*Your universe and my universe are both constructed. You cannot apply the rules of your universe to my universe—we have evolved differently and separately. You would struggle to understand us, and therefore, you will be resentful. You will feel isolated, certainly annoyed. In our universe, we don't get annoyed.*

*There are some practical similarities, though. In our respective constructed universes, we agree on most things—otherwise, we risk chaos. We agree on geography. For example, we agree on the location of your planet, and if you had the science, you'd agree on the location of our planet—Planet 42, we'll call it for now. It wouldn't work if I said the Grand Canyon was in Tasmania, or near Piccadilly Circus, while you insist it's in America. So on locations, we cooperate. We also agree on names, again, no point in me calling the Grand Canyon the 'Rather Large Hole', while you are calling it a 'Crack of Some Size'. Colours? We don't really know. I may call something red and so might you, but how can we know if it is the same colour. We sometimes agree on manners.*

*On protocols? Mostly we agree—don't murder, steal, defame etc. This is the area of most concern between us, but I am not here to discuss morality or ethics. I am here to frighten you. On some level, we all must be afraid of one another. It is the only way if we are to engage and survive.*

*In my constructed universe, I have little or no control over events. Neither do you in your universe. Knowing this helps. But nothing will save us. Our science is the same, ours is more advanced, and we could annihilate you quicker than you could us, but that is not what you have to be frightened of. What you must be frightened of is yourselves, much as it is for us. Weapons don't invent themselves.*

246

Robbie felt less responsible, perhaps, not as far as carefree, but it was like the feeling of 'impending freedom' he had on his last day of school before summer holidays. He had no recollection of writing the piece, and he wasn't confident as to its meaning. But it was on his computer, so one of him wrote it.

# Harry Fanshawe

*Wanted: Female. Maybe thirtyish. Intellectual engagement. Creative writing academic (Tommy) still as new, give or take. Describe (no adverbs) your distinguishing feature. Send to the Stalwart Hotel c/o Sophie on behalf of her brother. Will meet at the Stalwart. Signifier: RR.*

'That's it?' Elbow asked over the phone.

'That's it,' Harry responded, putting the newspaper back on his desk and closing the page he had read to Elbow.

'Expansive.'

'What else is there to say, what else can you say that isn't a *cliché*?' Harry took a bite out of his sandwich. He chewed twice and swallowed the mouthful virtually whole.

'No adverbs?'

'Certainly not.'

'Tough. Isn't "maybe" an adverb?'

'Perhaps.'

'And RR? Not Rolls Royce.'

'Red Rose.'

'She'll know that?'

'She'll figure it out, or not.'

'Don't you mean, "Female wanted"?'

'No.'

'And nothing so far?'

'Nothing. But still early days.'

'Here's hopin'.'

'Exactly. I'm relying on the *National Financial Review*'s readership to a large extent as a qualifier or filter, so not expecting an avalanche.'

'Okay. Who's Tommy?'

'That'd be me.'

'Fair enough. How long's it been running?'

'A few weeks.'

'No avalanche, then.'

'No, but also the response, if there is one, will be to Sophie at the Stalwart. I'm not expecting them to turn up here at my office.'

'Well let me know. Maybe the accountant has a sister or friend who might be fascinated with dentists, what do you reckon?'

'Very likely, I'd say. Everyone's fascinated with dentists.'

There was a knock at Harry's door.

'Have to go.'

'Right. See you later. I've got teeth to drill and root canals to perform. Pain infliction, don't you love it? By the way, does she bring the rose or do you?'

Harry hung up the phone, wrapped the remains of his sandwich and shoved the wrapped sandwich into his top drawer. He scraped together the crumbs on the surface of his desk with his hand and pushed them off the edge, onto his lap into the bin next to him. He swiped the back of his hand across his mouth to make sure he didn't have any crumbs or mayonnaise lingering. He opened the drawer again and retrieved a mirror to check his teeth. All clear.

There was another knock, this time softer.

'Come in,' he called. His voice wavered, and he hit the 'in' way too high— he didn't know why. It was Friday but late, and he wasn't expecting anyone. He'd already seen most of his students, at least those who had appointments.

His creative writing student came in, and he gestured for her to sit down. She did so and crossed her legs. She looked serious. She was wearing her shiny red raincoat as usual. He noticed her beauty mark/freckle and it fascinated him. Her coat fell open to reveal her tanned naked legs. He had to work hard not to linger on them. He had to work hard not to swallow or gulp or let his nostrils do anything un-nostril like, whatever that may be. It was almost as though she was inviting him to look at her legs. Was she? He had to stop this behaviour. It was unprofessional and unsettling.

He cleared his throat, if unnecessarily, and forced himself to not look at her legs and tried to stop thinking how she might be naked under her raincoat. Useless. The most guaranteed way of thinking about something you shouldn't be thinking about, was to tell yourself not to think about it. Stop thinking about her beautiful, naked, tanned legs, and how she might be naked under her raincoat, he told himself. Yeah, that was working. She was leaning over and retrieving something from her beach bag, if that was what it was, and so, wasn't looking at him for a moment. He tried to get his thoughts and eyes under control.

She didn't speak to him. She let her smile do the work. He looked at her to determine if he could look at her without any of these unprofessional thoughts zooming around his head. He looked at her face and felt she looked different in some way he couldn't nail. She retrieved from her bag a copy of the *National Financial Review* and put it on the edge of his desk while she continued to search in her bag. She produced a single sheet of paper. As far as he could tell, it had one sentence written on it. Her flash fiction piece, he assumed. She put the newspaper back in her bag, sat back and looked at him. He had seen plenty of flash fiction pieces comprised of one sentence.

'Would you prefer me to read this, or do you want to read it?' he asked, trying to sound composed. She uncrossed her legs. Composure, such as it was, evaporated for Harry.

There seemed such a familiarity to her. He somehow felt comfortable and uncomfortable at the same time. She had an allure that came with being confident. Most of his students were nervous and anxious. He didn't know if it was him that unsettled them or if they were unsettled for other reasons. He gazed at the beauty mark on her cheek, and it blurred as his gaze deepened. He felt he was falling, down, far down, into an unknown, unfathomable abyss.

He felt warm and observed the shards of sunlight in the room surround her blonde hair, creating a halo. There was no halo. He only imagined it. He wanted to touch her. He wanted to run his hands up her naked legs and under her coat. He thought of Beverly and felt sad, but then it had been some time since he'd felt anything like this about another woman. He somehow thought Beverly wouldn't mind, but that seemed like a justification. He tried to shut down his thoughts toward this woman sitting naked in front of him with her beautiful legs uncrossed.

She held the sheet of paper out to him and smiled a smile that risked causing his nostrils to do something untoward. He felt she was waiting.

The phone rang. It broke Harry's concentration. He held up his hand to his student and indicated he would take the call. She rested the sheet of paper on her lap. It covered her exposed thighs.

'Tommy, here.'

'Really? Sophie here, Tommy.'

'Oh, hi.'

'You doin' the Tommy thing at work now?'

Harry cleared his throat and tried to sound professional for his student's sake.

'What's up? I'm in a meeting.'

'You have a response to your ad.'

'Oh, that's good...Is it?'

'Don't know, depends on your take.'

'What did it say?'

'It's only three words.'

'Succinct then, that's never a bad thing.'

'Unless it's "fuck off loser".'

'Yes, unless it's that. Is it?'

'No, it says, and I quote, "My beauty mark". She's not who you think she is.'

'That makes no sense,' Tommy said.

'Why should it? Got to go. But good luck, your life's about to change, if you want it to.' Sophie hung up. She'd been back from Paris for a few months and was calm and sanguine, Harry thought.

Harry looked at his student. She looked back at him, and a small smile appeared on her lips. Not a 'knowing' smile, he didn't think, but then is there such a thing as a knowing smile? Wouldn't you have to assign knowingness to it for that to be the case? He smiled back and hung up the phone. He had met with this student several times and realised he hadn't looked closely at her before, apart from noticing her red coat and beauty mark, her blonde hair, her smile and the fact that she was stone motherless naked under her coat. He was losing control again. Nonetheless, she seemed different in a way he was unable to pinpoint. Something about her was different, maybe the way she'd done her hair or her makeup. He couldn't tell, but then he was aware his observational powers were less than perfect when it came to nuance. One thing though, she seemed more confident, more definite some-how. She wasn't nervous. Maybe she never had been, and he had imagined her nervousness. Or perhaps it was his nervousness. Maybe he had changed, altered in some way. He wondered, sitting opposite her, with that enigmatic beauty mark and the whole naked thing going on and her perfume filling his office, was she both the cause and effect? He felt inspired—there seemed no other word for it. 'Inspired' was wholly inadequate to describe the surge he was experiencing, but he understood it, and it worked to a degree. And it wasn't that important, the word 'inspired'. What was important was the feeling, the fact that he was having a feeling at all. She did this to him. Stupidly, he got it. He did know her, he thought. And yet, she was different in some way. She was one of the attendees at The Writers Circle. He felt something in his heart.

He took the sheet of paper from her and read the three words printed on it. When he looked at her after reading the three words, she smiled. He felt his lips curl into what he hoped would be some kind of reassuring smile and not a strained curling lip effect. Right at that moment, he realised something had happened to him. But what? It was then he noticed the long-stemmed red rose lying on his desk.

He was in The City of Angels, as Beverly referred to LA, a place where you arrive, walk out into the soft glow of the sun and disappear whenever you need to.

What happened next? He reread the three words. She stood and undid her coat. She didn't undo her coat. He fell in love with her. She knew she was in love with him. He spoke. She spoke. He disappeared as Harry and became Tommy. Who knows, but something happened next. Something always does.

# Robbie Carton

O'Brien was reported missing. Robbie looked over at O'Brien's empty cubicle. Robbie thought that even when O'Brien was sitting at his desk, he could be reported missing.

It was Robbie's first day back after his hospitalisation. He felt strange and out of place. He tried to settle, but he felt unsettled. He had a pulse at the side of his head. Bentley had cruised by and said, 'Take it easy. I want you to go home if it gets a bit, you know, much, on your first day. It's just accounting.' Bentley whispered so that others didn't hear him say 'It's just accounting.' Robbie's wound had healed, but he could feel a ghost bandage on the side of his head and a distant phantom throb. The words 'it's just accounting' might also have been the cause of the throb. The words 'it's just accounting' from Bentley were dangerously close to heresy and clearly something Bentley wanted only Robbie to hear, like it was their secret—Robbie felt less tense in some way.

Robbie had put some of the story together about O'Brien, or as much of the story Robbie had been able to discern from bits told to him by Gloria and Bentley, while he was in hospital and not thinking too clearly. It seemed O'Brien had finished his audit of the first mine, gone to the canteen and got drunk. Very drunk, according to eyewitnesses. The next day, without a trace of life on his face, if you don't count flies and no one did, there were too many to count, O'Brien left the first mine and headed to the second. Again, he finished the audit, went to the canteen, and got drunk. Very drunk, according to eyewitnesses. After everyone had retired for the night, he sat on the roof of his four-wheel-drive rental and watched the night sky move, while listening to the sound of vastness, and cried. This was according to the security guy who, during his rounds, found O'Brien in this state. The security guard got O'Brien back to his donga and onto his cot and left him to it. The security guard had seen people cry at the night sky before. It was always newcomers.

Next morning, with both audits completed and emailed back to head office and world order maintained, accounting-wise, O'Brien said his goodbyes to the staff and headed off down the track. He was never heard of again. His four-wheel-drive was found abandoned on the side of the track, almost at the midway point between the two mines, nestled in a dry creek bed. The keys were in the ignition. The car had a full tank. The tyres were inflated. There were two bottles of water on the back seat, one half empty. The car had started up when the police officers tried the engine. There was nothing wrong with the vehicle, but O'Brien was nowhere to be found. He had disappeared. The police announced, without a trace of irony, that there were no suspicious circumstances. There was no irony when it came to the mysteries of the outback. One of the police officers said, 'It is what it is', and that seemed to explain everything that happened in the outback. 'The bush is benign, but that doesn't mean what you might think it does.' The officer smiled and left it at that.

A search was mounted but nothing of O'Brien was found, not even his footprints, only the comings and goings of tracks made by wildlife. It was as though he got out of the car, floated off into the bush and vanished. When Robbie heard the news, he thought there was something expected about it, something predictable, and something that didn't surprise him. O'Brien hated being an informant. O'Brien hated being an actor, Robbie thought, and in the end, it got to him.

Robbie imagined O'Brien knew he was a fake and wanted to escape. No one in the office discussed it. Accountants are like that, prudent in the face of the inexplicable, or the explicable come to that. Prudence was the key to being an accountant, one of the keys. There were more keys to being an accountant than you could find on a piano.

Robbie hoped O'Brien had made it out of his fake life. He hoped O'Brien had succeeded. He felt O'Brien's pain for the first time. O'Brien had coveted the outback trip. Had O'Brien intended to disappear? Or did it occur to him after he got the opportunity to do so? Or was it the deep night sky that got to him? Robbie considered these questions. He thought it showed O'Brien was not a real accountant, in the sense of an accountant being authentically an accountant—as in predictable, unimaginative, and controlled. He was a qualified accountant, no one disputed that. He completed the audits, so no problem there. But it did prove O'Brien was a fake. Robbie considered though, that as a fake, O'Brien was authentic. Robbie hoped O'Brien made it across the Rubicon. Robbie hoped O'Brien had found a way out of the trenches for his own sake and for Robbie's.

Had any of O'Brien's spermatozoa survived in Gloria from the one time they copulated? Robbie pondered this question and considered whether he had understood Gloria, about her and O'Brien. Chances were Robbie hadn't understood at all. He wondered if O'Brien's spermatozoa were hiding or resting in some dark recess inside Gloria, waiting to recreate O'Brien—or those recessive genes of O'Brien that might have managed to survive Gloria's dominant genes. O'Brien would want to ensure his legacy in some form. Everyone does, or it is assumed everyone does. O'Brien would want to leave something of his original existence just in case. Robbie imagined O'Brien's phoney sperm hiding deep inside Gloria. He could see their tiny, slow white eyes blinking in the dark. They were innocent and happy. They were waiting. But did they know what they were waiting for, or what to do? Was their mission conscious or instinctive? Robbie imagined one of Gloria's eggs passing by them on an outing, and their little tails wagging with excitement. He saw their blinking speed up, and energy pulse through their tiny bodies as they anticipated their destiny. They made a funny high-pitched noise before shooting off after the egg. Robbie stood close to Gloria one time, so close he could hear her breathe, but he couldn't hear any high-pitched noises. Gloria had let him stand close to her. She didn't move away. It was as though she sensed Robbie needed closeness with her to listen. Maybe she hoped he would hear something.

Robbie knew Gloria wanted a baby. He couldn't say where he got such an idea, but it was something about her that raised his suspicion, or he heard a departmental whisper, or maybe Gloria had mentioned it. When she had climbed naked into his hospital bed there was no mention of the necessity for a condom, which, in the end, wasn't needed. But upon reflection, Robbie felt he'd let Gloria down. Not because he didn't, couldn't, have sex with her, but because she had an agenda that wasn't fulfilled. But then again, this was all speculation on his behalf. Why would any woman of Gloria's intellect and talent want to have a baby with Robbie, a man who was drunk way too much, and who wanted to disappear, and who lost things?

Robbie kept an eye on O'Brien's cubicle, which remained empty for some time, maybe weeks. Specifically, one month, five days and twenty-four minutes. Robbie had activated a running clock, which sat at the lower left-hand side of his screen. Robbie understood, as did every accountant, an empty accounting cubicle could not be allowed to exist permanently. It defied the natural order of accountancy-world.

Then one morning, a new accountant appeared, sitting in O'Brien's seat, working away at whatever O'Brien used to do. There was something about this that offended Robbie. This new accountant was sitting there with a demeanour as if he was in his rightful place, and not like he was new and tentative, as would be expected from any new member of the tribe. Robbie didn't like O'Brien much, but this guy annoyed him—the way he took over O'Brien's cubicle as though he owned it. No one introduced the new guy to anyone. No one bothered to make him welcome. Accountants didn't do that sort of thing, it seemed too personal and familiar, too overt, too avuncular. It was unheard of for accountants to make a fuss over another accountant. It turned out the new accountant's name was O'Reilly. And no one found it odd that he looked exactly like O'Brien, the spitting image. Order, in its many manifestations, was restored. Accounting was relentless, impersonal, and sacrosanct, and 'order' was its religion. The work must go on, by any accountants, but it must go on, and accountants were there to see it did. Accountants know there must not be an accounting pause or hiatus because, if there was, if only for a few seconds, the world would know nothing untoward happens when the business of accounting stops, and that would spell the end of accountants.

Robbie noted there was a slight pall of disappointment in the air during O'Reilly's first week, but after that it was replaced with the usual pall of disappointment that permeated the accounting department when 'order' was returned. Everyone was smiling, some were grinning, and some others were inexplicably chirpy. Chirpy accountants? Robbie thought nothing could turn an accountant's stomach faster than chirpiness among one's brethren. 'Check your chirpiness', might be an accountant mantra, if accountants had mantras, which they didn't unless you count, 'Don't panic, it all adds up in the end'.

Robbie opened a new page on his computer.

*An undiscussed pall of disappointment hung over the department. After two days it lifted. It was replaced by the usual reassuring undiscussed pall of disappointment, and order in the department was restored. Everyone settled and carried on, satisfied in the re-establishment of the status quo. Chirpiness was checked. Accountants took comfort in routine, in familiarity, in the primacy of order. They were unsettled by change or alteration. Everyone was satisfied with the fact that O'Reilly and O'Brien could be identical twins, indeed doppelgängers, so long as it wasn't discussed, acknowledged, or scrutinised. What was more important, was that accountancy continued.*

Robbie closed the page and didn't send it to anyone.

He put the uncanny identical resemblance between O'Reilly and O'Brien down to nothing more or less than Bentley's sometimes bizarre recruiting decisions, where being the best candidate for the job on the day was equally important as some other unnecessary, if challenging, attribute. In this case, Bentley would have chosen O'Reilly because, in all respects, he was identical to O'Brien. For further proof of Bentley's mischievousness regarding departmental recruitment, look at the fact that Bentley had recruited Robbie, which Robbie considered amounted to as good an example as you will find—QED, or *quod erat demonstrandum*, as Bentley would prefer. Robbie suspected Bentley of being a closet anarchist, and this made Robbie smile. Robbie might be the only person in the world who knew this about Bentley. On the other hand, he could be wrong.

Robbie caught Bentley's eye the morning O'Reilly took up residence in O'Brien's cubicle, and gestured toward O'Reilly, then back to Bentley with an eyebrow movement that begged the question about O'Reilly. Bentley took Robbie's lead and looked at O'Reilly then back to Robbie and held eye contact for long enough to communicate to Robbie it was inexplicable or inscrutable. He did this with a blank face, relying on holding a stare with Robbie, but in that stare Robbie and Bentley understood each other to the exclusion of all others in the department. Then Bentley returned his attention to whatever he was working on, indicating nothing more than his stare had conveyed, which was nothing and everything. Bentley had a new lunch box sitting on his desk.

Robbie looked at O'Reilly for some time. He turned his attention to his blank screen and typed: *That which does not kill us, makes us stronger.*

Robbie sent Friedrich Nietzsche's famous line to Bentley and watched out the corner of his eye to see if Bentley made any gesture of recognition. Bentley kept working and made no indication whatsoever he had read

Robbie's email. Robbie knew he would have.

Robbie felt unnerved that O'Brien had made a run for it. What unnerved Robbie was not knowing if O'Brien had made it or not. Was he a better person? happier? content? Was he a different person, or had he failed in his attempt to escape and disappear from his life?

*Reinvention might not be possible*, Robbie typed on a clean screen then highlighted it and deleted it. He then typed, *Lasciate ogne speranza, voi ch'intrate—Abandon all hope ye who enter here.*

Robbie sent this Dante Alighieri quote from Alighieri's seminal four-teenth-century poem, *Divine Comedy*, to Bentley. Bentley kept focused on his computer screen. Robbie felt sure he saw Bentley nod, but he couldn't be sure. It may not have been a nod—not a conscious nod. He didn't know if Bentley was reading his email. He hoped Bentley read it and agreed with the quote. He hoped Bentley's nod was a nod of significance and not an acciden-tal nod, or worse, not an actual nod, a non-nod. Robbie came to respect that Bentley had many talents, not the least of which was that he could execute a non-nod with aplomb.

Robbie loved Dante's poem and hoped he might write something of equal significance one day—he never expected to. Robbie knew he spent far too much time gazing into the *abyss* and fighting monsters to write something of such significance. He'd long ago abandoned all hope in the world in which he lived.

An email notification from Bentley appeared on Robbie's screen. It pinged.

*I read this. Interesting. You were in hospital at the time. You sent it to me.*

*B.*

*PS. Sab corrected a few errors. She hopes you don't mind. She loved the faux science. She said ignore her corrections if you prefer.*

Robbie saw there was an attachment and he opened it. It was another story. Another story he had no idea he'd written, or that he'd sent to Bentley. He automatically accepted all the changes Sabrina had suggested, without checking any of them.

### Keep Your Head
### By
### Robbie Carton

*Ever since the head transplant, I haven't been feeling myself, well that's not surprising. My number is 4442, and they have removed my sense of smell. So I can't tell you what the room I am confined to smells like, maybe it has no smell, but I can't tell you that either. Nothing particularly memorable about my number, except for some reason I keep saying it over and over in my head, my new head to be accurate, and it feels like it has made a groove in my new brain and my tongue feels rough, a bit like it has been rubbed against a sharp tooth filling relentlessly. 4442, 4442, 4442...4442 is not my name, just my number. My name is, well, let's leave that for now. I don't want to tell you my name. There's no big secret, it's just that it feels strange to say my name. My name feels theoretical. I wonder what part of me is represented by my name. I need time to adjust myself to some of these things.*

*They confine me in this sterile room. I don't mean sterile as in there is nothing much in it, although that is true as it happens. No, it is 'sterile', as in bacteria-free, I hope. I can't be exposed to any germs or viruses. The anti-rejection drugs are severe and have knocked out my defences. It is the only way to stop my head from attacking my body. It is the complete opposite of other transplants, like in the case of liver, lungs, heart etc. where the danger is that the body rejects the new organ. Not in my case. The danger is the new head will initiate an all-out attack on my body. 4442.*

*My wife has visited twice. It is a whole ordeal. She must be stripped and scrubbed from head to foot and dressed in sterile clothing. They allow me sexual contact with her but with surgical gloves and a sterile condom. We are not allowed to kiss for obvious reasons. Besides, she breathes through a mask attached to a tube that supplies her oxygen from outside the room. The earlier numbers died, swift, ugly, and excruciating deaths. It was only as they neared the first thousand that things started working better, and the mortality rate declined. 4442, 4442. The first attempts were crude and experimental—the heads won.*

*I feel sad and lonely, and alien most of all. They tell me it's normal but what's normal? How normal can anyone be with someone else's head on their shoulders or someone else's body under their head? And how do they know what's normal? They have still got their own heads. It started to occur to me the other* day, how do I know the doctors and surgeons have their own heads? I can't stop the tears, even though they aren't technically my tears.

After the first one thousand or so, they started to get much better results, and I have every chance of surviving. I use the word 'surviving', and I use the personal pronoun 'I' but that is arguable. It is debatable just which 'I' I am and 'survival'? The best that can be said is that I am not dead, at least not in the traditional sense, but do 'I' any longer exist, am 'I' dead? Or am I not dead? 4442. My original head is dead. Four thousand four hundred and forty-two. It hasn't escaped my notice that 4442 ends with forty-two—the famous Douglas Adams number signalling the answer to the big question. I've never been superstitious, but I am now. Is that me or him?

I have been experiencing some odd thoughts. I don't know if they are my thoughts, though. There's not much to do here, and I don't feel like reading or learning anything. I'm feeling, well it is difficult, but I feel antagonistic, but this makes no sense. My brain, that is my old brain, died. It grew one of the terminal tumours that started spreading through all populations several years ago. They recommended a head transplant as a matter of some urgency. I feel resentment toward my old brain, as though it was weak, not tough enough, and succumbed to the tumour. Like it didn't bother to put up a fight, like it knew it could be replaced, so it didn't try.

I don't know whose head I got. They don't tell you. You can't know whose kidney or liver or heart you get, so why would they tell you whose head you're getting? They remove your face and surgically impose it on your new head so you look the same, with the proviso your new bone structure will be different from your old bone structure and, therefore, while you look near enough the same there will be subtle differences. Differences that remind you, you aren't you. These differences are affecting my wife too. I can tell by the way she looks at me. I think my nose is bigger, which might be ironic, given I can't use it to smell. I have different coloured eyes. Mine were brown, and now I have blue eyes. These things are not important, they say. You are alive, and you look pretty close to yourself. But when I look into a mirror, I don't see me. At least I seem to have more hair, and I look a bit younger. I wonder for a moment who my donor was and how he is now influencing my life.

I guess, as they tried to convince me, you are who you are because of your memories regardless of whose brain you house them in. I can't say I found this comforting, but what choice is there? You remember who you are throughout your life, and yet we all, those still in possession of our own heads, are largely *blissfully unaware that, apparently, you are who you are because of what you remember. So they have developed this somewhat crude and rudimentary method of transplanting your memories from your now dead head to your new head. They must do this before the new head you are receiving has been removed from its body, which means you need someone who is in an induced coma but is going to die when the machines are turned off. They have to be dying of something below the epiglottis, like heart disease or pancreatitis. By the way, they cut just below the epiglottis, for reasons no one explained or thought to, and I didn't ask. You ask why not transplant the brain? The surgery would be way too complicated—you have to connect eyes and ears, indeed all the senses nearly. If the whole head is done, then the connections, while incredibly complex, are far less in number. So, obviously, your donor's head, eyes, ears, nose, mouth etc. must all be healthy, and the brain must be in tiptop shape.*

*You might not get the same IQ as you had, but they say they try to match it with your own as best they can, though there are no guarantees. Anyway, as I say, they try to transfer as much of your memory to your new brain as is possible. This is inefficient though, as this technology is well behind the miraculous business of completing a successful full head transplant. They started this with pigs, and it wasn't necessary to transfer a pig's memory, so they spent less time on this part of the procedure. My brain started to suffer memory loss due to the increasing advancement of the inoperable tumour, so the sooner they got on with the whole business, the better.*

*But I have definite gaps in what I remember, and I know this because when I look at old photographs there are people, I don't recognise even though I am in the photo with them. This is a weird feeling. It feels heavy, like my brain has sunk to the bottom of its cranium cradle and I feel a bit foggy. They also can't guarantee I will not have some residual memories and thoughts still alive in my head from the donor. I know my donor was an engineer or builder of some sort. He built things and had mathematical formulas in his head and preferred redheads. We have something in common there. At least he wasn't gay, which would be a complication too far. I keep getting flashes of information or partial thoughts about all sorts of things that don't make sense.*

*They tell me smell will be the big problem. It is a powerful trigger for memories, and certain smells will trigger donor memories. This can cause mental deterioration and lack of balance, and so they dismantle your smell, which is one thing you lose. You might not think loss of smell is that great a price to pay for life, and it is damn hard to argue against that, but it is a big loss, much*

much bigger than you might imagine. 4442, 4442...Some of these rogue residual thoughts can be frightening, not that I want to kill people or anything like that. If truth be known, I had those thoughts from time to time with my brain.

I have a lot of sexual thoughts, more than seems normal, or normal for me, as far as I can remember. It is fascinating, looking into the sexual fantasy of another person. I was shocked, but then we all would be if we knew others' sexual fantasies. In the memory transfer, sometimes some memories come across incomplete. For example, yesterday while daydreaming, I was counting the number of times I've been to London. I was sitting in a vineyard on a warm day, with a summer breeze blowing across my face, and I was trying to count the number of times I'd travelled to London, but then I couldn't remember anything about London at all, except the names on the monopoly board.

They told me that with the assimilation drug regime and time, I soon wouldn't remember which are my memories and which are the memories of the donor, and that is the best it will be. The alternative is death, and as far as I know, death has its own limitations—such as no memories at all, yours, or anyone's. They tried to explain to me it is much like it is when you enter a witness protection program. You are the same person, basically, except you have a different persona you have to relearn and use.

You have to ignore your past and embrace your new future, except you can't leave everything behind. You remember things from the life you had to leave, your wants, your desires. You spend a lot of time wondering about who you were and who you are now, and mostly who you are now is made up. So the critical question is, 'Does my body have a new head, or does my head have a new body?' You miss a lot of things too. I do—I think that's why I'm so teary. They told me this would be the case, it is also, in part, the drugs working. So I'm trying to generate as many new memories as fast as I can, a new life I can cope with and develop. This is what they counsel you to do—move on, accept it, your old self has, by and large, gone, it's there by degrees, but it will be changed in remarkable ways. That's what they say in the counselling, but it's hard to accept, very hard. I'm not sure I have yet. You might think this is a fantastic opportunity to reinvent yourself, be a better person. But don't forget you are dealing with only some of your own memories and some of someone else's memories, and what if the donor wanted to be a different person as well? You would still fantasise over reinvention but now with someone else's head. The whole thing is enough to give you a headache.

They tell you that you must accept you are a hybrid version of you, your donor, and your new self. How much of your memories do you need to call *yourself who you were, to be authentically you as you were? They never answer these questions. They can't, they are learning too.*

*I look through new eyes, but eyes are eyes, they see, and that's about it. The same with ears. They don't see and hear things differently—they just see and hear. It's your new brain that is seeing and hearing things differently, you think. You can't be sure. When does this new brain belong to you? When do you feel it does? Immediately you come out of the anaesthetic? Not really. You feel pretty lousy at first as though, I said this jokingly to my wife, you've just had your throat cut.*

*Luckily, I remembered my wife, there was no guarantee. And I still seem to have a sense of humour. Whether or not it is mine, remains to be seen, but my wife laughed, sort of. It's an urban supposition that some head transplantees use the occasion to not remember their wife. No one knows what you remember— only what you tell them you remember.*

*I remember thinking the first time I made love to my wife with my new head, it had a feeling of 'first time' about it, for her as well, she reported. I saw in her eyes she looked at my face, my new face as though I were a stranger, her orgasm seemed more intense to me. I wonder if it has been a fantasy for her to have sex with a stranger. Am I a stranger to her? She is to me, at least in part, but not in looks, she looks the same. I look different to her, but that isn't enough, after all she could just close her eyes during sex and remember me as I was. I have the same penis so nothing new there. One of the memories I have is that she almost always closed her eyes during sex and that is what I noticed was different. This time she stared at my face (through her full-face mask) and into my eyes with some kind of alien intensity. For me it was like making love to an astronaut, not that I've done that. I heard her laboured breathing and her muffled orgasm. She made love to me like she never had before, at least as far as I can remember. It concerned me. Was she making love to me, or was she being unfaithful? She confessed it felt like she was being taken, only with her consent, if that makes sense. I remember how much I loved her before. I am glad of that memory. I cried after we made love the first time with my new head. I couldn't smell her. I remember what she smelt like, and I felt an intense comfort from that. I hope I never forget that smell even if it's not me, entirely, remembering it or smelling it.*

Robbie closed the file and sat still. He could hear the background noises of the department, the sound of accountants, both sexes, herding, foraging, hunting, picking their noses, adjusting their underpants, one of them peeling a banana. He listened to the sound of the silence between the noises. The sounds *absurdity* makes when it thrives. He heard Bentley talking on the phone, but Robbie only picked up the odd word. He heard Gloria laughing out loud, as though someone had told her a bawdy joke, or she'd told one to someone, or she'd adjusted the ribbon in her hair. Robbie could hear the sound of his own breathing and heartbeat. A gorilla moved across his peripheral vision, looking at some paperwork while he/she walked toward his/her desk. A gorilla with a desk, with a pink ribbon tied to its fur. The gorilla's fur not the desk, the desk had no fur. The office seemed normal to Robbie, at least superficially. Everything was normal or as normal as normal gets in the world. Yet it still felt bizarre and unnecessary and unnormal. Robbie couldn't experience anything, not even the 'unnormal'.

'Are you doing anything tonight?' Robbie felt like chewing some gum. He thought he could smell chewing gum, so his sense of smell had returned from wherever it had been, and it was at that moment he'd realised it had been absent. Robbie had never chewed gum in his life, and, as far as he knew, he had no idea what chewing gum smelt like, but he was sure he could smell it.

'Robbie? You okay?'

The voice lingered in his vicinity for a bit before it registered with him. He looked up to see Bentley standing next to him.

'Sorry? I was just...er...'

'Thinking...?' Bentley helped Robbie find the word he was searching for.

'Sorry?' Robbie tried to get himself concentrating. If he could stop thinking about chewing gum that would be a start.

'Thinking...you were thinking, lost in your thoughts, that sort of thing,' Bentley expanded.

'Yeah, probably...certainly lost, always lost,' Robbie said, finally engaging with Bentley. 'Well lost, well well lost.'

'I was asking if you happen to be doing anything tonight. I just had a text from Sab. She asked if you wanted to come for dinner. She's at the market and could pick up something tasty, she said.' Bentley held his phone in front of Robbie's face, and Robbie could see the text from Sabrina sitting over Sabrina's beautiful smile.

'You know, if you're free. No obligation. It's a bit short notice.'

'No, that'd be great. I'd love to, tasty sounds great.'

'Right then.' Bentley didn't stay for any further conversation. He headed back to his cubicle, texting on his phone. Robbie assumed he was confirming with Sabrina. Robbie felt honoured at that moment—feeling honoured was an entirely new emotion for Robbie.

Bentley stopped and turned back to Robbie. 'Did you want to bring someone? Sab's asking.'

'Thanks, but a bit short notice for that. So no.'

'Yes, quite,' Bentley replied and turned back toward his cubicle while finishing off his text.

Right at that moment, Robbie felt about as isolated and alone as he had ever felt. It wasn't that it was short notice to ask someone to come to Bentley's for dinner—that was always the case unless you were in a relationship, then you would have someone to bring. It was that Robbie had no one. No one he thought of as his, or who in reverse, thought of him as hers. That would be nice, he imagined. He felt alone because, at his age, he should have a relationship—someone he loved and was committed to. He'd like to be committed in a relationship. It would seem to be the least he could have achieved by now. He would have loved to answer Bentley with, "I'll just check with ... (insert name of wife, girlfriend, partner, or Sophie preferably)." He had no one.

His stomach groaned. He was hungry. He was looking forward to being comforted by Sabrina. She had the serene ability to make him feel okay about himself. She relieved the stress he suffered. It must be the reason Bentley was so 'okay' with being Bentley. Robbie glanced over to see Bentley oiling a bike pedal, then Bentley's phone rang. He took the call and opened a file on his computer. Bentley was at ease and had a confidence about him, in spite of the facts that Robbie considered would indicate otherwise, as in, he was an accountant working in a silly job, in a silly office, achieving nothing that made the world a better place. The same as Robbie. It was Sabrina. It had to be Sabrina who made Bentley the man he was. Wouldn't it be great if there was a Sabrina website where you could order a Sabrina clone? Robbie imagined if that was the case, it probably offered fine-tuning. Like you could order personality preferences and physical changes to suit, like striking red hair, perfect skin, maybe the odd freckle, a Sabrina smile. But then, he thought, he would be happy with someone genuine, someone to love, and someone who would love him. Robbie thought of Sophie, he always thought of Sophie, but this only made him feel sadder. He made a mental note to buy some flowers for Sabrina. Roses? Maybe not roses, that seemed a bit 'wrong message', and he was saving the roses option for Sophie. Tulips would work. Sabrina would love anything he chose.

Robbie opened the file of the 'Head Transplant' story again. He had no idea where it came from, and it provided no clue as to who he was and where he had been, or, more importantly, where he was going, if indeed he was going anywhere. But it did discuss identity and its origins and how you were the person you were.

He typed a new page,

*While all the characters are made up, their stories are true.*

He thought to send this to Bentley, but he was sick of sending his stupid thoughts and micro stories to Bentley. Bentley never complained, but he had every right to, Robbie figured.

Robbie had thought a lot about where his stories came from. They had some 'pickups' from his personality, his life experiences, but still, they had a life of their own. They had elements that were far from Robbie's life, as though they were determined to exist separately from their author, or in spite of their author, or in denial of their author. Robbie couldn't be sure, but he was often amazed at the dispirit content of his stories, and it was like he was reading them for the first time, no matter how often he read them. This both fascinated and confounded him. Most of the time he hardly recognised anything of himself in his work, and yet they were about him. Not him precisely but 'him' as a representative of the 'Robbies' of the world. In short, anyone who had ever felt confounded, tense, forlorn etc., and that was what disturbed him the most.

He reread the last paragraph of the Head Transplant story. The story had no ending, no formal ending that is, but then, having said that, it had made its points. He thought about smells and how powerful they were. He recalled how Sophie Fanshawe smelt. He thought if he could revisit that smell once more in his life, he might find some contentment. He didn't know how he could sniff her without causing her alarm, or her thinking he was a complete nob. Had he stumbled on a solution to life? The scent of Sophie Fanshawe would be so overpowering as to camouflage absurdity in the world, not eliminate it, which could never happen and should never happen, but force it to a small corner where its influence might be limited, or manageable at least.

He looked over at the nearest corner on the floor to see if 'absurdity' might be cringing there. It wasn't.

Later that day, sitting in his cubicle in the darkened office before he had to leave for Bentley and Sabrina's, he tried to put together some thoughts. He took a swig from the can of beer sitting next to his computer. Robbie still wasn't sure what had happened to him. He had vague memories that jumbled with other things in his life. Red Dust, Twinkling Lights, Loud Noise, Outback Silence, Columns of Numbers, More Columns, A Tarantula, Sophie Fanshawe, Paris, His Penis, A Feather Duster. He told everyone he felt fine. The doctors were convinced but recommended he seek 'advice'. They meant 'help'. He knew he wouldn't.

***

Upon leaving the hospital several weeks ago, or was it months? Robbie went back to his flat. He arrived late at night and remembered standing in front of his apartment door for some time before he opened it. He detected a tic in his left knee. He'd never had a tic before, and he wasn't sure how to spell 'tic'. He was exhausted. He had no idea what he was waiting for, or why he was standing in front of his door. It was like someone had nailed his shoes to the floor. For a shattering moment he couldn't remember who he was or where he was. But that passed. A huge food hamper sat in front of his door. He stared at it. He could see the card on top of the cellophane and knew who it was from because it said, 'Get Well Soon, from Bentley, Sabrina and the crew!' But also, because only Bentley would use caps for 'Get Well Soon' and finish with an exclamation mark, totally unnecessary in the context. And who were 'the crew'? It was unlikely anyone else in the office would have been involved, but it was typical of Bentley to generously include them. Why was a food hamper making him feel so depressed? It was a gesture of goodwill, sent with affection, meant to make him feel good. It was thoughtful, he'd been away for a long time, he'd have no food in his flat. A food hamper was the perfect gift. He saw Sabrina's influence all over it. He felt cared for, and this was new to him.

*Get Well Soon*. Robbie hadn't known he was 'unwell'…well, as unwell as he was. And was he still unwell? Would he always be unwell? He knew his life was not as it should be. He couldn't say what it should be because it had never been anything other than what it was. He couldn't say what it was or what it wasn't. When he wasn't 'himself', he was still himself. He worried he lacked stability, to say the least. Other-self, on the other hand, was always brimming with confidence. Annoyingly so. Other-self said he'd played cricket recently and scored a century and wanted to join something and mix with other 'other-selves'.

Robbie knew he had to do something about himself. He couldn't go on the way he was. He knew that. He knew he wasn't Austin Quinn. He knew other-self was happy with him being Austin Quinn. Robbie knew he had invented and tried on the persona of Austin Quinn to see if it worked—disappearing into someone else—but it didn't. *Wherever you go, there you are.* 'When he was not 'himself', he was still himself. 'Wherever you go, there you are,' he whispered. His moving lips almost touched the door. He thought he could kiss the door right now and it wouldn't seem strange. He put an arm out and leant against the door. He rested his head on his arm. He was over the hamper, literally and figuratively. But he appreciated the gesture. The gesture gave him some hope and a number of tins of food, and crackers, and beer.

He envied Bentley and Sabrina. They had each other and were in love and dedicated to each other. He thought if he had a 'Sabrina', or in his case a 'Sophie', he might be better than he was, or as good as he was. He might be healthier. Hold on, he might be a 'Bentley'. He smiled at the thought. Once, such a thought would have terrified him, but now he wasn't so sure. What was so bad about being Bentley, living a Bentley life? It wasn't as though being a 'Robbie' was working. When he thought about it, Bentley had a sense of humour. He got things. Bentley got Robbie more than anyone else in Robbie's life. Bentley understood things about Robbie that even Robbie didn't understand. The difference between Robbie and Bentley was that Bentley, in his modest way, was surviving, and prospering, which was a lot more than could be said for himself. Bentley had room in his life. He had room for Robbie's unreliability. He had room for Robbie's behaviour. *It was the best of times, it was the worst of times.* Robbie finally saw that he could celebrate both.

Robbie clenched his jaw, bent down and grabbed the cellophane wrapping. He picked up the hamper and opened the door. He stepped inside with a tic still in his knee. The flat was in darkness. It was hot, stuffy, and empty, apart from his furniture, a lamp and the birdcage. The bird was gone. Mail had accumulated inside the door. It was his. He stepped over it. He put the hamper on the bench in the kitchen and opened the fridge, exposing some half-empty takeaway curry boxes on one of the shelves. He could see some green mould inside the top of the boxes. There were three bottles of beer in the door. He took one and removed the top. He left the other two. He grabbed the takeaway boxes and threw them in the waste bin next to the fridge. He sat on his sofa in the dark drinking beer. The neon light flashed its comforting colours around him. On and off, on and off...like a heart-beat. He could hear the gentle ticking of the blue clock on the wall over the kitchen bench. It reminded him of how life continued, with or without you—relentless, dedicated, indifferent, mouldy. The ticking continued when he wasn't there. His presence was a matter of complete indifference to the ticking clock. And the mould grew and filled up spaces left unattended.

*** 

Time passed. How much time, Robbie couldn't say. He'd been to Sabrina and Bentley's place for dinner days ago, or weeks. He worked at the office all day and wrote all night. It was hot and he wore his tennis shorts. He opened his fridge and moved the two bottles of beer from the door to the front of the shelf, so when the door was opened, the bottles of beer would be the first thing visible. He placed a bottle of brown sauce between the two beers. He was in a hurry. Time was running out. Robbie sat at his kitchen table with his computer opened. The screen displayed the following:

*What Will Happen to You?*
*A Novel*
By
#$%&^*@*

He stared at the page for a few seconds. He had no memory of coming up with the title of his novel, but he liked it. He had a vague recollection of the story. He didn't know if he was still alive, or still in hospital in a coma, or in the parallel universe with Bentley, Sabrina, and Gloria look-alikes. He didn't know if he had ever been alive. And he didn't know if those thoughts were in his head or in his novel. He thought about Sophie Fanshawe. He wondered where she was at that moment. He always wondered where she was. He could smell her. He imagined her bladder was empty and his hand resting on her warm stomach. He could feel the heat from her skin. He could hear her delicate breathing next to his cheek. He hoped that whatever universe he was in, she was in the same universe. That would be something for him to hold on to at least. He wondered why there was no name below the 'A Novel by' line. Was he not sure who he was? Was he not sure what name to use? What was the importance of a name when it came down to it?

He sat motionless. The colours from the flashing neon bounced across his face and dark hair. He saw the story in front of him. He went to the top of the first page of the file and read the words on the screen.

*INT. AUSTIN'S APARTMENT—NIGHT*

*One hot summer's night, Austin Quinn, as he preferred to be called at night, sat alone in his apartment gazing at his computer screen in deep thought. It was late. He glanced up at the blue clock on the wall. It was 00.42. He turned his eyes back to the pulsing cursor. He watched it while he waited for inspiration, but all that came was perspiration. The light from the screen lit up his pallid face and made his Ken doll black hair darker. He wore a pair of cream tennis shorts. Sweat droplets ran down his chest and down the middle of his back. In his late twenties, single, and suffering from chronic loneliness, Austin Quinn hadn't written anything new for a long time. His life lacked form. He felt like he was a character in someone's novel. The thought that it was not too late to escape hovered at the edges of his mind.*

Robbie sat alone in his apartment, gazing at his computer screen. It was late. He wore only a pair of cream tennis shorts. Sweat droplets ran down his chest and down the middle of his back. He read the words in front of him, which had a vague ring to them, as though he had written them long ago but as someone else.

*The city rested during the sweltering nights. It ignored the stench from the rotting garbage on its streets. It ignored the strange birds in its parks. It watched the few citizens still in the city but it took no particular action against them. Not while it rested. Not in this heat. Your history, where you came from, how you existed before the city, these things were irrelevant. The only thing of relevance was, 'what will happen to you?'*

Robbie snapped out of his mesmerised state. He shifted his weight in his chair. He had no idea how long he'd been sitting still—minutes, days, weeks? His muscles ached. On the page in front of him were the words *A Novel by*

He moved the cursor to the next line down and selected '#$%&^*@*' and typed his name in its place. He added the words *'(Brown Sauce)'* as a subtitle under the title.

*What Will Happen to You?*
*(Brown Sauce)*
*A Novel*
*By*
*Robbie Carton*

Robbie had made a decision. He realised with clarity he wouldn't be any good to himself, to Bentley, to Gloria and especially to Sophie, or anyone for that matter, until he answered the question, 'What will happen to you?'

He scrolled to the end of the novel. He read the final paragraph.

*The city in which Austin Quinn lived was a place where things disappeared, and no one thought it odd. One night, Austin disappeared. His name was not Austin Quinn.*

*The End*

# From the desk of Bentley Herbert!

Hi, my name is Bentley Herbert. You will know me as various versions of this name, some shorter, some longer, some derivations and some misleading. My personal favourite was 'The Bertram Shandyman'. You have to celebrate Robbie's imagination. He was like a corrupt file. You never knew what he'd come out with, and neither did he.

I remain married to Sabrina. Like Robbie and every other accountant in the department, I must agree, Sabrina choosing me is unfathomable—it was unfathomable, but enough about that for now. My story such as it is, can be left for another time, *will* be left for another time. You are more interested in what happened to Robbie. I wish I could tell you, but as Robbie would say, 'I'd have to kill you if I told you. I had to kill the guy who told me'. A Robbieism, the last part, but I'll get to all that shortly. For now, I'd like to clear up some misconceptions.

To my knowledge, I'm sure there is no excessive nostril-flaring at the end of my sentences, and I do not have a habit of using air quotes. I especially do not hold my two fingers extended from each hand, in the air, at either side of my head and jump them up and down to emphasise what I'm saying. I did try to part my hair the wrong way once, that much is true, and I looked like a nob to be sure, which was Robbie's intention. Also, perhaps I'm guilty of the use of the odd Latin phrase *verum (true)*, but I get that from Sab who is a scholar, and she's been teaching me, and I'm sure I didn't overuse it, but maybe I did—*iam capta*, (point taken). Further to this, I don't have a magnifying glass, I don't collect stamps, and I don't know the first thing about brass, or the rubbing of it. Sab and I do go bushwalking with or without a banana in my knapsack, and I don't possess a peaked beanie, but I might buy one. Robbie thought to enhance me, and others, with various quirks and personality traits. It was his way of coping with his life at the office. And remember, he was a writer, he made stuff up. This whole account is made up, except for the parts that are true, as Robbie would say.

I suspect though, knowing him as I do, he'd probably be a little remorseful if everything he wrote and said about people he knew didn't make as much sense as he might have wanted or intended. 'You are not always in control of the narrative', he'd say, and in his case especially. He would add, 'Sometimes the narrative controls you'. Both these quotes were sent to me as emails in a running dialogue. He was probably right in both cases. Robbie thought deeply about the concept of story and how it affects us, as is evident in his prolific writing of short stories, or micro stories as he calls them. My personal favourite was *'Small Talk'*, where he portrayed us as friends and where he was the best of himself. The story made it onto the longlist of an international short story competition and received a 'Highly Commended', but Robbie is unaware of this fact. I'm glad he kept our respective names in the story. (**You can visit the author's website to request the 'almost' prize-winning final version, free.**)

I do think though, that Robbie would have had a modest hope. His hope would be that, on some level, some level important and profound to you, the reader, that it made some sense to you, and it had an impact. Maybe a lasting impact, and for the good. Always for the good.

Robbie Carton was, sorry, *is* a good guy. He had hope and was at pains to say in an email to Gloria and myself, 'Hope is the last to die'. Sophie said this one night in The Writers Circle. I remember Austin/Robbie made a note of it.

Robbie had some issues, to be sure, but then don't we all? And BTW and apropos of nothing much in particular, but I would have thought fire probably came after language. If you had fire then your gesticulations and grunting, as you would do in daylight, would have also worked at night, but only because you could see the person doing the grunting and gesticulating by the light of the fire. So, it can be hypothesised that fire came after language. People needed to develop language to communicate in the dark, because there was no fire to see their gesticulations, for what it's worth. Robbie liked this theoretical nonsense. He enjoyed questions without apparent answers. Questions based on twisted logic, or false premises containing bizarre links, or category errors as he preferred. He enjoyed flawed reasoning to prove something true, or not true. He enjoyed suggesting the answer to anything was 'Brown Sauce', but he was happy for you to choose any coloured sauce you prefer. He argued that annoyingly in life there are no right or wrong answers, while I might add, and stress, this does not apply to accountancy. I think Robbie suffered from the loss of his parents, who both died early and together, in Europe somewhere, I think. Was it in Holland? I'm not sure. He never spoke about them.

Robbie Carton is my friend. I wanted him to be less forlorn, tense, anxious and worried than he was. I wanted him to realise his potential, not so much as an accountant—I don't believe he would ever have found contentment as an accountant, as competent as he was—but as a successful writer, which was his true ambition in life.

Robbie had an appreciation of the absurdity of life, and how absurdity infected the living of life. He particularly liked how people stop noticing absurdity when it's everywhere. There's the story Robbie told about the lighthouse keeper when lighthouses, in times gone, used a cannon firing every hour on the hour to warn ships. The keeper was asleep one night when the cannon failed, and he woke and yelled, 'What was that?'

'Sometimes you only notice something in its absence rather than in its presence', as Robbie wrote and sent to me in another email along with the following:

*The first line of an actor's cv.*

*"Cast in the role of the Invisible Man, for the stage play of the same name, her performance was transcendental. It was like she wasn't even on stage." The Daily Planet.*

*Another critic effused,*

*"Her performance was so pitch perfect, it was like she was, well, actually invisible, and you couldn't tell she wasn't a man." Anonymous Drama Critic.*

Robbie had the sharpness of humour I wish I had. I'm sorry he couldn't find a way to use his talents to save himself. I'm being a bit prescriptive, perhaps he *has* found a way to save himself.

So, back to the question of what happened to Robbie. I know, as I'm sure you do by now, that Robbie Carton assumed the alias of Austin Quinn as his alter ego and, to a large extent, at least as much as we can work out and piece together, Robbie lived as Austin Quinn at night and by day, as Robbie. Austin Quinn, the one in The Writers Circle, was a Robbie invention. I don't suggest Robbie wasn't aware of this—he was. Maybe Robbie thought Austin, or someone similar, was the person Robbie thought to be if he could have disappeared from his life and start again. So he trialled it, as it were. He gave it a go, tried it on for size.

Robbie constructed a life and a story for Austin. He suggested a relationship between Austin and Sophie. Whether or not that happened in reality, I couldn't say. I suspect Sophie hoped Robbie would replace Austin permanently and Austin would disappear, but that didn't happen. Not in the way she wanted. She got some of her wish, at least half of it. Austin did disappear but unfortunately for Sophie and me, Sabrina and Gloria, Robbie also disappeared. Robbie's fascination with reinvention was all-consuming and, in the end, it did consume him. In his safer moments, he liked to say, 'Wherever you go there you are.' Robbie, as Austin in The Writers Circle, often said this when anyone's work was too autobiographical. This adage suggested on some level in life, that he suspected reinvention wouldn't work, but perhaps he was compelled to find out both as a person and a writer.

After Robbie's stint in the hospital recovering from what could be described as a partial breakdown of some sort, combined with a solid hit to his head as he crashed into a garbage bin, he returned to work. His seen-it-all-before doctor was aware of his habit of assuming the persona of Austin Quinn as his after-hours *doppelgänger* and thought it was 'cute but harmless'. The doctor suggested without much enthusiasm that Robbie might benefit from some professional help, someone to talk to. Robbie didn't heed that advice. I knew he wouldn't. Instead, he wrote it out of his system.

After he returned to work, he seemed to settle down, but he became increasingly obsessed with O'Brien's disappearance. Robbie couldn't leave it alone. He was desperate to know what had happened to O'Brien when he went to the outback mines. Robbie remained unsatisfied after O'Reilly started work in O'Brien's cubicle. Employing O'Reilly may have been a mistake, at least in regard to Robbie's sanity, but I was trying to help O'Brien. 'O'Reilly' informed me Robbie didn't speak or engage with him, as though Robbie couldn't deal with O'Reilly, as though O'Reilly didn't exist to Robbie and that O'Reilly was acting.

When Robbie had been back at work for enough time and appeared in good enough shape to fulfil his usual duties auditing the outback mines, I sent him back out there. I was tentative about it, but I also wanted him to feel like I, we, had confidence in him. I tried to boost his morale, and I thought the trip out there would be good for him. He liked the trips to the mines, and he told me he missed them. So I sent him. He filed his report, which was as professional and complete as was his habit. Then he disappeared. It isn't known if he disappeared while he was out there, or if he'd returned to the city to disappear. His last known sighting was when he said goodbye to the staff at the Paris mine, shook their hands and hugged some of them before getting into his car and driving off down the track. His four-wheel drive was found abandoned on the side of the track, notionally at the midway point between the two mines, nestled in a dry creek bed. The keys were in the ignition. The car had a full tank. The tyres were inflated. There were two bottles of water on the back seat, one half empty. The car started up when the police officers tried the engine. There was nothing wrong with the vehicle. But Robbie, in a mirror image of O'Brien's disappearance, was nowhere to be found. Like O'Brien, Robbie had disappeared without a trace. The police announced there were no suspicious circumstances. A search was mounted, but nothing of Robbie was found. And again, like O'Brien, his footprints weren't found, only the tracks of the comings and goings of wildlife. It was as though he got out of the car, floated off into the bush and vanished. The last known trace of Robbie was the dust tail his car threw up as he hit the dirt track, leaving the mine, and the staff waving goodbye to him. Some reported they felt as though he was saying goodbye for the last time. Others didn't give it much thought, and expected to see him again in a month as usual, and swore the barbeque, which had gone missing over the weekend, would be *in situ* for his return, come what may.

The police sergeant in charge of the investigation seemed resigned and made the point that, in the absence of any big disaster, like a bridge collapse, or a massive terrorist attack, or a natural disaster such as a tsunami or earthquake, often people would use the event to disappear from their lives. They sometimes used the outback to do it. With a little bit of planning, you could disappear into the bush, and if there were no suspicious circumstances, the police considered it not worthy of investigation. In the outback, people for thousands of kilometres know who you are, what you're doing and where you are, it's called the bush telegraph. Getting anyone to talk about it is another thing entirely. If people wanted to leave their life and no law was broken in the process, then it wasn't anyone's business, even the local wallopers thought this. It is what it is. The police sergeant was known for his raucous renditions of anything poetic. Such a person is known as a 'bush poet'. 'The bush is benign, but that doesn't mean what you might think it does.' The officer smiled and left it at that.

We had Robbie to dinner before he left on his trip to the mines. We told him about my promotion to New York and that Sab and I were transferring there to live, and that Gloria, as my current Deputy, was being promoted to head the department. I explained to Robbie how I had to go to New York to look at the job, and that was the reason I sent him to Paris at such short notice. He seemed happy for Gloria, and us. I told him Gloria would appoint her own Deputy. I said he should think about taking on more responsibility, should he be asked. That night he seemed relaxed, resolved, more so than seemed within his character. I found it unnerving. Perhaps he'd achieved some serenity, or it was the effect Sab had on him. Maybe, though, Robbie had a plan and had settled on what he was going to do, and he came to dinner as a way of saying goodbye. I miss him, more than I would have thought—as much as I would have thought.

At the bottom of the final report Robbie emailed from the mine before he disappeared, were the words 'Don't Panic'. They were at the end of the report, rather than was his habit of putting the word 'Panic' at the top of any paperwork he submitted. On this occasion the words, 'Don't Panic' were followed with the words, 'I apologise for everything'. It's a small point, but in the face of the mystery of his disappearance, you do start to examine every minor detail. I thought he was sending me a message and so I did as he requested. I didn't panic. I'm not sure what it was he felt he needed to apologise for.

We made inquiries. We reported him missing. We dealt with the police. Sab and I took a trip out to the mines but came up blank. We called his phone, which went to message-bank, then it stopped working altogether.

One late afternoon, Gloria and I checked out Robbie's apartment with the landlord's permission before he re-let it. After the landlord let us in, he left. We stayed in Robbie's apartment for hours, until darkness fell. We didn't speak. It was as though we were absorbing Robbie's life, his world, and his story. We thought he might speak to us in some mysterious way. He didn't. Or did he? We drank the beer in his fridge. Gloria wondered if he might have left the bottles there for us. They were on the top shelf at the front and between them was an unopened bottle of brown sauce—Robbie's well-known response to life's absurdities. Other than the beer and the bottle of brown sauce, the fridge was empty, cleaned out and clean.

As the dark crawled through Robbie's apartment like 'floodwaters creep down a dry riverbed', as he once described the passing of time, in one of his stories he wrote for the company newsletter, we absorbed the neon light searching the apartment. The landlord had told us when he first entered the dark apartment after the lease had expired and the rent had stopped, he saw a blue clock on the wall, an empty birdcage, a hand mirror on the kitchen bench, a sofa and standing lamp. I looked at the clock and saw it had stopped at 00.42. Gloria thought this critical number from Douglas Adams' book *The Hitchhiker's Guide to the Galaxy* was a clue or message from Robbie, as it was Robbie's favourite number. The chances the clock stopped at precisely 00.42 were too improbable to contemplate. This, and the brown sauce bottle, confirmed Robbie's intentions and his coded message. The landlord saw nothing else except a lot of white and brown mail on the floor inside the front door, and a manuscript in the middle of the room, abandoned as though someone had left their imagination on the floor to be covered in dust. On the title page he had read the following:

> *What Will Happen to You?*
> *(Brown Sauce)*
> *A Novel*
> *By*
> *Robbie Carton*

The landlord had gathered up the pile of letters in front of the door. He stuffed the letters into a garbage bag. He picked up the manuscript and was about to put it in the garbage bag, but hesitated. Instead, he left it on the kitchen bench. As he closed the door to leave, a puff of air must have caused the title page to break free and float to the floor. The landlord was gone, leaving behind the blue clock, the spaces between things (a topic close to Robbie's interests), and the empty birdcage, all in darkness. The title page of the manuscript was still on the dark, stained floor when we entered the apartment. The intermittent neon light flashed across the white sheet. It was as if Robbie, or his *non de plume* alter ego, Austin Quinn, or whatever name he has now adopted, had long gone and would never return. But had left his manuscript to be found by someone. Perhaps he thought *that* someone might be me.

Perhaps Robbie has disappeared and started again as someone else, or perhaps his existence was fictional, and Austin Quinn was the real Robbie Carton or vice versa, or perhaps I've made this whole thing up myself, or Robbie has imagined me, and I'm the invention of Robbie's fiction—a character in his novel. Or perhaps we are all characters in Sophie's novel. The postmodern Robbie Carton character would love this conjecture.

Gloria noticed the hand mirror propped up at an angle against the kitchen back-splash—it was held in place with some blu-tack. The blue and red neon light kept flashing through the apartment and words appeared on and off in the mirror, but they were in reverse. I wrote them down. They were *ecnarusnI gnoL eviL ?uoy ot neppah lliw tahW*. I held them up to the mirror, which had the effect of reversing them. We read them: *What will happen to you? Live Long Insurance.* This is a slogan posted all over the city. I smiled at Gloria, and whispered, 'It's Chinatown.' To Robbie, this line from the movie of the same name, summed up the absurd, surreal world in which he lived, or now didn't live. 'It's brown sauce,' Gloria countered.

I tried many times to get Robbie to come to The Writers Circle. I thought it would be good for him. Robbie never came, but Austin did. I told Robbie about the people there, about Sophie Fanshawe, who he already knew from the Stalwart, about Pamela, and Sophie's brother Harry, who preferred to be called Tommy, which he got from Robbie, as Austin. Austin had explained to Harry once that 'Tommy' was a good name for a writer. Robbie knew the group was using Dunleavy de Boston's character Austin Quinn as the character to form a story around. It was apparent Robbie chose Austin Quinn as his name because there were several creative people inventing a persona, backstory, and future, perhaps a life, for the same person, and maybe Robbie thought he needed ideas and imagination with the development of his persona. It's not without some poeticism that Austin Quinn, as invented by each member of The Writers Circle, should disappear in their narratives.

Robbie was a world unto himself, and it appears he has disappeared into it. I posed to him the question of '*What will happen to you?*', which was the prevailing creative stimulus question put in front of the members of The Writers Circle. The convenor admitted lifting it from the well-known advertising slogan plastered all around the city. The intention was to get everyone writing. Robbie didn't need this, though. He was always writing. I put the question to Robbie many times. I was trying in my primitive way to jolt Robbie into some kind of action, to take some control over his life. Eventually, Austin Quinn joined the group, but Robbie didn't.

I hope one day I will see Robbie again. I hope he's well and not only surviving but prospering as Robbie Carton or Austin Quinn, or whatever *Knight of La Mancha* he settles on. I like to imagine him off on new adventures, no longer 'tilting at windmills' or fighting his demons, but setting wrongs to rights with his usual charm and humour. I hope he finds his place in the world.

I thought for a long time about his manuscript we found on his apartment floor. I sent it to a publisher to see if it might attract interest. It did. A contract was offered within days. All we need is for Robbie to reappear and he will soon thereafter be a published writer—his life's dream. I sent an email to him to let him know about the publishing contract—I don't know if he got it, or if he was continuing to monitor his emails. There was no reply. I attended The Writers Circle along with Sophie, and Harry, and Pamela. Others came and went. Robbie might have contributed in a profound way, had I convinced him to come along as Robbie. I joined the Circle to get help with the company's newsletter.

Robbie was in love with Sophie. Robbie knew Sophie from his contact with her at the Stalwart, where he was invariably too drunk to do anything about advancing his interest in her. I do believe Robbie's interest in Gloria was fleeting, and then only to temporarily fill the hole in his heart that was reserved for Sophie Fanshawe. I believe he saw Gloria more as a trusted friend. She was someone who understood his humour. Robbie had a strong affection for Gloria.

Gloria has flourished in the department. She took over Robbie's responsibility for the mines. I sent her out when it seemed Robbie wouldn't be coming back. She excelled and suffered none of the angst that brought O'Brien unstuck and abetted Robbie's disappearance. And, as my replacement, she has settled well in her new position as head of the department, as I expected she would. Gloria misses Robbie as a friend and work colleague. Gloria confided in me that she had decided she wouldn't offer Robbie the role of Deputy. She was right. Robbie wasn't the person for the job. Flanagan got it instead. Gloria would never send O'Reilly out to the mines. She sent our resident gorilla out, minus the gorilla suit, although the people out at the mines probably wouldn't have batted an eye, had she turned up in her gorilla suit. One of Gloria's skills is that she understands people, and she is comfortable and confident in herself, and she knows O'Reilly would be at risk if he went back out to the mines. Did I say, 'back out'? I meant outback—a Freudian slip.

Gloria had a miscarriage.

Sab and I live on W57th Street, at least for a time, a couple of blocks from The Russian Tea Room. Sab is lecturing and continuing her research at Columbia University. She's popular among the faculty and student body alike. I'm concerned about Sab, she seems unsettled, and she is worrying about her mother back home who is unwell.

Walking down W57th Street a while ago, in the lunchtime crowds, I could have sworn I saw a glimpse of someone who looked a lot like Robbie on the other side of the busy two-way Manhattan street, but he disappeared into the middle distance before I got a good look. I did notice this person had untidy black hair. Both Sab and I keep a lookout, as though we expect Robbie to turn up one day. It seems like something Robbie might do.

As for Harry/Tommy and Pamela and Bronnie. This is complicated. It's true that Bronnie and Pamela swapped lives, but only for a few days. They quickly realised they preferred their own lives and personas. They missed their apartments and clothes and, once sober, Pamela wasn't keen to engage with Bronnie's boyfriend and make love to someone she didn't know, as exciting as it sounded over several martinis. Bronnie also wasn't keen on a 'dishevelled academic widower' as was an apt description of Harry/Tommy. So Pamela and Bronnie reverted to their own lives. It seems reinventing yourself as someone else is not as straightforward or satisfying as you might think. People invest a lot into who they are throughout their life, however flawed that may be. So they, Pamela and Bronnie, swapped back, but not before Bronnie, pretending to be Pamela, had turned up at the Stalwart with a rose to meet Sophie in answer to Harry's ad in the *National Financial Review*. Sophie didn't know who the woman was, but she did know she wasn't Pamela. Sophie was fascinated and happy to play along with the game. She figured something interesting happening to her brother was better than the status quo. So Sophie directed Bronnie, as Pamela, to Harry's office. But it was actually Pamela who went to Harry's office that day. Pamela and Bronnie had swapped back by then. This was a good thing, as Pamela, having met Harry/Tommy at The Writers Circle, liked him, and didn't mind at all that he was a dishevelled academic widower who was lost and needed help. So, in time, Pamela and Harry came to an understanding—Pamela was patient, and Harry took the time he needed. There was something about a red raincoat and a beauty mark? I don't have any more details, except to ask the question, on the day Pamela came to Harry's office with a red rose, was it Pamela who was different, as Harry thought, or was it Harry who was different? Harry found himself looking at another woman with more than passing interest for the first time since Beverly's death. Such a thing hadn't been possible until then. Pamela calls Harry, Tommy. Beverly had changed his name to Harry from Harold, and Pamela changed his name to Tommy. So Harry is Tommy, and the world remains largely undisturbed.

Pamela will never be Beverly, but that's a good thing. Harry and Pamela have been travelling together and, on one occasion, visited us in New York. We had lunch across from the famous, but now closed, Carnegie Deli on 7th Avenue, and the four of us took a selfie at Columbus Circle with Central Park in the background. You can see the pic online.

Bronnie, for her part, was intrigued by Pamela's idea of becoming an actor. She took a college course in acting and landed a role in an Australian soap, before taking up a starring role in an American sitcom. She lives in Santa Monica, just off Montana Avenue, behind Wholefoods where she shops. Bronnie has a perfect American accent. She wears her beauty mark every day. Her beauty mark and blonde hair have become her trademark, and young girls and young boys the world over are sporting beauty marks just like Bronnie's, or so I'm told.

The question of who sent the roses to Pamela and Bronnie's office remains a mystery. Pamela stopped thinking about it long ago. Pamela and Bronnie have both sworn off martinis for life.

Mel, Sophie and Harry's mother, lives in a lighthouse, which is automated and relies on a light, not a cannon. She keeps a white nanny goat. She milks the nanny goat every morning before she paints the lighthouse with watercolours. Mel paints with watercolours, not the goat. The goat hasn't demonstrated any particular interest in the arts, either before or after she's been milked. One of Robbie's favourite grammatical amusements—he liked a dangling participle. And the lighthouse was not painted with watercolours, a canvas was, which featured the lighthouse.

My attempts at writing haven't amounted to much, apart from editing the company newsletter and contributing to some of the writing, which, if

I do say so myself, was okay. Even Robbie was a little impressed. During my time in The Writers Circle, I managed a few short stories about which the only profound thing that can be said, I fear, is that they contain characters who all knew one another, who met regularly in support, and who liked one another but were seeking something else in life, or thought they were. Those that survived their universe were not much better off than those that remained at odds with their universe. A lot like life, as it turns out. My characters are all more or less forlorn, lonely, and tense—perhaps more so than I intended and obviously too much like Robbie. Austin once said to me about my writing, '*Wherever you go, there you are*', and I'm okay with that.

I feel forlorn about Robbie's disappearance. Could I have done more to help? I don't know. Did he need help? Should I have confronted him about his alter-ego Austin Quinn at The Writers Circle? Probably. But I didn't. It would seem like a betrayal if I did not go along with it. He trusted me to keep the fantasy in tack. Sophie went along with it too. She knew Robbie from the Stalwart. I haven't asked her about this, I consider it a private matter between her and Robbie. In the end, you have to do what you think is right. That's what I did, or tried to do.

I read Robbie's manuscript. It was profound in an absurd kind of way, but definitely profound. I laughed out loud at times. It's not a comedy as such. The absurdity highlighted the sadness of Robbie's characters. Not everything made sense. Not everything added up, which, I believe, would have been Robbie's intention—if you look too closely into the abyss… as he would say.

To quote Robbie's favourite saying, 'It's Chinatown', or 'Brown Sauce', as he often preferred. In the end, Robbie's novel made flashes of sense out of overwhelming nonsense, just as Robbie could do with one of his office emails. He subtitled his manuscript 'Brown Sauce'.

I spoke at length with Sophie when she returned from Paris. She said as a writer you have to get the relationship between the real author and the implied author, and between the implied readers and the actual readers sorted out before you can start writing. She came to appreciate this during her time in Paris. She came to understand this was the reason she had trouble remembering writing the words, because she was remembering as the author, when she should have been remembering them as her implied author—a fictional construct.

Sophie suggested that if you're reading this account, the chances are you have read a number of Shakespeare plays, and you're an inquisitive person with a secret. I believe, having listened to Sophie's prose in The Writers Circle, that Sophie knows your secret, like Shakespeare knew the secret of everyone in the theatre watching his plays—they were watching themselves.

So all that remains is to ask the 'What will happen to you?' question about Robbie, and the same question about Sophie, or all of us if it comes to that, including you, dear reader. There is no answer to that question. I can tell you Sophie came back from Paris determined to track down Robbie. I think she wanted to find out if she was in love with him.

The novel Sophie completed in Paris was rejected by her publisher, but was later picked up by a new publisher based in New York. It's in two parts. The second part she completed upon her return from Paris.

The film rights are under negotiation for both parts of Sophie's novel. The novel is a *roman à clef* centred round Robbie's disappearance and includes the people in Robbie's life, such as, Mel as Syd, Sophie, Gloria, Harry/ Tommy, Pamela, Bronnie, and Sabrina, all under other fictional names, and me as a character named Barnaby or the Barnster. Bronnie has agreed to play herself in a cameo providing she can do it with her natural hair colour and no beauty mark and uncredited.

It's the story of Sophie's personal journey to find Robbie. The search took her all over the world and ended in...Tears? Joy? Tears of joy? I'll let Sophie tell that story.

Sincerely yours (Latin: *Sincere vestrum*)

Bentley Herbert FCA, MBA.

VP International Finance

322 W57th St (A couple of blocks from The Russian Tea Room)

New York NY 10019

USA

One last thing...

I'm not permitted to say any more about Sophie's novel, but I am able to refer you to the *accountant's* mantra and say this:

*Don't panic, it all adds up in*

*The End*

# Acknowledgements

Maggi Miles, my editor, an unrelenting supporter, a true believer.

Others who gave time to read the manuscript, and who provided valuable input by laughing in the right places, more or less. Kerrie Jordan, Tony Jordan, Robyn Ormsby, Marg Scheil, and Sarah Sutherland.

**Literary References**

Douglas Adams, Martin Amis, Paul Auster, Ray Bradbury, Albert Camus, Lewis Carroll, Miguel de Cervantes, Donleavy de Boston, Charles Dickens, Bret Easton Ellis, William Golding, Ernest Hemingway, Alfred Hitchcock, James Joyce, Herman Melville, Haruki Murakami, Vladimir Nabokov, George Orwell, J. D. Salinger, Arthur Schopenhauer, William Shakespeare, Arthur Stace, Leo Tolstoy, Robert Towne and Tennessee Williams.

The line, 'Forget it, Jake — it's Chinatown.' is from the movie *Chinatown*. Written by Robert Towne, directed by Roman Polanski, produced by Robert Evans, owned, and distributed by Paramount Pictures. This quote reproduced with the kind permission of Paramount Pictures.

**Musical References**

'Alfie' by Burt Bacharach and Hal David. 'God Only Knows', and 'Wouldn't It Be Nice' by The Beach Boys. 'Nowhere Man' by The Beatles.

# About the Author

Gary N. Lines currently lives in Adelaide, a medium-sized city in Australia. He has also lived in Paris, New York, London, Melbourne, Santa Monica, Byron Bay, and Westport Connecticut on Old Mill Road.

This novel was written primarily in Santa Monica, California. But also in Hardwicke Bay, South Australia, and one laborious weekend in Grafton village in Vermont, together with many lost weekends in The Empire Hotel's bar, in New York City.

Gary holds a Master of Creative Arts from Flinders University.

As with *Doing Life In Paradise* Gary's debut novel, *What Will Happen to You?* is a work of fiction. Everything is made up—except that potatoes *are* grown in Australia, that's true. None of the characters exist or are based on any actual persons—any similarities are purely coincidental except for Dunleavy de Boston. If anyone knows of his whereabouts, please contact the author—the last time he was around, he nicked the barbecue.

### Also by Gary N. Lines

*Doing Life In Paradise*, a novel. (Published UK 2015)

Author website: www.garynlinesauthor.com

www.ingramcontent.com/pod-product-compliance
Lightning Source LLC
Chambersburg PA
CBHW020434030726
47495CB00006B/1793